Aliens

Zack Cool

CHAPTER 1

Strange Sound

Stories of spaceships and little green men talked about in an old local newspaper, Jacob read laughing along with the mention of the coronavirus virus while enjoying his pint of home-brew. Jacob had resided on the Moor for years, the only green and white he had seen was discarded rubbish by holidaymakers, certainly not aliens. Jacob walked the same route for years attending his ewes, enjoying the occasional frosty evening with a clear sky glimpsing a shooting star. Sometimes, without warning, engulfed by misty fog from the sea, creating a strange sound, as if the bowels of the earth were howling.

Jacob lived alone since his wife had passed away some years back from breast cancer. He reminisced reliving holding her hand while she took her final breath. Rosalind slowly released the grip on his hand, leaving him alone in this uncertain world of misery without her. Jacob, wiping the tears from his cheek, could not bring himself to seek romance again; he'd had known Rosalind all his life from when they attended school. Jacob fondly gazed to the mantelpiece where her ashes sat in the urn above the fire. He didn't need much to sustain him; a hundred ewes would keep him occupied. Grazing is not an issue on the Moor, Jacob had earned his right of free grazing from his father before him. He would be the last generation, he hadn't sired a son, something else missing from his life, sat at his oak kitchen table with the good book opened on Revelations. Jacob had no time for these people with their telescopes gazing at the stars searching for spaceships, he had gone out with the good book; told in no uncertain terms to go away by some foul-mouthed yobs. He sighed despondent, believing he knew the truth according to the message in the good book. Jacob smiled everyone to their own opinion, providing they did not harm his sheep, they can waste their time staring into space.

Jacob patted his faithful sheepdog Jack laying close to the hearth, hearing a strange sound outside. Watching Jack's ears perk, looking to the door growling. Jacob grabbed his shepherd's crook and torch venturing outside into a blanket of fog. Hearing the strange sound he had heard many times before over the years. Jack glued to Jacob's heels, they carefully made their way to the sound of breaking water, striking the rocks on the shoreline below. The further they ventured from Jacob's thatched house, the darker the sky became, more mysterious than the Devils curse, not a star seen through the fog. If Jacob hadn't walked this route so many times before he wouldn't have ventured towards the cliff edge. The sound of breaking waves increased in volume, finally reaching the fence separating land from death, with a vertical drop to the rocky shoreline below. Jacob patted Jack reassuringly, although Jacob wasn't sure something wasn't happening. Perhaps God had come to take him to join Rosalind he loved dearly. Jacob squinted at a blinding light vanishing into the distance, presuming blistering hot fragments of a meteor penetrating the darkness.

He sighed heavily, slowly finding his way home hearing the sheep bleating as he entered the house. Both he and Jack, his dog, were soaked from the damp fog. Jacob glanced to wear his wife's ashes sat over the fireplace, stared in horror they were gone. He walked closer to the mantelpiece seeing a neat ring of dust where the urn sat for four years. Jacob would never touch the mantelpiece, a sacred place in his mind where Rosalind resided. He looked to Jack for answers! Jacob concluded ashes would be no use to anyone other than God; perhaps, he had taken them. The only explanation Jacob could accept, couldn't imagine a thief stealing ashes; although he never locked his door and his gun is still in the corner with a box of cartridges. Jacob checked his tin where he kept his cash in the kitchen cupboard, the money is still present.

Jacob made a coffee pouring a few dried biscuits into Jack's bowl, placed on the floor by his water dish. He returned to the front room staring at the mantelpiece again in case he is mistaken, lowering his cup in the hearth and throwing more blocks on the fire. Jacob flopped down in his old armchair staring at the mantelpiece, sipping his coffee. Jack returned laying down by Jacob's feet. Jacob nearly always slept in his armchair, hating the bed ever since Rosalind had passed on, wasn't the same.

Morning came too quickly, Jacob disturbed by the light coming through the window. Quickly making him some breakfast, a couple of fried eggs, a rasher of bacon and a slice of crusty bread. Jack would have any spare scraps his master passed to him. Jacob would freshen with a cold wash in the sink is sufficient to wake him; he'd had his shirt on for a week and decided it would last one more day. Jacob stepped out into a bright day; the wind is always strong by the coast. He strolled across the Moor, carrying a bale of hay on his shoulder and a little supplement for his sheep. Threw the hay in the hay rack looking at the sheep around him, reckoning they were all there without counting individuals. He walked amongst his sheep looking for lame ones or any that looked under the weather. A sheep's life is hard on the Moor, and only the fittest survived.

He made his way back to the barn, noticing the half-dozen hens had managed to lay eggs in the laying boxes for a change; he wouldn't have to go on a hunting spree to discover their hidden location. Jacob returned to the house, pushing a barrow load of logs, delivered some time ago. There were no trees on the Moor where he lived. They had to come from some distance, or if Jacob is lucky, he could drive his old tractor down to the shoreline and collect driftwood and use for a source of heating. He usually traded with another farmer to avoid spending hard-earned cash.

He pushed the barrow through the front door into the living room, stacking the wood in the hearth glancing to the mantelpiece. Jacob froze to the spot! Rosalind's urn is there in its usual place. He pushed the barrow out of the house, glancing back again to the mantelpiece to reassure himself he didn't imagine. He walked into the kitchen, making a cup of tea sitting in his armchair, staring at Rosalind's urn, could he possibly be hallucinating, something strange is happening! Jacob sat there for nearly one and a half hours, not quite sure what he is waiting for. He quite expected something to happen; only hearing the clock chime 4 o'clock on the wall. Jacob walked to the window, moving the net curtains last washed by Rosalind before she died, looked out not knowing what he is looking for, he needed a sign of some kind, hearing the strange sound that accompanied the fog. Jacob grabbed his crook, Jack, his faithful sheepdog, came to heal. They strolled out of the house heading in the direction of the sound coming from the clifftop.

Jack paused laying down, Jacob glanced back. "What's the matter, Jack?" Jacob asked calmly, sensing the fear in the dog's eyes. Jacob knew the wasn't much that would frighten Jack; he'd seen off one or two trespassers in his time, leaving them with a message they wouldn't forget.

Jacob continued walking puzzled by Jack's reaction, listening to the sound, the strange noise coming from the sea shrouded in fog. Jacob reached the fence, two more yards, certain death awaited you on the rocks below. He squinted, trying to focus on a bright light heading into the heavens disappearing from view, he sighed heavily, slowly making his way home to the house.

Jack, sitting by the front door shivering, not like him at all. Jacob wondered if he is unwell he's six years old, remembering Rosalind picking him from the litter on a neighbour's farm. Jacob opened the front door, they both entered, he hastily walked in the kitchen; quickly prepared a warm broth. Soaking Jack's dog biscuits in his bowl, placing by the hearth throwing on a few more logs to increase the heat, Jacob couldn't imagine life without Jack. Jacob glanced to the mantelpiece smiling to see Rosalind's urn is still there. Jacob decided he would pay any price, sell his soul to the devil to have Rosalind in his life. Sat down in his armchair by the fire after making a large mug of soup, holding in both hands watching Jack devour his food. Jacob drifted off to sleep in the armchair with Jack resting his head on his master's boot. Jack listened to the wind howling; rattling the tin on the neighbouring shed roof. Jacob snored, oblivious to what is taking place outside dreaming of Rosalind making him tea in a spotless house, she insisted keeping, frequently scolded for coming in with dirty boots.

Jacob awoke with a jolt, morning had arrived. He had his cup of tea and a thick crust of toast with marmalade, a jar he was saving for a special occasion that never came. Grabbed his crook by the door heading out into a windswept morning grabbing a bale of hay from the barn, he carried on his shoulder across the Moor to the sheep rack. Jacob caught an old ewe with his crook sitting on her backside using his foot clippers, he trimmed her feet, ending up catching six more with the same problem. Jack, his faithful sheepdog, sat quietly watching, eating the clippings known as dog chocolate. Jacob carried on walking across the Moor for some distance suspecting he had a sheep missing, standing on a large rock he looked back to his flock; counting carefully discovering they were all there. He struggled across the windy Moor for over five hours, returning to the house. Jacob opened the door stood there shocked, not believing his eyes. The house cleaned from top to bottom, the dust on the mantelpiece surrounding Rosalind's urn had gone. The crockery which had sat in the sink for weeks is washed up and stacked on the draining board. Jacob went into the bedroom, scratching his head clean sheets on the bed, he looked from his bedroom window, sheets hanging on the line they were washed. Fresh clothes for him in a neat pile with a note, he could barely think, trembling as he picked up the notepaper: "Jacob, wash and change your clothes, you smell, from your Rosalind."

Jacob reads the note 5 times before dashing into the bathroom, removing his dirty clothes, taking a bath the first one in six months. He stepped from the bath, the large bath towels were there waiting for him, quickly returned to the bedroom, changing into fresh clothes. Jacob studied the note, definitely

Rosalind's handwriting. Perhaps God he surmised is allowing Rosalind to come from heaven and help him. Jacob never smiled so much, where every looked, no dust, he opened the fridge, cleaned, and with a plate of sandwiches wrapped in cling foil for him. He sat at the kitchen table; he had no idea what is happening? He didn't really care the thought that Rosalind is close is enough, made himself a pot of coffee, celebrating adding a little tot of whiskey. Jack sat beside him in his usual begging posture, Jacob smiled, casting a morsel of crust, Jack caught instantly.

Early the next morning Jacob attached his small trailer to his old Fordson N tractor, cranking the engine frantically until she spluttered into life. He turned the fuel onto TVO, he remembered his father acquiring this old tractor when he was a child, his father sitting him on his knee, allowing Jacob to try and steer. If it wasn't the fact his father had won the football pools, he entered on a whim one week, he wouldn't have this tractor; they could have never afforded in those days. Jacob kept her in memory of his father, he didn't use her very often, perhaps three or four times a year. He remembered courting Rosalind, she would love to drive this old tractor down onto the beach, the track is a little precarious; nevertheless, she managed, they would spend hours cutting and collecting firewood for the farm.

Jacob drove on with Jack sat in the trailer with the chainsaw and axe, steadily descended the old track taking them down onto the beach, which wasn't very big more stone than anything else. You could always guarantee after a good storm timber will have come ashore.

Winter approaching another week, and November is here, Jacob cut a load of timber watching a heavy mist approach from the sea. He quickly started his tractor heading up the track, returning to the farm. He unloaded the trailer into a small shed where he stored the wood to keep it sort of dry, removed his pocket watch the one his father gave him before he passed on. One o'clock lunchtime. Jacob sat at the kitchen table slicing a piece of bread, with a large portion of cheese and two pickled onions would do for lunch, smiling, remembering the times Rosalind would prepare him a lovely meal; he lived like a king in those days. He quickly washed the dishes something he hadn't done for some time, suspecting if Rosalind is watching, she would burn his ears if he didn't, after all the trouble she'd gone to-to tidy the house. He placed the dishes in the cupboard where they belonged. Jacob ventured outside, grabbing his old wheelbarrow loading with blocks, returning to stack by the hearth.

He smiled, hoping Rosalind wasn't watching, she would scold him frequently for pushing the wheelbarrow in the house with a dirty wheel. He quickly stacked the blocks against the wall, removing the barrow from the house checking there is no mud left on the flagstone floor. The misty fog is as thick as ever. Jacob heard the sound the weird sound of the earth in agony. He grabbed his crook, slipping on his waterproof coat; Jack, close to his heels. They set off towards the cliff fence, staying on the well-trodden path Jacob knew so well. For years he'd walked this path, hearing the same eerie sound hoping one day to discover where it's coming from. He stared into the mist, observing a bright light, almost beckoning him to step over the fence which he knew would be sudden death if he ventured further. Jack had come with him this time and not shied away from as before; Jacob bent down, patting him with reassurance. Jacob sighed heavily, slowly turning around walking to the house, finding the door open, quite suspected thieves, watching Jack run indoors barking, then silent, not a whimper. Jacob gripped his crook firmly anticipating trouble, although puzzled why Jack wasn't barking. He entered the property seeing Jack sitting in front of his chair, wagging his tail while Rosalind stroked him.

Jacob had prayed for this moment for as long as he could remember after Rosalind passed away. Common sense dictated, he is hallucinating, no one came home from heaven; she's in an urn on the mantelpiece. He watched Rosalind rise to her feet approaching him in her usual attire, knee-length skirt pinny tied around her waist with the blouse she loved so much, embroidered with roses. Jacob is frozen to the spot. "Jacob," Rosalind said calmly. "Your meal is in the oven I must go," she kissed him on the cheek vanishing into the mist.

Jacob came to his senses dashing outside, you could barely see a metre in front of you; he didn't know which direction to take. He called out, "Rosalind, Rosalind, come back, please!" Jacob quickly followed the trail to the cliff-top, watching the misty fog vanish as if sucked into a vacuum cleaner. He returned to the house opening the oven finding a beautiful meal, potatoes, meat and vegetables, with Rosalind's lovely gravy. Jacob would always profess to Rosalind, he'd only married her because of the gravy she made, which usually resulted in a wooden spoon around the ear. Jack sat patiently like a starving animal hoping his master would cast him the bone. Jacob is trying to understand what is happening; is this just his imagination, had he prepared the meal subconsciously.

Jacob loved Rosalind more than life itself, in fact, more than he loved God, which he thought a sin. He quite accepted the fact God could do anything. The Bible speaks of miracle after miracle; perhaps he sighed heavily suspecting he is wishful thinking. Why would God bother with him a simpleton? Jacob washed his plate, casting the bone to Jack, who dashed off to sit by the fireplace grinding away at the bone with nothing else on his mind. Jacob made a coffee sitting by the fire, watching Jack totally unconcerned Rosalind is here one minute and gone the next; nothing is making sense. Although Jacob didn't really care, providing she kept coming to see him, his life is complete with her. He through more wood on the fire still pondering events, he dared not say anything to anyone fearing incarceration; he doesn't believe what's happening, so why should others. Before Jacob realised, the morning is staring through the curtains quite a bright morning from what could be seen. He awoke to find a birthday card on his lap, wishing him a happy birthday from his beloved Rosalind.

Jacob ran into the kitchen checking the calendar, his birthday, and he'd forgotten, Rosalind hadn't. She'd remember things like that which he considered insignificant in the scheme of things. He only marked the calendar with market days. Jacob placed his card on the cupboard so he could look at it again and again with his mind returning to work. Jacob hoped the old Ram had sired all the ewes properly this year and were carrying twins. He'd changed the Ram which hadn't been quite so successful. He and Jack were eating him for the last six months a little like eating shoe leather; nevertheless, Jack didn't seem to mind.

Jacob grabbed his crook walking down the steep track to the waterline staring out to sea, he didn't know what he is looking for. Nevertheless, he surveyed for as far as he could see, walking towards the cliff face sitting on a large Boulder. Jacob is astounded watching a small area of misty fog appear about 5000 yards out from the shore, slowly approaching the beach. The misty fog couldn't have been more than 3 meters wide and perhaps as tall which he thought is exceptionally odd. The misty fog stopped at the shoreline; there is a sudden burst of brilliant light stepping from the light Rosalind. Jacob rose to his feet, immediately walking towards what appeared to be his wife, his deceased wife. She is dressed in a classic white boiler suit for a better description; there is not a dark piece of material on her figure apart from her footwear which is silver. Rosalind smiled, holding out her hand. Jacob accepted without fear of consequence for his safety, allowing Rosalind to lead the way into the mist which appeared to have a door. Jack stayed by the rock laying down, Rosalind glanced back-patting her leg. Jack immediately ran to join them as the mist engulfed them all, taking Jacob and Jack on a journey of discovery as they were about to find out. The misty fog cleared, Jacob found himself standing in a large construction under the sea; he could see fish through the windows swimming unconcerned around whatever he is in. Other male and females appeared dressed the same as Rosalind walking around the vast expanse of whatever kept the water out and them safe. Jacob wanted to speak and found he couldn't, Jack had vanished, no longer with them. He stood there, holding his crook watching his clothes disappear and replaced with the same as Rosalind is wearing and everyone else.

Rosalind spoke: "I'm created as your deceased wife, Rosalind, we will explain why Jacob all will become clear to you in time."

Finally, his mouth would work. "This cannot be heaven under the sea; this is devil domain, God lives in heaven above the clouds?" Jacob expressed unsure of anything any more.

Rosalind and the others studied Jacob's expression while Rosalind led him into another part of the construction. Everything is white, even the furnishings which were not dissimilar in shape to anything you could buy on the High St, he concluded. Jacob encouraged to sit down studying another person enter joining him and Rosalind. "I suspect you have many questions Jacob all can not be answered at the moment, as time progresses, you will realise we are telling you the truth, you may call me Peter."

Jacob studied him rather suspiciously: "If this is not hell, where am I, and how can this person be my Rosalind, she was cremated and on my mantelpiece?" Jacob asked calmly.

"We have been here since the construction of earth, we created the life forms on the planet, and some have evolved, unfortunately, not the way we anticipated."

"Are you saying God does not exist? Something I have believed in all my life and my parents, millions of other people and me. How do you discredit miracles, they do occasionally happen to the lucky few?"

Peter and Rosalind glanced at each other. Peter answered with a demonstration holding his hand out, resting the back of his hand on the table. Jacob watched the wedding ring Rosalind had lost when they were first married originally belonged to his mother, and her mother before that appear in Peter's palm. Jacob speechless looking at Peter and Rosalind, for answers, explanations to his questions. "A miracle I can perform, I can raise people from the dead such as Rosalind who sits before you. We have records of everything, everyone, every animal, every insect, every hair on your head, Jacob, we are the creators."

Jacob laughed: "I've heard talk, we came swinging out of the trees! God created everything in six days, resting on the Sabbath."

"Rosalind, remind Jacob of something only you, and he would know," Peter suggested.

"What happened between us on John Hickory's haystack Jacob, and what did you ask of me?"

Jacob rose to his feet, he knew exactly what Rosalind is referring to; she permitted him to make love to her for the first time, he proposed, and Rosalind accepted. "We did you know what and I asked you to marry me, you kindly accepted one of my best ideas to have you in my life."

"You need further proof Jacob," Peter asked, changing his appearance into Peter the fishermen from the Bible. Jacob collapsed into his chair. Rosalind held his hand. "You must believe what Peter discloses to you, I am Rosalind I'm created from her ashes, check her urn on the mantelpiece and see what you discover inside; although your Rosalind was cremated the traces of her essence, remain in our memory banks, and I'm her in every sense of the word."

"Are we to live together as man and wife," Jacob asked, puzzled by everything. He remembered watching a Star Trek movie at the pictures with Rosalind, there is someone called a shapeshifter on board could they really exist?

"If you wish Jacob or I would keep your house and provide your meals and assist you with any task of importance to you."

"What if someone sees you with me? My friends all know Rosalind died, I presume you don't want to become common knowledge; the world would be turned upside down, I should imagine if everyone discovered their religion is false. My next question what happens to me now I know? Am I to suddenly disappear, which wouldn't be such a bad thing, I would definitely be with Rosalind in heaven?"

"You are not to die until the allotted time Jacob, you are worrying over trivial matters. Anyone who observes Rosalind on your farm, may not remember her death, I can assure you; we control everything," Peter pointed to a large screen on the wall. "Watch the aeroplane Jacob 197 passengers will lose their lives today thanks to a terrorist bomb." Jacob watched the plane explode, he hadn't watched television for some years, since the one he had refused to work, never bothering to afford to replace seemed a waste of money. The only person that would watch television is Rosalind, and she's gone. "Couldn't you have saved them," Jacob asked, rather distraught.

"Of course, you are missing the point, the Bible was originally constructed as guidelines by my brothers and me, hoping the inhabitants of the earth would use the book as a guideline. Unfortunately, as you know your own history, we failed miserably; now we have nothing other than savages living on the earth."

"If you are truly the creators, this should be a minor problem for you to rectify. To be quite honest, I don't think you are the creators, you're probably an alien from somewhere," Jacob paused, remembering what is written in the Bible. "Although the Bible does not speak of any other beings; that would lead me to believe you are a government experiment, and you're hoping to trick a simpleton like me."

Peter projected a beam of light from his eyes, stunning Jacob. Jacob stood there, frozen to the spot. "I want you the first of every month to come to the beach with your tractor and manure spreader. You will wait for your manure spreader to be loaded. When the fog clears, you will take your machine to one of your grass pastures. You will spread the contents thinly over the ground you understand me, Jacob," Peter instructed in his firm tone.

"I understand," Jacob replied robotically. Rosalind glanced to Peter and nodded, walking Jacob along the corridor, she paused, waiting for the misty fog to engulf them both and they reappeared on the beach. Jacob stepped from the misty fog in his original clothes, Rosalind vanished, returning to where she'd come from. Peter is waiting for Rosalind to return. "That went better than I thought Rosalind," Peter advised. "He will comply, although he is extremely strong-willed; his love for Rosalind is his strongest thought, I read his mind easily."

"I agree Peter with your conclusion, I will have to repair the manure spreader; he hasn't used it for years since Rosalind died. He only has a hundred ewes, barely enough to sustain his living, I will have to improve the situation Peter. We must make him a little more efficient, he will never realise he is spreading cremated humans on his pastureland, excellent fertiliser."

Peters silver eyes shone, observed Rosalind's turned silver from the brown colour she projected while in the presence of Jacob. "Rosalind, proceed cautiously, he will not remember his visit here, I wiped his memory other than with you. You may experiment as you see fit with him. The human flesh we require for our home planets will be transported every month," Peter concluded, flashed his eyes, walking off.

Rosalind transported to Jacobs farm looking at the manure spreader, dressed in the same attire as Roslind would originally where when she is outside with Jacob, a brown boiler-suit. She started working on the old manure spreader far worse than she suspected. Jacob came over to join her surprised, although, for some reason, it seemed quite reasonable for Rosalind to be here. "We must have this working properly," Jacob, Rosalind insisted calmly.

"I am aware Rosalind, I have manure to collect from the beach every month it's free," he smiled. Rosalind grinned, trying to perform the same way as a human would in facial expressions. They spent the rest of the day working on the machine using spare parts from the old workshop. Jacob had an old Fordson major tractor, he used to use on the spreader. While he wasn't looking Rosalind touched the battery terminals charging the battery from her own life form. She walked over to the diesel tank in the corner of the shed drawing off 5 gallons and emptying in the fuel tank of the Fordson major. Jacob commented: "She'll not start, I suspect the battery is flat, I'll have to blow the tyres up, they look a little worse for wear," he complained.

"Jacob," Rosalind suggested, "I would like one of your coffees, you make me one, I'll finish off here join you in a minute," she smiled.

Jacob smiled, "you always were better with machines than me." He chuckled, walking to the house with Jack at his heels.

Rosalind waited until he is out of sight sitting on the driver's seat of the Fordson major. She pushed the starter lever, the tractor burst into life after the engine turned over several times, filling the shed full of smoke. She reversed the tractor to the manure spreader attaching along with the PTO shaft to discharge the machine in the field, allowing to spread and empty. The spreader would carry about five tons, which were ample for their requirements for the moment until the shipments increased in volume. Rosalind checked every tyre on the machine and tractor inflating to the correct pressure by touching with her hand.

Rosalind entered the house to discover Jacob with his large Bible on the kitchen table reading passages. He knew Jesus had restored life to Nazareth who was dead for four days, Jacob concluded four days or four years there would be no difference in Jesus's eyes; he could restore anything he wanted. Why bother with him a mere insignificant person in the scheme of things?

Jacob asked: "I presume you have met Jesus; he restored you to life, Rosalind?"

"Why ask the question if you already know the answer, Jacob? You have met Jesus, although you don't remember, do not concern yourself with trivialities we have a greater mission." Rosalind smiled confidently deciding to use Jacobs religious beliefs to work in her favour.

He exhaled closing the Bible, passing a mug of coffee to Rosalind sitting opposite. "I must say Rosalind you haven't aged a day; Jesus must have set your age at 20, you look no older, and I'm 43. Jesus has truly given me a present, we must not speak of this; something tells my mind you are to stay a secret? Is that correct Rosalind I can't show my friends you exist?"

"Think Jacob logically, how many widowers there are in the world today; why weren't one of them chosen? The world would be in turmoil if they learnt of my existence, I'm here for a special reason you are helping Jesus. Say no more please or he may take me away deciding you are undeserving of the gift." Rosalind knew Jacob wouldn't want that to happen, she had listened to his prayers begging God to return Rosalind for years.

Jacob is quiet for a moment, "I presume you will have to return to heaven in the evenings, we won't be like husband and wife again like the old days?"

"Sometimes I will have to return and others I will stay, depending on my duties, after all, I'm working for God you wouldn't want me to disobey him, Jacob, would you?"

Jacob shook his head: "No, you must not disobey his commands, I definitely don't want to lose you again, Rosalind. I heard the old Fordson major start I didn't think she would ever again, I heard you try the manure spreader I presume it works. December I have to collect a load from the beach of fertiliser; Jesus is generous, helping me grow grass for my sheep."

"Isn't he always." Rosalind smiled, walking into the bedroom, making the bed. Jacob nervously entered: "Will you be sharing this with me tonight, Rosalind?" Jacob asked, slightly worried, wondering what he should and should not do; he didn't want to offend Jesus or God or anybody for that matter and especially not Rosalind.

Rosalind smiled, "only if you take a bath, Jacob, I have clean sheets on the bed; your beard looks like rats tails, and your hair is not much better, wash thoroughly, and I will clip before retiring to bed this evening." Jacob smiled, she is speaking the truth, he hadn't bothered with his appearance or cleanliness since Rosalind died. He spent the next hour in the bath, scrubbing every part of his body shampooing his hair and beard twice for good measure. He wrapped a towel around himself, heading for the bedroom quickly dressing, finding Rosalind in the kitchen with sharpened dagging shears. Jacob sat on the chair, Rosalind carefully cut his hair and tidied his beard. He actually looked like a human instead of a Neanderthal. Rosalind quickly swept up the loose hair throwing on the fire giving off an awful smell for a moment. Jacob looked at himself in the mirror that had a crack across from Rosalind, and he playing a childish game in the kitchen when they first married, the ball hit the mirror on the wall. Both retired to bed, Rosalind placed her hand on Jacob's forehead, he immediately relaxed in a deep sleep. Rosalind, leaving to return to the spaceship, stepping into the misty fog outside the front door. She vanished reappearing in the spaceship concealed in a large crater, camouflaged so no vessel or radar could detect the ship. Peter is waiting for her arrival with Matthew, another brother of the 12 apostles as they name themselves thousands of years ago when creating the Bible; hoping to instil order in the humans, which failed as the centuries passed.

Rosalind, Peter and Matthew acknowledged each other with a flash of their eyes, which were silver now Rosalind had returned. They walked through the vast space ship watching human bodies processed into joints of meat, anything that wasn't to be used is incinerated by their engines and turned into powder, disposed of initially through their recycling chambers. However, human technology had progressed and would detect any discharge from the spaceship, now Jacob will solve the problem. Matthew asked: "Peter, we cannot permit the human race to continue destroying the planet. They are only good for feeding other creatures; let's destroy, our task will be finished and leave the Earth to regenerate and become what it was a beauty to behold."

"Stay positive, Matthew," Peter advised. "The human race has its uses such as feeding the young animals on other planets we are terraforming. Let us continue along this path for another five years, while we find a solution to transport the humans alive to our designated destinations. The animals can hunt tracked down the human and eat."

Rosalind remarked: "Five years is not long Matthew, we will find a solution to transporting humans alive over vast distances throughout the universe. Look what we've achieved, Jacob travelled with me and didn't die, we are making progress. Before if you remember Matthew when we tried to transport another living being, they were instantly destroyed because the transporter is only designed for us nothing else."

Matthew acknowledged with the flash of his eyes. "Difficult, we are trying various methods when I bring humans aboard for processing, none arrive here alive from Africa, our best hunting ground for humans. Of course, the odd aeroplane disaster and as long as humans keep fighting there will always be bodies to transport."

Peter flashed his eyes. "We will succeed Matthew remember when we came up with the idea of God's to control the humans. That worked very well for some considerable time. Rosalind returned to Jacob I fear he's realised you're missing." Rosalind flashed her eyes walking along the corridor she stepped into the misty fog. 6 o'clock in the morning she reappeared by the woodshed, splitting wood with the acts as Jacob stepped from the house, he smiled, observing her working. "I'll make the coffee and breakfast Rosalind," he called out laughing. She acknowledged his comment with a nod, continued splitting logs loading the wheelbarrow.

He returned to the house, bewildered by everything his life had changed from a routine of breakfast feed the animals go to bed, to catering for Rosalind again which is not a problem as far as he could see; he had something in his life he long for four years. Jacob looked from the window seeing the snow starting to fall. November and December were dismal on the Moor, he wondered if his old Land Rover would start, he hadn't used it all summer trying to save money. Jacob looked in his tin at the back of the cupboard realising he would have to grocery shop, he hadn't bothered to grow vegetables this year. He couldn't be bothered there was only him, quietly hoping he would die and join Rosalind. Things have turned out the other way round Rosalind has joined him which made him smile, opening his old sweet tin only to discover a wad of cash. Jacob had to look twice he couldn't believe what he saw, there were hundreds of pounds held fast by elastic bands; shopping certainly wouldn't be a problem he grinned. Suspecting God is trying to help him, although, couldn't remember God giving anybody money, he concluded puzzled. There again he'd never heard of anyone having their wife returned; perhaps God is operating differently now in the modern age.

Rosalind pushed the wheelbarrow to the front door, carrying armfuls of blocks, she stacked by the side of the hearth; not bringing the wheelbarrow inside as Jacob would. She closed the door on the weather, joining Jacob in the kitchen, sitting down to eggs on toast with a little bacon and a cup of coffee. Jack sat in his usual position, waiting for anything to fall off the table. Rosalind patted Jack tucking into her meal which she would discharge later in the day went Jacob wasn't watching, she didn't require food to sustain her essence. Rosalind, a member of the Zibyan collective, pure energy, something similar to radiation, although admitted no side effects to any other being unless provoked. A form of shapeshifter, they could take any form they wanted solid, or liquid made no difference. Their own planet situated behind Neptune several billion miles away, although with their propulsion system a simple matter of three or four days to their home planet, "Zagader."

Jacob cleared the table, Rosalind washed the dirty dishes heating the water with power from her hands. Jacob hadn't stoked the fire for the boiler to heat the water. Jacob heard a knock at the door. Jack ran in front of him barking, Jacob opened the door. Police officers were standing in the doorway in their wellington boots after walking across the Moor. "Jacob Walker this is your farm?"

Jacob answered abruptly, "correct." Jacob glanced over his shoulder, Rosalind is gone from sight. "We've had reports," the officer laughed, "of aliens, strange people wandering over the Moor have you seen anything?"

Jacob laughed, "three green men purchased a joint of lamb from me the other day."

The officer smiled: "Our sentiments exactly, we have more important issues; no little green men would come to this planet they would have to be mental," the officer laughed walking away.

Rosalind had returned to her spaceship meeting Peter and Matthew. "What's going on, Peter?" Rosalind asked.

Peter advised: "I watch the officers, a dozen of them scanning part of the moorland, none of our brothers and sisters have ventured onto the moor without my consent. I suspect it's what the humans call a hoax, someone's making up stories, continue as before Rosalind be on your guard."

Rosalind flashed her eyes to Matthew and Peter, checking the scanners aboard the spaceship, locating the police officers were some distance away from Jacobs farm. She reappeared by the old Land Rover where Jacob is standing with his head under the bonnet checking the oil. He glanced at her. "That was close, Rosalind! The old Land Rover won't start, the battery flat, I'll have to walk to the village," he frowned.

"Make the coffee Jacob leave the vehicle repairs to me, I hope you're driving across the Moor to the village otherwise the police will be arresting you. Your old Land Rover hasn't an MOT certificate or tax or insurance."

Jacob sighed, "as usual Rosalind you are correct I haven't bothered since you passed on. I can easily drive across the Moor. Is there anything you'd like from the shop if you can ever get the old beast working."

"Remember to say nothing to anyone Jacob about me, purchase essentials, say nothing out of the ordinary," Rosalind advised extremely concerned with recent events.

He returned to the house; Rosalind held the terminals on the Land Rover battery recharged, she climbed inside turning the key, the old diesel Land Rover burst into life. She drove to the diesel tank topping up parking the Land Rover outside the house. Jacob had made the coffee hearing the sound of his

Land Rover he couldn't help but smile. Rosalind could always make things right, watching her enter the house; she'd left the engine running on the Land Rover to warm the cab for Jacob. He kissed Rosalind on the cheek finishing his coffee, holding his old shopping bag. He climbed into his Land Rover steadily driving along the old track, which is actually shorter than going by road, allowing him to study his sheep. Jacob finally parked walking the mile to the village shop, which had changed since the last time he visited, into a self-service affair. He walked along the shelves with his basket looking at the price of food; everything is expensive, promising himself to grow vegetables next year. Jacob is shocked if he wanted an extra shopping bag he would have to pay. Instead, he had an old box the shopkeeper gave him; even more of a shock the groceries come to £50.

Jacob struggled to carry the box, and shopping bag the mile to the Land Rover; he'd purchase far more than he intended. The bags of flour were quite cumbersome, needing them to make bread. Jacob finely placed his groceries in the back of the Land Rover, heading home slowly across the Moor. Rosalind helped him unload, putting everything in the cupboards. Jacob noticed she'd already made three loaves of bread, he didn't dare ask how considering they were out of flour. She cut Jacob a large crusty slice with the smearing of butter and jam. He sat there as if he'd won the lottery drinking coffee gazing into Rosalind's beautiful brown eyes.

Rosalind interrupted his thoughts: "Sheep, you must check them, Jacob, I wouldn't be surprised if some have lambed." Jacob smiled slipping on his coat with Jack following close to his heels, he left the house. Rosalind already knew there were lambs on the Moor and had prepared several pens in the barn. She is finding this whole experience quite enjoyable, although she could be anything she wanted. Playing the part of Jacobs wife and helping on the farm is very interesting and thanks to their ability to extract information from anyone's mind, she could perform flawlessly.

Jacob hadn't walked very far before he could see several ewes with lambs; he quickly returned to the barn, smiling, noticing the pens already prepared, Rosalind is always one step ahead of him. He grabbed a four-wheeled cart, he used to tow behind his quad bike before that broke, now he had to pull the cart by hand. He sighed slowly watching Rosalind come from the back of the buildings on his old quad bike; she parked in front of him with a smug grin practising human facial movements to try and blend in.

He stood there shaking his head in disbelief, wherever Rosalind had come from he didn't care, his life is turning into a bundle of fun again like it used to be before she passed away. Rosalind attached the little trailer patting Jacob on the cheek, "don't belong I'll make the coffee." Jacob climbed aboard his old quad bike towing the small trailer, gathering three old ewes and six lambs placing in his trailer. He slowly returned to the barn placing the ewes and lambs in individual pens for the moment; giving each a little water, a few sheep nuts making sure the lambs could suckle before going in the house for his coffee.

Rosalind had already prepared lunch serving as Jacob walked in. He placed his hands either side of her face gently kissing Rosalind lovingly. Rosalind is somewhat surprised, she knew from the records Jacob and his deceased wife very rarely held each other or had physical contact. "Thank you for being in my life Rosalind," Jacob remarked, sitting at the table.

Rosalind smiled: "I'm pleased, Jesus allowed me to return." Maintaining her cover as an alien by making Jacob believe Jesus had returned her.

"Yes, praise the Lord," Jacob voiced. "I've never thanked God for a meal since you were gone, I'm surprised he even bothers to look down on me," he sighed slowly, enjoying his meal.

"Remember tomorrow what you must do, Jacob," Rosalind advised.

"I'll not forget Rosalind, I'll be on the beach at daybreak with the tractor and manure spreader; free fertiliser," he smiled.

"Tonight Jacob I have to return to heaven; only for one night then I will be with you by the time you've spread the manure tomorrow, breakfast will be on the table waiting for my husband."

"It's a long time since I've heard you call me your husband; warms my soul immensely Rosalind and you are my beautiful wife. I'm such a lucky man I must've really pleased God somewhere for him to return you to my life."

Jacob returned to his sheep to monitor and check if any more had lambed using his quad bike, and trailer pleased him immensely, saved a lot of walking. He watched the misty fog start to engulf the Moor. He dropped another bale of hay off in the sheep rack before heading to the buildings, hearing that strange sound coming from the clifftop. Jacob walked through the misty fog stopped by the fence on the top of the cliff, with Jack close by his heels, watching a bright light vanish.

Rosalind had returned to her spaceship discussing matters with Peter and Matthew. "I presume you are ready? Jacob will be on the beach around 8:30 PM in the morning."

Peter assured: "We are ready; he will have a full load, the maximum he can carry, five tons. We managed to acquire several hundred bodies, we processed and are on the way with the transport to the designated planets. What is the situation between you and Jacob; he appears to be extremely fond of you Rosalind."

"If all humans were like him, we wouldn't have a problem, I haven't detected unkind thoughts in his mind about me. Although at times he's a little suspicious, especially when I make things work and he cannot. I think the most difficult human thing to deal with is pretending to sleep; because we don't, I have to pretend until he's asleep then I can go about my business."

"I detect you are enjoying your assignment, Rosalind," Matthew remarked. "Don't become too attached, although I know highly unlikely; when we decide to eradicate the human race, he will be one of them remember that. Unless Peter and our other brothers and sisters find a way of instilling in humans, the necessity to work hand-in-hand with nature and not just greed and destroy."

"If that time comes before Jacob dies naturally, I may take him home, I enjoy his company," Rosalind remarked deep in thought.

Peter and Matthew glanced to one another considering Rosalind's remark. Peter responded, "he could not travel the vast distance in human form or withstand the prolonged acceleration. If we had solved the problem, we wouldn't be sending humans to feed the animals processed, would be far easier to ship them alive, for the animals to enjoy the chase, and add extra fertiliser to the planet's surface."

"I appreciate what you're saying Peter let's take one step at a time. I'm returning to the farm to ensure Jacob is on the beach ready for the consignment to be transferred." Rosalind flashed her eyes, stepping into the misty fog transporting to the farm. Although still dark outside their eyes shone like torches, she checked the tractor, and manure spreader is ready and returned to the house making breakfast. Jacob sat up in bed smelling bacon and eggs dressing quickly having a quick wash, he sat at the kitchen table enjoying his breakfast. "I haven't slept so peaceably for years now you're back in my life Rosalind, I couldn't wish for anything better," he smiled.

Rosalind kissed him on the cheek, "it's good to be home, don't forget fertiliser this morning Jacob."

"No, it's nearly 8 o'clock, I'll make my way down to the beach," standing up kissing Rosalind on the cheek heading out of the door to the tractor and spreader. The tractor started quickly much to Jacob surprise. Barely daylight the weather is overcast and beginning to snow, he pulled his coat tight trying to stay warm, standing up occasionally warming his hands on the exhaust pipe of the tractor. He finally made his way down onto the beach. He backed up to the water's edge standing by the tractor engine to stay warm the wind is quite vicious cutting along the coastline.

Jacob noticed the misty fog coming in off the sea, and the next minute engulfing the manure spreader and vanishing as if it never existed. He could see the spreader loaded to the brim with a powder. Jacob didn't bother to investigate the contents. He placed another piece of string around his coat, trying to stop the wind opening. He drove steadily up the steep track, the tractor struggling to gain traction, the stones were slippery coated in snow. Jacob breathed a sigh of relief, reaching the top travelling the short distance to the pastureland, spreading the fertiliser very thinly over the pasture. The tractor and spreader performed ideally much to Jacob surprise driving back to the shed. He parked throwing an old sheet over the bonnet of the tractor to keep the weather out of the engine.

Rosalind came from the house, grabbing Jacob's hand, he followed her indoors. "I fed the sheep Jacob and brought in another five ewes and their lambs. I think you should bring the rest of the flock in I've made room in the barn what do you think, husband?"

"I think you are a wonderful, clever wife." Jacob picking her up in his arms, kissing her gently on the lips. "We'll have a quick coffee; Jack and I will bring them in. You stay out of the cold, I don't want anything happening to you," he smiled reassuringly.

Rosalind is starting to enjoy the physical contact, some think totally unnecessary with her own brothers and sisters. They were pure energy created and programmed, mating is impossible in their pure form even if they shapeshifted, they could not participate in other species practices, strictly forbidden and futile.

Jacob patted Jack on the head. "Come on, let's have the sheep in while this weather persists, I don't want to lose any lambs." Rosalind watched them leave stepping out into the blizzarding snow sweeping across the Moor. Jack ran on finding the old ewes bunched behind large boulders. The sheep moved quickly; they knew they were heading for the buildings running on ahead of Jack. Jacob followed, shielding his eyes from the stinging snow. Rosalind had gone out, opening the gates watching the ewes run inside immediately starting to steam. She'd already placed a bale of hay in the rack and filled the troughs with fresh water at least the ewes could lambing comfort now. Jacob a few minutes later joined her at the barn. They both stood there watching whirlwinds curling into the air, twisting the snow in a never-ending dance. Jacob hugged

Rosalind, "thanks for opening the gates I quite forgot; the ewes looked settled, it'll cost a bit to keep them in. I'll have to purchase some creep feed and nuts for the ewes; hopefully, the hay will last until spring. I'd make silage, but I don't have the equipment," he frowned disappointed with his own performance. They ran back into the house followed by Jack, who had turned white, caked in snow, he shook himself by the fire laying down. Rosalind made a coffee, commenting: "I've mended the television, Jacob."

Jacob didn't bother to comment, Rosalind could walk on water there is nothing she couldn't do, she'd always been the same. She placed a hand on his shoulder. "Jacob, you think we should buy a round baler, you can make silage perhaps another tractor." Rosalind had already read his thoughts to ascertain what he really wanted for the spring and summer?

Jacob smiled, "I wish, I'll keep the ewe lambs back, time to increase my flock. I have to change the Ram, as regards affording that sort of equipment only in my dreams," he sighed heavily.

"I'm returning to heaven this evening Jacob, I will talk to Jesus, perhaps he will assist, who knows," she remarked, passing a towel to Jacob to dry his hair and face.

He frowned: "You can't ask God or Jesus for anything else, I have you I will manage Rosalind," he insisted drinking his coffee.

"We shall see Jacob," Rosalind voiced, walking to the far end of the kitchen removing an old shoe-box bringing back to the table, she lifted the lid. Jacob stared in disbelief filled to the brim with money, he didn't realise the money is collected from corpses transported to the spaceship, which they usually burnt having no use for the currency themselves. "Rosalind! Where has it come from?"

"Oh, something I'd saved over the years since I was a child. This is my nest egg, our nest egg I should say. We must purchase out of our area, no one will be none the wiser don't you think husband?"

"I will not touch your savings as tempted as I am; you struggled all your life scrimping to accumulate. I'll not waste your money."

"It's our money, there's barely enough here to buy a second-hand baler and tractor not forgetting the bale wrapper. This is our future Jacob," she insisted firmly.

Jacob gently placed his hands around Rosalind's waist, easing her down onto his knee. "You are a woman to behold; giving without reservation. When the snow has cleared if you insist, I'll look in the farmers weekly and see what's about, the best time to buy is now. Nobody wants a round baler while it's snowing," he chuckled.

She kissed him on the cheek, moving to the kettle boiling the water to make another drink, she glanced from the window you could barely see a few yards in front of the house. After tea, Jacob went out to check on his ewes, discovering two more had lambs he placed them in pens, returning to the house shutting the door on a miserable evening. Rosalind and Jacob watched television for the first time together in four years until the clock struck 11 o'clock, they retired to the bedroom. Jacob drifting off to sleep after Rosalind had placed a hand on his forehead.

She changed quickly heading for the spaceship in the misty fog transporter, waiting for her at the front door. Rosalind walked into the bowels of the spaceship where humans were processed to be transported by another spaceship. Everything is automated the carcasses would come in stripped of any clothing left on the bodies, and laser cutters would remove the flesh away, leaving very few bones to travel with the meat. The rest of the material is incinerated turning into dust, ready for Jacob to spread on the field. Once the flesh is processed, entered an instantaneous blast freezer to keep fresh while they waited for the transport ship which came every month.

Rosalind imagined Jacob on the conveyor on his way to be processed. She jumped, bringing herself back to reality, this is the first time she'd suffered a scenario thought, which is most disturbing. She knew she is fond of Jacob, but couldn't bear the thought of him used as animal food. She is determined there would be a solution, although she feared her brothers and sisters had already read her mind and would be concerned with her thoughts.

Peter joined her, "Rosalind your thoughts are irrational for a Zibyan; you will have to accept the fact if I cannot find a solution, Jacob will die like the rest of the human race. They are little more than rodents, destroying everything of beauty. What makes matters worse, we created these monsters through meddling with the genetics of the chimpanzee. Now the chimpanzees suffer at the hands of these hybrids; we will stop them, Rosalind." Peter walked off, not waiting for Rosalind to reply. Rosalind thought she must not make her thoughts available to all, although it would be challenging to have anything private in the Zibyan culture, everyone is designed to read everyone else's opinions to prevent hostility amongst the collective.

Rosalind returned to the farm, remembering to change her appearance stepping from the misty fog transporter by the sheep pens, watching Jacob come from the house. He commented, "you ever sleep Rosalind you're always up before me," he chuckled.

"How'd you know I actually sleep Jacob," she remarked, patting his cheek. "I'll make breakfast while you feed the ewes and lambs, I see two more have lambed during the night." Rosalind walked off towards the house, she wondered how Jacob would react if he knew who she really is? She realised she is contemplating things she usually wouldn't. Zibyans never considered any other race to be of any significance; they were little more than a plaything, an experiment. When she was programmed, history showed, they had created everything, they were the beginning, and the end should it come to that. Rosalind remembered her first sense of consciousness, fully formed as pure energy. She remembered the computer instructing her on her abilities, considering, she was only an hour from creation. Rosalind quickly gathered her thoughts; her mind is wandering, she didn't know why Zibyans didn't behave similarly to her. Yes, they could think and solve problems, never pondered on the past very often she considered the computer has designed their thoughts never to look at history unless essential.

Except where planet Earth is concerned, created initially as a breeding ground for various types of lifeform, after several millions of years of development; mutating creatures until they made the grave mistake of humans. Many debates were held, some Zibyans wanted them exterminated immediately, and others wanted to see what the outcome would be. Now Zibyans know! Humans were in the same category as rabbits and rats and would have to be controlled. Rosalind thoughts returned to preparing egg and bacon with fried bread for Jacob; her mind kept wandering trying to solve issues if they were real issues. Jacob entered the house kissing Rosalind on the cheek fondly, sitting down to his breakfast with a large cup of coffee. "I'm afraid I put the Ram into early this year, a silly bloody mistake," he cursed, "at least will have early lambs but it does create an awful lot of hard work," he frowned.

Rosalind patted him on the shoulder, "We will survive Jacob, may add a few extra pounds towards our future. Look what I found last week's farmers weekly; I went for a walk along the cliff enjoying the fresh air from the sea, someone must have dropped the magazine, how lucky," she commented, placing on the table in front of Jacob. He glanced up grinning knowing Rosalind had somehow acquired this, she is not a patient woman when Rosalind wanted something, is now; which made him laugh even more. Rosalind had read his thoughts pretending to be surprised at his laughter, as he opened the farmers weekly looking down the for sale section.

CHAPTER 2

Rosalind's in Control

Jacob noticed to biro marks highlighting, one round baler and bale wrapper. A little further down the page, an old 188 Massey Ferguson tractor four-wheel-drive with eight thousand hours on the clock. In brackets, bale loader available for this tractor along with muck fork and bucket. Jacob glanced to Rosalind, "I presume you've already purchased?"

"No, Jacob it must be your decision as well, I have to admit, when I was in heaven, I made contact with the small dealership in South Wales asking their opinion of the machines. What would they do for a cash settlement? I didn't want us wasting our time travelling," she remarked casually.

Jacob burst out laughing, "I presume you've worked out how we're going to travel there, my Land Rover isn't road legal as you reminded me."

"Well yes sort of, Jesus has arranged this for us, a little risky," she remarked, slipping on her coat passing Jacob his. She held his hand, leading him out of the front door into a misty fog; wasn't there earlier. Jacob suddenly feeling ill with the speed of travel; this is one of the problems Zibyans were trying to resolve when transporting humans over vast distances alive. Humans physiology couldn't stand the acceleration. Lucky as the crow flies; only three hundred or so miles away from where they lived on the moor. Jacob started to recover as he stepped from the mist into brilliant sunshine with Rosalind. She held his hand tightly, guiding him in the direction of the machinery dealership. She'd already travelled herself, making sure the equipment is sound to purchase before ever considering mentioning to Jacob. They entered the storage yard Rosalind showing Jacob the equipment. "Looks wonderful Rosalind for its age, can we afford it," Jacob sighed?

"Lead the negotiations to me, Jacob," she smiled, kissing him on the cheek, she walked off to the sales office with her shoe-box tucked under her arm. Rosalind entered the office, holding the sales rep's hand. She is now in control; she agreed the price she thought is fair, plus delivery to the farm over the next couple of weeks. The sales rep wrote out a sale ticket with a six-month warranty on the pieces of equipment.

Rosalind left the sales office enjoying the ability to manipulate situations, she had generally taken for granted. "I paid the salesperson they will deliver in a couple of weeks, come on, let's go home out of this miserable weather, starting to look overcast again Jacob," Rosalind smiled. Her facial expressions were becoming more comfortable to perform these days. They walked off into a small woodland stepping into the misty fog and were immediately transported to the Moor, Jacobs farm. He stepped from the mist falling over, struggling to control his sense of balance. Rosalind realised what is killing the humans in transport; their brains were being turned inside out in their skulls, their balance couldn't handle the velocity of travel.

Peter aboard the spaceship is receiving the information from Rosalind, realising if they sedated the humans while travelling, this might solve the problem and a way of transporting to the home planet for distribution as animal feed.

Rosalind helped Jacob into the house, sitting him by the fire in his armchair, making him a coffee; while he gathered his thoughts. She hoped no permanent damage is caused to him during transport as it had killed so many other humans. Rosalind left Jacob to rest venturing outside in the snow to check on the sheep; lambing appeared to be in full swing; 10 ewes had lambed. She carefully checked the animals, placing in pens marking each lamb with its own number so it would never be lost.

Jacob glanced to the mantelpiece looking at the urn with Rosalind's Ashes. He rose to his feet suspicious of everything, he opened the top of the urn Rosalind's Ashes were gone? Had Jesus or God re-created his Rosalind? Perhaps he is irrational, he concluded, and shouldn't be questioning the gift of Rosalind. Jacob realised for the first time in years, he's smiling, that is thanks to Rosalind, she made his life perfect or as perfect as it can be living on the Moor. He watched Rosalind come in from the cold, not in the slightest bothered by the plummeting temperature. "Do you feel better, Jacob?" she asked, concerned.

"Yes, thank you, I presume we travelled the distance in seconds and my sense of balance couldn't cope although it never affected you, Rosalind?"

"You must remember Jacob, I am accustomed to travelling at high speed; when you live in heaven that is the way you travel. God wouldn't have subjected you to the speed if he didn't think you would survive Jacob. That would rather defeat his plans for you which there are many, he will enlighten you as time progresses. What did you really think of the equipment Jacob are you pleased?"

"Very pleased; you selected excellently, I hope we have operators manuals with the equipment? I've never used a round baler only a conventional one. I have used a tractor and loader before when my dad hired one from a friend. One year there was so much seaweed washed up on the shore, a golden opportunity for free fertiliser, my father and I trailered it and stockpiled," Jacob reminisced. Rosalind smiled, "you have nothing to worry about Jacob; I've used a round baler and a tractor and loader before we were married, on work experience, and the bale wrapper which virtually operates itself," she assured confidently.

"That was years ago Rosalind things have changed," Jacob smiled.

She patted Jacob on the head. "Why do you think I selected that particular round baler, bale wrapper tractor and loader; because those were the ones I'd driven before," Rosalind actually chuckled for the first time.

Jacob shook his head; venturing outside to check the ewes and lambs once more before retiring to bed, finding more ewes had delivered. He marked the individual lambs and mothers penning them together, running short of space he realised before returning to the house with Jack close to his heels. He and Rosalind sat together on the old settee watching television until 11:30 PM, before venturing into the bedroom. Rosalind lay in bed kissing Jacob on the forehead, touching him with her hand he fell into a deep sleep. She immediately changed her appearance stepping outside the front door into the misty fog transporting to the spaceship, flashing her eyes to Peter and Matthew with the usual greeting. "We are running tests after we heard the conversation between you and Jacob; you must be very careful Rosalind, I think he's quite suspicious of everything," Peter suggested.

"I have Jacob under my control Peter, he's blissfully unaware of who I really am; he believes Jesus and God sent me to him, he accepts that explanation wholeheartedly."

Matthew suggested: "While we are all together, I would strongly recommend our next shipment of humans should come from the Arab countries. I have seen the way they treat animals, I want animals to have the opportunity to return the compliment."

Both Rosalind and Peter glanced to Matthew, surprised at his suggestion. "Nothing has changed for centuries Matthew what suddenly brings this to your urgent attention?" Peter asked.

"I have been here the same length at you two for thousands of years, we are fortunate we never age, or our powers deplete. I have watched the animal activists, try to protect the creatures of burden from punishment. Our fault Peter we made the donkey special allowing Jesus to use him to ride into Bethlehem on you remember?"

Peter turned to look at Matthew: "We have made many errors Matthew, my brother; we could use this situation to our advantage. We know Jacob travelled merely three hundred miles in our transport, which made him ill, not fatally thankfully. I suggest you try and transport alive Arab to hear; if he survives sedate him, and accumulate sufficient for the transport vessel, we will send live food to the animals to enjoy the chase. I think that is what's called sweet revenge by humans."

Both Matthew and Rosalind flashed their eyes, approving Peter's suggestion. Rosalind commented, "if you can't transport them alive Matthew to hear, I would suggest you send out a stun ray and discreetly render the individual unconscious, transport them here, and sedate for the journey to the home planet for distribution."

Matthew flashed his eyes frantically almost excited by the approval, disappearing to the rear of the spaceship to make preparations. Peter looked at Rosalind flashing his eyes, "you must return to Jacob before he wakes, although you appear to have the situation under control Rosalind. We were fortunate your experiment with Jacob showed us the way forward. I hear our collective praising your name," Peter flashed his eyes walking off in human form.

Rosalind made her way along the corridor, stepping into the misty fog immediately changing her appearance, reappearing by the sheep in the barn. Much to her surprise, Jacob is already out there shining his torch checking on his sheep. Jacob jumped, "I came out looking for you Rosalind you weren't in bed. I presumed you were here with the sheep. Where have you been?"

"Well if you must know Jacob, I ran away with a little green man who came to earth in a spaceship. Actually, I went for a quiet walk to gather my thoughts," she assured. "That reminds me, we are short of groceries Jacob you will have to visit the local shop. I will write down the list of things I want you to purchase for me," she patted his cheek. "I'll make breakfast." Rosalind walked off before Jacob could make another comment. He couldn't help smiling; he could never remember Rosalind quite so outspoken, but he didn't care; she is here making his life perfect and fulfilled.

Jacob entered the house finding his breakfast on the table, 3 slices of fried bread, each with an egg on top coated with baked beans. Jacob smiled pleasantly grabbing a crusty slice of bread mopping his plate, making sure there wasn't a morsel left. Jack had sat there waiting for a scrap, Rosalind opened the front door throwing a bone outside. Jack ran out to retrieve from the snow realising he is conned. Rosalind had shut him outside with the bone so he couldn't make a mess on the floor. Jack wandered off, laying between bales of straw crunching on his bone.

Jacob kissed Rosalind on the cheek, "I hope my old Land Rover will make it across the Moor, the snow may have drifted in places on the track," he suggested quite concerned, watching Rosalind place her thick coat on and gloves.

"I'll come with you Jacob, I've already thrown a shovel in the back of the Land Rover just in case," she smiled, displaying a human expression.

"Don't be silly Rosalind your freeze out there; I don't want anything to happen to you," he assured firmly.

"In which case, I'd better drive," she grinned quite enjoying using human facial expressions which she is now becoming accustomed to. Jacob burst out laughing following Rosalind out of the door. She climbed into the driver's side of the Land Rover, checking her memory banks. Selected four-wheel-drive starting the old diesel engine, studying a G P S map in her computerised mind of exactly where the track is under the snow. There were no visible landmarks left apart from the odd rock. Jacob sat there, astounded by her skill. She knew the Moor like him, but he'd never imagined she could drive the Land Rover on the old track when you couldn't see where it is in places, another miracle to behold he thought.

Rosalind left the Moor, driving on the snow-covered road. Jacob is absolutely shocked, she preached to him the vehicle wasn't roadworthy, yet she is on the side road heading for the shop. Admittedly he thought the chances of seeing a police officer were very slim in these conditions. Rosalind parked outside the shop, Jacob said nothing. They both entered Rosalind grabbed the trolley, and by the time he'd reached the checkout, there wasn't room to put anything else in. Jacob dreaded the bill suspecting to be horrendous. Rosalind smiled at the cashier when the bill came to £120 which Rosalind paid for in cash. Jacob had already started stacking the groceries into boxes provided by the store, glad to be rid of them. He slowly carried each box outside into the blizzarding snow, placing in the back of his Land Rover, pulling down the tarpaulin to prevent the snow penetrating.

Rosalind sat in the driver's seat again, Jacob sat there grinning, watching Rosalind select four-wheel-drive, heading back the way they came. She left the road cutting across the Moor, she could see faint tracks from where they came across to the shop, which made it easier to find their way home. Jacob had to ask: "I see it's okay for you to drive on the road with a dodgy vehicle and not me?"

She grinned, patting Jacob's leg, "I'm in full control Jacob of any eventuality, you've known me long enough, I only take calculated risks. I shouldn't imagine a policeman is within a hundred miles of the shop in these conditions."

He didn't bother to reply, looked across the bleak Moor barely able to see a hundred yards in front of him and somewhat relieved to be home. Jacob quickly carried the boxes of groceries into the kitchen for Rosalind to disperse amongst the shelving. He kissed her on the cheek venturing outside again to check on the ewes; only to discover another 10 had lambed, Jacob quickly checked their health and marked with a number, realising he'd forgotten all about Christmas, already, 31 December. Rosalind hadn't reminded him which he thought is strange; she always used to like Christmas. Jacob sighed heavily walking back to the house, finding Rosalind busily stacking shelves. "We didn't celebrate Christmas Rosalind," Jacob expressed concerned.

She smiled, "I thought I'm your Christmas present. Jesus wasn't born on 25 December, you know that is a made update for convenience Jacob, so why celebrate something false?"

He placed his hands in the air in the surrendering posture, kissing Rosalind on the cheek. She looked away continuing with her groceries, while Jacob sat by the fire with Jack by his chair.

Rosalind, enjoying living on the farm with Jacob immensely, in the thousands of years she'd been on earth; she had never ventured far from the spaceship only once betraying Mary Magdalene. She found humans extraordinarily boring and repetitive. They seem to be only interested in procreation, inflicting misery on another creature and destroying the planet, which supports their very existence. Jacob is different, she enjoyed his company, although he wasn't her own kind, he had good quality's, he is her pet to do as she pleased with. Although thought pet is being somewhat demeaning. She is quite surprised he hasn't tried to venture further than kissing, which male and female humans seem to enjoy participating in. Rosalind carried a mug of coffee to Jacob waking him, he'd fallen asleep in the chair. "Don't forget Jacob tomorrow fertiliser, I know the weather is foul if you like I will collect the fertiliser?"

"No, I can manage you sure it will arrive in these conditions, Rosalind?"

"Yes, the fertiliser will arrive, but this will be the last load for some time, I suspect it's nothing you've done Jacob there's a slight change of plans I believe."

"Oh well, we mustn't complain," he smiled, drinking his coffee quite suspicious of the whole operation.

Jacob and Rosalind retired to bed; she kissed him on the forehead holding his hand. Jacob immediately fell asleep.

Rosalind slid out of bed, changing her appearance walking to the front door; she stepped into the misty fog transported to the spaceship. Peter is waiting for her, "we have success Rosalind, admittedly Matthew has to transmit a stun ray; he managed to wipe out a Sahara Desert tribe in one mission. They are sedated the transport ship is due here in the next hour. They will be shipped alive and make conscious before dispersed amongst the planets for the animals to enjoy the chase. The humans will learn what it's like to be ill-treated, they will finally experience my writings of hell."

"I hope Peter the home planet will record events, I want to see the humans suffer the way they made the animals in their charge."

"I agree with you sister, I will summon you when the information arrives; we should have within seven days. The seventh-day, the sabbath as I named in the Bible, which the humans fail to observe in most cases. What are these thoughts in your processor Rosalind of experimenting further with Jacob? There is no need for you to subject your systems to intercourse; serves no purpose we know all there is to know."

"Are you instructing me, Peter, not to experiment further with Jacob? Have any Zibyan's attempted such a task to find out the fascinations? We have watched and experimented with humans. Not one Zibyan has actually experienced the information. If I find it displeasing, I'm sure the central computer will rectify my memory banks."

Peter and Rosalind flashed their eyes at each other in respect. Peter moved away, changing his form into pure light. Rosalind walked down the corridor stepping into the misty fog, changing her appearance transported to the sheep, noticing there were more lambs born during the night. She quickly marked and separated into pens before returning to the house. Jacob yawning coming out of there bedroom, watching Rosalind start to prepare breakfast. "There's no need to go out Jacob, they're fine, more lambs," she smiled. "Oh yes, don't forget, have your breakfast and head down to the beach; be careful the rocks will be slippy on the track I don't want anything to happen to you," patting his cheek. Jacob quickly devoured his breakfast, not wishing to be late for the Lord's work.

"I'll be careful," slipping on his thick old army overcoat along with his woolly gloves and cap, he stepped out of the house. He shielded his eyes from the blizzard removing the old tarpaulin from the bonnet of his tractor, struggling to get her to start. Finally, with a cloud of black smoke from the exhaust pipe, the old Fordson major burst into life. He steadily drove along the track slowly descending, feeling the tractor slipping and sliding a very precarious descent. Eventually reaching the beach, he drove some distance and parked where he had before. Jacob left the tractor running; he dare not stop the engine in case she wouldn't start again. He noticed the thick misty fog approach from far out to sea, engulfing his manure spreader. Jacob felt the tractor shudder as the load is placed in the spreader. He watched the misty fog vanish into thin air as if it never existed, he glanced back to see the spreader loaded with a fine powder. Jacob drove steadily along the beach looking at the slope he would have to climb, he selected a lower gear and opened the tractor throttle considerably; he attempted to climb selecting differential lock to increase his traction.

Rosalind had turned herself invisible, watching everything from the clifftop; she could see the old tractor is struggling to acquire sufficient traction. Jacob finally levelled out on top of the cliff heading straight for the pastureland, immediately

Aliens

discharging the contents of the manure spreader across the covered grass, turning the snow a grey colour where he travelled.

Rosalind returned to the house, she quickly changed her appearance waiting for Jacob to return. She heard him parked the tractor by the barn. Jacob quickly checked the ewes to see if there were any more lambs before dashing into the house. Rosalind helped him remove his coat hanging on the back of the door where it could drip without causing too much mess. "I shan't be going down there again with the tractor for a while Rosalind to dangerous; I didn't think I'd make it back," he remarked, sitting at the kitchen table. Rosalind made the coffee passing a mug to Jacob, she sat quietly opposite receiving a telepathic message from Peter. "The transport ship had left Earth's atmosphere, heading home with a live consignment." Rosalind didn't flinch, she didn't want Jacob to realise someone is communicating with her. The wind started to howl drifting the snow, Jacob hoped the thatched roof would hold fast in these conditions. Rosalind realised Jacob is anxious after reading his thoughts. She placed her hand on his forehead; he drifted off to sleep. Jack laying by the fire, glanced to Rosalind and looked away. Rosalind carefully carried Jacob to his armchair, positioning him comfortably. She changed her appearance stepping from the house into the misty fog transported directly to the spaceship many fathoms below the sea.

"What are you not telling me, Peter," Rosalind asked.

"I am concealing nothing Rosalind, although I am concerned this will be the first live shipment of humans, unconscious they are harmless. When they are awake, they are dangerous as you've seen for yourself."

"You notified the ship commander Peter of his cargo, only a matter of a maximum of four days, depending on the weight he's carrying. I foresee no problems. Here's Matthew approaching. What is your view Matthew," Rosalind asked.

"Peter is right to be cautious; we are dealing with the unknown. We have never transported live humans before; although they are sedated at the moment. Once they're on the designated planets and revived, who knows what will happen? We will have to wait for the information to be transmitted to us."

Rosalind enquired: "How many humans are on board the transport ship? They are in sealed containers, I presume Matthew?"

"Yes Rosalind and with a force field in place, anyone who left the containment area would be exterminated. We've only sent 200 as a test."

"We must remember; the atmosphere they are entering, when they regain consciousness is very thin, not formed properly at the moment. The humans will struggle to perform if they can't breathe adequately. We are not affected by such restrictions, don't forget, we can destroy with one touch. They are insignificant in the scheme of things," Rosalind assured.

Peter and Matthew flashed their eyes at Rosalind. Peter spoke, "we gain strength from your positive thoughts, Rosalind, I'm sure Matthew will agree everything you have said is the truth; although I do detest violence, except against violent beings."

Rosalind flashed her eyes; Peter and Matthew responded vanishing. Rosalind stepped into the misty fog waiting for her at the end of the corridor. She changed her appearance while transported to the farm. She checked the ewes and lambs and the thatched roof before returning to the house, hoping she can allay Jacob's fears. She smiled, noticing he's drinking a pint of his home-brew, sitting at the kitchen table. "Where have you been," Jacob asked in a serious tone.

Rosalind realised, he'd had more than one pint of home-brew by the slur in his voice. "Checking the sheep not sitting here drinking the Devils poison. One glass is sufficient, more is sinful Jacob," Rosalind remarked. She Grabbed the glass pouring the remainder down the sink. Before Jacob could move, Rosalind touched his forehead, Jacob is unconscious, she carried him into the bedroom, casting on the bed in an unceremonious action, disgusted with Jacob's behaviour. Jack, the faithful sheepdog, stayed by the hearth sensing Rosalind could harm him.

Jacob awoke the next morning with a hangover, he dressed and wandered into the kitchen holding his head; discovering Rosalind about to make breakfast pouring him a coffee. Neither spoke; Jacob is ashamed of himself and decided to break the ice with the words: "I apologise for my behaviour Rosalind."

"I'll check the sheep Jacob," she remarked, heading for the door, slipping on her coat, leaving Jacob to make his own breakfast. Rosalind discovered lambs appeared to be everywhere. She spent some time sorting out which lambs belong to which ewe. She would be glad when lambing is finished, and thankfully the air is decidedly warmer this morning. Rosalind fed the sheep returning to the house to find Jacob had made breakfast for her, which she didn't really want.

Nevertheless, she would have to consume and dispose of at a later date when he wasn't looking. She knew if she discharged the unwanted food, Jack would gladly eat quickly. Jacob said nothing pouring the coffee slipping on his coat heading outside. Rosalind grinned, placing her plate on the floor quickly. Jack cleared within seconds. She put the plate in the sink along with the other dirty cutlery and started washing up before Jacob returned.

Jack started barking, he could hear something. Rosalind glanced to the door slightly concerned, Jack wouldn't bark if Jacob is approaching. Rosalind cautiously opened the door she could see nothing and sensed nothing. Jack ran between Rosalind's legs heading across the Moor barking. Jacob came running to the house, "what's upset, Jack?"

"I have no idea Jacob, I can't see anything, can you?"

Jacob scanned after grabbing his binoculars from the window sill, noticing some distance ahead, Jack herding a ewe and two lambs towards the buildings. Jacob chuckled, "that old dog doesn't miss a trick and can count the flock better than me. I hadn't realised a ewe was missing." He went outside opening the pen, placing some hay and sheep nuts for the old ewe; she'd come home with two beautiful lambs. He marked them with a number marking the old ewe with a unique mark, so he knew she would have to stay; whatever happened she is not to be sold to valuable. Jacob returned to the house, mixing a bowl of food for Jack. Patting him, placing the bowl on the floor. He hadn't realised this is a bonus meal for Jack he'd already had bacon and eggs. Jack looked in his bowl less than impressed with what is on offer after Rosalind had fed him. Jacob embraced Rosalind taking her entirely by surprise, she rather enjoyed the closeness sending strange sensations to her mind; for the first time since she'd returned Jacob passionately kissed her. This is definitely different; she knew what he is performing, she'd watched hundreds of humans do the same. Although never experienced the sensation herself until now.

A week had passed Rosalind received a telepathic message from Peter, "he'd received a transmission from the home planet; she is to return to the spaceship as soon as possible." Rosalind moved away, patting Jacob's cheek. "I'm taking a walk Jacob down onto the beach, there isn't a chill in the air this morning. I need some fresh air," she smiled, slipping on her coat.

"I'll stay here Rosalind and look after the sheep; be careful on those slippy stones. I know the snow is starting to melt; we could still have more though, I don't think winters finished with us yet."

She smiled, leaving the house, walking to the end of the barn she stepped into the misty fog, transported aboard the spaceship. Peter and Matthew were waiting for her; they greeted each other with a flash of their eyes. Rosalind sat on something you couldn't see as if suspended without any support, Matthew and Peter sat similarly. They watched intently the whole wall became a film as if they were actually on the planet themselves. The naked humans were released from their unconsciousness, standing to look around. Firstly alarmed they were naked and secondly hearing the sound of what appeared to be ferocious animals growling in the vegetation. The human scattered into the undergrowth mothers and children alike; males grabbing sticks in their attempt to protect themselves from whatever they were facing. Not very long before screaming could be heard, they watched a woman torn apart by lions. Peter commented: "Excellent now the humans know what it's like to have pain in flicked it on them, without having any defence." They spent the next two hours watching humans torn apart by various animals. Matthew remarked, "a very successful mission, everything went according to plan. I must start and search for my next victims; finally, we have a use for humans not only feeding our pets but entertainment as well for our brothers and sisters."

Rosalind, Peter and Matthew glanced to one another, flashing their eyes, each going their separate ways. Rosalind changed and transported to the beach. She hadn't realised Jacob is stood on the cliff watching her step from the misty fog. Jacob quickly moved away, so she didn't see him walking back to the buildings with Jack. By the time Rosalind had joined him, Jacob is feeding the sheep and checking on the newly born lambs. Rosalind read his thoughts realising what he'd seen, deciding to say nothing for the moment and see what transpired. She could dismiss simply by saying that is the way she travelled from heaven. Whether he would, believe it or not, is another story. Rosalind returned to the house starting to prepare lunch. Jacob stayed outside with the sheep deciding to take a walk down onto the beach to make sure his eyes were not deceiving him. He slowly walked along the water's edge, the waves gently advanced towards the cliff. Jacob noticed Rosalind's footsteps suddenly appear in the sand heading to the track from the beach. He now had confirmation he didn't imagine things, he stood for a moment looking out to sea for any signs of a vessel. Jacob sighed heavily, slowly walking from the beach, returning to the farm buildings and his beloved sheep.

Rosalind called from the doorway. "Jacob lunch."

Jacob responded: "I'll be there in a minute." He wondered whether he should say anything concerning his suspicions; perhaps he should watch Rosalind a little closer before confronting her with his concerns. After all, he'd long to have his wife, why destroy something, he wanted by opening his mouth and probably saying the wrong thing. He entered the house sitting quietly at the table, enjoying his beautiful lunch. Rosalind reading his mind, understanding his past thoughts concerning what he saw. She knew this would fester in his mind; she decided to repel any suspicions he may have. "You noticed me returning from heaven, Jacob, and you never mentioned why? Are you keeping secrets from your wife now?"

He exhaled, lowering his knife and fork to the plate. "That's not what I envisage; when you go to heaven, I thought it would be vertical; not horizontal and coming in from the ocean in a misty fog."

"I should imagine, God and Jesus must be rolling about in heaven laughing at your comment Jacob; you have no idea what heaven is like. You only perceive what you think is right, not what God thinks is right. If I were you, I would dismiss your ignorant thoughts before I'm taken away from you again," Rosalind warned.

Jacob didn't reply; he continued to finish his lunch. "Thank you! I enjoyed immensely," Jacob moving from the table; slipping on his coat, grabbing his crook from by the door going outside. He jumped in his Land Rover heading across the Moor parked on the edge; he walked the mile to the shop. Jacob purchased a newspaper returning to his Land Rover, he sat catching up with world events, hoping there is something in there would give him a clue to what he didn't know. All he had his suspicions. Jacob noticed a small piece written about a tribe who lived in the Sahara Desert, had vanished without a trace; the only thing remaining is the animals roaming freely.

Rosalind reading his thoughts, Jacob wasn't the pushover she'd envisaged, she is convinced he is so in love with the Bible; he would believe anything she said to cover her tracks.

Jacob knew something didn't feel right; he just couldn't put his finger on what it is. Rosalind is correct how would he know how God operated? Why couldn't Rosalind come in from the sea in a misty fog, make no sense for her to travel here in full view? If she is seen by somebody, there would be an uproar. He exhaled, folding the newspaper placing on the passenger seat, he steadily drove home with more questions than answers. Jacob checked the ewes before venturing in the house. Rosalind sat watching television, Coronation Street, which made him smile; she used to be addicted to the program when they first married. Rosalind must be Rosalind, there could be no other explanation he concluded.

She smiled, placing the kettle on the stove, reading his thoughts as she made the tea passing Jacob a cup in his arm-chair by the fire. She returned to the settee turning the channel over on the television with the remote watching Emmerdale farm. Jacob nearly burst out laughing, this had to be Rosalind, another one of her favourite programs, although as far as he is concerned is an absolute load of tripe; the farming aspect is no longer there. Jacob fell asleep in the chair with Jack close by. Rosalind placed her hand gently on Jacob's forehead, changing her appearance, she walked out of the door stepping into the misty fog transporting her directly to the spaceship.

Peter is waiting, flashing his eyes: "You will have to be more careful Rosalind if you keep raising his suspicions, you could be in trouble. Although he couldn't harm you, he could direct the other humans to our spaceship location."

"Understood Peter, surprised he is suspicious or may have been just a stroke of luck as humans would describe."

"Now we can transport humans alive, you could actually dispose of him; we no longer need to spread human remains on land Rosalind."

"No, we don't know what will happen in the near future, I will keep him. I find the whole experience rather intriguing, he is quite unpredictable at times."

"I can't understand your fascination with one human male; he's not even what humans would call attractive. We certainly wouldn't rate him as anything other than animal food Rosalind. Perhaps you should stay away from the farm for a few weeks or permanently would be a better solution."

"Our brothers and sisters gave him to me, are you saying you have all changed your mind, I'm now to abandon my experiments, with Jacob?"

"Your brothers and sisters will not prevent you from carrying out whatever experiments you see fit. They are like me concerned you are becoming too involved with an inferior species of little value to the Zibyans. You are unlikely to discover anything we haven't already."

"That is why I am a higher grade scientist than you, Peter; that is how we discovered the best way to transport humans alive thanks to me, Peter!" She flashed her eyes, walking away, starting to understand why humans became annoyed, something she hadn't experienced before until now. Rosalind changed her appearance, stepping into the misty fog transporting to the beach. She stepped out onto the sand, slowly walking along the beach until she ascended the old track, carved in the cliffside hundreds of years ago by peasant farmers to transport seaweed for fertiliser. She finally reached the farm noticing Jacob checking the ewes, separating the final two ewes completing the lambing for this year. Jacob couldn't believe he hadn't lost a lamb a miracle in itself. Rosalind read his mind smiling at his thoughts not only of the sheep but her.

Jacob, without warning, scooped Rosalind up in his arms, she placed her arm quickly around his neck firmly, wondering what he's planning. She read his mind to ascertain if she is in danger or not. Rosalind smiled realising what he is trying to achieve now and had to make the decision did she want to go that far? She allowed Jacob to carry her into the house, he lowered her to her feet. Rosalind didn't know whether she is relieved or disappointed, he hadn't gone further. He kissed her very lovingly as he always did, there is nothing aggressive about Jacob in the slightest, which she quite admired. She quickly made two coffees while Jacob threw wood on the fire. She rejoined him carrying 2 cups; he sat in his armchair and Rosalind decided to sit on his lap, she never saw Jacob smile so much since she'd known him. Jacob started kissing her neck. Rosalind is intrigued she watched his fingers slowly unbutton her blouse, sliding his hand inside and caressing her. Rosalind had strange senses running through her, nothing is unpleasant. She jumped to her feet, holding Jacob's hand, leading him into the bedroom, she removed her clothes laying on the bed Jacob did likewise. Finally, Rosalind had experienced lovemaking which she didn't find an uncomfortable experience. However, from a Zibyans perspective, the sensation is similar to plugging yourself into the electric mains, she would receive the same tingling sensation, less the messy stuff.

They both showered and dressed, Jacob is now convinced this had to be Rosalind, Rosalind is reading his mind, pleased with the outcome, his suspicions had drifted off into the back of his mind. She made two more drinks sitting watching television for the rest of the evening; while Jacob went out to check on the ewes and lambs. When he finally returned, they retired to bed Rosalind placed her hand in his and Jacob entered into a deep sleep. She quickly changed her appearance heading for the door stepping in the misty fog transported to the spaceship. Peter and Matthew were both waiting for her arrival; they flash their eyes at each other in a pleasant manner. They sat side-by-side, watching more transmissions from the three planets they were slowly turning into replicas of earth. Rosalind noticed, the humans transported to the planets, still found time for sex, although they were likely to die soon ravaged by the wildlife. She couldn't understand the fascination and concluded it's because she wasn't human. She watched the two-hour transmission and about to leave. Peter commented, "have you finished experimenting Rosalind; there isn't much else you can do with him now he might as well go on the next shipment."

"No, I have not finished with him and may keep him till he dies a natural death; unless I decide to send him as animal food." Rosalind walked off, which is rather rude not acknowledging Peter or Matthew with the courteous eye flash.

Matthew and Peter appeared in front of her, inhibiting her return to the farm. "You may not leave the spaceship until we receive a courteous acknowledgement; you are aware of the rules Rosalind, no Zibyan may dishonour another."

Rosalind knew she couldn't overpower two, wondered why the thought had ever entered her mind. She flashed her eyes at Peter and Matthew. They moved aside; Rosalind continued stepping into the misty fog transporting to the beach.

On the clifftop, Jacob watched Rosalind step from the misty fog onto the sand. He returned to the sheep realising he would have to accept the fact he didn't understand heaven, or God and how things worked. He's a mere mortal in the scheme of things little more than an insect in God's eyes. Rosalind read his thoughts as she walked from the beach. She concluded the more times he saw her step from the misty fog, the less suspicious he would become. He would eventually accept, she would have to travel to heaven occasionally.

Rosalind approached Jacob kissing him on the cheek. "I'll make breakfast," she continued walking to the house, preparing breakfast. She would make believe she had eaten something before Jacob arrived; saving her discharging on wanted food. Although Jack thought terrific, he'd never lived so high and mighty before, only had scraps and dog biscuits.

Jacob came into the house, sitting down for a lovely bacon and egg breakfast. "I saw you watching me from the cliff, Jacob. Does it bother you? I have to travel occasionally."

"I must admit Rosalind I find it strange; although its God's wish and I'm a lucky man to have his wife, I will have to accept what is. I'm in no position to question what God decides is right or wrong," Jacob expressed honestly.

Rosalind smiled: "God will be pleased with your attitude. Jacob, you will see many strange things God performs, you are a privileged one; except what is and enjoy his glorious gift of me."

He smiled glancing to Rosalind, "you are surely a gift, turning my life away from misery."

"You may receive a greater gift of travel through the heavens, to a place far beyond your imagination; no other human has visited until they are dead," she suggested conjuring another experiment.

Jacob stared bewildered: "you mean, I will visit heaven, surely not until my allotted time?"

"The journey will not be easy Jacob you may suffer from travel sickness," she chuckled.

"Who will look after the animals, you can't leave them to starve Rosalind, wait until they are on the moor again," Jacob suggested trying to stop smiling.

Rosalind cleared the table washing everything in the sink. She dried her hands on the tea towel, slipping on her coat. "let us walked Jacob across the Moor," she remarked, looking out of the window. "Not a bad morning, I remember when we first met; you nearly walked my legs off across the Moor," she laughed checking her memory banks for information on Rosalind and her likes and dislikes. He smiled slipping on his coat, grabbing his crook opening the door Rosalind stepped out followed by Jack. They followed the well-worn sheep tracks carved out by animals over the centuries. The air is brisk with the grey covered sky in places; at this time of year, the weather can change in seconds. They walked for two hours, noticing the grass is recovering as the snow cleared. Jacob is desperate to have the sheep outside again; the cost of feeding them indoors is draining his profits. The only thing that killed lambs more than anything else is wet weather, cold they can stand hiding behind their mothers or rocks. Rosalind and Jacob returned to the farm deciding to release half the flock with the eldest lambs. The old ewes were keen the thought of eating fresh grass appealed to them, the lambs followed quickly. Rosalind suggested, "let's walk down onto the beach, you never know there may be a surprise there for you, Jacob!"

"You keeping secrets from me again, woman," he patted her backside, holding her hand. They strolled off towards the beach down the rocky track cut into the cliff face, finally reaching the sand. The smell of the sea air is always fresh and inviting to the nostrils. Jacob had spent some time down here when he was younger fishing catching mackerel and plaice. Rosalind suggested, "you should come fishing Jacob; good protein, I remember you bringing me fishing once, and we ended up behind that rock over there," Rosalind displayed a grin.

He chuckled remembering what had taken place and he still managed to catch half a dozen fish. Jacob scooped Rosalind up in his arms, carrying her towards the rocks. She struggled to escape. "I prefer the bed," she smiled.

"I know the old bones there not what they used to be, I prefer a little comfort." Jacob noticed the misty fog coming in from the sea, a narrow strip no more than 3 meters wide. Rosalind smiled realising Peter had prepared a welcome for Jacob and had agreed with her thoughts of transporting him. Rosalind encouraged, "come along Jacob nothing will harm you. You are with me." They both walked into the misty fog; within seconds they were aboard the spaceship, Jacob looked watching the fish swim past unconcerned. Peter appeared in his robe along with Matthew. Jacob believed he is in the presence of disciples dropped to his knees in respect. "Stand Jacob, I am Peter one of the Lord's disciples, and this is Matthew, you read his Scriptures not so long ago; we watched you from heaven."

Jacob stood with his head, bowed: "Thank God for returning Rosalind to me. I was wandering in the history of despair until Rosalind returned to me by our Lord."

"Jesus considers you worthy Jacob, one of the few who have not turned their back on the Lord. The world has turned into Sodom and Gomorrah. God will not permit this behaviour to continue."

"What is the Lord's command and I will obey," Jacob assured.

"When the Lord has decided; Rosalind will bring you to me again, Jacob. I have many tasks to perform, Rosalind will take you home where you may enjoy each other's company with the Lord's blessing." Jacob watched what appeared to be an angel, floating, approach Peter carrying fishing rods. The angel passed the fishing tackle to Peter. "A gift from me Jacob, I am a fisherman of men, you may fish the sea with Rosalind." Peter passed the fishing rods and wicker basket to Jacob and Rosalind. Jacob bowed to Peter and Matthew. Rosalind flashed her eyes to Peter and Matthew, escorting Jacob along the corridor into the misty fog. In a second they were on the beach; Jacob held his head looking out to sea there is nothing, only the waves lapping against the shoreline. Jacob walked to the cliff face sitting on a rock looking at the fishing tackle. Rosalind joined him, she could see from his expression her plan is working; there is no doubt in Jacob's mind about Peter or Matthew. "What happens now, Rosalind?" Jacob asked.

"Nothing, we continue as we are enjoying each other's company running our small farm. Although I think we should fish for a while don't you Jacob," she smiled, checking her memory banks on how to set up a fishing rod correctly.

Jacob set up his fishing rod casting out to sea; they spent the next two hours fishing each catching a large plaice. As Rosalind wound in her line for the last time, she caught a large cod. Jacob surprised, although he did notice she could cast further out to sea then he could. Jacob gutted the fish leaving for the Seagulls; they strolled back to the farm carrying what they'd caught. Rosalind started to prepare their evening meal while Jacob went outside, checking the remainder of his ewes and lambs. He sat on a bale of hay pondering what had taken place today, trying to imagine walking to the local pub telling his friends he is chatting to Peter and Matthew two disciples. Jacob envisaged the white van coming to collect him, laughed out loud with the old ewes looking at him suspiciously. Jacob slowly walked towards the house looking up into the clouds; the night is drawing in although a lot lighter than a few weeks ago.

Rosalind had prepared the large cod she caught. A banquet Jacob thought if he'd ever seen one. He tucked into his meal, enjoying every mouthful, bringing back memories of fresh fish when he used to spend a lot of his spare time on the beach fishing. Rosalind is reading his thoughts which were mostly about her and occasionally other things. After Rosalind had washed up, they sat together watching television until time to go to bed. Rosalind kissed him on the forehead, and Jacob is immediately asleep. She changed heading for the front door, she stepped into the misty fog transported to the spaceship. Peter and Matthew were waiting for her. They greeted each other with the flash of their eyes and sat watching the transmission of the way humans were behaving shipped to the newly terraformed planet. The males and females, along with some of the older children, had used large leaves to cover their modesty. The males had used rocks to sharpen bamboo into weapons.

Rosalind commented, "earth all over again remember the beginning?"

"Yes," Peter replied, "humans are certainly resourceful, especially the latest generation; they have learnt from their history books when undergoing education and are now putting it to practice."

Matthew suggested, "perhaps we should suspend shipments, we didn't intend the humans to kill the animals that rather defeats the object."

"They're not actually killing the animals," Rosalind advised. "They are only protecting themselves, their living quite happily on bananas and other fruits and catching fish from the stream. I don't think the adult animals are at risk at the moment."

Peter remarked firmly: "Humans are not wanted on these planets to colonise. They are merely food for the carnivores, I should have realised we have actually shipped carnivores; that's what humans are. I think we will return to the old ways;

shipped them processed and dispose of the unwanted leftovers on Jacob's farm."

Matthew agreed: "Unfortunate I rather hoped the larger carnivores would have eliminated the humans by now, humans are cleverer than we thought even without superior weapons."

"My next question brothers? I would like to take Jacob to see our creations. I must comment on your excellent betrayal of Peter and Matthew from the Bible we wrote, Jacob is instantly convinced."

"I think it may be inadvisable to try and transport Jacob conscious to our planets. We had tried before and failed. The only way we can succeed is by sedating before take-off; I will give the matter some thought Rosalind. You must return to Jacob, he is waiting for you on the cliff edge, you have been here for over six earth hours."

Rosalind flashed her eyes to Peter and Matthew. "Before you go, Rosalind," Matthew remarked, "humans are suffering from a new disease administered accidentally by their scientists; over 5000 have died already from the escaped virus. I have transported aboard before they are cremated. Arrange for Jacob to come to the beach in three days, I will have sufficient waste for his spreading machine to carry."

She flashed her eyes and continued walking stepping into the misty fog. She changed stepping out onto the beach to find Jacob had come down to meet her, which made her smile. He is becoming familiar with her coming and going from heaven Rosalind believed. She held his hand, watching him smile as they strolled along. "Jacob in three days, you are to come to the beach with the Fordson major and manure spreader; there will be a load of fertiliser for you, and in the near future you will be travelling into the heavens."

Jacob kissed Rosalind very passionately, which she hadn't received before from him. She eased away. "Jacob this early in the morning," she smiled, reading what is in his mind. Jacob placed his arm around her waist, they continued up the track cut into the cliffside. He looked at the other ewes and lambs desperate to be released and eat fresh grass. He looked up into the sky, deciding the weather is settled. "We'll let these go, Rosalind, they'll do better out on the grass than they will in here, save me feeding them every morning."

"You are correct Jacob sheep don't like restrictions." Rosalind opened the pens, she watched the ewes and lambs scurry off onto the Moor. Jacob looked at his second-hand tractor fitted with a loader and round baler and bale wrapper they had purchased for this season. "We must go shopping, Jacob," Rosalind advised holding his hand walking towards the house.

"I've never paid so many visits to a shop in my life Jacob," commented worrying about money.

Rosalind made the coffee reading his mind, she removed his old tin from behind the sugar. She'd already placed a large wad of cash in there, she passed the tin to Jacob. He almost spilt his coffee when he removed the lid; money jumped out onto the table so tightly packed in the tin. Jacob stared in disbelief, he is convinced he's short of cash, obviously not, he certainly wouldn't have to visit the bank which is a three-hour drive away. Jacob looked at Rosalind; she is the only explanation for the sudden influx of money. She shrugged her shoulders and grinned, Jacob burst out laughing. "We will go shopping Rosalind, perhaps buy you a pretty dress," he smiled.

"Jacob," she quickly reassured. "My clothes are made in heaven, should I require. Dresses are no good on the Moor, draughty, I prefer my jeans there more comfortable and overalls."

"As always you are practical Rosalind and I get to see your beautiful legs every night," he chuckled.

Rosalind smiled, slipping on her coat, Jacob patted Jack. "You stay and look after the farm, we won't belong." Rosalind drove the Land Rover slowly cutting across the Moor, checking the ewes and lambs on their journey to the shop, at least the snow had vanished apart from concealed crevices. Rosalind drove directly to the shop. Jacob is surprised considering the Land Rover wasn't taxed or insured to go on the road. Rosalind commented: "Don't worry Jacob, there is no police in the area."

Jacob wondered how she would know, guessed something to do with heaven, although he couldn't imagine Jesus being involved in breaking the law. He pushed the trolly; Rosalind plucked items from the shelves. The shop is quite busy considering there is a campsite not very far down the road. Otherwise, the shop probably wouldn't be here at all Jacob surmised. Rosalind had managed to spend over a hundred pounds, Jacob thought she is almost stocking up for world war three with the amount of flour she is purchasing. Jacob loaded everything into the back of the Land Rover, and Rosalind set off, leaving the road as a police car drove past on the main road. He watched Rosalind grin, she patted his leg, "you have nothing to worry about Jacob. Although I'm purchasing a second-hand Range Rover, you can use that to take me out, and the Land Rover can stay on the farm to be used across the Moor."

"And where is all the money coming from Rosalind, or shouldn't I ask?"

"You have a lot more money than you realise Jacob, you are like your father, a penny-pincher. Of course, if you're going to treat me horrible and not take your wife out. I can always return to heaven at least there, life is comfortable, and we want for nothing," she grinned.

"Where in the Bible does it say the wife takes control of your life; a wife is supposed to be dutiful to her husband," he smiled smugly.

"Don't you start quoting the Bible to me, Jacob Walker! Or you will be living on your own," Rosalind advised firmly, she parked outside the house, Jack is sat there in front of the door, daring anyone to try and pass him. Rosalind patted him, opening the door for Jacob to carry the boxes to the kitchen. Jacob is beginning to wonder whether this is actually his Rosalind; he could never remember her so strong-willed and determined to have what she wants. She still hadn't explained where the money is coming from. Rosalind read his thoughts, "the money is coming from my personal savings which you know nothing about, let that be the end of the subject Jacob, please." Rosalind quickly placed the groceries, grabbed her coat storming out of the house trying to behave like a female human would. She walked down to the beach, the misty fog approached, she stepped inside and immediately aboard the spaceship. Peter and Matthew were standing there waiting for her; they flash their eyes to one another with their greeting gesture. "Rosalind a few miles from your location on the farm, a mass grave discovered, you remember when the Romans disposed of the villagers. Now they are surveying the whole Moor in the hope of finding more graves and artefacts. This could become a serious problem for you at the farm."

"What do you suggest?" Rosalind asked.

"Matthew and I will frighten the archaeologist's make-believe the moor is haunted. One or two people will disappear, and become a food source for our animals and go on the next shipment. I know the police will search, and you will experience some disturbance. However, use your powers to blank their minds if you must," Peter suggested.

"I suggest Peter from what I can see from our scanners there are 10 people involved in the dig. We will take the whole 10 they will vanish. The police will immediately become involved, we will leave their clothes at the dig this will confuse the situation further. They may be led to believe this is a magical burial," Matthew suggested.

"Don't forget there will be helicopters flying searching the Moor, for signs of life," Rosalind suggested.

"One or two will have to have a malfunction, and their bodies will disappear. We will turn the Moor into the most undesirable place to live on earth if we must," Peter assured. "We cannot be beaten Rosalind the humans are nowhere near as advanced as we are."

"While you two are betraying God's; remember Jacobs flock of sheep, I don't want them harmed or him," Rosalind insisted. "Peter can you change the foreign currencies into sterling send a transformed sister or brother to a bank. They will exchange, remember not to take any more than £10,000 at a time. Otherwise, questions may be asked, never use the same bank twice," Rosalind cautioned. The three acknowledged each other flashing their eyes in respect. Rosalind walked into the misty fog at the end of the corridor and stepped out onto the sand, she glanced up to the top of the cliff seeing Jacob stood there, he came down the old track carrying two fishing rods and a basket. Rosalind smiled, she is becoming used to using human expressions, they appeared to come quite naturally now at the right moment. They smiled at each other, Jacob past her rod; within minutes she is casting way out to sea far further than Jacob could. Jacob presumed God is assisting with her cast. They stayed there for over two hours

Rosalind catching another cod, and he managed three mack-erel. Jacob gutted the fish on the beach, they packed their rods away, walking up the old track home to the farm. He and Rosalind watched a police helicopter flying overhead studying them for a moment and continued across the Moor. Jacob remarked: "I wonder what's happened somebody must be lost?"

"Probably," Rosalind opened the front door switching on the television in time to see the news, they sat and watched. The whole burial ground is taped off, forensics in their little white suits. A reporter is given a commentary: "Several people have gone missing excavating the burial ground, no one has any clues at the moment as to what has taken place here; the police are presently searching the Moor."

"There's your answer Jacob," Rosalind remarked, uncon-cerned, already knowing what had happened.

"I'll check the ewes and lambs, Rosalind, they're not used to disturbance like this."

"Okay, I'll have your tea ready in about two hours, don't be late," she smiled, watching Jack, the old sheepdog followed Jacob out the house.

CHAPTER 3

Keeping Control of the Situation

Jacob strolled with Jack close by his heels across the uneven ground, trying to avoid tripping on stones. Jacob could see the helicopter searching in the distance. Without warning the helicopter exploded descending to earth like a brick. Jacob stood there in shock, barely believing what he is seeing. There is no point in him trying to reach the helicopter it's miles ahead and the way it exploded, there would be no survivors he concluded. Jacob found his sheep huddled together, which usually meant there's a dog somewhere. He crouched down, holding Jack around the neck, he didn't want him running off until he knew what the problem is. Jacob noticed two police officers walking out of the gully. Jack barked, struggling to escape Jacobs grip. "Quiet Jack," Jacob ordered. Jack settled, although Jacob could feel him trembling. The police officers approached enquiring if he'd seen anyone and where he is from. Jacob pointed to where he lived. The officers smiled, continuing their search. Jacob steadily walked home via a different route to check all the ewes had stayed together; too difficult to count them while they were so unsettled.

Rosalind heard a knock at the door; she answered, standing there were two police officers the one female officer asked immediately. "Have you seen anyone suspicious around here recently, you probably heard, we are searching for missing persons."

"No, my husband is out on the moor tending his sheep; they tend to get a little upset when they hear loud noises, like helicopters. We saw on television what had happened."

The male officer looks strangely at Rosalind. "Jacob Walker! Didn't his wife die of cancer, who are you?"

Before the police officers could take another breath, Rosalind had stunned them both with a blast from her eyes. She watched the bodies vanish into thin air. She smiled realising Peter had transported them aboard the spaceship to be processed. Rosalind closed the door returning to prepare a meal for Jacob. Jacob removed his boots entering the house, patting Jack, "good dog."

Rosalind smiled, "how are the sheep, Jacob?"

"A little unsettled; I bumped into two officers; they're searching for those missing archaeologists or whatever they are. They have no business disturbing the dead; mind you, I wouldn't mind if they buried some of these yobbos, who come onto the Moor every year leaving, glass, tin and paper everywhere."

Rosalind glanced to him, "enjoy your meal Jacob; you never know what God has planned, you may see the evil ones disappear in your lifetime, who knows," she patted him on the shoulder.

"That would definitely be a sight for sore eyes. I haven't missed television, all you see is someone murdered; old folks assaulted and robbed of their money. Those people deserve to die. Sorry God for my outburst," Jacob continued eating his meal.

Rosalind made the coffee sitting on the settee, she switched on the television seeing a news reporter standing near the excavation, holding his microphone. "We've had an update from the police. Apparently, the archaeologists at the dig left their clothes behind when they were abducted or whatever happened. Now two police officers are missing searching the Moor for evidence of what has taken place. There have been reports from the public of spaceships and strange activity in the area. The last piece of news a police helicopter exploded; there are no survivors." Rosalind turned off the television.

"I suspect there will be more disturbance, Jacob. Don't forget in the morning, you must go to the beach there is a load of fertiliser coming for you," Rosalind advised; slightly concerned they would have to make sure there is sufficient fog to prevent helicopters from flying and spot Jacob.

"I hadn't forgotten Rosalind." They spent the rest of the evening watching television, not one of Jacob's favourite past times before they retired to bed. Rosalind incapacitated Jacob as usual by touching him. She immediately left the house stepping into the misty fog transported aboard the spaceship. Peter and Matthew were waiting for her to arrive; they flash their eyes to one another in a greeting. "Wise decision Rosalind disposing of the two police officers, adds more superstition to the already superstitious people in the area; they believe the Moor is haunted," Peter advised.

"I didn't have any choice, Peter, the officer, realised Rosalind is dead; he must have known Jacob to have remembered such an event."

Matthew confirmed, "there processed along with the archaeologists. I hope to process 500 humans before the next transport ship arrives. Perhaps we should invent an incurable disease and obliterate the human race."

"Patients Matthew, I'm sure the humans will destroy themselves by creating something they can't control," Peter advised. "I heard the conversation between you and Jacob, his attitude to his fellow humans, similar to ours when it comes to punishment for various crimes Rosalind."

"Yes, Peter, I think if he possessed the powers we do, he would annihilate most of the human race without hesitation; he is a good human."

Matthew confirmed: "Jacob is standing on the beach waiting for you Rosalind, you must go quickly and send him to the beach with the tractor and manure spreader. I will send the incinerated human waste before the search starts again for the missing humans, and they see Jacob." Rosalind flashed her eyes to Peter and Matthew, quickly moved along the corridor, stepping into the misty fog. Changing her appearance, she stepped onto the sand, Jacob held her hand. "Quickly Jacob the tractor and manure spreader; otherwise, the police may see you and ask a hundred and one questions you don't have answers for," she smiled reassuringly. They held hands running as quickly as they could to the farm. Jacob started the old Fordson major driving down onto the beach; he watched the fog cover everything, he couldn't see 10 yards in front of him in any direction. He felt the manure spreader flex as it is loaded and the foggy mist vanished instantly. Jacob started the tractor heading up the track until reaching the top of the cliff, headed off for his flat pasture. He quickly spread the contents of the manure spreader and returned to the farm. Jacob parked the manure spreader close to where the penned sheep were lambing. He moved the hurdles, stacking them in a neat pile until they were needed again. Rosalind climbed aboard the tractor they'd purchased with the loader. She cleaned out the old barn loading on to the manure spreader. There wasn't much, the sheep weren't in there long, just one load. She parked the tractor in the barn as a police Range Rover arrived. Jacob watched two officers step from the vehicle making a bee-line for him. Rosalind went off into the house out of the way.

"Jacob Walker, I believe, have you seen anything strange? Have you seen two officers today or yesterday?"

"Yes, when I was on the Moor there were two officers, I was checking on my lambs because of the disturbance; they're not used to a lot of noise. The two officers walked off in that direction," Jacob pointed, "I see no others, I wouldn't advise going over there with your vehicle it's boggy you'll be stuck."

The one officer smiled, "thanks for the information; you think someone could get into difficulties in the bog and disappear sucked under?"

"Probably at certain times of the year, but you'd have to be a real idiot to walk into the middle of a bog. Been there since the beginning of time, so what's been sucked underneath, God only knows. I shouldn't think police officers are that stupid; they would wander into the bog; even in wellingtons, you wouldn't get very far before they were full of water." Jacob watched the police officers drive off in the direction of the bog. Rosalind had listened to the conversation by turning herself invisible and is satisfied with what Jacob had said. She quickly entered the house, changing her shape into Rosalind, ready for Jacob to walk in.

Jacob ambled to the house, hoping the police wouldn't disturb his sheep, he opened the door to find Rosalind watching television holding up a cup of coffee for him to join her. They sat together watching the news, much as before the helicopter searching above. The presenter advised: "Tomorrow a hundred people were joining in the search walking the Moor and were under strict instructions not to bring dogs and disturb the wildlife or sheep."

He glanced to Rosalind, "I may bring my sheep back to the farm first thing in the morning Rosalind. I don't want them scattered over the Moor, in fact, I'll fetch them before night. I just about have time," placing his coffee on the table.

"Be careful, Jacob, can you manage?"

He smiled, "I can with Jack," he grabbed his crook from the door, slipped on his coat, heading out with Jack close at his heels. Jacob quickly set up a large pen inside the barn for his hundred sheep and lambs. He knew it would cost him money, but a better alternative than having them worried on the Moor by strangers, and could inadvertently herd them into another farmer section. Jacob grabbed a small sack with a few sheep nuts left inside. He started calling the sheep as he walked across the Moor. He could hear them calling; Jacob sent Jack off in a wide arc to gather the ewes and lambs. Wasn't many minutes before the ewes and lambs appeared to be together and quite happy to follow Jacob rattling the bag of nuts. They entered the barn without any trouble. Jacob emptied his bag of nuts in the trough at the end, making sure the water is turned on. He stood outside the pen, counting making sure he hadn't missed one; almost dark, placed a bale of hay in the sheep rack, he is only keeping them in tomorrow; while the crazy people walked across the Moor. Jacob is pretty convinced they wouldn't be found; the Moor had a strange way of making things disappear. This wasn't the first time someone had gone missing he recalled over the years and never found.

Rosalind came from the house, she stood there counting faster than Jacob could think, with her computerised brain. "They are all there, Jacob and the lambs," she smiled.

Jacob patted Jack, "good dog." Jacob scooped Rosalind up in his arms, carrying her to the house. "Put me down, you fool," she insisted. They retired to bed after having a large mug of cocoa. Rosalind kissed him on the forehead, he immediately drifted off into a deep sleep. She left the house, changing her appearance stepping into the misty fog immediately transported to the spaceship. Peter and Matthew greeted her with a flash of their eyes. "What are your plans, Peter?" Rosalind asked.

"I think I will send a thick fog and they will have to call off the search; however, they will only wait for a clear day to resume the search," Peter concluded.

"Have the humans we transported to the new planets been exterminated by the animals?" Rosalind asked.

"Yes," Matthew answered, "we won't make that mistake again. I prefer to send dead humans, we can freeze and keep fresh during transport and store on the home planet and distribute as necessary."

"Back to our present problem," Peter advised: "Permit tomorrow to go ahead, let them search the Moor, they will find nothing. Perhaps everything will calm down, and if it doesn't, we will have to take further steps."

"Agreed," Rosalind voiced. "Matthew, I think rather than unnerve humans by taking a large number from one area. You should have a snatch pattern around the planet. We should snatch one or two people from each town around the world; that way, it will look as if they are runaways, missing persons. Humans are always looking for those sorts of people on television until we decide to destroy the humans completely."

Peter intervened, "a sensible idea, however as much as we long to destroy the humans; our brothers and sisters on the home planet, are considering encouraging life on two more planets; once we have finished with the two were working on at the moment. I'm afraid which means we will need humans to continue feeding the animals for a while longer; probably no more than 200 years, we will have to see."

"Do we really need more leisure planets, Peter?" Rosalind asked.

"The collective has decided to increase our populace by 1 million; although we don't die. The collective wants to be prepared in case of an invasion. At present, we cannot be destroyed, the collective is thinking ahead in preparation for the unknown."

Matthew commented, "with four planets constructed similarly to early Earth; before we tampered with the DNA of chimpanzees, would be quite easy to hide in an emergency Peter if we were invaded."

"You must remember Rosalind, there are not many of us. Look at how many humans there are, their sexual appetite, leading to more procreation is swamping the planet, I suspect before long there will be another war. Hopefully this time they will wipe each other out; perhaps not completely but enough for them to realise their mistakes," Matthew suggested. He moved to the wall looking at a screen the size of a mobile phone he transmitted his thoughts. Peter and Rosalind watched on the screen on the other wall, individual humans and couples snatched from around the world and processed aboard the spaceship within seconds. The humans were joints of meat still quivering as they entered the freezer unit. Rosalind noticed Jacob is on the beach fishing waiting for her return. Rosalind smiled which Peter and Matthew thought is a strange and unnecessary distortion of the face. "I must return to the farm Jacob is fishing waiting for me."

Peter remarked, "you are becoming more human by the day Rosalind." They flash their eyes at each other, Rosalind walked down the corridor stepping into the misty fog. She changed her appearance stepping out onto the beach. Jacob picked up Rosalind's fishing rod, "I thought you could catch lunch while you are here," he chuckled, kissing her on the lips. He watched Rosalind cast her line out to sea, he thought for a moment, there'd be insufficient line on the real she'd cast so far out. "I wish I could cast like that Rosalind," he chuckled.

"It's all in the wrist action Jacob," she grinned, reeling her line in. Jacob watched a large cod, trying to break free. All he'd managed to catch with three miserable mackerel barely worth keeping. Jacob removed his penknife, killing the fish the minute ashore, gutting at the same time. The seagulls were hovering overhead they weren't going to miss the chance of an easy meal. Rosalind carried the fishing rods and basket Jacob struggled to carry the fish; he didn't think cod existed this big any more. He's pleased to return to the house and finally placed the fish on the kitchen table. He kissed Rosalind on the cheek going outside to check on his ewes and lambs again. Jacob could hear people he looked off into the distance across the Moor, watching them search for the missing archaeologists and the police officers. He's pleased he penned his sheep last night, at least they wouldn't be disturbed out there and possibly frightened into jumping in the bog or breaking a leg trying to run. Rosalind came out looking in the same direction as Jacob. "We are collecting our second-hand Range Rover today Jacob. God will transport us when there is no one watching."

"What about tax and insurance Rosalind, you haven't even told me what colour it is?"

"The colour is white, tax and insurance are taken care of, you have nothing to worry about. The vehicle is three years old ex-police vehicle and cheap. I will expect you to take your wife out for a Sunday drive occasionally," she smiled.

"Does it come with a blue flashing light," Jacob laughed.

Rosalind walked to the end of the building, watching the search parties, she could see further than Jacob or any human could. Rosalind returned to the house Jacob jumped on his old Fordson major transporting the manure they loaded the other day to his pasture and spread very thinly. People seem to be everywhere, helping with the search for clues for the missing persons. Jacob slowly drove back to the farm, parking his tractor and spreader, he entered the house. Rosalind immediately instructed: "You hold me tight Jacob, do not let go, it's time." Jacob gripped Rosalind kissing her neck, which she hadn't anticipated him doing, "stop it, Jacob, not now, be serious." In the blink of an eye, they were transported to Exeter to waste ground where no one is present. Jacob fell over, releasing his grip from Rosalind; he shook his head, feeling extremely dizzy. He struggled to his feet, holding Rosalind's hand. "This way, Jacob," she smiled, leading the way to the garage.

Rosalind collected the keys while Jacob looked around the vehicle, wasn't in pristine condition, after all, it's ex-police. Jacob slid onto the passenger seat suspecting Rosalind would drive which he didn't mind. Rosalind slid onto the driver's seat, starting the vehicle they headed for home. She called in at the shop, making Jacob push the trolley spending another hundred pounds on groceries. Jacob couldn't believe the amount of money they were spending, and still, they weren't short; the only conclusion he could come to is God is approving of everything taking place. Jacob loaded the groceries into the back of the Range Rover, hitting his ankle on the towing hitch; he glanced down, he hadn't noticed it before, at least he could tow the old trailer and take his lambs to market himself. They headed off across the Moor, Jacob asked, "why didn't you go the long way around on the side road?"

"I want to be nosy and see if those idiots have finished disturbing the Moor. We can release the ewes and lambs Jacob."

"Hadn't thought of that Rosalind," he replied quietly.

"Plus I can test the four-wheel-drive on our new vehicle," she smiled reassuringly.

"Not a bad ride Rosalind certainly more comfortable than the old Land Rover," he chuckled.

They finally reached the farm, Jacob carried the groceries into the house; while Rosalind placed in cupboards and in the fridge. She made them both a coffee while Jacob stoked the fire. He stepped outside, grabbing the wheelbarrow fetching another barrowload of blocks, leaving the barrow outside the door stacking the blocks by the fire. They sat together on the settee, drinking their coffee, watching the news on television. A reporter advised: "nothing has changed the search across the Moor had revealed no new clues, the police were baffled as to what had happened."

Rosalind smiled, "probably aliens Jacob we can blame them for everything," she patted his leg standing up, turning off the television.

He grinned, finding her comments rather amusing. "I'll release the ewes and lambs, Rosalind, I think they will do no good in a barn."

"I agree with you, Jacob can you manage," she asked.

He smiled, "yes, thanks."

Jacob and Jack went outside, he moved one of the hurdles, the sheep and lambs quickly left the barn heading out onto the Moor. They could freely roam, their only restriction, the pastureland which is set aside to make hay for the sheep to feed through the winter, totalling some 25 acres. Which Jacob like to get two cuts if he could. This year he hoped to have silage and hay now they had the equipment.

Rosalind had looked over the cliff noticing large quantities of seaweed had accumulated on the shore. She made her way to the barn finding Jacob stacking hurdles. "Jacob on the beach there appears to be a considerable amount of seaweed. I'll go down with the loader tractor, and you bring the manure spreader. We might as well take advantage, Jacob, you could chop it up into little bits with the manure spreader and leave it to rot in a pile; we can utilise it later then don't you think?"

"Sounds like my wife has an idea." He watched her sitting in the nice cab of their latest acquisition. She started the engine heading for the beach. Jacob started the old Fordson major feeling the wind cutting across the Moor, he hadn't a tractor cab to sit in to keep him dry and warm like Rosalind. Jacob sighed, thinking never mind and followed her down onto the beach.

Rosalind carefully using the forks on the end of the loader loaded the seaweed into the spreader. Jacob had to make four trips; there is more there than looked originally. Rosalind followed Jacob off the beach, she headed for the barn, and he continued to where he is stockpiling the seaweed. He started the manure spreader, he pulverised the seaweed leaving it in a neat manure heap; to be reloaded on the spreader at a later date when it had really rotted. Jacob returned to the barn leaving the tractor, he went inside the house, finding a coffee waiting for him on the kitchen table. He sat in his armchair by the fire and Rosalind perched on the arm, placing her arm around his shoulders. Jack started barking, which usually meant he had heard someone.

Rosalind look to the door quickly moving, and Jacob stood up. Jack is really upset by the way he is behaving, Jacob had determined, he couldn't wait to get out of the door. Jacob held Jack's collar carefully opening the door, another dog is wandering around without an owner or on a lead from what Jacob could see. "Hold Jack," Jacob instructed Rosalind. He ran over to his gun Cabinet removing the shotgun loading with cartridges; he'd had stray dogs before tearing his ewes a part or kill half a dozen lambs. Jacob about to destroy the stray dog. The owner shouted, "don't shoot! Don't shoot! Sorry, he got away from me," the young woman shouted, grabbing her dog, attaching his lead. Jacob lowered his shotgun. "How many of my animals has he killed," Jacob shouted, annoyed.

"None, my dog, isn't like that thank you," she stormed off towards the beach with her dog now on a lead. She obviously understood the message by the speed they were walking, he would shoot any animal that threatened his flock.

This is the first time Rosalind had seen Jacob angry to such an extent he would kill. She removed the shotgun from his hand placing back in the Cabinet. Jack sat by his master's heels, receiving a pat on the ribs. Jacob and Jack walked across the Moor, finding the ewes and lambs unharmed although bunched together. Jacob breathed a sigh of relief, slowly walking to the house. He looked across the Moor in the distance; he's about a mile from the road, which he drove to along an old track cut in the Moor some years ago. If you hadn't a Land Rover, you wouldn't venture from the road, Jacob had left it in that state to stop unwanted visitors. Jacob smiled realising he hadn't visited his post box, positioned by the road, no postman would venture to the house the road is so rough, their vehicles wouldn't make it. Jack jumped in the back of the Land Rover, Jacob drove the mile to his post box, discovering several brown envelopes, usually meant trouble. He didn't bother to open, slowly driving home to the farm, he entered the house carrying the post throwing the letters on the kitchen table. Rosalind immediately opened using her ability to translate into her own language, so she understood correctly what is written. "This one from Inland Revenue. They are warning you not to be late with your accounts this year; otherwise, you will be severely penalised, Jacob."

Jacob shrugged his shoulders, "I don't make anything anyway, I'm no good at accounting; Rosalind always used to do the books," he sighed realising what he'd said.

Rosalind removed an old book from the cupboard draw, sitting down while Jacob wasn't looking, she blinked her eyes twice and the accounts were up to date. "Leave it to me, Jacob, I'm Rosalind, I'm sorry I died I couldn't help it, not my fault the books were not kept in good order. Now they will be I'm back and back to stay," she commented trying to display an annoyed voice, which is not natural for a Zibyan.

"Sorry, Rosalind, my mouth is working without my brain in gear," Jacob gave her a hug.

"We have plenty of time, Jacob, you won't be paying any tax, don't worry, leave everything to Rosalind," she smiled. "Jacob put your coat on come with me. I'm taking you to see Peter; he has some questions for you."

"For me, a mere mortal, not much brighter than the sheep I raise," Jacob looked absolutely astounded at her remark.

Rosalind held his hand, they step from the doorway into the misty fog and within seconds they were aboard the spaceship. Jacob smiled, remembering his last visit. He saw Peter and Matthew approaching floating in the air. Jacob bowed in respect keeping his eyes fixed on the floor not daring to look at Peter or Matthew. Rosalind flashed her eyes to Peter and Matthew. "I have brought my husband, Peter, as you requested. Look upon Peter Jacob, you are not committing a sin." Jacob slowly raised his eyes looking at Peter the disciple in his robes, pictures he'd seen in churches and in books Peter looked exactly like that. Peter waved his hand, and seating appeared, Jacob is absolutely petrified. Peter invited him to sit down with the gesture of his hand, Rosalind guided Jacob to sit down by her. Peter asked: "Jacob, in the years you have lived on earth. How would you assess the human race?"

"The Bible says who among you is without sin cast the first stone. Although from my point of view, I think the people who hurt little children, murder without due cause and drunk drivers not forgetting the merciless terrorists, they should be exterminated. That's a personal point of view, not Gods."

Peter and Matthew looked at each other, Jacob thought he's now in serious trouble for speaking his mind; Rosalind gripped his hand reassuringly. "Jacob," Peter voiced calmly, "why did you not mention themes?"

Jacob shrugged his shoulders: "Possessions can be replaced, although I don't agree with stealing; you're not actually physically hurting anyone by taking their possessions; not a pleasant experience. I have had things stolen from the barn some years ago, only hand tools, but they were expensive to replace," he sighed heavily.

Matthew spoke: "Have you forgiven those who stole your possessions, Jacob?"

Jacob sighed. "They'll not return again to the farm hopefully, once I could forgive, twice I would not, I would like compensation if I could catch them of course," Jacob smiled.

"Wise words Jacob," Peter commented. "I can make this our rule for thieving, you can be forgiven once, twice will not be forgiven and your other remarks regarding punishment, will be applied, we agree entirely with your assessment Jacob."

Jacob didn't know what to say other than, "God's decision what happens to people, not mine, he created the world within six days, let him decide on the punishment."

Peter and Matthew vanished, Jacob jumped to his feet in shock. Rosalind grabbed his arm, "don't be alarmed Jacob they've gone to talk to God and discuss what they intend to do next. The world cannot continue the way it is Jacob, the human race is destroying everything. The planet was never designed to cater for skyscrapers or polluting vehicles to the extent it's suffering at the moment. Greed is prevalent among humans; you must see that surely, Jacob?" Rosalind held Jacobs hand leading him down the corridor, stepping into the misty fog. Jacob fell over as he stepped onto the sand, gasping for breath. Rosalind is hoping the more he travelled in their transporter, the easier the trips would become. She helped him to his feet, they held hands slowly walking along the beach to the top of the cliff, returning to the house where Rosalind made coffee for them both. Jacob sat deep in thought had he unleashed hell on earth through his own stupid comments; surely God would take no notice of what he thought?

Rosalind placed the cup of coffee in his hand, reading his mind and his worried thoughts. "Jacob, you have nothing to fear, Peter and Matthew are only God's disciples; he will make the final decision on what is to happen on earth, not them."

"Thank you, Rosalind, I'm a sinner like anybody else, I once found a £20 note on the Moor and kept it. I didn't hand it into the police," he frowned.

Rosalind actually laughed: "I don't think God would worry about such a trivial matter, Jacob. If that's your only sin, you have nothing to worry about, I know for a fact, you are a good man; otherwise, I would not have married you."

"I am blessed to have you with me Rosalind let God be the judge of the human race, not me. I'm going to check my ewes and lambs Rosalind."

Jacob slipped on his coat, grabbing his crook from by the door, Jack is by his heels. They left the house walking across the moor with a red sky in the distance, promising a better day tomorrow. Jacob walked for about half an hour, checking on his ewes and lambs, everything appeared to be in order. He hastily made his way home night is closing in, the Moor is nowhere you wanted to be in the dark there were so many trip hazards, even if you knew the place like the back of your hand. He breathed a sigh of relief, opening the front door with Jack his faithful sheepdog scurrying to lay by the hearth. Jacob removed his coat hanging on the back of the door along with his crook. Rosalind watching television the end of the news usually consisted of who'd been bombed today or who is murdered. She turned off the tv, pouring Jacob a cup of coffee and herself. They sat together, enjoying the final drink of the evening before they retired. They lay in bed together, Rosalind placed her hand on Jacobs, he immediately fell asleep.

Rosalind changed her appearance leaving the house transporting to the spaceship. Matthew and Peter were waiting for her. They flash their eyes at one another in the greeting ceremony. Matthew advised: "Jacob sees things in black and white Rosalind; however, we are implementing a snatch program using the information from the courts around the world to select from."

Rosalind commented: "The way I see crime soaring on television you will not have a shortage of candidates. I would advise the home planet to proceed with their plans and terraform two more planets. We certainly have sufficient food here for the animals to survive on until they become self-sufficient."

Peter look to the far wall, a screen displayed of two equally sized planets slightly larger than Earth. "Our brothers and sisters are creating a sun to warm the two planets. They can share the same sun. Once they have finished construction, we will send seeds we have collected over the years before some of the species became extinct thanks to humans. They will be planted on the new planets, once they are established, animals will thrive."

Peter and Rosalind followed Matthew to another part of the spaceship, a screen displayed on the wall listing the court cases pending of criminals. Matthew programmed his computer to snatch the named people if they were convicted by the court, once they were out of sight of anyone and transport them directly to the food processor. Matthew advised: "From what I can see and the calculations the computer has made, we should easily have a minimum of 300 humans, a week if not more. Rosalind I may need you to send Jacob down with the manure spreader at least twice a month until humans realise criminals are going missing. If our plan works should encourage humans not to participate in criminal activity."

Rosalind laughed, Peter and Matthew looked at her and the way she distorted her appearance, making the sound. "Jacob will never realise he may have resolved the crimewave on earth by his few heartfelt comments."

The three of them stood there, watching the conveyor system start behind a transparent shield. Humans were arriving convicted of their crimes by a human court. The on-board computer read their minds before eliminating to ensure they were guilty of the crime charged before transportation and processing. Rosalind smiled again, which Peter and Matthew found totally unnecessary to display in their presents. Rosalind flashed her eyes at them both. "Jacob has come to the beach with the fishing rods I must go." Rosalind walked along the corridor, stepping into the misty fog stepping out onto the sand. She picked up her fishing rod watching Jacob smile. "Come on, Rosalind, I've caught three already," he chuckled.

Rosalind looked to see what he caught, three mackerel. She cast her fishing line. Jacob watched it travel through the air until he lost sight suspecting it would end up in America or somewhere. Rosalind grinned reeling in laughing; she found the whole process very amusing and enjoyable, which is something the Zibyans never concern themselves with as a rule. Rosalind fighting whatever is on the end of the line, something significant that's for sure; finally, she brought it ashore a large tuna. Jacob could not pick it up; he immediately dispatched the fish and gutted. He ran up to the farm coming back with the Land Rover struggling to lift the pieces of fish in the back of the vehicle. "You were saying Jacob, you caught three fish?"

"I hope you know how to preserve Rosalind, six months worth of fish here?"

"Of course, you will have to go to the shop and purchased white vinegar for me lots," she smiled.

They returned to the farm Rosalind passed a wad of cash. Jacob shook his head in disbelief but didn't bother to question where it came from. He jumped in the Range Rover heading for the shop; this is the first time he'd driven this vehicle and very impressed, he enjoyed the comfort immensely saved his old bones from being shaken about. He cut across the moor rather than using the road it gave him a chance to look at his sheep. Jacob entered the shop; the shopkeepers smiled, recognising him. "Jacob, we usually see you twice a year what brings you here today."

"White vinegar, we have a large fish to pickle, I don't suppose you have large quantities of that?"

"I have 5. 1-gallon containers that's all I have in stock at the moment."

"That will do thank you." Jacob, paid placing the gallon containers in the back of the Range Rover. He steadily drove across the moor in no particular hurry enjoying his comfortable ride. Jacob parked outside the house carrying the white vinegar into the house. Rosalind had gone down into the cellar finding suitable jars to store the fish in. She is stood there waiting for him. "I presume you walk to the shop Jacob," she remarked sarcastically.

"No, I took the opportunity to check on the sheep," he grabbed her quickly, kissing passionately on the lips; she is taken entirely by surprise. "Don't pick on me wife," he chuckled, stepping outside to close the tailgate on the Range Rover. Rosalind topped the jars with white vinegar carrying them down into the cellar where they would stay cool at a constant temperature.

She looked around avoiding the cobwebs that had accumulated, evident to her Jacob never ventured down here since his wife Rosalind had died four years ago. Rosalind made her way up into the kitchen on the stone stairs. Jacob is in the kitchen, making coffee for them both.

Rosalind felt a sensation run through her circuitry in her mind; she had the urge to hold and kiss Jacob. She didn't resist and proceeded to satisfy her urge. Jacob is taken by surprise, enjoying her closeness to him. They sat smiling at each other, enjoying their coffee, watching the television occasionally glancing to the depressing news. Rosalind suddenly listened along with Jacob, the newsreader remarked: "Something strange is happening around the world; there is not an unaffected country. People convicted of crimes are vanishing without a trace."

Jacob jumped to his feet, clapping his hands, "wonderful God acts in mysterious ways," he laughed.

Rosalind had never seen Jacob so happy over humans going missing. If he only knew the truth, she thought. Although the experiment may be beneficial to see if crime is reduced around the world, she doubted. Rosalind received a telepathic message in her mind. "Jacob is required on the beach in the morning, Matthew had processed so many humans, he'd run out of storage for the incinerated parts," Peter advised.

"Come on now we must retire, you have a busy day tomorrow. You must go to the beach first thing with the manure spreader there is a load of fertiliser for you," she smiled confidently.

"How do you know Rosalind who told you?"

Rosalind pointed her finger upwards and her eyes. "Oh understood," he grabbed Rosalind's hand, leading her to the bedroom.

Rosalind immediately put Jacob to sleep, she changed her appearance leaving the house, transported to the spaceship. Matthew and Peter were waiting for her; they flashed their eyes in the greeting process. "You have been busy," Matthew Rosalind remarked, "you have a consignment already?"

"We did not realise how many court cases are held each day around the world, and how many humans are actually convicted, 99% of the time, the courts make the correct decision according to our computer; the transport ship will arrive in the early hours. Matthew has processed over 5000 humans. We have the seed for the new terraforming planets to travel on the return journey. Would you advise Jacob there will be two loads to spread today on his pastureland Rosalind? God has been extremely busy," he watched Rosalind laugh a strange expression for a Zibyan.

Rosalind looked to the scanner observing Jacob on the beach with the Land Rover it is raining heavily, she smiled, making Peter and Matthew look at each other bewildered such an unnecessary movement of her construction. Rosalind flashed her eyes stepping into the misty fog, stepping out on the beach climbing straight into the waiting Land Rover. "Jacob, you must come down to the beach with the manure spreader, there will be two loads today," she said with some urgency.

He smiled, driving off the beach quickly up the track to the top of the cliff and home. He ran in the house, slipping on his overcoat, returned to the barn starting the old Fordson major heading down to the beach; he parked waiting, turning his collar up, trying to shield his face from the bitter wind. Peter sent the first load of fertiliser carefully filling the manure spreader. The misty fog vanished. Jacob drove up the old track to his pasture, spreading the fertiliser and returning to the beach quickly. He saw the misty fog approach dropping another load in the manure spreader. Jacob absolutely soaked by the time he'd emptied the spreader and returned home parking the tractor. He ran in the house into his bedroom, changing quickly out of his wet clothes, fearing he may catch a chill. Rosalind made his breakfast adding a few secret ingredients of her own to ensure Jacob wouldn't catch a chill from the adverse weather conditions. Rosalind had cooked in fried bread with three rashers of bacon and three eggs and a whole tin of baked beans. Jacob enjoyed every mouthful sipping his coffee with Jack sat beside him. Jacob smiled, removing a piece of fat from the bacon, Jack swallowed without even tasting, which made Jacob laugh.

He commented: "Rosalind we can't spread any more manure on the pasture, I want the grass to grow ready for mowing; with any luck, we will be able to have one cut of silage and one of hay. If I had a trailer, I could stockpile the fertiliser God is providing and apply after the first cut of silage," he sighed heavily.

"That isn't a problem, Jacob," Rosalind advised calmly. "I will purchase you one leave everything to Rosalind, God knows what you need before you do Jacob," she assured. "Now I think about it Jacob you should have another second-hand tractor with a cab, you'll catch your death if you keep driving that old tractor."

"We've already had a tractor this year, I still don't know where the money came from to pay for it. I certainly couldn't afford a trailer or another tractor Rosalind; be serious otherwise, you will have a sin debt up to our neck, and the last thing I want to do is lose my farm, it's been in our family for four generations."

"Yes Jacob you will be the last generation, you have no children to carry on when you die."

Jacob flopped back down realising Rosalind is speaking the truth. "However, we may be able to change things, I will talk to God on my next visit to heaven and see what miracle he can perform," she smiled reassuringly. "In the meantime, you will have a second-hand tractor and trailer so don't argue Jacob. leave everything to your wife; she knows exactly what she's doing, you will not lose the farm you have my word."

He sat there very quietly; the tractor and trailer were quite possible. Offspring definitely not on the cards, he didn't think, short of a miracle. He and Rosalind had tried to conceive a child when they were first married, and nothing happened. Jacob suddenly smiled, remembering a story from the Bible about a woman conceiving in her old age. He decided to say no more on the subject in case he put his foot in it as he usually did. He would wait to see what plans Rosalind came up with to resolve the issue.

Rosalind slipped on her raincoat, stepping outside into sleet and rain cutting across the Moor. She stepped into the misty fog transported to Exeter. She changed her appearance into Jacob, walking along the road to the machinery dealership. Rosalind looked around selecting a 10-ton trailer three years old and another Ford tractor four-wheel-drive 125 hp which she thought would be ample for their needs. Still, in the form of Jacob, she approached the sales office paying for her purchases in cash, which she removed from her raincoat pockets. The salesman is quite shocked to see the amount of money she is carrying. She left their address for delivery, placing the sale ticket in her pocket. The salesman shook Jacob's hand, "will be delivered early next week our lorries coming your way. Thank you once again, Mr Jacob Walker, for your business."

Rosalind walked off down the road stepping behind a derelict building into the misty fog and vanished in seconds. She changed her appearance into her natural form transported aboard the spaceship. Peter is waiting for her arrival. "Rosalind your brothers and sisters are concerned with your plans. They are not concerned you are spending earth money which would only be burnt and turned into fertiliser if not spent. However, they are intrigued to know how you intend to introduce a human baby into your life with Jacob. It does not matter how you transform; you will not be able to carry a child?"

Rosalind laughed. Peter thought, totally unnecessary movement of her physique. "I am aware I cannot conceive, we were not designed that way an unnecessary process Peter. I intended to substitute a Zibyan for the purpose. You know we can transform and copy any shape we desire large or small."

Matthew joined in the conversation. "Your plan could be beneficial Rosalind; went Jacob dies there will be a Zibyan male already in place to take over and will eliminate the necessity for secrecy."

"Now I understand," Peter remarked. "A well thought out plan Rosalind. No human would be suspicious of events; everything would happen as they would expect. The only part that may cause a problem is introducing an infant without you actually giving birth."

"I will have to mate with Jacob once more, which is a disgusting process; pretend to conceive and convince him I am carrying a child. I will simply create the illusion of a bulge on my stomach. Jacob won't question anything as long as he believes God has intervened to make it happen," Rosalind smiled.

"You appear to have everything under control Rosalind," Matthew commented, flashing his eyes along with Peter acknowledging each other. Rosalind walked along the corridor, stepping into the misty fog transported to the front door of the house, she quickly went inside. Jacob is watching television drinking coffee; he looked up at her slightly concerned, "where have you been?"

"To purchase a tractor and trailer. I saw Peter concerning having a child, which I had failed to do over the years before I died. Apparently, there is something wrong inside of me. Peter has spoken to God, he will provide you with a son when we decide the time is right. There is no rush there is no time limit," she smiled patting Jacob on the head, making herself a coffee, sitting on the settee with him watching television. Jacob is grinning from ear to ear; he would have a son to carry on his farm; he kissed Rosalind on the cheek. They both sat back watching television listening to the baffled report of what had happened to the archaeologists; there is still no explanation for their disappearance. The case would have to remain an unsolved mystery for the moment the reporter advised. Jacob and Rosalind retired to bed she put Jacob to sleep, leaving the bedroom returning to her spaceship.

Peter greeted Rosalind with the flashing of his eyes. They sat quietly, watching a transmission from the home planet of developments and improvements, they would all benefit from in time. Matthew joined them. "Jacobs suggestion of how to select humans is turning out more successful than I anticipated Rosalind, the rate of crime is reduced by half unbelievable."

"We still need another transport vessel early next week. I'm pleased you found another way of transporting the fertiliser to the farm. The reports I'm having from the home planet are very favourable Rosalind, the animals are thriving on the flesh there receiving."

"Good, I must return to the farm; Jacob is waiting on the beach with the Land Rover. He is a very honourable human if the rest of the inhabitants were like him; we wouldn't have a problem. Although we wouldn't have a food source either," she commented deep in thought. She flashed her eyes to Peter and Matthew walking down the corridor stepping into the misty fog onto the beach and into the Land Rover. Jacob patted her leg, "If you weren't seeing St Peter Rosalind, I could be extremely jealous," he chuckled driving off. "What is the outcome over you carrying the child is it possible?"

Rosalind smiled looking at him, "anything is possible with God there is nothing he can't do; so why are such a silly question Jacob, you will have a son when he considers the time is right."

"That reminds me, Rosalind, what have you actually purchase; I shan't ask where the money is coming from, I suspect it's something to do with St Peter and Matthew."

"I have purchased a Ford tractor 125 hp four-wheel-drive, along with a second-hand Marshall trailer capable of carrying 10 tons with high sides. You will have to stockpile the fertiliser until you can use on the field, Jacob," Rosalind advised.

"Unfortunate I only have 25 acres of good pastureland to grow hay on."

"Don't worry Jacob," Rosalind assured. "You will easily acquire two cuts from the field this year with the amount of fertiliser you are applying; the first cut will be silage the second will be hay."

"I'll not argue with you, your usually right," he smiled looking forward to having a cab to sit in, rather than just his old coat to prevent the wind cutting him in half. They arrived at the house entered, Rosalind made coffee for them both while Jacob watched the news on television. The ancient burial ground the archaeologists were investigating is a crime scene and closed until the police had time to investigate further; not considered a priority, although people were missing. They weren't buried, they'd vanished according to the reporter. Jacob sat there, holding his coffee. "You had better check the sheep this morning Jacob, perhaps, take a bale of hay out," Rosalind suggested sipping her coffee. Jacob glanced to her surprise at her comment sort of implying he wasn't looking after the animals properly; nevertheless, he decided not to comment. He finished his drink slipping on his coat, walking out of the door holding his crook with Jack beside him. They walked for about 2 miles watching the steam rise from the old bog.

Jack started barking; Jacob scanned the perimeter close to him, noticing an old ewe and lamb adventured to close and stuck in the mud. Jacob patted Jack for finding. Jacob using his crook, hooked the ewe around the neck, easing her to safety. He retrieved the lamb, trembling with the cold. Jacob quickly rubbed the lamb, creating circulation before releasing to its mother, bleating furiously. Jacob stood there, smiling with satisfaction; he wondered if Rosalind had been informed by St Peter, one of his sheep were in trouble. He shook his head, smiling at his own daft thoughts, continuing to walk around the bog which is about 2 acres in size at certain times of the year, with thick rushes in places and bracken which sheep loved to get tangled in. Much to his relief, there were no more sheep in difficulty. Deciding to walk to where the old burial ground is, he walked across the Moor, wouldn't take him long and would give him the chance to look at his neighbour's sheep to see if they were any better than his. Jacob walked for an hour, finally approaching the burial ground fenced off by the police. He stood there for a while, wondering what happened to the archaeologists. There again, according to the news, people were vanishing from everywhere all around the world. The only part that made him smile, they were criminals which he thought a just punishment the less of them there are, the better he concluded.

He took a deep breath walking back across the Moor looking at his sheep; hoping to increase the flock by a hundred this year. Since Rosalind had returned, Jacob had no idea how much money he had. He left everything to her quietly praying she didn't make a mistake, she's spending thousands of pounds on equipment he didn't know he had. Jacob noticed in the distance standing on a small rise in the ground a tractor and trailer unloaded at the end of his track. Jacob cut across almost running with excitement. The machine looked virtually brand-new, and the trailer wasn't in bad condition at all; barely a scratch on the paintwork. The lorry drivers smiled as Jacob approached, "Jacob Walker, I presume," the driver asked.

"Yes," shaking the driver's hand, "I thought this wasn't due here until next week?"

"Slight change of plan, I have a machine to collect from the next town, you were on route, so it only seems sensible to drop your tractor and trailer off on the way."

Jacob signed for the equipment, Jack had already jumped into the tractor cab. The lorry driver set off to his next destination blasting his klaxons as he drove away. Jacob grinning from ear to ear climbed into the cab of his new to him tractor; massive compared to what he'd owned before. The only Fordson he had is the Fordson major, and the first track to his father purchased the old Fordson N petrol paraffin which he kept for sentimental purposes. Little use in this day and age; other than for joyriding and minor jobs and pulling an old wooden donkey cart trailer that would barely hold a wheelbarrow full of manure; he'd have to load by hand in those days.

Jacob worked out how to start the tractor. He set off with a jolt after releasing the handbrake, he closed the cab door deciding how quiet it is. He looked in the distance seeing Rosalind stood at the end of the track which he travelled down extremely steady, to avoid being shaken to bits by the ruts. Jacob had never had so many new toys on the farm in all his life. He realised he's getting on in years, he certainly wouldn't be able to continue with the hard work, that accompanied farming without assistance, from either people or machinery. Machinery, the better option they didn't argue you only paid for them once apart from if they broke down, very rare.

He parked the tractor and trailer by the barn. Rosalind stood there grinning, she is quite enjoying using human facial expressions. She could tell by the smile on Jacob's face he's thrilled with what she'd purchased for him. Jacob opened the cab door. Jack jumped out followed by Jacob, he immediately picked up Rosalind in his arms, carrying her into the house. She'd already made the coffee he lowered her to her feet grabbing his mug sitting on the settee. "You certainly know what to purchase Rosalind, the tractor sounds beautiful and the trailer is ideal for what we need, especially if the fertiliser keeps coming from God."

"I should think the fertiliser will keep coming at least for two more years if not longer, Jacob. Perhaps we should look closer to the farm and see if we can increase your pasture land, I appreciate it may mean moving the fence," Rosalind remarked.

"We wouldn't be allowed, Rosalind there are certain restrictions, although I own some of the land, and I have grazing rights on the rest like one or two other farmers. I think if we start stirring up trouble or try and bend the rules, they'll jump on us like a ton of bricks," he expressed concerned. Rosalind produced a map of what Jacob owned, she placed it on the kitchen table. "I found this in the records in one of your grandfather's old boxes. If you look at the 25 acres of pasture marked on the map here, and you do the calculations your find you are 5 acres short; you are actually entitled to 30 acres of pasture. You own that land, Jacob," she expressed firmly.

Jacob finished his coffee, looking at the map, he grabbed a piece of paper doing the maths. Rosalind burst out laughing, she'd never seen such a primitive way of working things out. She had calculated everything in her own mind in seconds. Jacob spent 10 minutes double-checking his calculations. "You're correct, Rosalind, I'll fence the area off tomorrow morning will you help me measure. If the authorities try to be difficult, we have the proof on paper, and you've accurately measured."

"Of course Jacob, you realise the solution would be; once we've measured. Move the right-hand perimeter fence to the new location, and we'd only have to use new wire on either end, two short distances because of the shape of the pasture."

He nodded, smiled in agreement, he remembered he had the old post-rammer around the back of the shed. He kissed Rosalind on the cheek ran outside; taking the old Fordson major off the manure spreader and attaching it to his old post-rammer. This would certainly make it easier to push posts in the ground; admittedly, after all the rain, they should go in quite easily. Jacob walked to the old air-raid shelter looking inside, finding the buildings still dry. He hadn't looked in here for years; discovering a stack of fence stakes. There must be a hundred or more, and roles of sheep wire, which he couldn't recall buying. Perhaps his father had and never told him, that went for the stakes as well. Jacob noticed a box on the floor covered in dust with a piece of paper trapped beneath. He removed the paper, the delivery note for the stakes and wire plus staples the date on the delivery note was the day before his father died. Jacob exhaled reliving memories of working with his father. Rosalind joined him patting him on the shoulder. Jacob nearly jumped out of his skin. "We appear to have everything Jacob to complete our task tomorrow, come on an early night a busy day tomorrow."

He smiled, placing his arm around Rosalind's waist, giving her a squeeze. They both retired to bed Rosalind immediately put Jacob to sleep. She changed her appearance going outside the only one that knew what she is up to is Jack, the sheepdog, he could say nothing to anyone. Rosalind set about loading the trailer with the fence stakes and wire; Rosalind is determined they would finish the project by the end of the day. She drove the tractor to the pastureland marking out in the dark day or night made no difference, she could see just the same. Rosalind placed the post ready to be driven in the ground in a few hours. She walked back to the farm, leaving the tractor and trailer there. Rosalind climbed aboard the old Fordson major with the post rammer attached taking to the paddock. She thought about starting work and realised Jacob would hear the noise, he would realise she wasn't the real Rosalind.

She returned to the farm at 6 o'clock in the morning, she started cooking breakfast and making the coffee, making sure she made sufficient noise to wake him. Jacob quickly washed and dressed coming in the kitchen kissing Rosalind on the cheek, sitting down to his breakfast, "you're keen this morning Mrs," he chuckled.

"Come on Jacob eat up, a busy day I want this job finished by 5 o'clock."

Jacob started laughing, "you know we can't complete that, probably take a week."

Rosalind placed her hands on her hips; she'd seen female humans do that when they wanted to make a point. "Jacob the fence posts are already there, so is the post rammer. The only thing stopping us completing the task is you sat there doing nothing. Daylight in the next 15 minutes, I expect you to be there with me working."

He stared in disbelief at her comment, watching her throw her pinny on the back of the chair, slipping on her boots and coat. There is no doubt in his mind she meant business and he better hurry up, or she'd be scolding him for the rest of the day. Jacob quickly drank the remains of his coffee, slipping on his boots and coat. He stepped out into the fresh morning, not quite a frost close enough. Jacob looked to the barn the tractor and trailer were missing and the post rammer, he looked to the pastureland some distance away there were the tractors sat waiting for him. Rosalind had walked on ahead, she wasn't going to be delayed by him, he ran to catch up with her. "Did you sleep at all last night, Rosalind?"

"Of course," she replied, holding the first post in place, while Jacob started the old Fordson major tractor positioning the post rammer. He drove the first post in the ground which didn't take many hits. Before lunchtime, they had all the posts in; quickly removed the staples from the old sheep wire on the original fence. They pulled across the field to the new boundary fence. They stretch the sheep wire to make it tight and re-stapled. Jacob looked at his wristwatch 4:45pm; the only thing left to do is lift the old posts out from the original fence, which would open the area up to 30 acres. Jacob breathed a sigh of relief, he's shattered, Rosalind looked as if she'd just made a cup of tea, not in the slightest tired from the day's events. "Tomorrow Jacob we can use the hydraulics on the old major, wrap a chain around the posts and lift them out the ground. If there are any good ones, we will save them. If not they can go on the saw bench and use for firewood," She ordered taking charge of the situation. Jacob didn't bother to argue, he's pleased to put his feet up; even Jack looked like he'd had enough of the day. They soon retired to bed, Jacob immediately went to sleep with Rosalind's assistants. Rosalind changed her appearance detaching the post rammer from the Fordson major. She grabbed a chain from the workshop and drove to the pasture land. She wrapped the heavy-duty chain around the first post, decided she couldn't be bothered it's dark no one would see what she is engaged in. Rosalind pulled out the unwanted fence posts by hand, taking a few seconds, leaving them lay on the ground. Jacob could collect them tomorrow and sort through what is right to keep, and what should be used as firewood. She drove the tractor back to the barn leaving their stepping into the foggy mist, she transported herself to the spaceship.

CHAPTER 4

Jacob Suspicions

Jacob woke up suddenly looking at the clock on the bedside Cabinet barely 3 o'clock in the morning Rosalind is missing. Jacob suspected St Peter may have called upon her or God to return to heaven. He quickly dressed grabbing a torch he left the house noticing the Fordson major no longer had the post rammer attached, a chain wrapped around the hydraulic arms. Jacob walked to the pastureland seeing the posts were laying on the ground. He shone his torch on his wristwatch just to confirm he wasn't dreaming 3:20 AM. "He muttered doesn't the woman ever sleep?" Jacob hadn't realised Rosalind had appeared behind him from the misty fog touched his shoulders, he's unconscious. She picked him up in her arms, carrying him to the farm, quickly undressed him placing back in bed and climbing in herself. Rosalind would simply say it Jacob said anything to her he must have been dreaming. Jacob opened his eyes, shaking his head, finding Rosalind laying beside him, he's in his pyjamas. Rosalind pretended to be asleep, Jacob decided to say nothing suspecting he's dreaming. He looked at the clock by the bed 5 AM sighing heavily he tried to go to sleep for another couple of hours at least.

Rosalind touched his arm, Jacob is in a deep sleep again. She went out into the kitchen, changing her appearance she transported to the spaceship. Peter is waiting with Matthew, both looking extremely concerned, Jacob may become conscious while she's away. "I have no idea what happened or why Jacob managed to escape my control."

Peter suggested, "I would put Jacob in a deep sleep at least until 10 o'clock in the morning, that way you can return to the farm to collect the posts yourself, and make-believe he overslept. Rather than jog his memory, he'd already seen the posts removed, Rosalind."

"Yes, I agree." Rosalind flashed her eyes at Peter and Jacob returning to the farm, she held Jacobs hand until she is convinced he wouldn't stir until at least 10 o'clock. She went outside taking the tractor and trailer across the field, not bothering to switch the lights on the tractor. Rosalind didn't need them; she could see perfectly well enough. Rosalind threw the old fence posts on the trailer checking the fencing once more, making sure they'd missed nothing. She checked the new pastureland for any signs of stones that would damage the farm equipment. She sent out blasts from her eyes, destroying any stone into insignificant fragments to prevent damage to the farm equipment in the future. She spent nearly 2 hours checking the newly added 5 acres. Now daylight, she drove back to the farm, rather pleased with her accomplishment. Rosalind went into the house and made breakfast and give Jack his bowl of treats.

Jacob came staggering out of his bedroom. "I have a stinking headache this morning, Rosalind," plonking down at the kitchen table looking at his lovely breakfast. He glanced at the clock, "you let me stay in bed, and we have all this work to do Rosalind?"

Rosalind shrugged her shoulders, "easier to do it myself Jacob than wait for you," she chuckled.

He grunted finishing his breakfast, slipping on his coat he went outside to find the trailer with the old fence posts loaded on the back. He recalled his dream remembering dreaming they were out of the ground last night now they're on a trailer? Jacob shook his head in disbelief; the woman is unstoppable; he could never remember Rosalind working so hard before. She came out to join him, "if I were you, Jacob, I would put the saw bench on the back of the old Fordson major and cut up some of these old posts; they will do for the fire," she smiled, patting his cheek walking over to find eggs laid by the hens overnight. Jacob asked, "Rosalind has God, Peter, or Jesus made you stronger than normal people?"

Rosalind turned to face him holding half a dozen eggs in her pinny, "he must have Jacob look I'm holding six eggs all on my own," she smiled walking back to the house realising, she'd been sarcastic.

Jacob attached the saw bench to his old Fordson major spending the rest of the day, sorting through what he wanted to keep and cut up the rest ready for the fire. He noticed two men looking at his pasture boundary alterations, suspecting officials. He walked down his old track cutting across as they'd finished measuring his extension to the pastureland. "Good afternoon Mr Walker," one official said politely, "we see you have extended your boundary; we've checked the measurements, you are within limits, but you must not go any further."

"How did you find out," Jacob asked puzzled. He watched the other official point his finger into the sky. "Satellite! Big Brother is watching you all the time," the official chuckled. Jacob watched them walk off, jumping in their Land Rover, driving off across the Moor, joining his old track and onto the road. Jacob suspected if the satellite is scanning the Moor, it would have seen Rosalind he wondered if the satellite worked in the dark, as he walked to the house. Rosalind is there to greet him on the doorstep, "officials Jacob?" she asked directly.

"Yes, apparently there's a satellite above us, perhaps they are trying to use that to find out what happened to the archaeologists." He shrugged his shoulders, sitting on the settee in time to hear the news. The reporter looked extremely stressed: "Governments are bewildered, people are going missing, once convicted of a crime. Some people think it's Gods way of removing evil from the earth; others believe it's aliens." There is a pause: "Just in! A group of terrorists have vanished engaged in a battle with Armed Forces on the Syrian border, no one has an explanation?" Rosalind calmly passed Jacob a coffee, trying not to smile. "I've already eaten Jacob; would you settle for cheese and onion sandwiches tonight, we need to use the cheese before it spoils and that goes for the onions," she commented walking into the kitchen.

"That will do fine Rosalind." Jacob turned off the television, walking into the kitchen sitting at the table. Rosalind commented, "tomorrow morning first thing Jacob; you must go to the beach, two loads of fertiliser take your new tractor and trailer, at least if the weather is bad you won't be affected your be nice and warm," Rosalind smiled.

"I presume you will be talking to St Peter or Matthew?"

"Why do you ask Jacob? Are you concerned, I'm here by God's will only. You must remember I descended from heaven, I have to receive spiritual instruction. If you wish to live alone again, Jacob, I can return to heaven and never come back to see you if that's what you really want?"

He lowered his sandwich to the plate, "whatever gave you that silly idea Rosalind; my life has never been so fulfilled until you returned. I'm inquisitive that's all, you must remember I am a mere mortal. I'm unsure of what you are, you look like my wife, you behave like my wife some of the time. Things happen around here that I find suspicious, you must understand Rosalind, I'm waiting to wake up from a dream," Jacob spluttered in somewhat of a panic, thinking he may be losing Rosalind.

"Finish your sandwiched Jacob," Rosalind advised pouring him another coffee. "As long as you want me to stay, I will stay," she smiled reassuringly.

"That will be forever until I die," he sighed heavily dreading the thought of passing on now he had Rosalind in his life. He wondered would he rejoin Rosalind in heaven, although the Bible states quite clearly until death do you part, so technically you are single once you're dead. That thought did not impress him in the slightest. Rosalind is reading his mind, she had become accustomed to Jacob in the short time she'd known him; there definitely is a familiarity. They both retired to bed Rosalind immediately put Jacob to sleep. She stepped from the house into the misty fog transported to the spaceship, greeted by Matthew and Peter, with the flash of their eyes. They sat watching the wall turning into a screen; their brothers and sisters on the home planet selected to speak, for the mass, a hundred in total.

"Peter is your earth name which we will continue to use as a reference, including your brother and sister, Matthew and Rosalind. You realise Peter, Matthew and Rosalind you have resided on earth since its conception to be colonised. You watched and encouraged some species to exist. The humans were a gross error of judgement on our part; we should have left everything alone and not interfered with the chimpanzees and created a hybrid."

Matthew advised: "They are serving a purpose, food for the terror formed planets, the animals seem to survive quite well on human flesh until they are established and can regulate their own numbers."

"You, Rosalind you are providing a valuable service, associating with the human for the purposes of disposing of waste. Noted in the interest of our advancement, you have made plans for a Zibyan to play the part as offspring for the human Jacob. Excellent in theory, a vote is yet to be cast by the collective to approve. Although once we have a Zibyan in charge of the farm, this will open up new opportunities which we can explore at a later date. This will have to be discussed, with the firstborn. He is presently engaged in the search for fragments of our creators on another planet."

The screen vanished. Peter remarked, "from the information I've received from the home planet. There are plans not only for two more planets to be terror formed. Now they are considering six more planets. I do not see the purpose, although I am one of the many, my opinion is ignored on the grounds, I am too close to the subject they considered."

Matthew expressed, "I agree with your analysis. We appear to be copying the humans, one earth government, destroying thousands of acres of land to construct a railway line from one end of the country to the other. What will they do when there is nowhere to grow anything to eat. People are starving now, and still, they destroy the ground that feeds them; perhaps the humans are on a suicide mission, Peter?"

"We will have to wait and see. Jacob has come to the beach, prepared to transport waste products fertiliser onto the trailer. I can actually see him smiling a strange facial expression sat in his cab while the rain pours down and for once, he's not getting wet," Peter commented.

Rosalind smiled, flashing her eyes to Peter and Matthew walking to the misty fog stepping inside. She changed her appearance stepping onto the beach, opening the cab door on Jacob's Ford tractor sitting on the passenger seat. Jacob had discovered the tractor had a heater and six years old it still worked. He kissed Rosalind on the cheek, feeling the trailer loaded. She patted his leg, "come along Jacob you have two loads, we are so lucky to have fertiliser, it's given to us many farmers have to purchase their own."

He nodded in agreement, backing up to where he'd tipped the seaweed to rot, he released the tale board on the trailer running back into the cab, he tipped the fertiliser in a pile, quickly lowered the trailer and shut the tailgate. Rosalind jumped out of the cab running for the house to prepare breakfast for Jacob. Jacob drove down on the beach again enjoying every moment of driving his tractor, no wind screaming around his ears, he wasn't wet apart from when he ran to open the back of the trailer. The window wiper work so Jacob could see where he is going; there's certainly nothing wrong with today so far. He waited patiently watching a misty fog come from miles away across the sea and empty fertiliser in his trailer. Jacob drove to the manure pile again, emptying his newly acquired trailer driving to the farm parking, dashed in the house looking forward to his breakfast. Rosalind had really laid on a lavish breakfast, fried tomatoes, fried bread three rashers of bacon and three eggs and two sausages. Jacob exhaled, "I'll be as fat as a pig when I've eaten this lot Rosalind, but I'm not complaining."

"Jacob, I purchased a hundred ewe lambs 12 months old the farmer is retiring. I sort of jumped in and purchased the whole lot; you said to me the other day you wanted to increase the flock well we have."

Jacob, drinking his coffee, almost choked. Rosalind patted his back. "Are you, insane woman!" He shouted. "We haven't that sort of money to spend especially after you purchased equipment recently."

"I wish you'd stop panicking about money, we can easily afford, remember I do the accounts, not you and I wasn't going to miss a golden opportunity to increase the flock. Plus the ewe lambs you're bringing on yourself this year. Anyway, the lorries arriving at midday."

He continued eating his breakfast. "I'm sorry for shouting at you Rosalind. Do I know the farmer?" He asked calmly.

"Mr Clydesdale, he specialises in white-faced. Mr Clydesdale suggested you bring our flock off the Moor when the others arrive, while they sort themselves out and recognise each other and hopefully stay out of trouble."

"After a breakfast like that, I don't think I could walk across the Moor," Jacob expressed tapping Rosalind's backside as she walked past which made her grin. She knew a loving gesture by a human. Jacob stood up, walking to the door, slipping on his coat, grabbing his crook. "Come on, Jack, we've work to do don't blame me; it's Rosalind's fault," he chuckled. Jacob and Jack walked across the Moor until he located his sheep and lambs. "Away, Jack," Jacob ordered. Jacob watched Jack bunch the sheep, they slowly followed Jacob to the farm buildings. Rosalind had already set up a large pen to hold the sheep and lambs. He smiled, watching Rosalind empty a bag of sheep nuts in a trough at the far end to encourage the sheep to enter. The sheep and lambs run past him more interested in food than they were trapped. Rosalind came out, he shut the gate on the pen. Jacob commented, "we have several lame ewes and lambs, I'll clip their feet while we have them tightly penned."

Rosalind watched how careful Jacob is handling his sheep, clipping their feet, spraying each one with a disinfectant to try and keep the foot rot away, the same applied for the lambs. Rosalind noticed the lorry carrying their new flock slowly making its way up the rutted track, nothing the driver wouldn't be used to around here. The lorry parked, the driver climbed out quickly, opening the rear of the lorry dropping the ramp watching the ewe lambs run for freedom; they immediately started to eat the grass. Jacob released his own flock; there's an awful lot of bleating, which is expected. The lorry driver past Jacob some paperwork and left the farm in a hurry for his next destination. Jacob exhaled watching the sheep and lambs slowly walk off into the distance, munching every blade of grass they could find. He prayed the new flock would stay with the others. He placed his arm around Rosalind's waist, giving her a kiss on the cheek. "There are some nice you lambs you chose wisely, I couldn't have done better myself," he smiled. They walked across the Moor to the enlarged pastureland. Jacob noticed how much difference the fertiliser had made to the one section before they extended the pasture. "Perhaps I should spread a couple of loads of fertiliser on the 5 acres, you can see the difference plainly; the other 25 acres are coming on nicely," he remarked.

"Yes Jacob," Rosalind agreed looking into the air, "it will rain later today help wash the fertiliser in the ground."

They returned to the farm attaching the manure spreader to Jacobs ford tractor. Rosalind using the loader on the other tractor loaded the manure spreader. Jacob spread everything he'd stockpiled on the 5 acres extended pasture including the seaweed. They both stepped from their machines in the farmyard. Jacob commented, "with any luck, we'll get an early crop of silage." Rosalind smiled in agreement rather enjoying operating farm machinery and working with the animals. For thousands of years, she'd stayed aboard the spaceship apart from travelling to the home planet occasionally and betraying Mary Magdalene, thousands of years ago. She had never experienced earth and its real beauty until she shaped shifted into the form of Rosalind and became Jacobs wife. Rosalind checked her memory banks, discovering, she once had a vegetable garden. She walked around the back of the house to a fenced-off piece of ground realising it hadn't been touched by Jacob. He joined her. "Sorry, Rosalind I know you used to love growing vegetables. I'll see if I can start the old Rototiller and prepare the ground for you," he sighed, feeling disgusted with himself for allowing Rosalind's garden to deteriorate.

"I will start the Rototiller you never could; you and that machine have a love-hate relationship," she grinned walking to the garden shed. Rosalind removed the Rototiller quickly reading the manual from the database, so she knew exactly what to do. Jacob stood there watching; Rosalind is correct she opened a tin of petrol tipping a little in the machine, pulled the starter cord, it burst into life after sitting there for four years, Jacob couldn't believe it. She allowed the machine to warm for a minute. "There, you are Jacob." She watched him start to rotavate her garden, she grabbed a rake from the shed, removing any weeds left on top of the soil to the compost heap, where they could rot. Rosalind is determined to experience growing things herself, rather than allow her technology to perform the task for her. Peter and Matthew aboard the spaceship, were tuned into her thoughts along with the home planet, intrigued by her insistence to experience the way humans performed first hand rather than watch.

Jacob spent an hour going over and over Rosalind's garden until he'd pulverised the soil into submission, extremely fertile because of its peat content. Jacob placed the rototiller in the shed pleased to see the garden the way Rosalind always kept it pristine. "Sunday Jacob, you can take me out to a garden centre, and we will see what's available to purchase. I don't have any seeds or plants. I definitely want to grow a few rows of potatoes so don't suddenly have a bad back," she chuckled, enjoying the human form of teasing; she had studied from her memory banks and watching humans perform. Jacob is thrilled, he loved Rosalind beyond measure the first time around. Since she had returned from heaven, she's even more perfect in his eyes. "You will have whatever you want Rosalind," he smiled contentedly, closing the little gate on her garden as they left. Jacob and Rosalind returned to the house sitting by the fire watching television. A newsflash: "A hundred prisoners from New Orleans have vanished without a trace from their cells. Prison officers have carried out a thorough search and can find no trace of an escape." Rosalind watched Jacob smile; she already knew where the prisoners had gone, and Jacob would spread their remains in due course.

Jacob made Rosalind a cup of coffee, leaving her to watch the television. He returned shortly passing her a cup. "I'll check the sheep Rosalind I don't want them wandering off too far," he smiled. She smiled, watching him slip on his coat, grabbed his crook and Jack joined him at the door. He stepped out into a breezy late afternoon spending the next two hours finding his new ewe lambs. They'd all ventured some distance trying to find fresh grass. Jacob would willingly fertilise, although not permitted on the Moor. He walked back to the farm taking two bales of hay and a bag of sheep nuts on the back of his quad and trailer, driving across the Moor to where he'd left the sheep rack. Jacob came to a conclusion, his sheep were psychic. Jacob had barely cut the bales of hay and placed in the sheep rack before he's swamped by bleating ewes and lambs. He grabbed the bag of sheep nuts, making little piles walking across the Moor for a short distance encircling the sheep rack. Jacob watched the ewes and lambs devouring everything placed on the grass, what little there is of it.

He climbed aboard his quad with Jack jumping on the carrier, slowly drove away, deciding to visit the post box at the end of his track and see what the postman had left him. Jacob opened the box, a handful of letters mainly brown, which usually meant official. He sighed slowly placing the letters in his coat pocket heading back to the farm parking the quad bike in the barn. Jacob and Jack went into the house, Jacob removed the letters from his coat pocket, passing to Rosalind. She opened each letter studying the contents. Rosalind smiled, lifting a cheque. "The Inland Revenue is refunding you £10,000 Jacob, there's been an error over the years in their accounting."

"About time I had something out of that lot," he smiled sipping his coffee. "I suppose that means a trip to the bank in Exeter, they've shut all the little branches where father used to go. We might as well have the day out and see if we can find you some plants and seeds for your garden," he smiled.

"That's the first idea you had today I like," Rosalind smiled. "Will go first thing in the morning, Jacob, we can leave Jack in charge your look after everything, won't you, Jack."

Jack barked as if he knew what Rosalind is saying wagging his tail frantically. Jacob and Rosalind spent the rest of the evening watching a little television and deciding what they would grow in her garden. They had agreed before retiring to bed they would purchase two rose bushes to brighten the place. Rosalind always wanted roses at the front of the house and died before she'd achieved her goal according to Zibyan records. Rosalind placed her hand on Jacob's forehead as he lay in bed. Rosalind left the room, changing stepping into the misty fog transported aboard the spaceship. Peter and Matthew were waiting. Matthew advised: "I am to return on the next transport ship to Zagader, I am summoned by our brothers and sisters. Peter will stay with you, I am to stay on Zagader for one earth calendar month to lecture our brothers and sisters in person. They want to see for themselves staying on earth for thousands of years has not altered any of our abilities and conviction to Zagader."

Rosalind displayed a human frown which is observed by Matthew and Peter. "I find that request rather strange Matthew, why now when we arrived thousands of years ago. If the request had been made, say after the first thousand years, I could understand, but after 9000 years or more," she paused.

"You sound like a human suspicious of everything, perhaps we should send you. You appear to be in greater need of attention then Matthew," Peter advised.

"You mean we cannot think Peter individually? What happens if there's a crisis, and we operate as a collective? Some are affected, some are not? We will not survive if you have no individuality. The collective is good; although we must operate individually, should the emergency arise," Rosalind suggested.

A large screen appeared on the wall members were listening from the home planet. "Rosalind, your intelligence has surpassed our expectations. We presume your association with Jacob has assisted you in thinking as an individual and not as a collective?"

"Yes, brothers and sisters, I have to think and assess the situation on my own. Waiting to consult Matthew or Peter or the home planet would take too long; Jacob would notice the delay in my decision-making processes, and so would anyone else. You all know the human brain is not dissimilar to our own; other than totally inefficiently used. They are not so stupid as to realise something isn't quite right if you don't answer your question quickly; unless you can think of a reason for delaying." A delayed response from the collective while they assessed everything Rosalind had said. "You have merit in your assessment, we will reprogram so we can all operate individually if necessary in an emergency. Otherwise, we will stay and operate as a collective and enjoy the warmth of each other's thoughts," The screen vanished from the wall. Rosalind watched Peter and Matthew stand to attention, while hoods engulfed their brain, giving them the ability to operate outside the collective without reprisals should the emergency arise.

Matthew and Peter look to one another after the hoods were removed and Rosalind. "Sister, you're not bothered by thinking and acting on your own?"

"You will find rather strange, I certainly have I'm still adjusting but the more you practice, the easier it becomes; I still prefer to be connected to the collective."

"Now I understand," Peter remarked, "why you have embraced the facial expressions of a human and participated in other activities. I see the merits of your actions, and so do the home planet now. Our programming is slightly altered; we can understand why you behave the way you do to be more efficient in the task you have set yourself."

Rosalind flashed her eyes, walking down the corridor stepping into the misty fog, stepping out by the front door. She glanced across the Moor, although not totally daylight, she could see walker's with their rucksacks following the path. She entered the house to find Jacob, making breakfast. "Rosalind, I'm 43years old, you know; how old I'll be before I die?"

"Why do you ask?"

"What is the point in having a son if I'm too old to teach him anything. I don't mean to be pushy, I will be about 49 before he is five years old and approaching 60 before he will be willing to learn. If I'm lucky enough to make 70, he will be barely old enough to take over the farm legally."

"Considering I won't die, I will be here to teach him. I know as much as you if not more Jacob; do not concern yourself. You could even live to 100 with my assistance," she smiled reassuringly.

"I suppose you're right Rosalind, although I would really love some time to play with my son and show him the way of the world, as you rightly pointed out you know more than me. You have God on your side. I will have to accept what is given I don't have any choice," he sighed slowly sitting in his old armchair. "I promise you, Jacob, you will have a son long before you pass away into history. Maybe the case you don't pass away at all. God may have other plans for you," she smiled.

Jacob grinned, "that would certainly be a miracle to behold, although I suspect society would soon realise something strange is going on if I outlived everyone else."

Rosalind kissed Jacob on the cheek flicking through the television channels until she found Emmerdale. Jacob laughed; he couldn't stand the programme going into the kitchen to have a glass of home-brew. He sat contentedly pondering on all that is said; contented with the thought, he would eventually have a son and perhaps a daughter if he is lucky.

Rosalind is reading his mind, she hadn't realised he may want a daughter as well, which quite surprised her, nevertheless nothing that couldn't be achieved she decided. Jacob had one more glass of home-brew; deciding that's enough, he remembered the last time Rosalind had scolded him. He finished his drink kissing Rosalind on the cheek and retired early to bed. Jack, the faithful sheepdog, stayed by the fire, enjoying the warmth.

Rosalind switched off the television going into the bedroom. She kissed Jacob on the forehead rendering him unconscious. She walked from the bedroom, changing her appearance, Jack watched curiously for a moment then turned his head away, resting on his paws. Rosalind stepped out of the front door into the misty fog transported to the spaceship in seconds. Matthew and Peter greeted Rosalind with the flashing of their eyes, and Rosalind responded likewise. "Well, Peter, I'm sure you've read my mind, and Jacob's regarding children?"

"Yes, you can understand his concerns; he's ageing like all humans, thankfully. Otherwise, the world would be swamped; we are fortunate they haven't worked out what is wrong with their DNA sequence; otherwise, they would live forever, perish the thought."

Matthew commented: "I've ordered a transport ship, should be here within three days, I have more human corpses than I know what to do with, send Jacob with the trailer tomorrow Rosalind there will be two loads."

Rosalind cautioned: "How many humans have you processed this month, Matthew. Don't forget humans are not stupid; they are searching now trying to discover where the missing humans are going. We do not need them searching the sea where our spaceship is located. If we are discovered, although we can defend ourselves, it could possibly ruin everything."

"I have processed 5000 snatched from all over the world, most prisoners convicted of murder."

Peter insisted. "No more Matthew suspend operations for a month, allow the humans chance to calm down. The home planet has stockpiles of flesh for the animals, and with this consignment, you shouldn't need to do anything for two months."

Matthew suggested: "Peter if you listened to the transmissions of governments around the world, although they are concerned people are missing; they are rather pleased we are taking prisoners. Not only is it lowering the crime rate; but emptying the overcrowded prisons. The humans will not search very hard providing we don't take any of their leaders. I think we have nothing to be concerned about."

Peter glanced to the wall screen appeared displaying an aircraft carrier 20 miles to the south of them with helicopters flying with sonar scanning the seabed. "I think you are mistaken Matthew in your assessment."

Matthew looked at the screen. "This does not compute, the information I am receiving state something different from what we see, why?"

"Because Matthew," Rosalind answered. "Humans have tricked you into believing one thing and doing the opposite. Haven't you learnt any think Matthew in the time we have studied humans? They are devious, not trustworthy; they are hunting for us, something has given them a lead to our location; check your computers, Matthew."

Matthew vanished. Peter looked at Rosalind. "You are more experienced Rosalind at thinking as an individual, do you have any suggestions?"

"Yes, programme a Russian launch computer to send a missile towards the USA, and allow it to explode short of reaching land. The carrier will head for home or the Russian border it doesn't matter which way it goes providing it leaves this location."

Peter immediately turned: "Computer, you heard the conversation implement."

The computer spoke: "Missile launched from Russian submarine close to the Russian border. The aircraft carrier Abraham Lincoln has received orders to head North effective immediately."

Peter and Rosalind looked at the screen on the wall noticing the helicopters returning to the aircraft carrier, watching the ship change direction. Rosalind flashed her eyes at Peter walking down the corridor stepping into the misty fog, stepping out onto the beach seconds later. Rosalind smiled, seeing Jacob coming down the track on the beach with the old Land Rover, he stopped passing Rosalind a fishing rod and kissed her on the lips. She smiled in appreciation, casting out to sea as far as she could. Jacob tried to cast as far as Rosalind and failed miserably. She tried not to grin. Jacob commented, "if you catch a shark Rosalind, you can deal with him." Jacob watched Rosalind's rod bend under the strain of hooking something; he watched her reeling in another large cod, he sighed profoundly realising he stood no chance against her. Jacob dispatched the fish and Rosalind grabbed Jacob's fishing rod. She cast passing it to him, "now reel in slowly and see what you catch Jacob," kissing him on the cheek.

Jacob laughed, "you cheat Rosalind, you have the strength of God with you." Jacob found his rod bending and something on the line he reeled in slowly struggling, unlike Rosalind, he spent the next 20 minutes trying to land whatever is on the end of his fishing line, only to discover a conger eel. Jacob immediately cut off its head using the shovel in the back of the Land Rover. Rosalind laughing watching Jacob throw the eel in the back of the Land Rover along with her cod. Jacob drove to the farm with Rosalind still expressing a smile, he carried the still wiggling conger eel into the kitchen along with the cod. "Jacob there will be two loads of fertiliser tomorrow morning. Now off to the shop purchase more pickling jars if you can and more white vinegar please." Jacob didn't argue he kissed Rosalind on the cheek dashing out of the house, leaving Jack with Rosalind. He climbed in his Range Rover driving across the Moor, checking on the sheep as he travelled, relieved to see the flock is staying together and not separated. He finally reached the road driving the mile to the shop, entering to the sound of a buzzer on the door going straight to the counter. "Do you happen to have any pickling jars and more white vinegar?"

"I haven't been asked for pickling jars for years, these modern people wouldn't know how to pickle, I have three boxes left. I thought I would never sell how many do you want?"

Jacob smiled, "I will take the lot at the right price and another gallon of white vinegar, I'm pickling fish."

"There are 10 jars and lids in each box if we say £10 a box that's £30 for the lot plus the vinegar?"

"That's a fair price, I know they cost more than that, we're doing each other a favour here," Jacob smiled handing over the money, carrying the boxes to the back of his Range Rover, plus another gallon of white vinegar. Jacob drove off steadily watching people walking across the Moor, at least they were sticking to the correct pathways and not wandering amongst his sheep. Jacob parked outside the house. Rosalind came out opening the tailgate on the Range Rover, carrying a box of jars inside, while Jacob moved the other two returning for the vinegar. Rosalind had already prepared some of the cod and the conger eel. She quickly filled the jars after washing them thoroughly in the sink. Rosalind topped up with vinegar she finally sealed preparing them for the next stage before going into storage. "Jacob, after you've dealt with the two loads of manure tomorrow you can take me shopping, we can pay the £10,000 cheque into the bank and go to a garden centre," she smiled.

He didn't respond, the thought of driving to Exeter is not his idea of a good time, although he appreciated he'd have to pay the cheque in at the bank. Jacob went outside, taking a walk to his pasture land surprised the way the grass is growing, almost on steroids, he thought. Even the 5-acre extension, the grass had caught up and is the same length as the other. Whatever God is sending down is exceptionally potent, if the loads kept coming the way they were, he'd have ample to spread on the 30 acres; once he'd taken a cut of silage which the way things were looking would be in a couple of weeks if not sooner. Jacob smiled, walking across the Moor, finding his flock of 200 ewes, plus lambs. The lambs were progressing nicely and wouldn't be long before they were in the market. Jacob continued walking finding himself looking at the old burial ground where the archaeologist vanished. He couldn't believe they were all evil and taken by God, there must be other forces involved? If they were all females, they could have been kidnapped, but a mixed group. Jacob started walking back to the farm, dropping to the floor like a stone as an Air Force jet appeared to try and cut his head off; the noise is horrendous. The pilot shouldn't be flying this low with sheep on the moor, they would scatter every direction in a panic. Jacob picked himself up, heading for his flock of ewes discovering they'd all bunched together by the bog. He and Jack pushed them away to safer ground; Jacob is relieved none were harmed. He and Jack made their way home stepping inside the house, Rosalind already knew what had taken place. "You heard the jet, Rosalind?"

"Yes, Jacob, I thought he is taking the thatch off the roof, I didn't think they were permitted to fly that low?"

"Not at this time of year anyway, they occasionally do but not that low," Jacob advised calmly deeply concerned.

Rosalind switched on the television. The diversion peter and she set up in the spaceship to occupy the carrier had worked; ships were travelling north on a heightened alert basis. Jacob commented: "One of these days somebody's going to do something they regret and nothing will be left but ashes. Perhaps that's the way God is going to cleanse the earth," he frowned.

"If you were God Jacob how would you resolve the issue, all people seem to do is bicker and argue, seems to be the greatest pastime and to see who can inflict the most pain on the other," Rosalind remarked making a coffee.

Peter and Matthew were both listening to the conversation transmitted by Rosalind's mind, intrigued to see how Jacob would resolve the issue. "I think the first thing if I had the power," he chuckled. "I would melt their electronic equipment that controlled the nuclear weapons, make them inactive; no idiot could press the button and inflict pain and suffering on innocent people."

"You mean something like a virus Jacob?"

Jacob looked to Rosalind: "virus what you mean how would that work?"

"Haven't you ever seen or operated a computer Jacob?"

"No I've seen them in the bank, I watch the typist at work, in some offices at the cattle market."

"A virus is like having a cold, or the flu makes you inactive unwell. You know I died of cancer that's a sort of virus to explain in simple terms."

Jacob smiled, kissing her on the cheek. "Yes give the bloody computers cancer virus, then they couldn't launch the dooms-day devices around the world. I think all countries should be affected they'd be in the same pickle," he chuckled.

Peter and Matthew aboard the spaceship had listened to the conversation realising Jacob simplistic idea may be beneficial; they would wait to speak to Rosalind when she came aboard the spaceship in the evening.

Jacob and Rosalind watched television for the rest of the evening before retiring to bed, where she put Jacob to sleep. She stepped from the house into the misty fog boarding the spaceship. Peter and Matthew were waiting. They had already worked out a plan and were waiting to discuss matters with Rosalind. They greeted each other with the flash of their eyes. "Rosalind, we have formulated a plan it would serve two pur-poses. One to immobilise nuclear weapons and the other to keep countries busy trying to solve the problem and not look for us or worry about people going missing."

"Explain your plan," She said cautiously.

"We can use their own Internet against them; not only will we paralyse nuclear weapons on land at sea and ships and sub-marines. To enhance Jacobs idea further, we would also include the banks where their money is kept. We estimate it would take them at least two Earth years to resolve the problem; the virus will also affect their satellites."

"Where would you insert the virus whichever country you choose will automatically be blamed and could start more confrontation."

Peter look to Matthew as if they were short of an answer. "Where would you suggest," Peter remarked.

Rosalind smiled, Peter and Matthew looked at her, strangely displaying a human expression. "Insert the virus in satellites simultaneously. We should have a worldwide effect in a matter of minutes. Their antivirus software will not recognise what is sent as a threat until it is too late, and the computers destroyed along with the microchips. If they attempt to launch the nuclear devices will explode before take off."

Peter instructed the computer: "Implement Rosalind's instructions effective immediately."

The computer responded: "Implemented."

"I'm returning to Jacob he is outside filling his tractor with diesel, preparing to come to the beach." Rosalind flashed her eyes to Peter and Matthew they responded likewise. Rosalind stepped into the misty fog transported to the farm. Rosalind shouted across the yard, "Jacob, I'm making coffee before you go."

"Okay," he smiled, walking to the house seeing the television is on with newsflash written across the screen. He sat quickly, watching. Rosalind joined him with the cups of coffee the presenter advised: "Most countries around the world have suffered a catastrophic computer failure on their weapon systems, even ships at sea are suffering from the same virus. The Ministry of Defence has no explanation at the moment."

Jacob smiled glancing to Rosalind: "That will give them a headache for a few weeks" he chuckled, "if they spent the money on curing cancer and other illnesses rather than on weapons; the world would be a better place."

"Off you go, Jacob God is waiting, don't forget you have two loads this morning, he is generous do not upset him," Rosalind smiled.

Jacob placed his cup on the table, walking briskly out of the door, followed by Jack. Jacob opened the cab door Jack jumped in followed by Jacob. He drove down onto the beach, parked, seeing the misty fog approach feeling a load of fertiliser shake the trailer as it loaded. Jacob drove to where he is stockpiling, tipped the load, returning collecting the next load emptying and finally parking by the barn. He returned to the house with Jack finding Rosalind had changed into a pastoral blue dress, wearing her fur-lined coat holding her favourite handbag. "Hurry Jacob, change you're taking me out, I have the cheque for the bank." Jacob stared in disbelief; he'd never seen Rosalind look so beautiful. He quickly ran into the bedroom, finding a suit already laid out on the bed for him; he hadn't worn that one for about five years he thought, changing quickly. Jacob opened the front door for Rosalind and the Range Rover passenger door. "I'm driving Jacob thank you." Jacob laughed, climbing in the passenger side while Rosalind walked around to the driver's door. Rosalind set off slowly down the drive, Jacob glanced to the front door of the house seeing Jack sat there quietly.

Rosalind drove very steadily they were in no rush, and Jacob felt like a trussed up chicken in a suit. Rosalind could see him looking at her; she is reading his thoughts. Some she thought rather explicit what he would like to do with her. After travelling for some time, Rosalind found a parking space. They walked to the bank paying in the £10,000. Continued walking down the road, Jacob holding her hand, which she found quite a pleasing sensation. She steered Jacob into a large garden centre where she purchased a variety of seeds two rose bushes, plus some winter vegetables and seeds. Jacob loaded their purchases into the back of the Range Rover. Rosalind steadily drove home, finding Jack still laying on the front doorstep. Rosalind parked the Range Rover leaving Jacob to unload while she made the coffee and changed into her working clothes.

Jacob grabbed the spade digging two holes one either side of the front door, placing a little manure in each and planting Rosalind roses. She came outside, holding a mug of coffee looking at his handiwork smiling. He accepted the coffee leaving Rosalind to sort out her own vegetable garden that is a taboo area for him, other than preparing the ground. Rosalind planted everything she wanted. She received a telepathic message from Peter, "To bring Jacob to the spaceship; he is to travel to visit Zagader. The inhabitants would stay invisible and betray themselves as spirits, such as suggested in the Bible to avoid any confusion."

Rosalind quickly asked telepathically, "what about the animals, Peter?"

He responded telepathically, "I will shapeshift into Jacob and Matthew will become you for the few days you are away, a new experience for us both."

Rosalind returned to the house, washing her hands in the sink. "Jacob, you are travelling to heaven tonight. Peter and Matthew will look after the farm you have nothing to worry about," she smiled confidently.

Jacob looked shocked, "what do I wear? How long will we be gone?" He asked, extremely concerned.

"You need nothing, miracles will take place the minute we start to travel; your clothes will be replaced; you only need to stay by me, and you will be safe. You will be the first person alive to see the other worlds God has created," she advised with confidence.

Jacob sat down in his armchair. "The first cut of silage in two weeks Rosalind, who will feed Jack? Look after my sheep," he panicked slightly.

"Leave everything to Rosalind; you really think I would allow everything you've worked for to be destroyed. Ye of little faith. I can feel God's displeasure already at your comments Jacob, you should be ashamed."

Jacob bowed his head. "Sorry Lord; earthly possessions have no place in heaven in your eyes; excuse this poor mortals stupidity."

"Time to go, Jacob, hold my hand. Stay here, Jack." Rosalind opened the door they stepped into the misty fog and within seconds were aboard the spaceship. In the seconds they had travelled, Jacobs clothes had changed into a spacesuit, he looked about himself puzzled not expecting to be wearing anything other than a robe as he'd seen in the Bible pictures. Jacob said nothing, Rosalind held his hand, leading him through the vast spaceship lying beneath the water. Suddenly they travelled vertical boarding another spaceship. Rosalind immediately placed her hand on Jacob's forehead rendering him unconscious, suspecting if she didn't, he would be dead within a few minutes. Rosalind awoke Jacob after three days; the spaceship is slowing down, preparing to dock on Zagader. She supported Jacob's arm, steadying him to his feet. He looked from one of the windows observing an Earth-like planet. "Are we home already?"

"No, this is one of God's planets where animals and vegetation are not destroyed by interfering humans. When a creature or human cease to exist on their own planet, they are transported here in spirit form to live in tranquillity, and other planets designated by God the creator."

Jacob exhaled trying to understand everything Rosalind had said, seeing stars in the distance. Rosalind felt the spaceship moving to land on the planet; she quickly rendered Jacob unconscious again until they'd landed safely, she feared the sudden acceleration and deceleration would destroy him if he is conscious. Rosalind felt the spaceship settle, watching her brothers and sisters unload the containers of flesh for storage and turned themselves invisible, so Jacob would not see them. Rosalind awoke Jacob stepping into a misty fog. They travelled away from the spaceship, stepping from the mist on a shoreline. Their spacesuits had gone, they were now wearing robes which made Jacob smile, convincing him this is definitely God's country. Zagaders atmosphere slightly thinner than Earths, Jacob struggled for a while to breathe properly. "Where is everybody," Jacob asked, looking to a starry sky although, daylight.

"All around us Jacob they are in spirit form, you cannot see them because you are alive; if you were dead you would be one of them," She answered calmly.

Jacob watched a lion come running from the jungle, he quickly picked up a rock in a panic taking a defensive posture. Rosalind grabbed his hand: "No, Jacob, the lion won't hurt you. You must remember this is heaven, and God controls the animals." The lion growled walking off into the jungle, Jacob breathed a sigh of relief, noticing a coconut fall striking a rock. He ran over quickly, drinking the milk laughing. He split the coconut completely in half, passing one half to Rosalind. She smiled pleasantly watching Jacob eating. Jacob asked, "Rosalind, are we permitted to swim? I haven't for years the water is always freezing at home."

She nodded, watching Jacob remove his robe running into the sea completely naked. The water extremely warm,

Jacob found himself surrounded by dolphins. He could never remember being so happy before other than when he married Rosalind. He looked into the water, watching the fish nibbling at his feet which tickled. "Come on, Rosalind," he shouted, waving his arm for her to join him. Rosalind checked her memory banks immediately understanding how to swim, receiving concerned messages from her brothers and sisters; they never ventured into water other than for experimental purposes.

Rosalind stepped out of her robe, running into the water naked swimming to join Jacob. Her Zibyan, brothers and sisters watched intrigued, they'd seen humans perform in water many times before and considered a way of cleansing the body of bacteria, which Zibyans didn't possess. Rosalind and Jacob spent half an hour swimming around finally returning to the beach. Both laying on the warm sand; much to Rosalind surprise Jacob started making love to her. She had thousands of messages entering her circuitry concerned, she is allowing Jacob to perform a sexual act on her.

Jacob rolled off, jumping to his feet running into the sea; Rosalind followed to cleanse herself without Jacob realising. Her mind exploding with messages and questions. They both finally returned to the beach, slipping on their robes holding hands, they walked along the beach. "This is truly heaven Rosalind," he smiled, noticing bananas growing, he ran over pulling two from the bunch appeared to be ripe. He passed one to Rosalind. "You have it, Jacob, I'm not hungry; thank you," she smiled with satisfaction. She had achieved what she wanted Jacob to visit her home planet and for him to travel here without dying. "Where are we sleeping tonight?" Jacob asked, placing his arm around her waist.

"Where ever you want Jacob, here on the beach or in the mountain's over there in the distance look," she pointed.

Jacob looked into the distance seeing a hazy blue mountain, "I suspect it would be extremely cold up there?"

"No, the temperature stays the same weather night or day Jacob." Jacob looked surprised at her comment suspecting the temperature to fall during the evening and night. They continued walking, watching the sun slowly set. Jacob asked, somewhat concerned, "if we stay out here, Rosalind, what about the animals I don't want to be a lion's dinner, thanks."

"They won't bother you in the slightest Jacob, they have no interest they are all well fed; their hunting instincts are suppressed for the moment." Rosalind held his hand, easing him down to sit on the warm sand. She removed large banana leaves rolling into a pillow for Jacob to rest his head-on. He lay down, she touched his forehead and Jacob is unconscious. Her brothers and sisters immediately materialised, no longer invisible, asking Rosalind questions about her experiences. Rosalind spent the rest of the evening, talking with her brothers and sisters, explaining the sensation of physical contact with a human, she would not recommend; although humans appeared to enjoy immensely.

By 7 o'clock in the morning, Jacob woke stared in disbelief, Rosalind's brothers and sisters vanished. Jacob rose to his feet kissing Rosalind on the cheek removing his robe, he ran out into the sea, he couldn't understand how warm the water is and eventually rejoined Rosalind; who somehow miraculously had acquired bacon and eggs on a plate. Jacob sat on the sand, enjoying his breakfast suspecting God could produce whatever he wanted. Don't be stupid and ask a question he thought. Jacob finished his breakfast, Rosalind removed the plate and utensils from his hand. Jacob watched them vanish. Rosalind laughed, "one of the spirits you can't see prepared your breakfast this morning."

"Oh," Jacob replied, trying to stay calm in an otherwise crazy situation. Jacob watched the misty fog appear before him and Rosalind, she encouraged him to enter. Rosalind instantly sedated Jacob while they travelled several light-years to the next terror formed planet; for the Zibyans to experiment on and create another replica of Earth, minus the human infestation. Rosalind eased Jacob from the misty fog into a clearing amongst palm trees and other spectacular vegetation. Jacob wasn't feeling well, the atmosphere is thinner still on this planet, he sat down trying to breathe. Rosalind surmised whether it would be possible to implant a Zibyan intelligence into a human. Her brothers and sisters were reading her thoughts and were considering the possibility. Although at the outset could not see the benefit of doing so; they needed more feedback from Rosalind on her assessment. After half an hour, Jacob had calm down and could breathe satisfactorily, although he couldn't move quickly before he became breathless. Rosalind considered her last thought, Jacob would not be Jacob if they transplanted a Zibyan brain into his human body; besides she liked Jacob the way he is not predictable. Rosalind taken by surprise discovering a shelter constructed suspecting by the humans, they had transported here as food for the animals. Jacob cautiously entered the bamboo construction. He noticed a carving on a piece of bamboo: "Help we are dying." Jacob glanced to Rosalind alarmed. "What is this Rosalind?"

Rosalind focused on what he is reading: "I don't have an explanation, somebody playing silly games, I suspect children's spirits."

Aliens

Jacob sat down in the makeshift chair someone had made out of bamboo, looking from the construction, he noticed a panda sat quietly eating. Jacob rose to his feet; he now had a horrible feeling inside; this may not be gods creation. He walked briskly closely followed by Rosalind. Jacob could hear the faint sound of water running; he quickened his pace finally coming to a waterfall noticing in the clear water human remains, a skull, in fact, the whole skeleton he presumed. He sat down pondering, trying to find an explanation for what he is seeing. This is definitely more than Childs play now. He couldn't envisage God, Jesus, Peter or Matthew involved in a murder.

Rosalind slowly sat beside him. She asked calmly, "what conclusions have you come to Jacob?"

"I'm trying to find a logical explanation and can't, God would not permit such a thing."

"How many times Jacob in the Bible has God lay waste to humans standing in the way of his chosen people? What happened to Sodom and Gomorrah? God chooses who lives and who dies, not you or I. He decides how they die according to their behaviour. If they are good, they become a spirit if they are evil, the animals enjoy their flesh, they die a slow and painful death. If you cannot accept God's chosen path, then I suggest you burn your Bible Jacob," she expressed firmly hoping he would accept her explanation.

Jacob sat quietly, considering what she'd said; he knew she spoke the truth regarding Solomon Gomorrah. The Israelites were favoured by God, he made the path for them to follow. "I cannot argue with your logic Rosalind since you have spoken to the Almighty and his disciples, I'm in no position to question. Please take me home to the environment I understand, until my allotted time."

Rosalind held Jacob's hand, watching him look one more time at the skeleton lay beneath the clear water. The misty fog appeared Rosalind encouraged Jacob to step inside. She immediately sedated him wiping his mind of what he'd seen, very regrettable she thought, not her plan at all. Within seconds they had travelled light years returning too Zagader her home planet. She helped Jacob to his feet. Many of her brothers and sisters materialised in front of Jacob, wearing robes. Jacob stared in disbelief, one young woman approached him not dissimilar to Rosalind. "Welcome to heaven Jacob, you were chosen to see his glory," she produced in the palm of her hand an orange, "enjoy, the fruits of heaven."

"Thank you," Jacob smiled, excepting the fruit; he watched the orange peel itself in the palm of his hand. He plucked segments slipping into his mouth, enjoying. Jacob glanced to the sky seeing angels flying around him male and female from what he could see. Rosalind realised he'd calmed down considerably, although she had attempted to wipe his mind of the last stressful event without damaging his brain, she knew he's still very unsure of everything. As suddenly as the Angels had appeared, they vanished along with the others in robes leaving Rosalind and Jacob stood there alone. Jacob sighed heavily, "I apologise, Rosalind, I'm shocked to think God would allow people to be eaten by animals."

CHAPTER 5

The Journey Home

Rosalind and Jacob stepped into the misty fog taken aboard the spacecraft. Jacob asked, "I don't remember much about travelling here. I would like to look out of the window if possible at the wondrous creation of God."

Rosalind held Jacobs hand, taking him to a large observation window. "If you start to feel ill, Jacob, you must tell me immediately. You must remember spirits can travel at any speed, human flesh cannot, and the last thing I want is you to become a spirit before your allotted time," she advised kissing him on the forehead.

He nodded. The spaceship started to accelerate; Rosalind had already asked the captain to reduce the forward velocity for a while. She would sedate Jacob whether he approved or not. Otherwise, it could take several Earth years to travel the distance. Rosalind had insisted the crew remain invisible to Jacob while they travelled to earth. She spent several hours checking systems becoming rather bored travelling at such a slow speed, felt she could get out and walk quicker to earth. Rosalind realised a human assessment that made her smile. She's about to return to Jacob stepping from the corridor, she noticed another Zibyan sat by him impersonating her. Rosalind had never felt outraged before anger is not part of the Zibyan culture; they always were cold and calculating in their decision-making. She turned herself invisible to Jacob and stayed out of view of the sister impersonating her. She accepted the fact the Zibyans shared their thoughts, and there wasn't such a thing as possession of an item. Although at this precise second Rosalind experienced human jealousy for the first time, which shouldn't happen, her construction should not permit. She suspected since she is thinking as an individual and not as a collective, this may be the cause of her outrage.

"I don't know what's come over you Rosalind," Jacob remarked, "you've never been this affectionate before," he chuckled.

"We are married, Jacob, let's enjoy each other," the female impersonating Rosalind suggested.

"Here and now Rosalind," Jacob asked surprised.

"Why not," removing her space suit laying on the floor. Jacob removed his suit, making love unknowingly to an impostor. Rosalind watched intrigued, she couldn't blame Jacob in the slightest as far as he is concerned it's her. When they finally finished the Rosalind impostor rose to her feet dressing in her suit kiss Jacob on the forehead; saw Rosalind, the impostor vanished instantly. Rosalind chased after her intending to administer harm, abruptly stopped by other members of the crew. "I am a commander Rosalind you do not own anything, and neither do we; remove the incompatible thoughts from your mind and return to Jacob." She immediately changed into Rosalind, walking down the corridor to find Jacob asleep. She touched his forehead to ensure he would stay in that state for the rest of the journey, telepathically instructing the commander, "increase their speed. Jacob is now unconscious."

Rosalind is receiving messages of concern from her brothers and sisters, concerning her aggressive thoughts towards another sister, who only sampled what is permitted to anyone if they wished. Rosalind realised she would have to calm the situation, or she could be taken from earth and made to return to Zagader. Rosalind telepathically apologised to everyone explaining. "They were new sensations she hadn't experienced before and maybe, very beneficial should the Zibyan nation be under attack sometime in the future."

Rosalind waited for a response, she is thinking as an individual like a human. Her mind suddenly filled with answers of approval at her explanation, she could be extremely beneficial should an unsavoury situation arise. Rosalind smiled, looking out of the observation window, she stayed there for the whole length of travel which is three days. Rosalind awoke Jacob in preparation to transport to the other ship.

The transport ship positioned under the water linking to the other ship. Rosalind and Jacob were greeted by Matthew and Peter. Jacob immediately bowed his head in respect to what he believed were two disciples of the Lord. Matthew instructed: "We require your trailer; there is more fertiliser for you, Jacob coming from heaven in the morning."

Jacob glanced to Matthews expression, which appeared to be lifeless unlike Rosalind's. "I will Park on the beach at 8 o'clock, Sir."

Rosalind escorted Jacob along the corridor into the misty fog, they stepped out by the front door of Jacobs house already changed into their original clothes. Jack inside by the fire, they'd only been gone eight days; most of that spent travelling. Jacob is having re-occurring thoughts almost like nightmares of dead bodies. He asked directly, "Rosalind the fertiliser God is supplying is it the remains of humans?"

Rosalind made the coffee using powdered milk, they would have to go to the shop tomorrow. "What do you think, Jacob? You have sat there watching television; condemning unruly humans, in some cases condemning them to death. Why are you so surprised God may listen to your opinion when he gives you the gift of travel to see the beauty of his creations. I am surprised at your attitude Jacob after what God has given you," she advised with authority.

Jacob exhaled he realised he couldn't stand against God's wishes, no matter what he did. God created the earth, stipulated in the Bible; he'd met Peter and Matthew visited God's homeworlds. He personally wasn't responsible for killing anybody, he is merely making use of the fertiliser. "I'm sorry," Rosalind easing her down onto his lap.

"You've had more than your fair share travelling home," she smiled, getting up. "After you transport the fertiliser in the morning, we're going shopping Jacob," she ordered. Jacob slipped on his coat, grabbing his crook from the back of the door, deciding to check on his ewes and lambs. The lambs would soon have to go to market for store lambs, he couldn't fatten them up here. Jacob stepped from the house followed by Jack; they quickly walked across the Moor, trying to check on the sheep before nightfall. Jacob is rather pleased with what he could see, surprising how things change even if you're only away for a few days. The lambs were progressing nicely, and perhaps next week would send them to market. He slowly walked back to the farm sitting by the fire after feeding Jack. Rosalind had made Jacob a sandwich until they have gone shopping tomorrow. They retired to bed Rosalind touched Jacob's hand, he fell into a deep sleep. She changed her appearance stepping from the house into the misty fog, transported to the spaceship. Peter acknowledged flashing his eyes as Rosalind had. "I see you have explained to Jacob the fertiliser is humans?"

"Yes, he's far from stupid Peter after seeing the skeletons which were unfortunate. I would have hoped the Lions would have crunched the bones to nothing or the hyenas, I suspect it's because they fell in the water. He appears to believe it's God's wish and continuing to dispose of the waste, we are fortunate he believes the Bible." Rosalind and Peter watched Matthew appear carrying a large suitcase which is filled with money they discovered when he opened. "You can use this to improve the farm Rosalind; otherwise, will be incinerated," Matthew advised.

"I will have to conceal from Jacob, I appreciate Matthew. There are many improvements I wish to make in the coming months, one will be a computer, and the old generator needs replacing. I have to confess I find it extremely pleasurable involved in the farm, good experience for whatever may lay in our future," she smiled.

Peter remarked: "Jacob has come down onto the beach with the trailer, you had better join him, Rosalind." They flash their eyes at each other, and Rosalind walked down the corridor carrying the large suitcase. She stepped into the misty fog, changing her appearance stepping out onto the beach. The morning air extremely fresh she thought, tying the suitcase to the hydraulics of the tractor, there wasn't room in the cab for her and the suitcase. Jacob opened the cab door for her, she climbed in quickly shutting the door. Jacob had the heater running in the tractor, he looked somewhat worried. She scanned his thoughts, "No, I'm not moving out Jacob," she chuckled, watching him grin. "May I know what's in the suitcase," he asked hesitantly.

"A present from God that's all you need to know. I have to keep some secrets from you, Jacob," she chuckled teasing him. They felt the trailer shudder as Matthew tipped the first load into the trailer. Jacob started the tractor heading up the track reversing to his manure pile, he tipped the fertiliser on the existing pile and continue to the beach after Rosalind stepped from the cab releasing the suitcase going in the house. She went down into the cellar hiding the suitcase behind two large barrels. She ran up the stairs returning to the kitchen, making two coffees switching on the television as Jacob came in. He sat beside her watching the TV displaying more depressing news of fighting abroad, and women and children suffering. Jacob muttered, "this has to stop Rosalind. God must intervene, they are better off dead than suffering like that," he exhaled.

Rosalind patted his leg, "God is watching everything Jacob watch what happens in a minute."

The reporter appeared in front of the camera: "The guns have stopped the rocket launchers have exploded? Why I have no idea; hundreds of soldiers have vanished into thin air?" Jacob watched the female reporter place a hand to her mouth in shock, bewildered by what had taken place. Jacob stared at Rosalind. "You knew exactly what's going to happen, Rosalind, how?"

"Very simple Jacob; you remember the last conversation we had regarding missiles and rockets, you suggested we give them a virus. God has approved your idea. Now when armies release weapons of mass destruction, they will merely explode if they try to launch," she smiled with satisfaction. "Yes, Jacob, there is another load of fertiliser for you tomorrow at 8:30."

"How many innocent people have died Rosalind," he asked somewhat in a panic.

"None! Anyone who fires upon helpless women and children is guilty in God's eyes, you have read the Bible! What does God advise regarding children?"

"I know the passage you are referring to Rosalind; I cannot fault his decision. There is nothing so innocent as a child until the parents warped their minds with subversive behaviour."

"If all humans were like you, Jacob God would not have a problem. Come along, turn the television off Jacob were going shopping," she smiled.

Jacob patted Jack, "look after the place we won't belong," he smiled, stepping from the house walking down the yard to the Range Rover accompanied by Rosalind. "I'm driving Jacob," she insisted which made Jacob laugh.

They drove across the Moor, looking at his lambs. "We will have to send them soon to market, they can go next week; they should make a reasonable price for store lambs," he smiled.

"I think you need a new sheep trailer the one you have is rotten Jacob, it's a wonder it stays together."

"That will cost more than the lambs fetch at the market," he advised deeply concerned with her money spending. "You appear to forget Jacob we had a £10,000 rebate; plus the money I've saved. I'm also buying a computer and a new generator. You might as well be upset with my spending all at once rather than in phases," she grinned, mischievously; human expressions she enjoyed immensely watching the horror appear on Jacobs face at what she'd said.

Jacob exhaled suspecting he wasn't only arguing with Rosalind probably with God who is definitely on her side. Instead of driving to the shop, Rosalind continued for several miles, in fact for over an hour coming to an agricultural dealership. She smiled pleasantly observing a row of sheep trailers. Rosalind grabbed Jacobs arm dragging him along. He had to admit, he is beginning to enjoy spending money, although petrified they could ill afford the expense. The thought of a new trailer which would be easier to load is quite appealing. Jacob and Rosalind looked inside several; deciding to take a double-deck trailer which the Range Rover would easily pull. Jacob stood there watching Rosalind count out the money. He watched over £5000 vanish from his savings. The dealership fitted the number plate on the rear of the trailer and Rosalind backed up like a professional hitching to the new trailer. Jacob couldn't stop grinning the woman is a menace or should he referred to her as an angel. Jacob shook the sales rep's hand climbing into his Range Rover, Rosalind drove off whatever she attempted she is exceptionally professional at. She finally parked alongside the shop. He pushed the trolley while Rosalind plucked items from the shelves. The shopkeeper commented: "I managed to acquire more pickling jars for those just in case moments Jacob."

Before Jacob could speak. "We will take them," Rosalind advised. "How many boxes?"

"I have five boxes of 10 in a box, and I have 5 gallons of white vinegar."

"We will take everything." The shopkeeper looked absolutely shocked at her comment not suspecting Jacob to want any more jars or vinegar at the moment.

Jacob grinned loading everything in the Range Rover. Rosalind paid and joined him. Rosalind drove around the road this time gently entering their drive, trying not to break anything travelling across the ruts. "Tomorrow Jacob after you've moved the load of fertiliser, I will come down onto the beach and load the trailer with stone. You can fill these ruts in their becoming ridiculous and will damage your vehicles, if not repaired, no one will ever want to come here," she expressed firmly.

"That's the general idea, Rosalind," he advised biting his tongue trying not to lose his temper. "I don't want strangers on the farm. If I repaired the track, make it so easy for criminals to drive to the farm."

"If you were on your own Jacob, I could understand your point of view; now you have God's protection, you really think anything will happen. Whoever attempts to rob you will end up in your trailer as fertiliser," she affirmed without hesitation.

He exhaled not responding, guessing would be futile. Jacob detached the trailer from the Range Rover a brand-new shiny Ivor Williams which stuck out like a sore thumb; rutted track or not if anyone caught sight of it he thought it would be stolen in minutes. He went into the house to find Roslyn had made the coffee, he placed one box of groceries on the table, going outside he carried in the pickling jars and vinegar. "You must be planning another fishing adventure with this amount of jars and vinegar Rosalind."

"I happen to know, you like pickled cabbage and pickled onions, yes we can pickle more fish if we desire."

He sat quietly, drinking his coffee after switching on the television. Jacob remarked, "Rosalind, you realise taking stone from the beach is sort of illegal."

Rosalind placed her hands on her hips, pretending to be an annoyed human female. "Stay in the house tomorrow Jacob. I will move the fertiliser and repair the road myself! I don't need you at all to help, I didn't realise every stone is counted on the beach, and once the sea washes over what I've removed, you won't know the difference."

"Rosalind that maybe the case, they will see what you placed on the track, will stand out like a sore thumb. Some nosy official will only have to test and check the beach before they realise what we've done. Do you have to go looking for trouble," he emphasised annoyed.

Rosalind left the house realising Jacob had a valid point. She jumped in the Range Rover driving off joining the main road. She hadn't travelled far before she came across road repairs, they were removing old tarmac. Rosalind parked on the side of the road the gang Foreman came over. "3 miles up the road," she explained. "I have an old track full of ruts would it be possible for you to tip one or two loads on the track, I can fill the ruts in myself with the tractor." Rosalind had seen studying humans, they used a form of inducement, which is cash. Rosalind removed a couple of hundred pounds from her pocket watching the mans face light up. "I'll follow you with the next lorry load show me where you want it tipped, that'll buy you three loads," he smiled. Rosalind quickly calculated that would be sufficient to fill in the potholes. She sat quietly in her Range Rover, waiting for the lorry to be filled. She steadily drove off with the lorry following, she turned into the track parked, pointing to the track, put her thumb up, the lorry driver blasting his horn in acknowledgement and Rosalind returned to the farm.

Jacob heard the tractor and loader start, he came dashing out thinking someone is stealing his tractor. Rosalind, changing the manure a fork for the bucket so she could scoop up the road planings. Jacob looked down the drive seeing the lorry load of road planings, he smiled at her resourcefulness. Rosalind would not be beaten under any circumstances, he decided, grabbed a shovel walking down the track. Rosalind joined him with the tractor filling the ruts with a little discarded tarmac and Jacob levelling with the shovel. Rosalind had to remember to switch the tractor lights on so Jacob didn't realise she could see in the dark. They carried on working until 11 o'clock in the evening, which is ridiculous really, Jacob thought afterwards. They could have finished the next day; nevertheless, the job is finished, and his back felt like he'd been run over with a steam roller, he could barely walk. Jacob hobbled to the house going straight to the bedroom, changing into his pyjamas, falling asleep on the bed instantly. Rosalind fed Jack all the waste products she'd accumulated through the day. Jack had never had such a good life before Rosalind arrived; he's living like a king. Rosalind went into the bedroom, touching Jacob on the forehead, ensuring he wouldn't wake too soon. She changed her appearance stepping outside the house into the misty fog and transported to the spaceship deep beneath the waves.

She hadn't been there long discussing issues with Matthew and Peter when their scanner alerted them to an intruder on the farm. Rosalind looked, noticing someone reversing up to their new sheep trailer. She remembered what Jacob had said, why he hadn't repaired the track to help stop unwanted visitors. Rosalind immediately returned to the farm while Peter extracted the two thieves turning them into fertiliser to be collected by Jacob in the morning. Rosalind realised Jacob couldn't find a strange vehicle on the farm; otherwise, he'd be really suspicious of what had taken place and probably involve the police, which she definitely didn't want. She climbed in the van after detaching their sheep trailer, quickly driving down the road only to discover she's chased by a police car. Rosalind drove for several miles from the farm deciding to drive off the cliff, changing into a fish swimming away as the van entered the water. Peter had already realised what Rosalind had done sending the misty fog to collect her. She shapeshifted back into the form of Rosalind stepping into the misty fog transported to the spaceship.

Peter remarked: "You really can think as an individual Rosalind, the police car didn't realise you driven off the cliff. They carried on along the road, trying to catch the van. Perhaps you should listen to Jacob Rosalind this incident wouldn't have occurred."

"Agreed! Nevertheless, with our technology, humans are no competition for the Zibyans," she smiled, which always made Peter concerned, she's copying humans to frequently in appearance and actions.

At 8:30 Jacob drove down onto the beach with his tractor and trailer, collecting a load of fertiliser transporting to the manure pile, he tipped returning to the house. Rosalind already there with his breakfast ready. Jacob commented: "Somebody came to the farm last night Rosalind there are strange tyre tracks in the dust. I bet they were after my Ivor Williams sheep trailer, why they didn't take it I don't know. I forgot to lock it to one of the posts with the chain."

"Well if anyone came up here who wasn't invited, they certainly won't make a return visit," she advised calmly; switching on the television and quickly changing the channel, after seeing a crane lifting the white van from the sea and divers boarding a small boat. Rosalind thankful she drove at least 5 miles away from the farm so there'd be no connection.

Jacob finished his breakfast patting his leg for Jack to follow, he went out of the door saying, "I'll check on the pasture to see if we can sneak in an early cut of silage and I'll check the ewes and lambs," he smiled, closing the door. Jacob walked down the old track to the road, in places he could see the strange tyre marks which were not from his vehicle.

Jacob walked across the Moor until reaching his pastureland 30 acres. He's pleasantly surprised since he'd spread fertiliser on the pasture it had come on in leaps and bounds. There is definitely sufficient for one cut of silage, and hopefully, one cut of hay before the end of summer. He had plenty of fertiliser in stock thanks to God and unruly humans who God incinerated. Jacob sighed slowly continuing to walk across the Moor coming across his flock of sheep. He definitely needed to take the lambs to market; they wouldn't improve any more there's insufficient grass, he wanted his ewes to rest before the Ram is introduced again. He suddenly realised he needed a new Ram he wasn't going to start interbreeding. Jacob and Jack returned to the farm. He began to set up a large pen to separate ewes and lambs; there would be at least 2 loads in his new sheep trailer. Rosalind came out realising what Jacob is preparing, she knew he had every intention of keeping the ewe lambs back that were born last year to increase his flock to around 250 breeders. Rosalind suggested: "Jacob, you know it's at least a three-hour drive to market; do you know exactly how many lambs you're sending?"

"None of the ewe lambs; I can't remember how many others there are, I'll find out in the morning it'll be an early start. Early next week, I want to take the first cut of silage Rosalind with your help," he smiled. "Why don't you bring them closer to the farm Jacob? Better still separate the ewes and lambs tonight, we'll have an early start in the morning."

"Okay," he kissed Rosalind on the cheek. Jacob set off across the Moor with Jack, spending an hour rounding up his flock returning to the farm. Once the sheep were penned. The laborious job of separating ewes and lambs started. The ewes were easy to sort out; the lambs were a different story. After they'd finished sorting lambs, Jacob discovered he had 25 for market which is a load. Jacob fed and watered the lambs going to market in the morning, although they were more concerned with trying to escape back to their mothers, who hadn't a care in the world they'd wandered off looking for fresh grass. Rosalind and Jacob returned to the house, Jacob is shattered, and after a quick cup of coffee, he went to bed. Rosalind touched his forehead, making sure he wouldn't wake until 4 o'clock in the morning when they'd have to set out for the market with their lambs once they'd loaded.

Rosalind changed her appearance stepping outside the house into the misty fog immediately transported to the spaceship, Peter is waiting for her. "Is it essential for you to be so involved with Jacob Rosalind," Peter asked, concerned.

"You're not jealous! Are you, Peter," Rosalind laughed, displaying another human expression.

Peter quickly search through his memory banks, discovering the meaning of jealousy which is not Zibyan practice. "I find your remark out of order. I am certainly not jealous as you call it of anything Rosalind. Although you did display your jealousy when the Zibyan female practised on Jacob aboard the transport ship; explain your behaviour!"

"I thought it's pretty obvious you have access to my thoughts, along with the rest of the Zibyan collective. I am hiding nothing I merely practised a human reaction. You appear to forget Peter, although we are designated male and female when we are constructed; we are actually neither. We are whatever we wish to choose to betray. If I wish to be a male Zibyan, I could as you can become a female Zibyan."

"Why are you stating the obvious Rosalind why are you telling me something I already know. I think you are trying to separate yourself even further from the collective to pursue your own interests, which would be highly inadvisable if you wish to continue to exist," Peter warned firmly.

Rosalind looked to the wall watching the screen appear, members of the home planet were visible. "If I am to be accused as Peter has suggested, I recommend you order me to Zagader on the next transport ship my brothers and sisters. Peter is correct! I operate as an individual and not as a collective some of the time. You cannot operate as a collective when you work with humans on a one-to-one basis."

A member of the home collective spoke: "Peter, we sense your brain cells are functioning irrationally. We order you to connect to the main computer so the errors can be corrected in your thought pattern. Rosalind, we are monitoring everything; we are permitting you to continue with your experimentation, operating as an individual; we accept your explanation; this may be a beneficial asset in the future."

"Thank you, brothers and sisters, I can assure you I only have the collective success as a top priority nothing else."

"Rosalind, you will be interested to hear, we have named one of the six planets Rosalind and another Jacob. A vote was cast not including yourself Peter or Matthew to avoid impartiality."

"The only word I can use brothers and sisters is thank you, which is a human saying and I'm sure Jacob if he ever knew, he would be extremely pleased with your decision, his name will live on after he's passed away."

The firstborn on Zibyan rose in the air advising: "Jacob may not cease to function, you know Rosalind we created the human DNA. We can prevent his ageing, and the only way he would cease to operate is through an accident once we've altered his DNA. This would give him the same life expectancy as the Zibyan, what is your view?"

"I'm sure Jacob would be pleased; however, he couldn't stay here on earth the scientists would imprison him experiment on him trying to work out why he wasn't ageing or dying. The solution would be to transport him to his name planet around the normal age a human would die. We know we can transport him we've already proved with the last transport."

The firstborn Zibyan spoke: "You are correct Rosalind in your analysis, something we had overlooked. We keep considering the humans as insignificant, they are not they are extremely intelligent. Jacob has served our collective by disposing of waste and you Rosalind sacrifice yourself for the well-being of our collective; we will speak again on these matters."

Rosalind flashed her eyes in respect of her brothers and sisters who responded likewise. She walked along the corridor, glanced back and flashed her eyes to Peter, who had come away from the main computer after having his brain cells checked for defects. She stepped into the misty fog walking into the house, finding Jacob sat at the breakfast table drinking coffee. "I thought I would have to leave without you Rosalind, nearly 4:30. I've already loaded the lambs come along," he insisted worried hoping his lambs would fetch a reasonable price. "I'm driving," Rosalind insisted. Jacob shook his head, not bothering to argue climbing into the passenger seat and Jack sitting by his feet.

Rosalind drove very steadily, finally reaching the market. They quickly penned their lambs taking the paperwork to the office. Rosalind remarked: "I hadn't better be seen with you Jacob it may cause questions to be asked when you bump into old friends, don't you think?"

"Yes, I understand Rosalind," he kissed her on the cheek watching her run behind the cattle shed. The next minute a misty fog appeared and vanished, he knew she'd gone home.

Jacob left the cattle market around lunchtime, his store lambs had fetched a reasonable price. He drove steadily, stopped in a lay-by to purchase flowers on the way. He finally reached the farm parking the Ivor Williams chaining to a post; he grabbed the flowers from the passenger seat entering the house.

Rosalind had made him a lovely lunch; he often wondered how she knew what time to make a meal for, guessed God is telling her. She kissed him lovingly on the lips excepting the flowers, she knew this is a human custom. She placed the flowers in a vase on the table, giving them pride of place while Jacob enjoyed his roast lamb roast potatoes and vegetables. After lunch, Jacob ventured outside looking at his mower, hoping it would survive another year, he purchased it 10 years ago, and it stood out in all that time. He attached the mower to his Ford tractor which almost dwarfs the mower, drove to the pasture and started cutting certainly quicker this year having the extra horsepower really made the mower moved quickly. By teatime, he cut the 30 acres returning to the farm taking the mower off. He fought through the stinging nettles finding his hay tedder attaching to the back of his tractor. Rosalind had already come out while he is mowing attaching the round baler to her massy tractor and loader. Jacob walked over to the old articulated trailer the floor is almost rotted away; he'd used reinforcing wire to patch in places. The tyres look perished, he hoped she would last another season.

They returned to the house, watching television for the rest of the evening, finally retiring to bed. Rosalind placed a hand on his forehead, making him unconscious. She stepped from the house into the misty fog transported to the spaceship. Matthew waiting for her. "Rosalind; Peter has ventured to Egypt as an experiment."

Rosalind smiled, "I hope he discovers what he's looking for, I'm sure it's something scientific, Peter has always been that way inclined."

Matthew flashed his eyes, "you are correct Rosalind he has the notion, humans have hidden a nuclear facility which we were unaware of, he's investigating in person."

"When is the next shipment for Zagader Matthew?"

"Next week now we have expanded the planets we are terraforming; there will be more animals to feed some have bred already, and we are transporting the young between planets to save genetically engineering others.."

"We are harvesting the grass turning into silage, we will be able to spread a considerable amount of fertiliser on the pasture once we've completed the task." The alarms sounded in the spaceship something coming aboard; as Zibyan in distress which is unheard of. Peter had materialised on the floor, not moving. Rosalind and Matthew ease Peter to the wall where the main computer linked to him. They watched the screen appear playing the information extracted by the central computer from Peter's mind. He had inadvertently connected himself to a nuclear device buried beneath the ground in Egypt far out in the desert, causing his power supply to be drained rapidly. The facility in question is unknown to the Zibyans. Peter suspicions were correct there were secret installations they were not aware of.

Rosalind casually walked to the invisible control panel. "Computer, turn everyone who's working in the facility into animal food and annihilate the facility." Matthew and Rosalind watched an explosion and a mushroom cloud from the nuclear facility. They walked to the processing unit watching bodies turned into joints, and the on wanted parts incinerated stored ready for Jacob to spread on the field. The computer advised: "Peter's life force will be repaired in 24 earth hours."

Rosalind and Matthew flashed eyes at each other. She continued walking along the corridor, changing her appearance stepping into the misty fog, stepping out by the front door of the house. Jacob is sat watching television. "Rosalind, a nuclear facility has exploded in Egypt; they estimate a thousand people killed; terrible," he expressed drinking his coffee.

"Accidents will happen, Jacob," she smiled. "Have you checked the moisture content of the grass you cut yesterday?"

"No, I get the message! I'm on my way if it's fit Rosalind, I will row up into rows ready for you to bale." Jacob left the house climbing aboard his Ford tractor with a lovely cab to keep the wind off him. He drove steadily to the pastureland jumping from the cab, he twisted the grass in his hands, checking the moisture content. The wind had really done its job, Jacob started rowing the grass ready for the round baler. Not only is the wind blowing warm air, but the sun is also shining for a change which made him think of flystrike on his sheep; realising he would have to dip them soon to protect them against the flies. By lunchtime Jacob had rowed the 30 acres returning to the farm, he detached the tedder. He backed up to the old trailer attaching going into the house to have lunch. Rosalind had made sandwiches. "I've already eaten Jacob. I thought you could do with cheese and pickle today."

"That's fine, Rosalind."

"I'll start baling Jacob; you come with the bale wrapper, once I've baled everything, we can transport the round bales and stack outside the barn. They won't hurt left outside, and you can spread more manure to encourage the grass to grow ready for haymaking."

Rosalind left the house climbing in the cab of her massy tractor and loader towing the round baler to the field. Her computerised mind read the operators manuals in seconds understanding how everything operated. She set off producing bale after bale. Jacob, with the bale wrapper, had followed behind collecting the bales and wrapping them in plastic. By teatime, she had baled the 30 acres. Jacob could never remember Rosalind so proficient with farm machinery, she's excellent at repairing things that were for sure, operating he couldn't remember.

Rosalind had returned to the farm detaching the round baler connecting the bale grab to the loader. She returned to the field as Jacob had finished wrapping the last bale. Rosalind started loading the bales on the old rickety wooden trailer. Jacob had returned to the farm detaching the bale wrapper, heading back to the field to attaches tractor to the old wooden trailer. Jacob stared in shock; the trailer had collapsed bent in the middle the trailer a wreck finished. He watched Rosalind drive past him looking annoyed. She tore off down the drive in the Range Rover as if on a mission, not bothering to speak to him. Jacob returned to the house, there's nothing he could do they haven't a trailer suitable for moving round bales. He sat there drinking coffee, watching television. Hearing the Range Rover return, Rosalind entered the house playing the annoyed housewife, placing her hands on her hips. "Jacob you should have replaced that trailer years ago! I purchased a new one will arrive in the morning; we will continue clearing the field. God has loads of fertiliser waiting, we need the field cleared to spread on," she insisted.

Jacob retaliated! "You must remember Rosalind before you returned, and God appears to have an endless supply of money I couldn't afford the diesel for the tractors; let alone purchase any new items. The rickety old trailer my father purchased, we've repaired it year after year to make do. That's all we can ever do here make do; you should remember that Rosalind," Jacob annoyed, walking out of the house and across the Moor followed by Jack. The twilight evening air is fresh, and the mist is coming down. Jacob didn't care he could walk the Moor blindfolded he thought, following the well-worn sheep tracks would take you to one destination or another. 9 o'clock in the evening before Jacob finally stepped through the front door of his house. Rosalind wasn't there he wondered if he'd said too much. The front door open, making him jump, Rosalind had fetched a barrow load of blocks for the fire. She pushed past him stacking the wood against the hearth, finally shutting the door, making a coffee. "Sorry, Rosalind, I didn't mean to sound off," Jacob exhaled.

"I suggest you drink your coffee Jacob and go to bed, we have a busy day tomorrow the trailer will be here by 9 o'clock."

Jacob laughed, "you sending me to bed without any supper as punishment!"

Rosalind smiled, "no, I quite forgot; you'll have to put up with bread and cheese. I'm not cooking anything now. Your own fault for storming out," she expressed enjoying the argumentative situation something Zibyans never participated in. Rosalind placed the bread and butter on the table opening the cupboard removing a block of cheese.

Jacob sat quietly slicing the crusty loaf spreading a little butter and a slice of cheese. Rosalind placed a bowl of food down for Jack by the fire. Half an hour later Jacob went into the bedroom changing for bed, and Rosalind followed pressing a button on the wall switching off the old generator, which she intended to replace it is totally inefficient and half the time struggled to supply sufficient power. She knew Jacob hated her using it, cost him money in the form of diesel, he would usually sit in the dark with a candle using the Aga to cook on rather than the electric cooker. They had a freezer down in the cellar which the generator would keep cold if it ever ran long enough. Rosalind went to bed, touching Jacob's forehead stepping from the bedroom, changing going outside stepping into the misty fog and transported aboard the spaceship.

Peter is standing there waiting to greet her, flashing his eyes. "Rosalind, I am pleased to see you. I thought my existence would end, I'm fortunate to have sufficient power to return to the spaceship."

Rosalind flashed her eyes, "you have recovered, a misfortunate error on your part Peter. You should know not to touch radiation it conflicts with your construction after the thousands of years you have existed, you make such a silly mistake!"

"Thank you, sister, for reminding me. I am not Jacob to be chastised and argued with; you must remember to switch off your human behaviour when you come aboard a Zibyan spaceship Rosalind."

"My error Peter we have both made mistakes," she smiled.

"Rosalind, send Jacob in the morning we have at least 10 tons of fertiliser waiting."

Matthew appeared, flashing his eyes to both. "An explosion in China a volcano has erupted unexpectedly 300 people are missing."

"How unfortunate," Rosalind chuckled, knowing exactly where the corpses were processed.

Peter remarked: "Rosalind is it necessary for you to distort your features when not with Jacob, serves no purpose aboard a Zibyan spaceship."

"You are argumentative Peter; this is not the Zibyan way." Rosalind watched the screen appear on the wall with many of her brothers and sisters looking at them. The firstborn spoke: "Have you caught a virus, Peter? Why are you criticising Rosalind? She is in female form for the benefit of us all. Her facial expressions are essential to maintain. She is assigned to Jacob to dispose of our waste to create replicas of the earth for Zibyans, it is written in our creator's memoirs."

"I didn't realise I am argumentative, I will link to the computer again and see if there is a defect," Peter remarked walking across the room attaching to the wall, allowing the computer to examine his mind.

Rosalind flashed her eyes to Matthew walking down the corridor stepping into the misty fog; transported to the farm. Jacob sat at the table drinking coffee. "To the beach Jacob a load of fertiliser; once we move the round bales you can spread what we've stored, and hopefully, the grass will grow, we may be able to achieve three cuts."

He kissed Rosalind on the cheek dashing out the door attaching the 10-ton trailer; he drove down onto the beach watching the misty fog appear, feeling the fertiliser dropped into his trailer. His Ford tractor easily pulled the load up the track, backed up to the pile of manure which is now becoming quite a heap. Quickly emptied, heading for the farm. He parked the trailer by the barn detaching waiting for whatever Rosalind had purchased to move the round bales. Jacob noticed a lorry parked at the bottom of the track. He guessed that is the trailer; he drove with his tractor down the drive, shocked Rosalind had purchased brand-new, which must have cost a fortune. Jacob attached the bale trailer steadily driving to the field and parked. He walked back to the farm Rosalind came out of the house. "Your coffees on the table Jacob; I'll start loading the bales," she smiled patting his cheek, which made him smile everything appeared to be back to normal whatever normal is these days.

Rosalind climbed in her tractor driving to the field smiling at the new trailer she'd purchased, she's rather enjoying everything. The negotiating to purchase things arguing trying to outwit your opponent most pleasurable to her operating systems. She carefully loaded the plastic-wrapped round bales onto the new trailer. Jacob had his coffee and walked to the field, sitting in his warm tractor cab. He drove to the barn Rosalind followed with her massy tractor unloading stacking neatly against the barn. They returned to the field, fetching another three loads before they were finished. Rosalind fitted the manure bucket to her front-end loader on the tractor.

Jacob parked the brand-new trailer inside the barn and attached his old manure spreader. Rosalind loaded the manure onto the spreader, Jacob quickly spread on the pasture land. He had managed to cover the whole 30 acres with a thin layer of fertiliser, hardly sufficient to make any difference he thought. Now he would spread the fertiliser that God sent directly onto the field, which would boost the growth even more. He parked the tractor and spreader by the barn and Rosalind followed with her tractor. They went into the house at 4 o'clock in the afternoon. Rosalind pressed the button on the wall hearing the old generator come to life. Jacob commented: "I haven't checked the diesel have you, Rosalind? I suspect the old generator is getting low by now."

"No, I thought you could manage that small task Jacob," Rosalind suggested firmly.

Jacob didn't respond, sighed heavily walking out of the door, walking around the back of the house to an old shed watching the blue smoke from the exhaust situated on the roof. Jacob checked the diesel tank outside the shed, almost empty since Rosalind had returned, they'd use 50 gallons of diesel which concerned Jacob considerably. There is no need to keep running the generator; they could boil the kettle on the Aga and cook most of the food. Jacob went inside the shed he stopped the generator checking the oil topping up; she's a little low although the engine would stop if the oil became too low. Why would Rosalind want a new generator; this old beast had served him for many years and still running. Jacob is beginning to think he's allowing Rosalind to walk all over him; yes, it's great having your wife back, but at what cost. He suddenly imagined Rosalind taken away, sent a shudder down his spine; he would have to be extremely tactful when discussing the issue. Jacob returned to the house, Rosalind knew precisely what he's thinking. "I suppose you're going to moan I use the generator too much? I don't know why you're worried; money isn't an issue, you have God on your side. I wish you'd accept the fact, Jacob," she advised with confidence in her voice.

"So you are suggesting, we should abuse Gods generosity and not be frugal?"

Rosalind exhaled imitating human behaviour. "At times Jacob I could easily strangle you. You need a mobile phone at least we could order the diesel without having to drive to a phone box! I'm buying a computer tomorrow, we should be able to operate off Wi-Fi."

"You will not purchase anything else without discussing with me first Rosalind please," Jacob stared daring her to defy him.

"Don't you threaten me, Jacob Walker! God will strike you dead; everything I do is with his approval. I don't need yours," she expressed firmly storming out of the door, she is becoming addicted to confrontation. Rosalind jumped in the Range Rover driving off 11 o'clock in the evening before she reached Exeter; entering an all-night store. She purchased a computer, and a mobile phone Jacob would not beat her; she is a supreme being, she would do exactly what she wanted regardless of her mission.

Jacob had made himself coffee when he heard the generator cut out the diesel tank is empty; he sat by the fire watching the shadows of the flames created dance around the wall. He pondered on what Rosalind had said. God had approved who is he to argue with God! Jacob lit a candle opening the good book reading a few passages which warmed his heart immensely. He hoped God wasn't too annoyed with him after all he's not without sin, thanks to Adam and Eve.

Rosalind drove to an all-night garage filling the Range Rover with diesel and slowly driving home, arriving at six in the morning. She opened the front door to find Jacob asleep in his armchair with the good book still on his lap. Rosalind read his thoughts realising the generator is out of fuel. She went outside to the main diesel tank filling a 5-gallon tin emptying in the generator tank. She knew the engine is self bleeding. Rosalind went back into the house and pressed the button on the wall. The generator spluttered into life, she tapped Jacob's cheek, "come on sleepy." Jacob stared, wiping his eyes on the sleeve of his jacket. "Say nothing, Jacob," she advised. "Forget what happened, trust me and trust God. That's my last word on the subject."

Jacob nodded, watching Rosalind go outside come back in with a box showing a picture of a computer on the outside. He sighed, deciding to say nothing. He watched Rosalind remove a mobile phone from her pocket plug into the wall socket to charge. "I will order diesel later Jacob the tank holds about 500 gallons I think?"

He nodded, "far more than we need, going cheap at the time, father purchased at a farm sale. I don't think we have ever had more than 200 gallons in there and that lasted three years."

"I will purchase 400 gallons later on. You had better fill the sheep dip and prepare the fencing. We have to dip the ewes and lambs otherwise you know what will happen Jacob flystrike."

He nodded. "I will let you know when breakfast is ready. Come on, move," Rosalind smiled, patting his cheek as he went out of the door followed by Jack. Jacob found the hosepipe attaching to the water tap placing in the top of the dipper. He remembered his father had built the sheep dip on an embankment so they could drain the dipper, by removing a plug further down the embankment; one of their smarter ideas he smiled. Jacob fitted the plug, turning on the water. He walked to a dilapidated storage shed, removed the chemicals to put in the water to stop the flies laying eggs on his sheep and ewe lambs. He slowly poured the chemicals, which cost him considerable money. He watched the water disperse the chemical, turning the surface a strange colour of mauve. Jacob heard Rosalind call. He smiled walking to the house sitting down to 3 pieces of fried bread each with an egg on to sausage and three rashers of bacon. "I thought you needed a good breakfast, Jacob, we have a lot of work ahead of us while you're finishing breakfast, I'll go with Jack and bring the flock in," she smiled reassuringly.

"You sure you can manage Rosalind," he asked, surprised at her suggestion.

Rosalind displayed her displeasure expression. "Sorry," he voiced. "Off you go, I didn't mean to criticise or question your abilities," he sighed.

"Jack," Rosalind called opening the door with him following. Rosalind checked the pen gate is open. "Come on Jack," she insisted with a firm command; jumping on the quad bike with Jack sat on the carrier trying to keep his balance as she speeded across the Moor until she located the flock. Jack jumped from the quad carrier instinctively knowing what to do. He soon had the flock gathered with Rosalind staying back with the quad and Jack steering the sheep who appeared instinctively to realised they were going to the farm. Jacob is waiting patiently smiling, watching the way she had guided the sheep very professional; they finally had them penned.

Jacob slipped on his waterproofs to avoid becoming soaked from the splashes the ewes would create when they dived in the dipper. Jacob stood there holding a poll, he'd made with the V in the end; so he could push the ewes heads under the water to ensure no part of the animal is left vulnerable to flystrike. By lunchtime, they had dipped everything; the ewes and lambs wandered off bleating shaking themselves furiously trying to remove the terrible smell and surplus water off their fleece. Jacob removed his waterproofs walking down the embankment he removed the plug, allowing the sheep dip to drain away and soak into the ground. Rosalind had returned to the house. She set up the computer on a small table by the window, attaching the receiver Wi-Fi for the computer. The signal wasn't very strong but sufficient to operate. The same went for the mobile phone; she'd already ordered 400 gallons of diesel which she paid for over the mobile by money transfer. She knew the money from the lambs would have gone into the bank by now, so they could easily afford the purchase. The diesel would arrive tomorrow, she suspected Jacob would not be impressed with her decisions. Nevertheless, he would have to like it or lump it as humans would express.

Jacob came into the house seeing the computer by the window on a little table, he didn't ask any questions he'd never own one or operated one. He noticed the mobile phone not having a clue how to operate; he could manage the phone box down the road without any trouble. The mobile phone rang. Rosalind answered. Peter from the spaceship she wondered why he's contacting her via mobile phone. "Rosalind, come to the ship tonight decisions have been made, I will explain later," Peter ended the call.

Jacob asked, "who is that?"

"Peter," she responded frostily.

"What did he want?"

"God business, not yours," walking off into the kitchen. Jacob beginning to wonder whether his relationship is falling apart. Rosalind's attitudes seem to have changed and not for the better. Rosalind is reading his thoughts realising she is displaying too much aggression towards him inadvertently, although she had to confess, she did enjoy teasing and arguing. Jacob sat on the settee turning on the television. Rosalind came over sitting on his lap; she knew this is the way the female humans behaved with their husbands. Rosalind tried to think of a reason to excuse her behaviour, remembering what human females experience once a month. "I'm grumpy Jacob it's that time," kissing on the cheek hoping he would accept the explanation.

He kissed her on the cheek: "Nobody's perfect, I'm sure God knows."

"I've ordered the diesel we have plenty of money, arriving tomorrow."

"That's okay if God is in charge of everything, I have nothing to worry about," he smiled briefly.

Rosalind touched Jacob's forehead; he immediately fell asleep. She pressed the button on the wall turning off the generator. Jack watched intently resting his jaw on Jacob's boot as Rosalind left the house. She stepped into the misty fog transported to the spaceship miles out to sea.

Peter is waiting for her with Matthew. Rosalind could sense something is about to happen, desperately reading their thoughts for a clue; gathering it's something to do with women. She is receiving mixed-up messages, almost as if Peter and Matthew's thoughts were scrambled to prevent reading. Rosalind watched the screen appear on the wall observing several brothers and sisters, including the firstborn of their collective. He was created by the central computer; initially considered a mistake, a malfunction by the creator. The Zibyan creators no longer existed after a freak accident, their flesh construction could not withstand the heat from the volcano which erupted. Only the central computer remained protected by an energy shield. The central computer realising the creator's deaths are his error; attempted to create an improved shapeshifting version of the creator's design composed of pure energy.

The firstborn looked to Rosalind, "we have made a decision Rosalind without discussing or informing you. We suspect your opinion would be biased if we included you in the decision of our collective."

Rosalind flashed her eyes to everyone, and they did likewise. "I'm surprised, in fact, intrigued, why you have isolated me from the decision-making process. I look forward to your explanation," she answered calmly.

"You are aware Rosalind of the mistake we made creating humans from chimpanzees, we are now transporting human flesh to other planets to feed the animals."

"I am aware I am part of the process. I've been here from the beginning with Peter and Matthew, I played the part of Mary Magdalene for a time, and later we introduce the Bible for good measure."

"We are not prepared to subject as Zibyan to become a child and submissive to Jacob, although your idea is based on logic."

Rosalind didn't know quite what to say. "Jacob will not have anyone to leave his farm to once he's gone. The farm will be sold or taken over by the National Trust who own the Moor."

"We the collective have decided, you will be replaced Rosalind with a human female under our control. The Science Department has decided they are ready to experiment. Matthew has located several females matching Rosalind's description; they will have their brains reprogrammed. One will stay with Jacob and the others transported to Jacobs planet."

"Jacob is no fool he will know immediately, it's not me and reject your idea. I presume you will pick such a female that can carry a child and give Jacob the son he requires to carry on the farm?"

"We are aware Rosalind there may be difficulties; you will remain at the farm invisible until we are satisfied everything is working the way it should."

"What about finances? The human Rosalind will not understand and certainly won't be as efficient as me," Rosalind expressed calmly.

"We suspected there would be some resistance on your part, you have operated as an individual for some time which is taught us many things. Your experimentation has not gone unnoticed, and you were honoured with a planet in your name."

"The information you are expressing is contradictory; you are dissatisfied with human behaviour, and we are shipping loads of their flesh to feed our animals on various planets. Why would you want to save Jacob, he's human?"

"We have watched you perform with Jacob, he has no aggression in him; he doesn't want to send it animals to market, although he has to out of necessity to survive. The creator's central computer as advised he is the closest resemblance to the original creators of them and us."

"If I understand you correctly. You are trying to reconstruct our own creators from the main computers records? Do we have any DNA in which to construct the original Zibyan race we are named after in honour of them?"

"Not at the moment, they were destroyed in the explosion, of year zero when the planet erupted unexpectedly. Those that did remain soon died at the moment of our creation, which was considered a mistake at the time, yet we are still here honouring our creators."

"You are the firstborn in the year zero; surely you realise, you the firstborn, who has watched everyone after you created. If there is a way to raise the original creators of us, we would have done it long ago why subject the Zibyan collective to a never-ending reminder of our failure."

"You have not listened to your brothers and sisters recently. A bone fragment has been found of an original Zibyan. Our brilliant scientists are trying to extract DNA as we speak."

"Has no one learnt the lessons of meddling! For 9000 years plus; we watched the humans destroy the planet earth even when we instilled religious teachings in the hope to control them; we failed miserably. Apart from in a few and I think you could possibly count them, on one hand, Jacob is one of them."

"We have decided Rosalind you will be replaced by a human once she is programmed. 4 more females will be impregnated by Jacob and transported to Jacobs planet where they will be nurtured until they give birth. We will alter the DNA of the offspring in the hope to create our creators."

"Why not take samples from Jacob; there is no need for him to mate with anyone. Transport to Zagader and inseminate the females there," Rosalind suggested running out of ideas to put a stop to what she considered to be a crazy idea.

"Rosalind, your thought pattern is clouded; do you not think our scientists have considered that possibility? If Jacob breeds on earth and the females made pregnant, we have a guaranteed success on their arrival."

"I have thought as an individual, and I think as one now. I'm advising the Zibyan collective not to attempt to create our creators from in theory a human DNA. I will have great pleasure in telling the firstborn, I told you so if you fail!" Rosalind expressed firmly.

"You will not only be chastising the firstborn Rosalind but your brothers and sisters who are in agreement with me and the computer." The images vanish from the wall. Peter and Matthew looked to Rosalind. "You are treading a dangerous path, Rosalind the collective have decided the individual is insignificant now. A decision has been made you must wholeheartedly comply."

CHAPTER 6

Uncharted Ground

Rosalind followed Peter into another section of the spaceship. Encased in a transparent jelly substance were five females all resembling Rosalind. Snatched by Matthew made unconscious and transported to the spaceship in preparation. "Computer," Rosalind asked, "what are the chances of Jacob accepting any one of these females?"

"Once I have wiped their memory and instilled the original Rosalind, we have an 80% chance of success."

"I would have expected at least 99.9% computer from you, what is the issue?" Rosalind asked rather please with the computer's answer.

"If I were wiping your memory banks, I would have 100% success rate; humans are different. They resemble our creators, they are organic, you are not you were created by me."

"I have a solution computer," Rosalind remarked, watching Peter look at her listening intently.

"I am listening, Rosalind, I have computed everything, I am the central computer I created you."

"Yes, computer! Have you considered, I bring Jacob here? Set aside a room make it familiar to a human, and allow Jacob to meet the new Rosalind here? At least that way, we can control the environment and the situation, give you some indication of whether your work is successful or needs refining."

"I agree with your analysis. If necessary, we can subdue Jacob to prevent him from rejecting the females selected to travel to Zagader. If he shows signs of rejection with the four for the home planet. The fifth one, supposed to carry his seed here will be destroyed, and you will have to continue living with him until we find another solution."

"When will you have the females ready computer?" Rosalind asked suspecting Jacob would not easily be fooled.

"The first one will be ready in an hour. I will prepare a room as you have suggested Rosalind, returned to the farm and prepare Jacob for travel to the spaceship in one hour."

Rosalind flashed her eyes at Peter walking along the corridor, stepping into the misty fog returning to the farm. She awoke Jacob where she'd left him. He jumped and yawned while Rosalind made coffee. "You are visiting Peter this morning, he is rather fond of you, unfortunate he can't travel here from heaven," she smiled reassuringly.

Jacob smiled: "Before I've had my breakfast," he enquired somewhat surprised.

Rosalind smiled, quickly preparing a sandwich of cheese and onion, which would make his breath smell awful. Jacob, blissfully unaware of what is about to take place, finished his sandwich. Rosalind held his hand they step from the doorway into the misty fog arriving aboard the spaceship. Jacobs clothes had changed, he's now in a robe the same as he wore when he travelled before to heaven. Rosalind led Jacob into a furnished room, hot coffee was already on the coffee table. "I shan't belong Jacob," she smiled sweetly leaving.

Jacob believed he is in a secluded room when, in fact, Rosalind and the others could see everything. Matthew transported the first woman into Jacob, supposedly programmed as Rosalind by the computer. Jacob stood up. "Who are you? I haven't seen you before?"

"I'm your wife Rosalind silly man, you've eaten cheese and onion sandwiches, your breath is disgusting," she proclaimed.

Rosalind watching with Peter and Matthew trying not to grin. "You look like my wife," Jacob expressed calmly, "but you're not?"

The computer sent down an invisible ray, connecting to Jacob's brain and the woman trying to betray Rosalind. Within seconds they were on the floor mating. Peter and Matthew walked away along with Rosalind. "Computer, you have failed," Peter expressed. "The only solution is to allow Jacob to mate with the four; no the five and send them all to Zagader and leave Rosalind with Jacob for the moment."

"I agree! Organic brains are difficult to reprogram, this female is performing correctly. Unfortunately, Jacob knew she's not Rosalind. Jacob can stay here till tomorrow morning by which time he should have mated with the five successfully. I will store the females here until I am satisfied they have conceived. I have transmitted our decision to the collective they have agreed with my analysis. Collect Jacob tomorrow Rosalind." The war displayed the firstborn on Zagader along with several other Zibyans. "I believe you have something to say to me Rosalind," the firstborn suggested.

"No, there is nothing to say; the evidence speaks for itself. I'm returning to my duties you have partially succeeded. You will have five candidates to ship to Zagader and onto Jacobs planet and in nine months; we shall see."

The firstborn vanished from the wall along with the others. Peter advised, "be careful Rosalind do not criticise the collective."

"I am aware Peter," she smiled walking along the corridor stepping into the misty fog appearing outside the front door. She noticed the lorry coming up the drive, he is carrying diesel, she presumed. He filled the diesel tank and left. Rosalind took several tins of diesel to the generator fuel tank filling, should last for a month she decided.

She grabbed the crook from the back of the door with Jack close to her heels; she walked across the Moor, finding the sheep grazing contently. Rosalind sat on a large rock, isolating her thoughts from the collective as she trained herself to do for some time. She wondered what she is trying to achieve? Although had to chuckle at the comment from the female about Jacobs breath. Why did she want him for herself? They couldn't breed successfully, they weren't even constructed the same. Once his lifespan is reached, he would die. He could be re-created by a Zibyan like she had with Rosalind, but it wouldn't be the same. The only solution would be to alter Jacobs DNA, so he didn't age. When he reached the age of 80 or 90 transport him to the planet named, "Jacob," where they could stay together for eternity.

Rosalind realised what she is thinking and shocked by her conclusions. This is not the Zibyan way she concluded, patted Jack rose to her feet, walking towards the house, enjoying the solitude much like Jacob. For the first time, Rosalind felt lonely missing Jacob; a ridiculous sensation, she knew humans suffered from the effect but not Zibyans. Rosalind sat watching television; she watched her two favourite programs turning off the tv, feeding Jack. She left the house stepping into the misty fog transported aboard the spaceship. Peter and

Matthew were watching Jacob and the fifth female mating. Matthew enquired, "you have experienced the mating process, do you think it's something we should practice as a form of experimentation?"

"From my own experiences, no! I can't see the collective ever agreeing to the practice; it serves no purpose pleasure is not a necessity in the Zibyan culture. I do know our creators would procreate similar to humans to create likenesses of their selves occasionally. According to the computer records, they vary rarely practised the procedure; that's why they didn't survive. I suspect they didn't travel to other planets very often or consider colonising elsewhere. Something went terribly wrong, and they were destroyed by a volcano. I'm surprised the computer didn't react in time to protect them."

The firstborn appeared on the wall, accompanied by others. "You have studied the computer records of our creators Rosalind. The fragment of bone recovered has the DNA of one Zibyan creator. When the females give birth, we will implant the Zibyan DNA, which will slowly modify the human DNA and produce a creator."

"Firstborn the one who carries the knowledge of everything. Have you considered the possibility our creators at the outset rejected our form as a mistake? If you create the creators, and they extract events from the main computer and come to a conclusion; we are still a mistake! They may wish to destroy us?"

Peter and Matthew looked to Rosalind and the firstborn, the others were silent. "Your individuality may have detected an error in our assessment. I as the firstborn watched the last flesh Zibyan ceased to function and helpless to sustain his life. We the collective have concerned ourselves with rectifying a mistake, we believe when, in fact, the mistake is not our making, only circumstances beyond our control. However, we will continue along the path we have chosen for the moment and will monitor closely, prevent what you have suggested Rosalind taking place." The firstborn and the others vanished. Peter turned to Rosalind, "I am fascinated by the way your mind works outside of the collective, although you are still working for the collective as an individual Rosalind."

Rosalind looked in the room where Jacob is with the final female to be shipped to Zagader. They were mating like rabbits she thought, turning away disinterested and partially annoyed it wasn't her, she thought irrational on her part. Matthew removed the final female into storage, where she would stay nurtured by the computer until it is established she's pregnant. Rosalind went into the room, Jacob laying on the bed. The computer had put him to sleep wiping his memory of any event, cleansing his naked body from top to bottom. Hence, there were no traces left of his endeavours. Rosalind lay beside him realising she had secured her position on the farm for some time with Jacob.

The alarm sounded off in the spaceship. Rosalind jumped to her feet looking at the screen noticing a lorry and several men herding Jacob sheep about to load. Peter had acted swiftly, paralysing the men transporting aboard to become fertiliser. Rosalind walked down the corridor stepping into the misty fog, she is transported to the lorry's location. She encouraged the sheep along the path to their own part of the Moor. Rosalind stepped into the misty fog, transported to the farm. Collected a bag of sheep nuts, returning to the ewes. Rosalind making sure they were on their own part of the Moor before she emptied small piles of food. She walked towards the lorry, hoping she had discouraged the ewes from investigating other parts of the Moor.

Rosalind climbing inside the lorry after lifting the loading ramp and securing. She studied her memory banks which provided her with instructions on how to drive the lorry. She set off along the narrow Moor road, parking the lorry in a lay-by some 10 miles from the farm and sent a blast from her eyes into the back of the lorry, the straw ignited. Rosalind stepped into the misty fog vanishing to the farm.

She now realised someone needed to be on the farm all the time, she would stay on the farm and collect Jacob in the morning. Rosalind took the decision the sheep needed to be sheared, they required their wool removed, they'd had several days of rain hopefully sufficient to wash out the awful smell of sheep dip. She quickly rounded the sheep with Jack returning them to the barn penning securely. She ran into the house removing the electric sheep clippers starting the generator. Rosalind could see plainly, although in the early hours and dark. The sheep seem to behave more peaceably as she removed their fleeces. Rosalind is racing the clock shearing a sheep at the rate of one every 30 seconds using her limitless energy and speed. When she'd finished shearing, she bagged the fleeces ready for collection they were virtually worthless, nevertheless would help prevent flystrike.

6 o'clock in the morning Rosalind drove Jacobs ford tractor and trailer down onto the beach and parked. The misty fog appeared, she stepped in travelling to the spaceship finding Jacob in his little room drinking a hot coffee. Rosalind entered, smiling. "You sleep comfortably, husband," she asked, watching him smile.

"I must have dropped off like a log Rosalind; I don't remember anything, I must have been exhausted, sorry."

"I'm pleased you've rested Jacob, work to be done; come along," Rosalind insisted leading him down the corridor stepping into the misty fog. He stepped out onto the sand in his work clothes seeing his tractor and trailer loaded waiting for him. They climbed aboard with Jacob driving returning to the manure heap. He emptied the trailer, driving to the farm. "I don't know what's happened Rosalind, I'm still exhausted, I think I could sleep for a week."

Rosalind, jumping from the tractor cab while Jacob parked in the barn. Rosalind went into the house making coffee for them both. She sat quietly waiting for him to join her, she could hear him pushing the wheelbarrow transporting logs to the house for the fire and Aga. She turned on the television, as much as Jacob denied he liked the TV. She knew he enjoyed the news, especially if criminals were punished or vanished, he knew where they were heading.

Jacob sat beside her. "Rosalind," he asked cautiously. "Would it be possible for us to afford a second-hand manure spreader. The one we have only carries five tons and most of God shipments coming 10-ton loads. I could easily spread directly on to the pastureland rather than tipping from a trailer, and you have to reload."

Rosalind felt herself laughing, Jacob sat there, bemused at her behaviour. "I'm sure I can arrange something for you, Jacob, I'm not used to you being efficient," she chuckled making more coffee for them both. "I have a confession, I've sheared the sheep, bored missing you while talking to Peter."

"You're joking. I hate that job my back thanks you immensely," Jacob kissed Rosalind passionately on the lips. "I hadn't noticed I must see my sheep in the morning."

After checking the sheep early the next morning; Jacob and Rosalind climbed into their Range Rover heading to the machinery dealership. Rosalind had already visited the cellar placing money in her large handbag and coat pockets.

They travelled for some time noticing a second-hand manure spreader. Rosalind pulled over to the side of the road for them to investigate. They both slowly walked around the machine; massive is an understatement Jacob thought. He dreaded the thought of what it would cost. The sales representative came from the office noticing their interest with a broad cheesy smile. "Good morning sir madam. £2500 plus the dreaded VAT of course and she is yours delivered, providing you live in this country," he chuckled.

"2000 for cash," Rosalind voiced.

"2250 delivered."

"Agreed!" Rosalind voiced counting the money from her handbag. The sales rep astounded to find someone carrying that amount of cash. "The spreader will be delivered tomorrow," the salesperson assured after realising they weren't very far away from his location. He had a lorry heading in that direction anyway, so he could kill two birds with one stone.

Jacob couldn't stop grinning, proud of the way Rosalind handled the deal. The spreader wouldn't have to go through the books everything paid for in cash. Technically the machine didn't exist, which made Jacob smiled even more not having to fight with the taxman, who he would personally spread on his field without reservation. They drove steadily along the road towards home. Rosalind suddenly changed direction heading down a narrow Lane which opened up into a small trading estate. Jacob looked at the sign where she parked. 'Generators.' He had rather hoped she'd forgotten the idea, obviously not!

Rosalind stepped from the Range Rover grinning looking at the expression on Jacob's face. Jacob listened to the salesperson explained to Rosalind. "The generator, you're interested in is extremely fuel-efficient, when power wasn't used, the generator would automatically switch off and restart if power is required." Jacob, like the sound of that himself, his old generator ran all the time whether creating electricity or not. With the specifications, Rosalind had selected the new generator cost £4000. Jacob thought her handbag would have to be extremely deep to carry that amount of cash.

Rosalind emptied her handbag there is £3000 left inside, she emptied her coat pockets, removing another thousand, delivery is free. The salesperson wrote out a sale ticket. The generator would be prepared and delivered early next week. Jacob decided today had been extremely expensive and hoped, his ewes could produce six lambs each to cover the cost, he still hadn't purchased a new Ram.

Rosalind smiled as they left the establishment. Jacob followed sliding onto the passenger seat of the Range Rover. She is waiting for him to say something, she could read his mind as she drove towards home. Within an hour, they were back on the farm. Rosalind made the coffee, Jacob sat quietly at the kitchen table with Jack by his heels. Nobody spoke a word, Jacob finished his coffee muttering, "I'll check the ewes, Rosalind. I have to purchase a Ram from somewhere," he sighed heavily. Jacob left the house watching the lorry driver way from the farm after collecting the sheep wool.

"You don't need a Ram till October Jacob, there's plenty of time to find one," Rosalind suggested calmly. He didn't reply, walked out of the door with Jack following him closely. Now the beginning of June Jacob is particularly concerned the weather is decidedly warmer, which would encourage flystrike. He knew he'd dipped his sheep, but no guarantee would resolve the issue. Rosalind is concerned, turned herself invisible following Jacob as a precaution. She suspected mating with five females in 24-hours a strain for Jacob, although he didn't realise what he is performing.

Jacob spotted his neighbour walking towards him with his sheepdog and crook. Jacob immediately ordered, "Jack, lie down and stay." Jack complied immediately, Jacob carried on walking, shaking Thomas's hand. "long time no see my friend how's life treating you."

"Not as well as you from what I hear at the shop," Thomas chuckled and sighed. "I'm selling up Jacob I can't make a living, and I'm getting on in years; my son is not interested, he's gone off to work in the city, you can't blame him."

"That is the last thing I expected you to say, Thomas, I'm sorry you have been a great neighbour. Sometimes I wonder why I bother," Jacob sighed.

"I suppose you wouldn't be interested, Jacob? I only have 10 acres of land plus my grazing rights which would naturally become yours plus a small house."

Rosalind could see the advantages of having more grazing rights and another property, which could be used by the Zibyans. She quickly materialised in a deep gully to the left of them, walking out, making Jacob jump and Thomas. "I didn't see you come in Mrs," Jacob voiced. "This is Thomas, our neighbour he's packing up more's the pity."

"So this is your secret Jacob you have married again, you kept that bloody quiet," Thomas chuckled.

Jacob realised he'd have to be extremely careful what he said concerning Rosalind, Thomas came to the wedding when he married Rosalind the first time. "We met, quite by accident, Thomas, she was walking her dog, and I threaten to shoot it as you can imagine it was love at first sight." Thomas burst out laughing.

"I'm pleased to meet you, Thomas; strange I have the same name as Jacob's first wife Rosalind," she smiled. "Jacob would like the chance to purchase your smallholding, Thomas. I have some savings I'm sure you would prefer a cash deal," Rosalind smiled.

"You're my kind of woman," Thomas voiced cheerfully. "Do you have a sister?"

Jacob glared at Rosalind, almost saying with his eyes. "Have you lost your bloody mind, woman?" She could read his thoughts which were not very pleasant at this precise second; she is absolutely shocked.

"Nice to meet you, Rosalind," Thomas voiced cheerfully. "I'll put some figures together and will discuss matters further. Jacob knows my land, he'll show you around. I must go I have a doctors appointment my old bones, aunt what they used to be," he chuckled walking off.

"Have you lost your mind, Rosalind," Jacob asked, annoyed. "I'm not taking out a mortgage to buy another smallholding."

"Firstly, I never asked you to take out a mortgage. I can pay for the farm myself without you. I can live there, and you can live on your own farm." Rosalind watched Jacob's eyes enlarge, shocked by her threat.

"You're not serious Rosalind, live separate lives?"

"Why not! I don't want to live with a backward farmer who doesn't look forward and take every opportunity that presents itself. Thomas only has a smallholding 10 acres and a rickety old house. What he does have is access to free grazing lots of free grazing which would benefit your ewes. You're not short of equipment any more. Sometimes, Jacob, I could hit you over the head with a bucket," she emphasised. "Besides I think God has a use for Thomas's old house, I don't have all the details, but I'm sure he will let us know."

"Oh, I didn't realise Rosalind, sorry if its God's will, let it be done," Jacob smiled. "I will leave you to organise everything as usual." They held hands walking home to their farm. Jacob sat quietly, watching television while Rosalind made drinks, he suspected Thomas would want between 160 and 280,000 for his property. Jacob knew he's lucky if he had 10,000 in disposable cash. Not forgetting everything recently purchased by Rosalind and him. He couldn't blame her entirely, he is the one who suggested the new manure spreader.

Jacob sighed slowly looking at the television listening to the presenter explain. "Over 2 million people had vanished over the past year without a trace." Jacob wondered what percentage of the humans were transported to him to dispose of on his pasture. He listened to the presenter explaining: "Crime had fallen to an all-time low and terrorism virtually non-existent at the moment." Jacob exhaled pleased in some respects and saddened in others.

Rosalind passed him his drink. "Don't worry about the money, Jacob, I have plenty to cover the cost. Besides, when you have a son, there will be land for him to make a living on. And before you ask not yet," she smiled. "Perhaps in nine months, we shall see; I'm making no promises." Already conjuring a plan in her mind. Somehow she would convince the collective to keep one of the females here to give birth, she would take the child and raise; after all, Jacob is the father.

"Are you with child," he asked, surprised.

"That is for me to know and you to wait and see, I promise nothing," she grinned with satisfaction at her cunning thoughts. Jacob kissed Rosalind very passionately rather excited about everything now. More land a son; excellent equipment, plenty of sheep what more could he asked for, not forgetting God and the fertiliser.

They both retired to bed rather early for a change; Rosalind switched off the television going into the bedroom. She touched Jacob's forehead; he is instantly unconscious. She stepped from the house, patting Jack stepping into the misty fog and in seconds aboard the spaceship. Peter and Matthew were waiting for her. "Rosalind, you know the firstborn will not accept your idea. Purchase another farm is a good idea our brothers and sisters could use the house as a refuge point before boarding the spaceship."

"We shall see Peter; the firstborn does not require five children to experiment with to transfer DNA from the creator's bone to humans."

Peter commented: "You are presuming what the collective will require Rosalind, they will find that an insult."

The far wall displayed a screen, the firstborn and several of his brothers and sisters appeared. "Rosalind I have considered your proposal; you are not demeaning a Zibyan which we would not accept to become a human child. If five males are growing inside the females, you may have one. If one is a female Jacob will have to accept that to continue his farm."

Rosalind grinned, making the firstborn and the others stare at her facial expression. "Firstborn let's hope everything works out successful for everyone. I believe the five have conceived and we should know within the next 24 hours what the females are carrying. Jacob must be extremely fertile for all 5 to conceive," Rosalind remarked. "Of course firstborn should your experiments not be fruitful you could always try again, Jacob will be here, there is an ample supply of females on earth. There is always the possibility a female child may accept the new strains of DNA substantially better than a male."

"You are correct Rosalind your individuality provides you with clear thinking and planning for the future. I have considered what you have said and will discuss with our scientists. If there is a female child, I will take her, you will have to accept a male." The firstborn vanished with his brothers and sisters. Rosalind burst out laughing watched by Matthew and Peter astounded at her behaviour. This is not the Zibyan way to behave. Peter asked with some urgency, "are you unwell Rosalind? Do you need the main computer to stabilise your thought patterns?"

"No, Peter! I displayed human behaviour, sometimes I forget where I am," she grinned walking down the corridor stepping into the misty fog, appearing by the front door. Rosalind entered to find Jacob sat at the breakfast table, eating toast and marmalade. He asked with some urgency, "has God approved us conceiving a child?"

"All indications, you will have a child in nine months; sex is undetermined at the moment Jacob, you must obey Gods request without hesitation. Otherwise, you will lose everything," she assured with confidence. She watched Jacobs smile broaden; all he wanted is coming true as far as he is concerned. "I'm going to see Thomas today, Jacob to finalise the deal. You stay on the farm and look after our flock," she instructed. "Don't forget your manure spreader arrives today."

Jacob, kissed Rosalind on the cheek, grabbing his crook and raincoat from the back of the door. Jack close to his heels, ventured outside with Jacob briskly strolling across the Moor in search of his sheep. Rosalind went down into the cellar locating the suitcase with the money in; she counted out 160,000, placing in shopping bags. Rosalind left the house stepping into the Range Rover, she drove the 3 miles to Thomas's farm venturing down along drive, wasn't in much of a better state than there own. She parked outside the front of the house; thankfully, this one had slates on the roof and not thatch. Although she considered the windows need replacing, the woodwork is rotten, and the farm buildings didn't look in a much better state. He had an old tractor, she guessed Jacob would love to play with and trailer, plus other odds and ends of old farm machinery; scattered around. She noticed in one pen, a lovely Ram, which she thought would be great for Jacobs flock. Thomas invited Rosalind in the house; he could see the two shopping bags, which puzzled him to start with until he saw the money. His eyes almost popped out of his head. "You weren't joking when you said you'd pay in cash Rosalind," he expressed surprised. "The Mrs has gone shopping, she would have loved to have met you, Rosalind," he smiled warmly.

"I'll come straight to the point Thomas. 160,000 in these two bags; I want everything the house the 10 acres, the machinery and the Ram. I believe you already sold your ewes?"

"Yes, they went yesterday I sent them to the market, I'm saving the Ram until next week that's why he's still here."

Rosalind held her hand out for him to shake. "Do we have a deal, Thomas?" She already knew the answer is no.

"You put another 100,000 on the table, and you can have everything lock stock and barrel," he smiled with confidence.

"I'll not argue with you, Thomas Jacob would never forgive me if I haggled with his friend. 100,000 is neither here or there," she assured. "I'll fetch it now you contact your solicitors and have deeds of ownership transferred to Jacob Walker, Thomas."

Thomas smiled: "I can see you are a woman of your word," shaking her hand confidently. "You collect the money, and I'll phone my solicitors while you're gone. The Mrs will be overjoyed, she can't wait to move. We have a little cottage with a small garden where we can grow our vegetables, and she can grow her bloody flowers; she's moaned about for years," he chuckled.

Rosalind walked out of the house. She drove home running down into the cellar, removing another £100,000 from the suitcase, Rosalind would have to speak to Peter for more cash, they were running short. Within half an hour, she returned to Thomas's property towing the Ivor Williams trailer to bring the Ram back to their farm for the moment, while the deal is finalised.

Thomas is counting the cash in the house, Rosalind picked up the Ram with one hand placing him in the Ivor Williams sheep trailer. Thomas came out to assist surprised she'd already loaded the Ram. He laughed, "no wonder Jacob married you! You're not frightened of anything or hard work by the looks of things." Thomas gave a receipt for the £260,000 shaking her hand warmly, "You can do what you like we won't be here much longer Rosalind, I know Jacobs had his eye on my old sit up and beg tractor for years," he laughed.

"Thanks, Thomas, enjoy your retirement." Rosalind waived driving off towing the Ivor Williams trailer transporting the new Ram for Jacobs farm. Rosalind drove steadily up the drive. Jacob, sat on a bale in the barn watching her approach puzzled why she had the Ivor Williams trailer on the back. He looked through the slats as she parked observing a large white-faced Ram. Jacob is grinning from ear to ear, Rosalind is unstoppable he concluded. She stepped from the Range Rover smiling, she is so used to performing human facial expressions; came almost naturally to her now. "All ours Jacob, including the old tractor and equipment. He sent his ewes to the market yesterday; that doesn't matter, we have enough we have over 250 breeding ewes." Jacob grabbed Rosalind taking her by surprise, kissing her very passionately. Expressed excitely, "You are a wonderful wife, two farms, a son or daughter soon, and I'm closer to God now than I've ever been."

"You know the old saying Jacob, don't count your chickens before they're hatched," Rosalind cautioned. She pointed in the direction of the road. "I think you'll find your manure spreader has arrived Jacob." Jacob jumped on his Ford four-wheel-drive tractor heading for the bottom of the drive. He reversed hitching the manure spreader to his tractor and connecting the PTO shaft which worked the spreader. Jacob signed for the spreader, the lorry driver carried on with his journey. Jacob steadily drove to the farm. Rosalind had already gone inside, making lunch for him. Jacob joined her if he grinned any more, his jaw would break Rosalind concluded. Placing the breadboard on the table with cheese and onion and a block of butter. "You realise we'll have to starve now Jacob we are destitute." She found herself laughing; she'd made a joke; this is a new experience altogether. The Zibyans had no sense of humour, never programmed as a necessity. She watched Jacobs serious expression for a moment until he realised she is joking. He continued spreading his butter, placing a large slice of cheese on the bread slicing onion, making his eyes water. Rosalind made coffee passing one to Jacob, she moved to the television switching on sitting down with hers. "Aren't you eating Rosalind Jacob," asked concerned.

"No, I have to watch what I consume," she expressed calmly suspecting Jacob would put two and two together leading him to one conclusion.

"Okay." Rosalind sat quietly, watching the news. The presenter advised bewildered: "2000 Russian soldiers had vanished from the face of the earth. Russia had suspended military operations pending further investigations as to what has happened."

Rosalind had received a telepathic message from Matthew. "Jacobs spreader is required in the morning."

"8:30 in the morning Jacob with your new spreader on the beach."

"Okay," he smiled, having a chance to use his new spreader. He finished his lunch going outside, giving the machine a thorough greasing and inspecting for any faulty parts. After all, it's second-hand; unusual a farmer would sell something that's in good working order. Unless he is desperate or wealthy and purchased a new one. He filled his tractor with diesel, checking the oil, he couldn't stop smiling. He could never imagine in his wildest dreams farming could be this easy, as long as you have the equipment. Jacob walked across the Moor eventually coming to Thomas's farm, looking at the old sit up and beg Fordson, his father and he had envied for years. Thomas came out seen Jacob looking at the tractor. Thomas patted Jacob on the shoulder. "Why don't you drive her home," he chuckled, "she's yours."

Jacob smiled, "thanks, Thomas, you sure you don't mind?"

Thomas climbed onto the seat of the old sit up and beg; he pressed the button the P6 diesel engine spluttered into life. Thomas reversed out of the shed topping up with diesel. The engine had a sweet sound a distinctive sound. The old tractor had hydraulics, and a PTO, one of the last built before this Fordson model was discontinued. Thomas warned, "remember, she has a high gearbox." Jacob nodded climbing aboard waving to Thomas as he drove away, heading along the road, not cutting across the Moor.

Rosalind is reading his thoughts, she wondered how someone could become attached or interested in a tractor. Humans are strange, she thought, turning off the television. She suddenly is alarmed reading Jacobs thoughts, stopped by a police car. Rosalind turned herself into a Seagull, flying the short distance to where Jacob is parked on the side of the road.

Two policemen were looking at his tractor, one removing his notepad. The two officers suddenly vanished into thin air. Jacob staggered backwards in shock; quickly climbed aboard his tractor, continuing along the road as fast as he dare travel. Rosalind flew back to the farm, changing from the Seagull into Rosalind. She watched Jacob part the tractor in the barn alongside his other equipment. His expression is white as if he'd seen a ghost. "Rosalind," he stuttered, "I've…"

"You don't have to explain Jacob, you will have to learn you are protected. The officers in question were corrupt. They were about to attempt to extort money from you so you would avoid conviction. Their fertiliser should be extremely potent," she smiled, grabbing Jacob's hand, leading him into the house. Rosalind poured Jacob a small whiskey after reading her memory banks of what humans use to steady their nerves, which Zibyans weren't afflicted with. She realised the police car a little close to the farm for comfort. Rosalind kissed Jacob on the forehead rendering him unconscious. She stepped from the house, checking no one is watching. Rosalind transformed into a Seagull, flying to where the police car is parked. When she is sure, no one could see her, she turned into a police officer slipping into the car, hearing the radio calling the officer's name. Rosalind quickly drove some miles winding down the car window. She changed into a Seagull flying off as the car went over the cliff, dropping into a salty grave. She flew towards the farm, watching police cars with their sirens screaming driving along the coastal road searching for their colleagues.

Rosalind landed on the beach stepping into the misty fog, transported aboard the spaceship. Peter and Matthew were waiting to greet her. Rosalind flashed her eyes in response to their greeting. "You made the right decision; Peter snatching the two police officers. The last thing we need is snooping humans around the farm, and especially our new acquisition. I explained to Jacob they had criminal intent, he accepted that excuse willingly."

"Unfortunately, Rosalind, the police car has a tracker fitted and alerted the police to wear the car went over the cliff. Thankfully the glass shattered when the vehicle collided with the rocks beneath the sea. They will search for the police officers bodies for a few days. The way you drove the car over the cliff gives the impression; they were travelling too fast to make the corner safely."

The firstborn appeared with some of his brothers and sisters on the far wall. "Rosalind the collective is pleased with the new acquisition, once modifications have been made inside the house, we can use it for a variety of uses."

"Firstborn how many planets do you intend to colonise, you have selected six will there be any more?"

"Rosalind, you already know the answer. The females Jacob impregnated are carrying four males and one female. The next transport ship will arrive shortly; you will keep one female until she has given birth to a male child. The others are to be transported to Zagader and onto Jacobs planet where they will reside until they have given birth, the females will be disposed of, and the infants cared for by the Zibyans and the DNA transferred from the creators bone fragments."

"I understand firstborn if you are successful in transferring the creators DNA to the infants, where will they reside? I presume in the laboratories or do you intend to accelerate their growth?"

"Why do you ask Rosalind I detect your individual thinking has reservations?"

"Firstborn I would recommend you do not dispose of the females. I would alter the infants DNA while the mothers are sedated and return the infants to their mothers. They will be producing milk for the infants and will care for them more efficiently than a Zibyan."

"What are your intentions with the female that gives birth to Jacob son? Are you disposing of her?"

"No, I will use her as a nanny, after reprogramming her mind, the child will thrive better on its own mother's milk than supplements firstborn."

"Rosalind, the main computer is fascinated by the way you think as an individual, your suggestions are sound, we will implement. Peter and you Matthew support Rosalind, she has shown her true loyalty to the Zibyan collective with her suggestions and ideas," the firstborn vanished.

Matthew looked on the screen. "Jacob has come to the beach with his manure spreader. I must go and prepare the load," he flashed his eyes to Rosalind walking off. Rosalind flashed her eyes to Peter heading down the corridor stepping into the misty fog and onto the beach. She climbed into the cab to avoid becoming wet the heavens had opened, which is good would increase the grass growth. Jacob asked, "how are Peter and Matthew?"

"They send their greetings Jacob. I have some excellent news for you in nine months, you will have a son; tests have been carried out, and God has approved."

Jacob kissed Rosalind very passionately, holding her close as the misty fog loaded the manure spreader. Jacob slowly drove up the cliff face track, reaching the top. Rosalind step from the cab heading for the house. Jacob continued driving along to the pastureland operating his manure spreader for the first time. The machine worked perfectly spreading a thin coating over the lush grass. He returned to where he'd stored the last trailer load of manure leaving his tractor and manure spreader there. He walked to the house to find Rosalind had cooked him a lovely breakfast. "Rosalind, I think we should spread the one load we tipped from the trailer the other day before we purchased the spreader; might as well go on the field it will help the grass grow; you want me to load or you?"

"I will load the manure," Rosalind insisted. Jacob laughed at her insistence. Rosalind left the house starting her Massey tractor with the loader driving to the manure pile. She loaded Jacob spreader returning to the shed. Jacob walked from the house kissing Rosalind on the cheek, carrying on and spreading the load of fertiliser on the field. Jacob returned, leaving his tractor and spreader by the barn, he checked on the Ram Rosalind had penned, had plenty of water and hay to eat. He returned to the house, collecting his crook and Jack; he set off across the Moor in search of his flock of sheep. Jacob, surprised to encounter at least 10 police officers walking across the Moor one approached him. "I presume these are your sheep," the officer asked with curiosity.

"That's right I'm carrying out my daily check, what brings you to the Moor," Jacob inquired suspiciously.

"Two officers went missing yesterday, they haven't been found. We still don't know what happened to the 10 archaeologists; where having a walk across the Moor see if we can find any evidence of anything happening. People always seem to vanish on the moor, especially stupid holidaymakers as if we haven't got enough work to do," the officer smiled walking on.

Peter called after him "if I find anything, I'll give the police a ring."

The officer answered back, "thanks, I wouldn't hold your breath."

Jacob continued walking, looking up in the air he could see a drone flying very quietly. He looked back towards the farm, witnessing another drone. He almost felt like there is a noose around his neck if the police ever tested the fertiliser he's spreading, they would realise it is human remains. According to Rosalind, he had nothing to worry about Gods protecting him, and from what happened yesterday, he has no reason to doubt her word. Jacob walked through his ewes satisfied they were all okay, he slowly headed for the farm finding Rosalind sitting on a bale feeding the Ram carrots. Jacob burst out laughing, kissing Rosalind on the cheek. "You realise drones are flying over the Moor Rosalind."

"Don't worry so, Jacob God has everything under control. If he ever decided to open the gates of hell on humans, they would be obliterated in seconds."

"I bumped into police officers on the Moor searching for those archaeologists and the two missing police officers. I have to confess it makes me nervous Rosalind."

"Jacob changing the subject. The house where Thomas lives, we are going to make improvements, specially designed for spirits to reside; before they travel on to heaven. You have no objections, do you?"

Jacob shrugged his shoulders, "If that's God's will; we have no use for the house. Only the farm buildings the 10 acres plus are grazing rights. I don't think there's any need to increase the flock were making hard work for ourselves."

"One last thing, Jacob; when your son is born, we will have a nanny to look after him. This means I will be free to help on the farm, and before you ask God is covering the cost," she chuckled, which made Jacob laugh at her screechy voice.

"I will not argue with you Rosalind; you have given me more than I expected out of life, and to think I am helping God cleanse the earth of evil."

"Jacob, the child, will have to be borne in heaven; God's wish, so he may bless the child before he comes home with his mother."

"There can be no better blessing for our son's arrival than to be in God's presence; we are truly blessed by the Lord, amen."

Rosalind patted Jacob's cheek-kissing him. "You may not see any difference in my shape, Jacob. God is preventing the world from knowing the event at the outset," she assured with confidence.

"Praise the Lord, he is blessing me this very day, and my wife and the forthcoming event of a son, amen."

"You would make a good disciple Jacob; you never question God's decisions, you are truly blessed." Rosalind walked round the back of the house looking at her vegetables growing, cutting a cabbage. Jacob joined her; he'd never seen vegetables grow so rapidly, almost as if they were on steroids. The rose bushes he planted at the front of the house were continuously in bloom. Rosalind would very often deadhead, and the next minute a new bud is bursting into flower; the fragrance is outstanding smelling of lemon.

Rosalind returned to the house, preparing a meal. Jacob jumped to his feet; Rosalind is shocked by his sudden movement. "Rosalind we have to purchase a cot and baby things you know," he chuckled. "I'll have to decorate the spare room. Where is the nanny going to sleep?" Jacob rushed into the kitchen, grabbing his tin, taking a wad of cash dashing out of the door before Rosalind could say a word. She heard the Range Rover start leaving the farm, she shook her head, smiling like a human in disbelief at Jacob's behaviour. She is trying to decipher his confused thought pattern; his mind is running wild with what he wanted to do for his son and his lovely wife.

He steadily drove across the Moor, not using the road, finally parking outside the shop. He grabbed the trolley with enthusiasm, selecting a tin of mauve paint it is on offer and brushes plus a roller. Jacob looked along the shelves, deciding, better wait before purchasing anything else in case Rosalind disapproved. At least now he could prepare the spare room which hadn't been used since he's a kid, he dreaded to think what it is like inside.

Rosalind had already entered the room cleaning thoroughly in minutes; the speed at which she worked while Jacob wasn't there is incredible. The old vacuum cleaner almost caught fire; never worked so hard before. Jacob came into the house, seeing the bedroom door open; he cautiously entered. Rosalind had mopped the flagstone floor there is nothing that needed cleaning. He heard Rosalind empty in the bucket in the kitchen sink. "Jacob take the old bed out it won't be needed; we will purchase a new bed for the nanny and a cot for the baby; the nanny will sleep in the same room as your son Noah."

Jacob came running into the kitchen, "Noah!"

"God's wish, you wish to argue with him, Jacob?"

"Praise the Lord what an honour for him to choose to name my son Noah." Jacob returned to the bedroom, dismantling the old bed taking outside to be disposed of when he had the next fire disposing of rubbish. He hastily returned to the bedroom, stirring his paint using the roller, he applied. Rosalind had made him sandwiches which he ate while working, he's too excited to stop. Rosalind received a telepathic message from Peter. "Matthew had emptied a jail in the USA of murderers, Jacob's manure spreader is required in the morning."

Rosalind switched the television on in time to catch the news, a prison guard interviewed outside the prison. "They vanished; I have no explanation. 2000 prisoners gone where?" The prison officer held his head in disbelief. "You heard it first on CBS News." Rosalind quickly turned the television off. "Jacob I'm going for a walk, I need some fresh air, shan't belong."

"Okay, just be careful Rosalind you don't trip in your condition," Jacob cautioned. Rosalind walked from the house along the side of the barn and round the back summoning the misty fog. Instantly transported aboard the spaceship. Matthew and Peter awaiting her arrival, flashing their eyes at each other in a greeting posture. "Matthew, I think you are making it pretty obvious there's an alien force on earth. Plane crashes in the sea, and the occasional cruise liner is fine. You have emptied three prisons this year the next thing you find; we have police everywhere and soldiers. The human race is not completely stupid. They may possess things we have not discovered and could actually be tracking us right now," Rosalind suggested.

Peter looked at one of the scanners. "Rosalind there is landing craft heading for the beach, what does this mean?"

"Ready weapon systems," she advised calmly. "This may be a military exercise, trying to keep the soldiers fit and healthy and alert. Take no action and watch what's happening. I must return to Jacob. Don't discharge our weapons unless you consult me first," Rosalind ordered. However, she is not in charge but is concerned this could ruin everything for everyone. She ran down the corridor stepping into the misty fog, changing her appearance returning to Jacob in the house. He smiled, hearing the front door open, and Rosalind step inside. "Jacob, soldiers, are coming on landing craft towards our shoreline, does this happen very often?"

"No, I think it's all to do with the missing people, I shouldn't think it's anything to worry about. Only the government trying to make out there doing something for the press to report."

Jacob placed his paintbrush in the paint tray, kissing Rosalind on the cheek. "Stay here I won't be long," he smiled. Jacob left the house Rosalind is reading his mind, he's going to confront the officers advising not to frighten his sheep. Rosalind thought that would be a futile exercise. The Armed Forces are not likely to take any notice of him. Jacob met the senior officer coming up the track from the shoreline. "You are about to enter my property what is your business," Jacob asked, seriously; watching the accompanying reporter grab his recorder from his pocket.

"We are on exercises were also searching for missing persons haven't you heard the news?"

"You're about a week late," Jacob advised. "Police officers walking the Moor yesterday. I walk the Moor every day of the week if I'd found any evidence or anything suspicious, I would have reported it to the appropriate authorities. If you and your toy soldiers upset my ewes, the army will be receiving a bill."

The reporter recording everything, trying not to grin. The captain looked very frustrated, trying to bite his tongue and not say a wrong word. "We will be cautious, you must remember Sir 10 archaeologists have gone missing and four police officers recently all in this area."

Jacob laughed: "None of them could probably find their way out of a paper bag. The Moor is notorious for strangers getting lost. I hope you haven't ruled out they've probably been taken by an alien ship which landed the other week." The reporter is laughing. The captain turning a beetroot colour by the second, walking past Jacob, Jacob remarked, "if you get lost, stay in one place, it will make it easier for us to find your bones and don't disturb my sheep."

The reporter took a photograph of Jacob still laughing as he followed the captain across the Moor, holding his compass. Jacob looked from the clifftop seeing the landing craft returning to their ship. Rosalind had turned herself invisible listening to everything Jacob had said. She had never known him to be so assertive and determined to protect what is his. A religious man or not he would stand his ground on certain issues she concluded.

Rosalind sent a telepathic message to Peter. "All is well."

Rosalind quickly returned to the house ahead of Jacob, making a coffee by the time he'd returned. Jack had stayed in the house by the fire. Rosalind passed the mug of coffee to Jacob sitting on the settee turning on the television. Jacob hadn't realised a drone is flying above when talking to the captain. He's even more surprised understanding his conversation is recorded by the drone and transmitted directly to a television station. They sat there watching the reporter laughing at Jacob having a go at the captain. The presenter commented: "I wouldn't like to cross that farmer, he is quite prepared to take on the British commandos."

Rosalind patted his leg, "well done, Jacob, you stand your ground for what you believe is right. I finish the painting while you were gone," she smiled.

Jacob moved to look in the spare bedroom, bewildered how she could have done so much painting in the short time he's away. Not realising Rosalind's abilities as an alien far surpassed any human could achieve. Jacob kissed Rosalind on the cheek. "You are such a wonderful woman to have in my life. I must go with Jack and check my ewes," he sighed heavily. Jacob grabbed his crook and coat stepping out of the door, followed by Jack. He followed the route the soldiers had taken realising they were heading for the bog, Jacob caught up with them. "Captain, stay out of there," Jacob warned, "you will lose your soldiers, I'm warning you; I know this land better than you."

The reporter, recording everything; the captain determined to show his authority off. "You go men search thoroughly." They'd taken barely 5 paces, four of the men were up to their waist in water, sinking slowly. Jacob stretched out his crook, one soldier grabbed, and the other soldiers attached themselves to Jacob to secure him. He eased each soldier out of the foul-smelling bog. The drone is above filming, sending the information directly to a news station. The Captain stood there open-mouthed, embarrassed beyond belief; not expecting the bog to suddenly swallow his men. The men that were trapped were okay apart from being wet. The captain said nothing, not even thank you, walking towards the road where the archaeology dig is some 2 miles ahead. The reporter patted Jacob on the shoulder. "These young officers never learn," he commented. "I would hate to be in his shoes when his commanding officers finished with him."

Rosalind is sat on the settee watching television, a blow by blow account of what took place on the Moor, transmitted directly to the 24-hour a day news station. She had never considered Jacob anything other than kind, would never think him a brave man prepared to risk his own life to save another. She pondered for a moment realising it is written in the Bible. If only the rest of the human race is so diligent as Jacob in their behaviour.

Peter and Matthew had watched events unfold, and the way Jacob had behaved. Matthew is very tempted to snatch the captain and turn him into fertiliser along with the soldiers, deciding not to it would only cause more problems for Rosalind and Jacob.

Jacob slowly walked along the well-worn sheep track heading for the farm, he noticed the postman parked at the end of the drive and drive off. Jacob change direction heading for his post box walking past his 30 acres of pasture land which appeared to be a beautiful deep green colour and proliferating. The weather had assisted lots of rain, and of course, God's fertiliser certainly boosted the growth. Jacob finally reached his post box retrieving a large brown folded envelope with the return address of, "Scrimshaw and Scrimshaw," solicitors across the top. Jacob hoped something to do with the new farm Rosalind had purchased, he tucked the envelope inside his coat to prevent the rain damaging. Jack didn't appreciate the rain, although it went with the territory of a sheepdogs life. Jacob finally entered the house, he passed the envelope to Rosalind. She immediately opened; deeds of ownership of Brook Farm. "The farm is ours Jacob there's a letter inside. Thomas Simmons has left the property. The keys are with the solicitor ready for you to collect from their Exeter office."

Jacob looked at his wristwatch 11:30, "not today Rosalind will go in the morning, Wednesday should be acquired day in town. A thought you could buy some baby things a cot, we might as well get prepared rather than leave everything to the last minute," Jacob grinned.

Rosalind smiled, "as you wish Jacob don't forget early next week the generators arriving; it won't need to go inside the shed, comes with its own casing to stand outside. We only need a coupling to connect the power to the house and of course, the fuel line from the diesel tank. As a just in case situation, I think we leave the old generator set up and connected.

Make a new fuel line to the new generator that way if one fails; we will have the other as a backup, we don't want problems in the winter if we have a young child here."

"I would suggest fitting solar panels the problem is I have a thatched roof, I suppose we could fit them to the barn roof?"

"The generator; the authorities can't see, solar panels on the roof they can Jacob. We don't want them asking where the money is coming from do we," Rosalind insisted.

"No, shall we have a snoop around the new farm," Jacob chuckled.

"Yes, might as well a miserable day, now the weather is closing in. Will not harm to check around the buildings," Rosalind remarked, slipping on her coat and Jacob doing likewise. Jack already sitting at the door to make sure he wasn't forgotten. Rosalind patted him, "come along Jack new farm for you to run around on."

Jacob didn't bother to ask who is driving; he climbed into the passenger side with Jack by his feet. Rosalind drove steadily down the drive and along the road, and eventually down the Brook farm drive to Brook farm, their new acquisition.

Jacob stepped from the Range Rover standing in the small porch, he slid his hand along the top beam, grinning. "That's where everyone keeps their spare key for an emergency." Rosalind smiled, watching Jacob unlock the door. Thomas had left virtually everything even blocks by the fire ready to be lit. There wasn't much difference in size or layout other than the fact this house had slates instead of a thatched roof plus it had a loft conversion when there a fire some years ago. They ventured around the back of the house, finding the old generator shed. Jacob laughed the same set up as he had initially and a converted 50-gallon barrel, to use as a diesel tank. The cost of laying electric cable to this house or his own is horrendous that's why they both use generators. Jacob stood on the small bridge spanning the brook, carving its way across the Moor, little more than a ditch in places.

Nevertheless, the water never stopped flowing and always pure. Jacob noticed a hand pump in the house suspecting that's where the water for the sink came from. Jacob wandered into the barn seeing an old international conventional baler and bale sledge, and acrobat turner, and an old waffler tedder; he already had the tractor at home.

The wooden tipping trailer had seen better days along with the old four-wheeled hey trailer. Jacob noticed the mower an old finger knife international; they were the best mower of their day would take a lot of stick before breaking. Jacob saw Thomas had left him half a rick of hay which made him smile. Jacob burst out laughing, coming across the old trailed muck spreader made by Massey Harris and still look serviceable, all the chains were oiled and everything greased. Jacob realised if it wasn't for his good fortune to have Rosalind and God on his side. He would have nothing to laugh about and wouldn't be much better off than Thomas, and certainly wouldn't be able to purchase Thomas's farm. Jacob asked, "Rosalind what plans does God have for the farmhouse?"

"Don't worry about anything, Jacob; the house will be looked after kept clean and tidy. No one would dare come onto the property without your permission or God's otherwise they'll end up on the 10-acre pasture land; we haven't inspected. Come along." Rosalind held Jacob's hand, which made him smile they walked along for some distance coming to a flat piece of ground, needed rolling Jacob decided after walking across. The grass quite lush thanks to being fenced-off like his own to prevent the sheep invading. Jacob shut the gate tying with a piece of string as an extra precaution in case walkers left it open, although they shouldn't be in there at all, not part of the footpath. They slowly returned to the Range Rover. Jack running around sniffing everything new territory, and now his. He christened every post he could find. Jacob thought Jack must have a bladder the size of a diesel tank. Jacob checked he'd locked the door in the house quietly smiling to himself, excited by their new purchase. Jacob sat in the Range Rover with Jack between his feet. Rosalind headed for home across the Moor commenting. "Jacob if you drive steady with your tractor and manure spreader, I think safer for you to travel to Brook farm across the Moor. You can see there used to be an old track here many years ago. What I don't want to happen, you confronted by police when you transport the manure spreader down the road, especially when the holidaymakers are here. They haven't a clue how to drive a vehicle correctly in the countryside," Rosalind smiled.

CHAPTER 7

An Unexpected Event

Jacob spent the rest of the day checking their equipment preparing for the final cut of hay, although the way the weather
is performing, he may get a final cut of silage before the frosts
come, not only from his 30 acres but from Brook farms 10
acres as well. Rosalind comes from the house carrying a hot
mug of coffee. Jacob sat on a bale, wiping his hands on an old
rag; they were plastered in oil and grease. He is determined to
look after the equipment, oil and grease were far cheaper than
new parts his dad always preached. "Jacob tomorrow morning
there's two loads of fertiliser need collecting, I think you will
have to stockpile until we removed the hay from here and
Brook farm don't you?"

Jacob nodded: "Yes, that's the only solution at the moment;
as soon as we've cleared the fields, I will apply the fertiliser.
We may achieve a final cut of silage before winter sets in; at
least the ewes this year will have ample hay and silage which
should produce a better lamb with any luck."

Rosalind received a telepathic message from Peter. "The
female carrying Jacob son had miscarried, and Matthew processed her for fertiliser." Rosalind immediately studied her

memory banks of how human females behaved when they miscarried. "Jacob, I have to go to heaven, I'm unwell something is wrong inside, I feel it."

Jacob jumped to his feet in a panic. "What can I do Rosalind tell me." Jacob noticed the misty fog arrive, and Rosalind stepped in; she vanished in seconds. Jacob sat on the bale, crying. Rosalind aboard the spaceship with Peter and Matthew watched the state of Jacob alarmed. Rosalind commented, "I haven't any choice if the female has aborted and she is now fertiliser. I couldn't let the pregnancy continue in Jacob's thoughts, he would have expected an infant in nine months."

Peter suggested, "we could select another female and artificially inseminate her Rosalind?"

"I don't know what the answer is Peter at the moment, let Jacob recover from this crisis first then we will take whatever steps are necessary to achieve what we want."

The three aboard the spaceship watched Jacob broken-hearted, sit by the fire in the house drinking his home-brew. Rosalind understood he's trying to numb the pain that humans suffer from. She suspected he would be unconscious shortly from the amount of home-brew he is drinking. Rosalind had not anticipated Jacob been so disturbed by the event; after all, a natural occurrence in many human females.

Much to Peters, Matthew and Rosalind surprise a screen appeared on the wall. The firstborn and some of his brothers and sisters betrayed. "Unfortunate Rosalind; we have watched with interest you and Jacob perform your various duties, far more entertaining than the rest of the human race put together. However, they do make excellent animal food for our pets."

Rosalind smiled, "as you can see, firstborn Jacob is extremely distraught. I haven't any other choice for obvious reasons other than to play the part after receiving information from Peter; the woman had failed to produce a son."

"Rosalind, the central computer has carried out calculations and a risk assessment. Listen to what he has to say and make your decision. You will be experiencing new events for as Zibyan."

"Rosalind, I have carried out multiple calculations and scenarios. I have always considered impossible for a Zibyan female to conceive or carry a replica of themselves. However, we now have an opportunity to experiment further because of your familiarity with Jacob. Link yourself to me, I will make some minor adjustments, and we will see what transpires if you wish to test the theory."

"Will, any of my abilities be affected computer?"

"You will still be able to shapeshift and be invisible in an emergency; however, I can't calculate what I don't know and for how long."

"Will Jacobs contaminants affect me long term, after all, I will be carrying an alien in my body structure?"

"Again, Rosalind, I have no answers we have not permitted experimentation of any kind on a Zibyan it is against our creator's law. However, since we are trying to create the original creators of the Zibyans. The firstborn and other brothers and sisters have agreed I suspend the law temporarily."

The firstborn spoke: "Rosalind since we have no need to produce replicas because we don't die. I'm permitting along with my brothers and sisters for you to experiment on this one-time occasion only. The central computer will monitor you constantly, store the findings in the event you are successful. The Zibyans can use again if an emergency scenario ever occurred. You will be in the memory banks of every Zibyan created and your sacrifice."

Aliens

Rosalind walked to the wall standing with her back against the central computer, linked to her for several minutes. Peter and Matthew watched. The firstborn and his brothers and sisters had vanished, they achieved what they wanted with the consent of Rosalind to participate.

Rosalind stepped away from the wall flashing her eyes at Peter and Matthew walking down the corridor. She stepped into the misty fog appearing outside the front door of the house. She entered seeing Jacob unconscious, he'd consumed so much home-brew. She carried him into the bedroom, removing his clothes, placing in bed and stepped outside; attaching the trailer to the Ford tractor descending to the shoreline. Matthew had already received her telepathic thoughts preparing to transport the fertiliser to the trailer. Rosalind transported two loads to the manure pile. She parked the trailer detaching the tractor and attached the mower. Rosalind determined to make sure they didn't lose any chance of a good crop while Jacob comes to terms with what he thought had happened. Rosalind drove to the field cutting the 30 acres driving on to Brook farm cutting the 10 acres there. Almost midnight when she'd finished not as that mattered to Rosalind she could see in the dark with or without lights. Rosalind, drove steadily back to the farm watching the ewe's eyes light up like beads of orange light. She attached the tedder filling the Ford tractor with diesel. Jacob had already greased all the equipment, so she went back into the house. She could hear Jacob in the toilet violently sick, he'd already made himself a coffee he'd left on the kitchen table.

Rosalind made herself a drink not as if she really needed one, although she had to keep the pretence she is Rosalind, his wife. Jacob staggered from the toilet, noticing Rosalind. She placed her finger to her lips. "We can try again Jacob, not the end of the world; although it might be if you continue to behave in this manner," she cautioned. "How do you think I feel and all you can do is drown your sorrows."

Jacob flopped in the chair holding his head which is screaming; he sipped his coffee looking to Rosalind with his bloodshot eyes. "I heard the tractor what's going on," he asked quietly.

"I've transported the fertiliser to the manure heap. I attach the mower cut the 30 acres and the 10 on Brook Farm. I've attached the tedder ready to spread the grass tomorrow weather permitting. What have you done? Lay in bed feeling sorry for yourself, Jacob. It's no different for me as it is for an animal to miscarry. I would have thought you were used to the situation, long before now," she scolded.

"I'm sorry, the last thing I expected to happen, I thought God is in control of everything?"

"Jacob!" She emphasised. "We are insignificant in the scheme of things in God's eyes. He promised you a son and a son you will have whether it's tomorrow or in 20 years, it will happen; now pull yourself together we have a farm to run. God has repaired me so I can try again when you've had a bath, and the hay gathered." Rosalind lifted her eyebrows after searching her memory banks of female facial responses indicating encouragement.

Jacob finally laughed realising God is in charge. Rosalind commented, "the child was only a seed, Jacob, barely a month." He kissed Rosalind on the cheek nearly 5 o'clock in the morning, Rosalind made breakfast. Jacob sat watching television drinking a cup of coffee still with a headache resembling someone hitting him with a sledgehammer.

After breakfast, Jacob went to check his ewes with Jack close at his heels. Jacob had taken a small bag of sheep nuts with him hoping to encourage the ewes to venture onto Brook farm. Jacob decided they would have followed him into the gates of hell in pursuit of sheep nuts. He stopped short of the farm placing neat piles spread out over quite an area leaving the ewes to clean up. He continued walking on to the pastureland on Brook farm; although only cut a few hours ago, the warm morning air is starting to wilt the grass. Jacob burst out laughing, hearing the Ford tractor coming. He opened the gate suspecting Rosalind had come to spread the grass trying to make it dry quickly ready for baling. He wasn't wrong, she drove through the gateway and started spreading. Jacob left her to it slowly walking back to the farm attaching the old sit up and beg to the new hay trailer Rosalind had purchased. The tractor would be ideal for this operation to save time changing equipment. Jacob hoped if the weather would stay pleasant for the next 2 to 3 days they can bale the hay and stack in the barn on either farm.

***

Peter and Matthew from the spaceship had transported to Brook farmhouse, not needing a key to enter; unlocking the door with the power of their mind. Peter commented: "Ideal for visiting Zibyans; 4 would be the maximum in here I think. They could travel invisibly so there shouldn't be any issues, will provide the recently created Zibyans with the opportunity of seeing the real earth, with a human infestation, they will learn from our mistakes first hand."

"I have to agree with you, Peter 4 would be the maximum; we have two ships a month visiting earth. Each party would have a two-week stay to sample what's actually happening here rather than seeing it by transmission."

Rosalind sensed they were in the house she stopped the tractor, knowing Jacob had gone home. She entered the house they greeted each other with the flash of their eyes. "We have decided Rosalind we will permit 4 to visit at a time. We will be here probably for hundreds of years, so there is ample time for everyone to visit. If the firstborn continues to expand and colonise other planets, we will definitely need humans to feed the animals."

"I like the number four around figure 2 male and two female. We must keep the balance equal, although we can change our sexes when we are first created by the central computer, our real designation is decided then." Rosalind flashed her eyes, leaving Peter and Matthew returning to the tractor. She headed for the 30 acres to spread the grass to dry, ready for baling.

Peter and Matthew return to the spaceship to report to the firstborn and other members of the collective.

***

Jacob fenced off a lush piece of grass at the side of the barn for the Ram to have fresh grazing until his allotted time to service the ewes. Jacob wondered whether he should purchase another Ram is he asking too much of this one? Jacob looked across the Moor suspecting Rosalind wouldn't be finished until lunchtime. He returned to the house, preparing lunch for her after all; she is working as hard as him. Jacob heard the new generator start when he plugged the kettle in; the machine is far more efficient than his old one burning far less diesel, he didn't have to switch it off at night it automatically shut itself down when no power is required for the house.

Rosalind came in at 12:30 noticing the lavish lunch Jacob had prepared for her, although she didn't need to eat it would have been rude of her not to pretend to enjoy the food. They sat enjoying their lunch together Rosalind commented, "I expect you to have a bath this evening," trying not to grin she knew Jacob would get the message; she could sense his hormones were on fire much like the old Ram outside.

"I shan't forget," Jacob smiled.

She is not impressed with the mating process; however, she had decided to attempt to carry a male child in her form wondering what the experience would be like, never attempted by a Zibyan she would be the first, and last according to the firstborn. Rosalind finished her lunch venturing outside to her garden, smelling the roses planted by the front door. The vegetables were coming on in leaps and bounds; she had plenty of carrots, cabbage and cauliflower, would have to be cut soon. Rosalind ventured along the top of the cliff taking the footpath, the afternoon air is warm with a gentle breeze, for once, she didn't need a coat. Rosalind paused, looking across the water to where she knew her spaceship rested in a deep crater, created by a volcano thousands of years ago. Rosalind decided now is the time she wasn't going to wait until the evening, she wanted it over with quickly. She entered the house; Jacob is in the bath. "Jacob in the bedroom now," she ordered walking off into the bedroom changing her appearance, she's naked lay on top of the bed waiting for him. Jacob came into the bedroom with a towel around his waist, his eyes almost fell out of his head. Rosalind laying on top of the bed naked. Jacob didn't need any instructions he made love to her instantly. Rosalind lay there accepting what he is engaged in, apart from the pleasant electric shock feeling passing through her form; that is the only enjoyable part. Finally, he relented, rolling over on his back.

Rosalind exhaled, quickly dressing while Jacob wasn't looking. She left the bedroom going outside for some fresh air, not enjoying smelling a sweaty human body. Rosalind would know in a few hours if Jacob seed attached to her construction, a matter of a few months, she could repel the infant satisfying Jacobs needs and of course the Zibyans. They would have a human-controlled by Zibyans to run the farm.

Rosalind wouldn't be surprised if the firstborn decided may be beneficial for Jacob to meet with an accident. She had to admit her assessment of the situation did not impress her in the slightest. Rosalind could see in an hour the sun would be set and the evening air is becoming decidedly cooler. She checked the grass spread earlier in the day, definitely need moving again tomorrow; a laborious job but necessary to make good hay for the sheep. Rosalind returned to the house finding Jacob had made tea placing on the table. She looked at his expression she'd seen before reading Jacob thoughts; there is nothing but love and admiration for her. They finished tea sitting to watch television Rosalind touched Jacob's forehead he's instantly unconscious. She changed her appearance stepping outside into the misty fog transported to the spaceship.

Peter and Matthew were waiting for her. They greeted one another with the flashing of their eyes. Everyone turned to look at the news displayed on the wall. "Offshore drilling around the coast is to start early next year in an attempt to find more oil." The presenter presented a map of where the expiration holes were to be drilled very close to the spaceship. Rosalind commented: "That's not going to happen. Otherwise, we will have to relocate our spaceship."

Matthew suggested, "I suppose we could show them where the oil is, that way they would stay away from where we are. I could make a little oil leak from the earth's crust, they would naturally investigate. The central computer estimates 5 trillion barrels, that should keep them occupied for a while."

"Let's wait and see Matthew, I don't want to release any more pollutants on the earth unless absolutely necessary. You never know perhaps the activists may convince governments to use electric vehicles; admittedly, there will still be diesel used on farms unavoidable at the moment."

"What about the aeroplanes they are totally inefficient, they pollute more than any other mode of transport. They have the solution but won't implement; strange humans, all about money, not the environment or the future" Rosalind expressed.

"How many times have we had this conversation over the centuries? If they weren't amusement for the Zibyan collective, we would have destroyed them thousands of years ago," Peter remarked, waving his hand the screen vanished from the wall. "Your condition Rosalind link yourself to the central computer for him to monitor."

Rosalind placed her back against the wall; the central computer attached to Rosalind's brain. The central computer responded: "Jacobs seed has moved to the artificial womb; you are growing two seeds, one female one male. I have transmitted the information to the firstborn and your brothers and sisters." The computer released Rosalind, she stepped away from the wall surprised by the information; suspecting nothing would grow inside her, considering she is pure energy.

The central computer advised: "Rosalind you must consume three earth meals a day, the proteins will be transferred to the seed. Otherwise, the infants have no way of surviving;

you are pure energy they are not at the moment. However, we are venturing beyond any experiments carried out, and quite possibly the infants may draw power from your life force. You have nothing to be alarmed about Rosalind, I can replenish any energy they use of yours."

"Thank you computer most unexpected developments," Rosalind confessed, not relishing the thought of some alien draining her life force to sustain their own.

The central computer insisted: "Rosalind, do not confess your condition until one earth calendar month has passed; otherwise, he will be extremely suspicious."

"Understood computer; have you transmitted to my memory cells what I must and must not do to safeguard the infants?"

"Yes, you must allow at least one Earth hour to pass before safety protocols will permit the information to your memory cells, a safeguard implemented by our creators to protect us all from unauthorised invaders."

"Excellent." Rosalind flashed her eyes to Peter and Matthew, noticing Jacob on the beach with the Land Rover, and fishing rods waiting for her to return. 7 o'clock in the morning and the tide is coming in. Rosalind changed her appearance stepping into the misty fog and out onto the beach. Jacob had already cast out passing Rosalind her rod, "A lovely morning Rosalind I thought we could do a little fishing before we fluff the grass again to help it dry."

Rosalind grinned, "you'll only be angry if I catch something bigger than you, Jacob."

Jacob smiled watching Rosalind cast her line, he thought her reel would catch fire the speed the line is leaving the spool. Rosalind started winding in her rod, almost bent double, she is laughing at the top of her voice she knew she had something big on the hook. Jacob stood there, holding his rod frustrated and burst out laughing. He removed his penknife, preparing to dispatch whatever she is winding in. Finally, the fish revealed a large cod. Jacob dispatched gutting and taking to the back of the Land Rover. They packed away their fishing gear, returning to the farm with Rosalind grinning enjoying teasing Jacob with human facial expressions. He carried the fish in the house, placing on the kitchen table kissing Rosalind on the cheek. "I'll go and fluff the grass if it dries well today we may be lucky and bale tomorrow who knows."

Jacob climbed aboard his Ford tractor heading for the 10 acres first on Brook farm, the crop is slightly thinner there and would dry quicker. Once he'd finished, he moved onto his 30 acres the grass is marginally lusher there and would probably take an extra day to dry out. Jacob loved the smell of grass turning into hay, he watched the sparrows and starlings following him up and down the field, catching any morsel the tedder disturbed. The sun is quite warm, Jacob felt through the cab glass. By 4:30 in the afternoon Jacob had finished, hoping by tomorrow morning they could prepare to round bale the hay and transport to the barn to keep it dry before the weather changed. He filled his tractor with diesel ready for the pending job the next day preparing the grass in rows for the round baler to perform its task. He's pretty confident they could proceed, he started the old sit up and beg driving to Brook farm leaving the trailer and tractor by the field. He walked back to the farm, noticing Rosalind fitting a roll of net wrap in the round baler. "Great minds think alike Jacob," she smiled, "bale the 10 acres at Brook farm first and by the end of the day tomorrow, we may be able to start the 30 acres here will have to wait and see."

They both retired to the house, shutting the door on the day's events. Rosalind had made a salad from vegetables in her garden and boiled some potatoes slicing melting cheese and butter in between. Jacob enjoyed his meal immensely.

Rosalind is less impressed although she had to obey the computer's instructions; otherwise, the seed she is carrying would die. The thought of having to contain food products in her structure did not impress Rosalind in the slightest. She couldn't expel for five hours according to the computer; otherwise, the nutrients would not be extracted efficiently.

Jacob cleared his plate, cutting another slice of crusty bread lavishing with butter and a large slice of cheese. He sat there, smiling away, enjoying his food. After watching the television with a mug of coffee until 10 o'clock, they retired to bed.

Rosalind touched Jacob unconscious until morning. Rosalind changed her appearance stepping outside the house into the misty fog and aboard the spaceship expecting to find Matthew and Peter were waiting for her. She hadn't sensed anything wrong and is beginning to wonder what is going on. She glided around the spaceship until she came to the processing unit for humans to be transferred into joints of meat for their pets on other planets. "Rosalind," Peter expressed, "some of the humans have trackers fitted which means the humans can track us."

"Computer, expel the humans fitted with trackers, to an island at least a thousand miles away from here," Rosalind ordered without hesitation. "Peter why did you delay in taking action, you may have given away our location! Computer." Rosalind requested, "monitor any approaching vessel or aircraft. Prepare the spaceship for immediate departure in the eventuality we are discovered; or if you consider they are far enough away from our location, create a malfunction aboard there craft and destroy. Bring the bodies here, providing they are not fitted with trackers." Peter and Matthew stood there; Rosalind's individuality had taken control.

The firstborn appeared on the wall, "Rosalind you are a strength amongst the Zibyans; the collective thought processor is defective. Central computer, revise your programming to become more efficient," the firstborn vanished.

"I have to return to the farm Peter, I have a busy day ahead of me."

Matthew questioned: "Rosalind surely your priority should be the well-being of your brothers and not a human?"

Rosalind turned to face him, "I think you need both to link to the central computer, your thought patterns are defective. Fortunate I came aboard when I did otherwise the humans would have detected our spaceship." Rosalind turned walking off along the corridor changing her appearance stepping into the misty fog, stepping out by the barn to find Jacob rechecking the equipment to make sure there were no defects; the last thing they needed today is a breakdown.

Rosalind held out her hand, "breakfast Jacob," she remarked, looking in the sky, "nice day today, Jacob, let's hope everything goes to plan," she smiled. Jacob held her hand they returned to the house Rosalind quickly made bacon and eggs with fried bread for them both, she had no choice now she had to eat. Jacob quickly finished his wiping his mouth, he kissed Rosalind on the cheek, "I must check the sheep, take a mineral block out this morning the ewes have to stay in tiptop condition it will soon be time for breeding." Rosalind nodded, watching him walk out the door, followed by Jack. Jacob collected a mineral block from the shed and walked across the Moor, finding his sheep had worked out he now owned Brook farm and were enjoying the fresh grass. He put the mineral block on a flat stone cut away some of the plastic covering. The ewes surrounded him eager to sample what he'd placed on the rock. Jacob quickly cast his eyes over the flock returning home, looked at his wristwatch, not quite 10 o'clock.

Jacob climbed aboard his Ford tractor and drove to the pastureland at Brook Farm. He set his machine to make rows of hay ready for Rosalind to join him. 11 o'clock she arrived and started round baling the hay. The crop is quite sparse; it wasn't long before she completed the task; there weren't that many bales in there. Rosalind detached the round baler from her tractor, Jacob started up is sit up and beg Fordson attached to the new hay trailer. Rosalind quickly loaded the hay-trailer and Jacob drove to Brook Farm. Rosalind stacked the bales inside the spacious barn although slightly dilapidated it would keep the hay dry. They made three more trips to the field and finally cleared. Jacob drove off with his Ford tractor to prepare the 30 acres for Rosalind to round bale. 9 o'clock in the evening they'd finished deciding to leave the hay bales out overnight.

Jacob had barely finished his coffee before his eyes were shut. Rosalind touched his forehead, making sure he wouldn't wake. She went outside sensing there is rain in the air, she set about clearing the 30-acre field making sure their hard work is not ruined. She finally stacked the last round bales in the barn by 5 o'clock in the morning. Jacob, come staggering out, hearing the sound of the tractor. He staggered back, shocked to see the hay is inside. He watched the sky light up with flashes of thunder and rain pouring from the heavens. "Make the coffee Jacob I'm nearly finished," Rosalind suggested. He nodded, running off towards the house to avoid getting soaked. Jack stayed with Rosalind; she immediately discharged what she'd eaten over five hours ago, and Jack quickly cleared up the mess. Rosalind patted Jack, he's a means to an end. Rosalind went inside followed by Jack. "You watched television Rosalind, I'll prepare breakfast you must have worked all night. Silly bloody woman you should have woke me; out there on your own you could have had an accident then where would I be?"

"I had God's help, why should I need you," Rosalind commented.

Jacob exhaled, "sorry, I worry about you."

"I know Jacob, my priority is the hay wasn't ruined. I went outside after waking for fresh air, I could smell rain approaching, I quickly cleared the field."

"I suppose the best thing to do today if you feel up to it Rosalind, spread the manure we have on the 30 acres. I think there are about five loads stockpiled, what do you think?"

"Yes, I'll fit the bucket to my Massey tractor and loader, you attach the manure spreader to your Ford." They both went outside Rosalind using the quick release mechanism on her loader, change from bale grab, to bucket reconnecting the hydraulic hoses. Jacob attached the manure spreader to his Ford tractor; raining heavily and Jacob dry inside the cab which always made him smile, after years of getting soaked on old cab-less tractors. They both drove to the manure pile; Rosalind quickly loaded him, and Jacob spread the manure across the recently cleared 30 acres; in the end, he spread six loads very thinly. They both returned to the farm parking the machinery, dashing inside out of the rain. Jacob commented: "I hope God has more fertiliser soon I have another 10 acres requires coating with fertiliser," he chuckled.

Rosalind made the coffee surprised, like Jacob to see Peter materialise in the house. Peter had the common sense to change his appearance into St Peter from the Bible, so Jacob wouldn't realise who he is. Jacob immediately bowed. Peter spoke: "Jacob God has heard your words, you descend to the beach with your manure spreader, there you will receive two loads go now, he awaits your arrival." Jacob didn't question he ran out of the door; both Rosalind and Peter heard Jacobs tractor start. "There must be a good reason for you to materialise here, Peter," Rosalind asked curiously.

CHAPTER 8

Uncertain Times

"Yes, the central computer suspects the humans aboard an aircraft carrier have worked out how to listen in on our communications. That is why I've appeared in person, we don't know whether that includes telepathy or not?"

"Oh, I suggest either you or Matthew turn yourselves into a Seagull. Fly to the aircraft carrier and turn yourself invisible, find your way through to the communications room and listen to what is said. You may be concerned over nothing; however, we need to know and urgently Peter, I can't go in my condition."

"No, Matthew and I both appreciate the sacrifice you are making for the collective; I will go."

"Whether there is evidence or not Peter, sink the aircraft carrier and accompanying cruisers, there might even be a submarine. This will create suspicion another superpower is involved and should take their attention away from us. I think the central computer will have to come up with new ways of communicating if what you find is any threat to us."

Peter nodded vanishing to the spaceship in preparation to implement what Rosalind had suggested. Jacob had turned the tractor radio on singing away, transporting the second load of fertiliser to the 10-acre field on Brook Farm. Rosalind could hear the tune in his mind, which made her chuckle, another human expression she had adapted, although she had more pressing problems at the moment to deal with.

The transport ship is on the way from Zagader with supplies and 4 Zibyans to stay on Brook Farm. The ship would return home with more human flesh to be distributed to the animals on various planets. Rosalind sat watching television a news helicopter is filming the aircraft carrier and support crafts. The aircraft carrier burst into flames along with two other support vessels. The cameraman aboard the helicopter recorded mines floating in the sea. Rosalind smiled, Peter had excelled, old-world war two minds had sunk two support craft and an aircraft carrier. Rosalind switched off the television and suspected Matthew would be extremely busy aboard the spaceship, processing flesh. Jacob would be acquired tomorrow to fetch another load of fertiliser. Peter appeared in front of Rosalind, changing his appearance into St Peter in case Jacob came in. "Rosalind, they were tracking strange sound waves they had no idea where they originated or heading in the direction of our spaceship."

"Good, we must be more vigilant Peter the human's technology is moving forward in leaps and bounds. Perhaps it's time for us to leave Earth and operate from space. The humans still couldn't detect us because of are cloaking ability, and there's no reason why we couldn't harvest human beings from there."

"Should I contact the firstborn and discuss your suggestions with him, Rosalind?"

"Talk to the central computer first, he can assess the danger far more accurately than we can." Rosalind flashed her eyes to Peter, and Peter responded, disappearing.

Jacob came into the house whistling, he hadn't tried to whistle for years. Rosalind found the whole situation very amusing, she is taken entirely by surprise when Jacob started dancing with her. "You're in a good mood, Jacob."

"Why not! I have a beautiful wife I don't get wet any more when I drive the tractor, I have double the acreage, and hopefully, soon I will have a son?"

Rosalind smiled, patting his cheek, "I may have twins who can say what is planned, Jacob."

"Praise the Lord, I would be truly blessed to receive one child; two would be beyond expectations."

"Oh yes Jacob, there's more manure tomorrow for you, maybe one load or two I'm not sure at the moment," Rosalind smiled.

"Great! I must check the sheep, I shan't belong," he smiled kissing Rosalind on the cheek seeing Jack sat at the door waiting for him. Jacob grabbed his crook and coat, briskly leaving the house his mind full of expectations. He thought his life was over before Rosalind returned, and for him to be blessed by God to have so many gifts. Machinery, more land is unbelievable; Jacob had never considered himself unique in any way. He struggled to come to terms why God had chosen him; when they were far more worthy people on earth, he's sure.

Jacob found his sheep close to Brook farm, taking a drink from the Brook. The four Zibyans staying on Brook farm had turned themselves invisible to ensure their safety while they explored. Jacob thought he could hear whispers which sent a chill down his spine; almost panicking at one stage, not realising the Zibyans were following him intrigued. Rosalind is reading Jacobs thoughts. Suddenly realising her brothers and sisters from Zagader had arrived at Brook Farm. Rosalind climbed into the Range Rover driving across the Moor to Jacob, sat on a rock listening intently to the whispers, trying to decipher what is said, suspected, he had succumbed to the wind enchanting his mind, making him believe ghosts existed.

Rosalind stepped from the Range Rover. "Brothers and sisters do not torment my husband before you ascend, or God will be displeased," Rosalind warned. She knew the Zibyans would transform; she hoped into something sensible after all the newly created brothers and sisters were barely 8 days old.

Jacob stood, holding his crook, with Jack sat by his heels. The Zibyans transformed into almost transparent figures. One of them spoke: "Sister Rosalind, we meant no harm, we are waiting to ascend to the heavens. Thank you and Jacob for providing a sanctuary for us; we will leave you in peace." The four Zibyans vanished.

Jacob sat back down on the rock dumbfounded at what he'd seen; he thought he's going mad for a moment, hearing whispers in the wind. Rosalind kissed him on the cheek holding out her hand, "come along, Jacob, let's go home."

Jacob sat in the passenger seat with Jack by his feet. "Rosalind those are spirits ascend into the heavens?"

"Yes, why do you ask Jacob?"

"Why do they call you, sister? And you call them sister and brothers?"

"We are all God's children, Jacob; surely you realise that. God selects the good to ascend as angels the others you saw what happens to them," she advised firmly.

"Oh yes, I haven't forgotten; how long before they will ascend into the heavens, Rosalind?"

"Approximately two weeks; this allows the spirits to see how bad the human race behaves before they ascend into pure love and happiness for eternity. That's where I was before God permitted me to return to my loving husband," she smiled reassuringly.

Jacob grinned for the remainder of the journey home; Rosalind assessed what he's thinking realising he is perfectly satisfied with everything she'd said. They went inside the house sitting down watching television. Rosalind remembered she'd have to eat something to sustain her foetuses, she didn't feel any different structurally patting Jacob's leg. "Do you fancy cheese and onion sandwiches tonight, Jacob?"

"Yes, excellent I'm not that hungry Rosalind."

Rosalind made the sandwiches sitting by Jacob realising, she should have picked something else; although she never consumed food to sustain her being. She had sensors which were horribly affected by the onions, she considered the cheese to eating raw human flesh which she'd never tried either. She consumed what she'd made quickly making a coffee, she could tolerate at least it would wash her sensors clean of the other rubbish she'd eaten.

They retired to bed Rosalind touched Jacob's forehead he is unconscious until morning. She changed her appearance stepping into the misty fog transported to the spaceship. Matthew and Peter were sitting watching the monitor on the wall displaying the four Zibyans walking out across the Moor. They had changed their appearance into hikers so they wouldn't look out of the ordinary to anyone. Rosalind joined Peter and Matthew flashing her eyes. Rosalind commented, "I wouldn't have thought they'd have ventured out especially in the twilight, admittedly they can see in the dark, but that's all they are not absorbing the full beauty of the planet."

"I'm inclined to agree with you," Matthew remarked. "Serves no purpose if it wasn't for the fact they could see in the dark it would be hazardous what are they trying to achieve? I cannot read their thoughts?"

Peter asked suspiciously, "computer, what is their designation?"

"They are classified only the firstborn is aware they are the latest creation to join the collective."

Peter and Matthew looked to Rosalind, hoping she had the answer. "I know nothing and obviously neither do you two. Central computer why are we not permitted to know the designation of the four Zibyans?"

"There have been some changes to the collective. The firstborn is ensuring we are adequately prepared for attack or invasion; these are the first four who specialise in combat."

"Computer this is not the Zibyan way. We are peaceful except where humans are concerned the collective agreed they should become animal food as and when required, what has brought about the sudden change?"

"Your individuality Rosalind has proven to the collective you can solve issues without consulting anyone, or asking for approval has proved beneficial. The firstborn has sent the four Zibyans to test their skills on earth, they are programmed with earth records and the ability to destroy if commanded."

Matthew spoke: "Central computer; the Zibyan collective was established by our creators, they were a non-violent race. I, Peter and Rosalind have stayed on earth for thousands of years upholding the Zibyan existence. The collective is stepping beyond our creator's teachings. We meddled with chimpanzees creating what we have now an infestation of humans. The collective agreed to leave alone and not interfere initially until they started destroying the planet and every other beautiful creature upon it. The collective agreed we created the humans, they are our problem and therefore must be removed or at the very least controlled. Nowhere in the creator's teachings have we ever been advised to create a military structure; this is a breach of all the Zibyans stands for."

Rosalind clapped her hands. "Well said Matthew, although I doubt we will be listened to in the slightest, it appears we are insignificant but not for much longer," Rosalind suggested.

Peter look to Rosalind, "what can we do; we are one in 2 million our views do not count. We have seen the devastation of war first-hand, and the misery created."

"Before we act Peter and Matthew, we must see what the four intend to do." They sat watching the screen. The four stumbled across two tents wild camping. The occupants were sat around a campfire which is illegal on the Moor, one couple per tent. "I know what they're going to do; torture the humans I will stop them. I don't mind if they are you mainly executed but to torture is not necessary, in this instance."

Rosalind ran down the corridor changing into a hiker's outfit stepping into the misty fog and transported close to the wild campers sat around the fire. Rosalind stepped out of the darkness walking into the light of the fire. "I thought you should know the authorities are on the way someone has reported you having a fire; I would pack up and leave quickly."

The two couples rose to their feet quickly packing away their tent and equipment, realising they would be fined and probably locked away for the night if captured. One female said, "thanks, we owe you one."

Rosalind advised: "If you follow this sheep track," she pointed. "You will end up on the main road within a mile, walk slowly, otherwise, you could trip on a rock." Rosalind stamped the fire out while the wild campers vanished into the darkness. "You 4 Zibyans show yourself," Rosalind ordered. The four Zibyans materialised wearing their hiking outfit. Rosalind pointed to the misty fog they stepped in; she had telepathically ordered. Within seconds they were aboard the spaceship, changing their appearance into a natural Zibyan. Rosalind is surprised, Peter injected the 4 as they arrived with interferon, designed by the central computer, in the event a Zibyan lost control and had to be contained until the problem is resolved in their thought patterns.

The two males and females Zibyans floated in the air, they were powerless barely functioning. Rosalind smiled at Peter and Matthew. "Peter you acted correctly on this occasion and probably saved a battle. We would have had difficulty controlling them, more likely; they would have one they have been programmed to kill, but not us thankfully."

"I don't know why you are so concerned Rosalind over humans; considering we sent live humans for the wild animals to feed on some months back."

"There is a difference Peter; the humans had ill-treated the animals, the humans deserve to understand pain and suffering. They could argue, the animals could not. However, that will not happen again. Humans are processed by Matthew on earth and shipped out as processed meat."

The firstborn appeared with some of his brothers and sisters on the large screen. "Explain yourselves," he insisted.

"I think it should be the other way around firstborn; you explain yourself. You have violated the principles of the collective? The central computer advises because of me and the way I operate, as an individual and could be beneficial in a war situation. A highly unlikely scenario to happen considering I know of no other being as powerful and as intelligent as us?"

"Your individuality Rosalind, many would like to possess. The central computer has tried to program others like you we cannot. We have looked to the humans for a reason they act individually not as a collective in most cases. The central computer has determined you either can be an individual, or not which is extremely frustrating for the central computer, not able to mimic your thought patterns in others; which all your brothers and sisters agree would be beneficial."

"Firstborn I perform the way I do out of necessity. Otherwise, Jacob would not have accepted me as his wife. Individuality is a trial and error process; you have to learn in stages and not be programmed with all the information at once."

"Central computer reprogram the 4, to the way a normal Zibyan would generally be. I set you a task Rosalind you are a scientist in your own category; find a way for Zibyans to perform efficiently as individuals." The firstborn vanished with his brothers and sisters.

The four were immediately connected to the central computer their memory cells were wiped and reprogrammed, within an hour they were transported to Brook farm to continue their studies. Rosalind looked to the monitor seeing Jacob walking along the clifftop; she suspected looking for her according to his thoughts. She flashed her eyes at Peter and Matthew stepping into the misty fog, she joined Peter holding out her hand. They walked along together, enjoying the early morning fresh air and the gentle breeze coming in from the sea. Rosalind concluded: "The fresh air makes me hungry Jacob, let's have breakfast," she smiled, holding his hand encouraging him back to the house. She set about cooking bacon and egg fried bread and tomatoes. Jacob sat at the table, enjoying his breakfast. Rosalind cautiously devoured hers, for once, her senses were not sending conflicting signals to her mind. Jacob smiled, kissing Rosalind on the cheek, "I'm off to check the sheep, Rosalind."

"Wait for me! I'm coming this morning, and it's about time I had my own crook," Rosalind complained, slipping on her coat. Jacob went to the far end of the kitchen hidden behind a large cupboard is a brand-new shepherd's crook, he eased it from behind the crockery cupboard offering to Rosalind. She grinned not realising it is there, she never looked behind the cupboard. "Thank you, Jacob." They set off across the Moor both now looking like shepherds.

Rosalind noticed one of the females reprogrammed approaching; she had transformed into a young woman wearing hiking clothes. Rosalind is concerned why she is on her own and not with the others. The females spoke, "good morning," continuing to walk as if she didn't know Rosalind, changing direction towards the shop over two miles away. Jacob pointed with his crook, "over there, Rosalind."Rosalind hurried Jacob along, she wanted to cut across the Moor in the direction of the shop to see where the female is heading. She tried to read the females thoughts, which appeared to be jumbled and confused, rather alarming. "The sheep look ok Jacob; let's cut across towards the shop we could do with some exercise, well I could anyway," she smiled, "I have to keep fit in my condition." She knew by saying that Jacob would agree to anything.

"As you wish Rosalind," gently placing his crook around her neck pulling her closer to him in a loving gesture. Rosalind set a brisk pace Jacob is struggling to keep up with her, catching a glimpse of the female some distance ahead engaged in a conversation with the human male. The female jumped in his car, Rosalind watched them drive off together. Rosalind stopped in her tracks telepathically contacting Peter.

"Intervene immediately and dispose of the male. Oh, I quite feel faint Rosalind professed we better go home Jacob," she briefly smiled.

Jacob looked extremely concerned. "Are you okay Rosalind you needn't of set such a fast pace; you shouldn't exert yourself so much." Jacob supported Rosalind home, insisting she rests while he carried on with his chores around the farm.

Rosalind received a telepathic message from Peter: "He had the female aboard the spaceship; the male is deceased and becoming fertiliser. The central computer will examine her brain cells; there is an error somewhere which must be discovered before any more Zibyans are created."

Rosalind responded telepathically: "Excellent Peter." Rosalind sat deep in thought, wondering if somehow the main computer had picked up a human-computer virus, after all, everything that happened here is transmitted to Zagader and processed by the central computer. Any decisions were filtered through to the secondary networks to administer the instruction. "Peter," Rosalind, ordered telepathically. "Send the four home to Zagader if one is malfunctioning the remaining three could possibly be infected as well."

Peter responded telepathically. "Matthew and I have been discussing your thoughts and agree with you, Rosalind. I've already transported the 3 aboard the spaceship and suspended, they are inoperative the four in total."

"I am surprised and pleased Peter and Matthew, you are starting to act as individuals in a crisis."

Matthew remarked: "The superpowers are up to their old tricks creating germ warfare, one of the components escaped, they've named the coronavirus most world powers are rather excited by the viruses abilities to weed out the elderly and sick. An unfortunate error of judgement; the elderly are the ones who know how to look after the planet properly, not like the younger generation. I suppose we mustn't complain they make good animal food if nothing else."

Rosalind is quite alarmed, "is there an antidote Matthew?"

"No, probably take the humans up to 2 years; there is no rush they want the virus to deplete the elderly and anyone else who has a lingering illness."

"Peter can you make something to protect Jacob from the virus, I don't want him to die, admittedly he is fit and well but you never know how this virus will affect anyone; obviously the humans don't."

"Why bother he's not essential! Admittedly, he has uses, in hindsight, yes I will create a vaccine for him give me one Earth hour and transport him aboard the spaceship."

"Excellent Peter."

Jacob came in the house seeing Rosalind making coffee. "I thought I'd told you to rest woman," he scolded. Rosalind did not answer passing him his cup of coffee. Jacob turned on the television listening to the news, the coronavirus is in every country. "There's no escape Rosalind, we are lucky we live on the Moor. That reminds me I've taken a walk down to the pasture, we may be able to acquire another cut of silage; nearly the end of September if we don't take it now it will be too late Rosalind."

"We are doing nothing Jacob until you have visited Peter; God has decreed you are protected from the coronavirus in case you come in contact."

Jacob looked surprised, "I wouldn't worry Rosalind the virus won't come on the Moor. Holidaymakers won't bother to travel, especially at this time of year. Besides the virus has been around for months and I'm still okay."

Aliens

Rosalind grabbed Jacob's arm, opening the front door, pushing him into the misty fog along with her; they travelled instantly to the spaceship. Before Jacob could gather his thoughts, Peter had already injected him without Jacob realising. Jacob immediately bowed his head in respect to Peter. "My Rosalind disturbs you, St Peter, with a trivial matter I am not unwell."

"I am not St Peter, my name is Peter, I am merely a disciple of the Lord. He decided you would receive protection Jacob be silent on the matter."

"I apologise for my stupidity Peter, I am not ungrateful for anything God provides me with."

"Go, Jacob, you have three days in which to gather your crop before the heavens open, God controls everything do not disrespect his judgement."

Rosalind escorted Jacob down the corridor into the misty fog returning to the farm. Jacob fell over feeling dizzy from travelling so quick, he slowly recovered to stand smiling. Jacob kissed Rosalind on the cheek climbing aboard his tractor heading for the 30-acre pasture land which he cut very quickly. Moved on to the 10 acres at Brook farm deciding there wasn't much grass but what little there is he would have. Jacob returned to the farm swapping over the mower for the tedder ready to row the grass tomorrow for Rosalind to make silage bales. Jacob returned to the house late afternoon he hadn't bothered to stop for lunch; cutting the grass is more important. Peter had warned him the weather is going to change shortly.

Rosalind is sat watching television, a severe earthquake in China estimated as many as 10,000 people could be trapped if not dead. Rosalind suspected by the time they cleared the fields of silage more fertiliser would be waiting for Jacob.

Rosalind advised: "Your lunch dinner and tea is in the oven," she chuckled.

Jacob burning his fingers removed the hot-plate from the oven, making a coffee sitting at the table hearing the signature tune of Emmerdale Farm. He knew Rosalind wouldn't move until the end, making him smile. After half an hour, Rosalind made herself a coffee sitting at the table as Jacob mopped his plate with a crusty piece of bread. "I presume you cut everything Jacob and we can bale tomorrow?"

"Yes, there isn't much there, more on the 30 acres than the 10. We could do with silage bale racks two would be sufficient; you think we can afford them, Rosalind?"

"Of course, we'll have a look at what we want on Friday after we finished with the silage." They watched television together until 11 o'clock retiring to bed. Rosalind decided not to go to the spaceship tonight, everything had been taken care of as far as she's concerned, most of all Jacob was protected from another man-made virus, she knew initially harvested from animals to use as germ warfare

Morning came quickly, Rosalind had gone outside at 5 o'clock in the morning, checking the tractors and filling with diesel. She fitted the bale wrapper to the old sit up and beg tractor. At least Jacob wouldn't have to change equipment halfway through the day. She drove the situp and beg Fordson parking outside the 30-acre pasture. She returned to the farm going in the house, making breakfast as Jacob came out yawning from the bedroom, sitting at the table. Rosalind had made him bacon and eggs, which is sufficient she thought for the day along with a mug of coffee to wake his brain up she hoped.

Jacob grunted after eating his breakfast, kissing Rosalind on the cheek running outside climbing aboard his Ford tractor.

He rowed the 30 acres of grass into neat rows for Rosalind to bale. Rosalind followed him climbing aboard her massy tractor taking the round baler. She started baling, didn't take long for them to cover 30 acres. They only had 50 bales in the field moving on to the 10 acres at Brook farm they only achieved five bales; nevertheless, it would all count.

Jacob drove back to the farm with his Ford tractor, attaching the new Hay trailer leaving in the 30-acre pasture land. He started wrapping the bales with plastic. Rosalind returned to the farm with the baler parking in the barn. She drove to the field with her tractor and loader and bale grab, stacking bales on the trailer. Jacob stopped wrapping the bales taking the load already wrapped bales to the farm. Followed by Rosalind so she can unload and stack them in a neat pile. By 9 o'clock in the evening, they had finished. Jacob is absolutely shattered collapsing on the bed that's where he stayed until morning. Rosalind joined him in the bedroom, ensuring he wouldn't wake up. She travelled to the spaceship greeted by Matthew and Peter with the flash of their eyes. "Is there something wrong with the spaceship Peter, I know she's been sat here for thousands of years?"

"The seawater appears to have affected the outer skin, especially ran the propulsion system. The firstborn suggested we return to Zagader where the ship can be repaired, we replace with a new one. Otherwise, we may never leave earth in the spaceship if she deteriorates any further."

"You could send the craft home on autopilot Peter and stay at Brook farm until the new craft arrives. At least if it did disintegrate on the journey home, you would be unharmed from the explosion."

The firstborn and his brothers and sisters appeared on the far wall: "Rosalind you seem to question every decision we make. The central computer determines the spaceship is safe. However, deteriorating slightly considering the thousands of years the spacecraft has been subjected to seawater; plus all the other chemicals the humans dispose of in the sea, thinking no one will know. I'm surprised the ship has lasted so long."

"Firstborn I am not criticising your decision, I am merely stating, Peter and Matthew, my brothers if left on earth at Brook farm they would be safe and not subjected to the possibility of the spaceship failure. Their contribution to the Zibyans collective is immeasurable, although the central computer has their brain cell patterns to transfer to another Zibyan in the event they should be destroyed! Why take the risk in the first place?"

"Central computer has all the records transferred from the spaceship to Zagader?"

"I am presently engaged in the process firstborn."

"When you have completed the task, what else must be done before the spaceship can take off?"

"I estimate we still have over a hundred tons of fertiliser in storage, should be removed to lessen the stress on the craft."

"Why are you holding back a hundred tonnes what is the purpose? Jacob would have spread on the farm if you'd have requested computer?"

"I am using as ballast to maintain the spaceship's concealment beneath the sea."

The firstborn thought for a moment. "I presume if the ballast is removed, you will float to the surface?"

"The spaceship will stay submerged using engine power and the other tanks containing seawater. However, it will place extra strain on the structure if maintained for any length of time."

"Central computer," Rosalind suggested, "if I arrange for Jacob to come down on the beach in the evening. You could surface under darkness unload the hundred tons which are only 10 loads for Jacobs manure spreader and take off for Zagader?"

"Excellent," the computer responded.

"I'll arrange for Jacob to come onto the beach at 9 PM. I will instruct him there is 10 loads computer."

"I will prepare the spaceship in preparation for this evening."

The firstborn commented: "Once again Rosalind your individuality has served the collective with your quick thinking, excellent," the firstborn vanished. Rosalind flashed her eyes to Peter and Matthew, leaving the spaceship for the last time, she stepped into the misty fog arriving outside the front door. Jacob is already making breakfast. She kissed him on the cheek, "Jacob, you are to be on the beach with the manure spreader at 9 PM. There are a hundred tonnes of fertiliser arriving and must be spread, you should be finished by midnight at the latest."

"Why the urgency?"

"Are you questioning God Jacob? I am carrying your son and daughter," she smiled.

Jacob immediately hugged Rosalind, "praise the Lord I am truly blessed this day. I will be on the beach at nine have no fear Rosalind, I will do whatever God wishes." Rosalind sat down to bacon and eggs and fried bread, she had no choice other than to eat to maintain nutrients for the foetuses growing inside her.

After breakfast, Jacob ventured outside attaching the manure spreader to his Ford tractor greasing and oiling everything, finally filling his tractor with diesel. Whatever happened, he couldn't let God down after all his prayers were answered, a son and daughter. Jacob set off across the Moor with Jack close at his heels. He wanted to check his sheep were okay; they were even more critical now than ever before; his son and daughter's future, he realised smiling. They would each have their own farm, now he understood God had worked everything out for him.

Jacob is pleased to find his sheep were now grazing both farms, which is ample grass for the stock he's carrying. He steadily walked home please with everything he'd seen. The only thing he noticed is one or two crazy walkers on the footpath in September when the wind cut across the Moor with a vicious bite at times. Jacob realised the seasons were changing, every month is different from when he was a child, making it difficult to calculate what he should do; not like the old days when his dad was alive.

Rosalind is checking her garden to see what is available to eat. She quite enjoyed growing to produce the old way without technology. However, she smiled realising she had cheated slightly by using some technology forcing the plants to grow far quicker than usual. She sent a telepathic message to Peter. "If when the spaceship attempts to escape earth, shows any signs of malfunction; you and Matthew should eject and transport to Brook farm where you would be safe."

Peter responded telepathically. "Thank you, sister, for your concern. Matthew and I have already prepared an escape plan should it be necessary. Like you, we are not so sure the spaceship will hold together."

The rest of the day is quite uneventful, Jacob had walked to the shop so Rosalind wouldn't realise. He hoped to purchase a large bouquet of flowers and an enormous box of chocolates. He slowly walked home to the farm. Rosalind hadn't realised he'd gone, she is too preoccupied running calculations in her mind as to whether the spaceship would hold together or not. Jacob entered the house Rosalind smiled after reading his thoughts. She kissed him softly on the cheek, "thank you, Jacob, the flowers are beautiful and chocolates you're spoiling me."

Jacob sat watching television; he had this strange feeling inside something is odd. Rosalind is behaving quite fidgety, which is unusual for her. Jacob glanced to the clock on the wall, 6:30 PM. Rosalind went outside, Jacob followed concerned watching Rosalind attach the 10-ton trailer to her massy tractor. "Why are you doing that, Rosalind?" He asked suspiciously.

"In case something goes wrong with the spreader or your tractor, the trailer will be a backup, at least we can still receive the fertiliser from God."

"You've never bothered before Rosalind; why now?"

"Something special is happening Jacob, I am not permitted to tell you. God's business, consider yourself fortunate I am here carrying your children. No one else on earth as ever had their wife returned."

Jacob walked off sighing, looking over the cliff out to a calm sea, he continued walking visiting the post box finding half a dozen letters, mainly brown envelopes as usual. Jacob walked across to his pasture land, opening the gate. The sheep were on the other side of the moor and certainly wouldn't realise he'd open the gate on the pasture land. Jacob looked across the Moor the sun is going down in a beautiful fiery red display. He returned to the house, placing the post on the kitchen table. Rosalind opened, there is nothing of importance only companies trying to sell Jacob their products. Jacob sat and watched television very uneasy about everything, and he didn't know why, almost as if the end of the world is coming, realising what a stupid thought, why would God give him so much and then take it away in a flash.

He looked at the clock on the wall 8:30. He slipped on his coat, glanced to Rosalind, who briefly smiled. Jacob went out of the house, climbing in his tractor cab with Jack sitting on the passenger seat. He descended to the beach quite dangerous driving in the dark down the cliff track, seeing lights in the distance, feeling the first load in the spreader. He headed up the track in all haste he had 10 lows to dispose of, and from what Rosalind had said he should be finished by midnight at the latest; which presumably meant something. The last thing he wanted to do is disappoint God he would feel a failure God is entrusting him to perform the task, and he would not fail.

Rosalind had turned invisible standing on the clifftop watching proceedings. She could see the enormous space-ship clearly floating. She watched the ship change shape in preparation to leave Earth, now understanding human fear. Jacob finely left the beach with the last load heading for the pastureland.

Rosalind watched the spaceship glow taking off for the first time in thousands of years. She crossed her fingers, watching the spaceship disappear into the clouds hearing an almighty explosion.

CHAPTER 9

The Journey

Rosalind telepathically tried to contact Matthew and Peter after hearing the explosion. Finally, she listened in her mind to Peters telepathic message: "They had lost one pulsating engine leaving the Earth's atmosphere, another ship is dispatched from Zagader to rendezvous halfway home; they would exchange spacecraft there, he and Matthew were to return to Earth."

Rosalind smiled another human expression she had adopted; she replied telepathically: "Safe journey." Rosalind entered the house turning on the television, hearing more disturbing news about the escaped coronavirus over a million dead. She wondered how long the human scientist would delay in presenting a cure to the populace?

Rosalind recalled from her memory banks, watching for four years Jacob crying some nights for the loss of his wife Rosalind, before she miraculously appeared, stating God had returned her to life. Her shape-shifting abilities had enabled her to conceive a female and male foetus for experimental purposes, now steadily growing inside her, providing she maintained her eating programme to ensure nutrients reached the foetuses.

Jacob came running in. "What the hell was that noise Rosalind I thought it would break the Windows on my tractor?"

"Nothing for you to concern yourself with Jacob. God is in control as you will discover as time goes on," Rosalind grinned.

"Come along, Mrs bedtime! I think it's nearly one o'clock in the morning," he picked up Rosalind in his arms carrying her into the bedroom laying her gently on the bed. She kissed him, Jacob immediately rendered unconscious. She walked into the kitchen, making herself a sandwich under normal circumstances she didn't need to eat, Rosalind was pure energy. However, since agreeing to carry Jacob's offspring for the benefit of experimental purposes, Rosalind had no choice other than to consume food. Rosalind sat eating cheese and tomato sandwiches watching television quietly, she would have transported to the spaceship. Unfortunately, the new spacecraft is still on its way from Zagader, once the new one had arrived, she could at least associate with her brothers and sisters.

Rosalind looked at the clock on the wall nearly 6 AM, she realised the food she consumed had been inside her for over five hours. She grabbed Jack's bowl and discharged the unwanted food from her system. Jack devoured everything, returning to the hearth and the dying fire, only a few embers remained burning. Rosalind, turning off the television rather bored, threw a few more blocks on the fire and started to make Jacob's breakfast. Rosalind made him bacon and egg on fried bread and some for her, she would have to keep eating to provide the foetuses with nutrients.

Jacob came staggering from the bedroom, sitting down to his lovely breakfast. Rosalind joined him becoming accustomed to the flavours passing over her sensors. Rosalind poured two coffees moving to sit on the settee watching the 7 AM news. The whole world is shutting down from the coronavirus; she wondered would it be beneficial now for the Zibyans to take control of the entire Earth. The human's nuclear capabilities and other weaponry were paralysed to some degree, although the humans had nothing that would affect or damage a Zibyan.

Jacob kissed Rosalind on the cheek, "I'm off to check the sheep; that reminds me we have to buy another Ram from somewhere Rosalind, we have over 250 ewes, too much for the one Ram to handle."

"I'll check on the computer Jacob and see what I can find suitable to service the flock," she smiled. Jacob walked out of the door, followed closely by Jack; he strolled across the Moor, walking almost to Brook Farm before discovering his sheep. Jacob sat down for a moment on a large boulder glancing across to the barn on Brook Farm, deciding to take a closer look at what Thomas had left him in the way of sheep feed. Jacob strolled towards the buildings in worse shape than his own. He put his shoulder to a door forcing open much to his surprise there were half a dozen mineral blocks. Jacob quickly removed one, pushing the door shut walking out onto the Moor. The sheep almost sensed Jacob had something for them surrounding him instantly as he lowered the mineral block down onto a stone, removing the plastic from the top. He realised one block is insufficient they'd be fighting all day to gain access. Jacob quickly returned to the old building removing another block placing down some distance away from the other; didn't improve matters much, but at least they'd all get a look in before the end of the day.

Jacob started walking across the Moor in the direction of home, noticing a group of teenagers approaching screaming and shouting loud enough to wake the dead; he couldn't say anything they were on a public footpath meandering across the Moor. Jacob suspected they were on holiday although the world is shutting down from the coronavirus, they must be the remanence of holidaymakers from the campsite 2 miles away, totally inappropriately dressed for walking the Moor. Jacob hoped they wouldn't venture close to Brook Farm realising the property is empty and break-in. Rosalind is reading his thoughts carefully to make sure Jacob wasn't in any trouble, after watching a program on television, of a group of teenagers assaulting a member of the older generation for fun.

Jacob discreetly watched the teenagers take the right fork on the public footpath which would take them very close to Brook Farm. He sighed, deciding to cut around out of their view back to Brook Farm, didn't want them setting fire to his hay, he'd seen one or two of them with cigarettes which didn't matter on the Moor at this time of year, however in a barn of dry hay is a different story.

Jacob remembered when he was a teenager playing in the barn on the bales of hay and later on in life with Rosalind, which made him smile. Jacob concealed himself, noticing the teenagers had left the footpath heading towards the farm, there were six in all three boys and three girls. Jacob couldn't understand why the girls were dressed the way they were; they must have been freezing in such short skirts, blouse and an open anorak. He watched them enter the barn the girls without hesitation remove their clothes laying in the hay. Jacob heard a vehicle approach, Rosalind, in her Range Rover, the teenagers quickly dressed scurrying from the barn to Jacob's relief, at least if they lit a cigarette out there wouldn't cause any damage only to their lungs.

Jacob walked across, joining Rosalind in the Range Rover, "what brings you here Rosalind?"

"Checking the property Jacob there are still holidaymakers walking across the Moor, there aren't any spirits in the house at the moment to monitor. On the subject of the house Jacob I think we should arrange for the window frames to be replaced, don't you?"

"I suppose... We could do without the cost."

"Let me worry about the money Jacob, not you. You concentrate on looking after the farm. I found a Ram not far away; he comes with a pedigree like my husband," she chuckled.

"And what did he cost me?"

"Only £2000, after I'd finished negotiating will fetch him this afternoon Jacob."

Jacob exhaled not bothering to argue with Rosalind, he knew he needed a Ram whatever happened. Rosalind drove steadily towards home, reversing up to the Ivor Williams, Jacob attached to the Range Rover, they went inside to have a cup of coffee and a light snack which Rosalind had already prepared. Jacob asked, "how you feeling Rosalind, you know?"

"As far as I can tell the twins and me are fine." Rosalind finished eating her sausage sandwiches slipping on her coat followed by Jacob. They sat in the Range Rover heading for the other end of Dartmoor, entering the driveway of Park farm, because of the coronavirus Rosalind had transferred the money directly into Mr Johnson's account. The Ram was left penned for them to collect, so there is no personal contact. Jacob quickly loaded the Ram noticing Mr and Mrs Johnson down the other end of the yard, he waved and shouted, "thanks." Rosalind and Jacob immediately returned home.

"We might as well release both Rams Rosalind, where only three weeks away from October, I'll fetch the ewes," he smiled.

"Okay Jacob will leave this one in the trailer to you return then left them all out together the Rams won't fight with any luck." They quickly placed marker crayons on each Ram.

Jacob promptly set off with Jack heading towards Brook Farm where he'd last seen the sheep, noticing smoke coming from what appeared to be a building. Jacob quickened his pace approaching the premises from the rear peering through the wall where a brick is missing. He couldn't believe his eyes. The teenagers had returned lit a small fire, the girls were naked, the boys were taking pictures on their mobile phones. Jacob noticed bottles of wine. Jack barked and growled, the teenagers quickly dressed running from the buildings across the Moor, leaving the fire burning and the discarded wine bottles. Jacob promptly stamped out the fire before it spread, the teenagers weren't far from the barn full of hay it would have only taken one spark, and the lot would have gone up in smoke. Jacob grabbed an old bucket taking water from the brook pouring over where the fire was burning to ensure it wouldn't ignite again. Jacob patted Jack as they left Brook Farm, herding the sheep towards home. Rosalind noticed them coming releasing the Ram from the Ivor Williams trailer and the other from the barn. The Rams ignored each other for the moment more interested in the ewes than each other. "You should have seen what I saw Rosalind the younger generation get worse. I don't remember us being so bad," he sighed.

"Not for much longer Jacob changes are coming, the Lord has had enough I can assure you," she patted his cheek holding his hand, leading him to the woodpile. She passed him the axe with a grin. "I'll make the coffee."

Jacob reacted trying to pat her backside she moved quickly, he missed, she continued on to the house, for the first time feeling movement inside her, she checked her memory banks. The central computer had placed all the information available on the behaviour of foetuses in her programming, so she understood exactly what was taking place. Rosalind realised, within another three days a new spaceship would arrive positioning in the same place as the old one ideal location for their activities. She'd have access to the central computer; with his abilities, the computer could examine her operating cells check on the foetuses. Rosalind was suffering from a strange sensation, her circuitry was increasing its sensitivity around the foetuses, which under normal circumstances, anything foreign invading her would be discharged without a second thought. She sat on the settee watching the television with a cup of coffee, heard the faint sound of Jacob splitting wood. Rosalind wondered why the teenagers were wandering across the Moor? The government had placed a lockdown on non-essential travelling. After reading Jacob's mind and understanding what had taken place, she determined the teenagers had no business participating in silly activities, endangering each other's health and everyone else they came in contact with.

Rosalind left the house. "I'm taking a walk Jacob I need fresh air," she smiled, patting his cheek heading down to the beach. Rosalind scanned the area for any signs of activity there were none. She shapeshifted into a seagull taking off gliding along the cliff, finally coming to the caravan site, she circled high above catching sight of the six teenagers entering a caravan, she glided on the sea breeze landing on the caravan roof. Rosalind turned herself invisible flying through an open window in one of the bedrooms, she watched from the open doorway, one teenager had linked his mobile to the television.

The girls were laughing drinking beer, watching themselves perform. The teenage boys weren't much better, the girls had taken the mobile from one of the boys well they performed. Rosalind transmitted a controlling thought to the six teenagers. She read their minds individually realising their parents had gone shopping for groceries. Rosalind decided it would be a suitable punishment for the teenagers to be discovered by their parents engaged in sex. She instructed the 6 to remove their clothes and to start performing, she could see the parents returning just a matter of a few seconds. Rosalind watched them enter the large static home, discovering what was taking place between their teenage children.

She left the static home through the open door listening to the parents screaming at their children. She thought about executing the six, considered it a futile exercise while the spaceship wasn't here to process the flesh. She had logged their home addresses so Matthew could collect them at a later date for processing. Rosalind shape-shifted into a seagull flying back to the farm transforming behind a large rock on the beach, sensing the foetuses moving back into position. Rosalind realised shape-shifting is not a bright idea while in this condition, she would have to stay in the shape of Rosalind as much as possible to avoid causing injury to them. She looked to the shore noticing Jacob fishing, she crept up behind him, making him jump. "I think all the fish have gone on holiday Rosalind, I've been here for an hour and not had a bite," he sighed.

"Let me cast for you Jacob," she smiled, taking the rod from his hand winding in and casting out, she passed the rod back to him. Jacob started winding in slowly, "I think I've hooked a battleship," digging his heels into the sand with his rod bent nearly double, he spent the next half hour struggling with whatever is on the end of his line. Rosalind stood there grinning watching him struggle. "I'd better go home and make the tea Jacob hopefully you'll be coming home before dark," she chuckled, enjoying teasing Jacob. Jacob continued to struggle. Finally, he realised what he'd hooked an octopus a large octopus. Rosalind, without hesitation, dispatched the octopus with a knife to the brain. Jacob stood there, he'd never seen anything so strange in his life. "I presume we can pickle an octopus, Rosalind?"

"Of course, you will have to nip to the shop, I'm short on pickling jars. I have plenty of vinegar in stock," Rosalind remarked cutting the octopus into manageable pieces while Jacob ran back to the farm to fetch the Land Rover; there was no way they could carry the octopus home there was too much of it. Jacob finally returned to find Rosalind had finished dissecting, she helped Jacob load into the back of the Land Rover along with the fishing rod. She checked her memory banks on how to pickle octopus correctly. Jacob left Rosalind at the house jumping into the Range Rover, he headed for the shop across the Moor checking on his sheep at the same time. He was about to enter the shop noticing a minibus drive past, he recognised some of the occupants the teenagers, Jacob smiled one less problem on the more he concluded entering the shop. "I suppose you don't have any pickling jars?"

the shopkeeper laughed, "I bought them, especially for you, I guess you'd want more eventually, I have six boxes."

"I might as well take the lot," Jacob paid, carried the boxes to the back of the Range Rover taking a box of chocolates and a bouquet of flowers. He drove steadily looking at his sheep again on the way home watching the two Rams busily serving the ewes. Jacob parked outside the house greeted at the door by Rosalind, who'd already read his mind excepting the chocolates and flowers kissing Jacob gently on the lips. "You keep spoiling me, Jacob. Did you manage to acquire some more pickling jars," which she already knew the answer to?

"Yes, you put the kettle on I'll carry in."

Rosalind received a telepathic message from Peter: "They were landing tonight, come aboard, we have many things to discuss."

Rosalind finished pickling the octopus waiting for the jars to cool, she carried them down into the cellar where the temperature was constant. She had spent some time down there cleaning using the old shelving to stack her jars on.

Jacob sat drinking his coffee, watching the news the coronavirus appeared to be out of control. The Prime Minister was pleading with everyone to follow the scientist's rules to avoid infection; Jacob presumed everybody was deaf or stupid. Rosalind patted him on the shoulder, "Jacob I noticed a considerable amount of firewood had washed ashore, while it's pleasant don't you think you should cut a load? I could bring your Ford tractor down with the trailer, you bring the Fordson major with the saw bench on, we could cut a load in a few minutes."

"Okay, good idea I usually leave everything to the last minute wait until run out or snowing, the weather is pleasant today let's make the most of it."

They both left the house, Rosalind, taking the tractor and trailer and Jacob the tractor and saw bench along with his chainsaw in case some of the wood was too hefty for him to carry to the saw bench. They spent two hours Jacob soaring the timber and Rosalind throwing onto the trailer, she thought she could cut the wood quicker with a beam from her eyes than the saw bench. They'd soon cleared all the decent timber from the shoreline steadily returning to the farm. Rosalind tipped the wood in a pile by the woodshed parking the equipment in the barn by Jacob saw bench. Jacob was quite worn out; he looked to Rosalind who appeared as healthy as ever, he suddenly remembered she was pregnant and shouldn't be lifting heavy blocks onto a trailer. Jacob stopped in his tracks. "Rosalind I'm so sorry, I don't know why it slipped my mind you're pregnant, you shouldn't have lifted those blocks. I should have gone on my own," he scooped her up in his arms carrying her into the house gently sitting her on the settee.

"Don't fuss, Jacob, I'm perfectly healthy. I'm just in time to watch Coronation Street, so you make the coffee," she grinned. "You can take a walk across the Moor check on the ewes and Brook Farm."

Jacob passed her coffee, selecting his crook from the back of the door, slipping on his coat setting off with Jack running close to his heels. Within half an hour, Jacob found his sheep by the old bog, he could see his two Rams had been fighting; both had blood on their heads. "Away, Jack," Jacob commanded. Jack would soon move the sheep away from the bog. Jacob stood on a rock, counting his sheep as they funnelled along the pathway in a neat row. Jacob breathed a sigh of relief they were all there. Jacob walked on once he is sure his sheep were safe, finally reaching Brook Farm discovering builders had already moved in replacing the window frames in the old house.

Jacob sighed, Rosalind certainly didn't let the grass grow beneath her feet, Jacob had never known a woman to be so impatient; mind you, with the coronavirus raging around the world, should imagine the builders were pleased to have a secluded property to work on. Jacob walked across the Moor until he came to a location with elevation, giving him a view of the campsite some miles down the road, the car park is empty, he suspected everyone had gone home. Jacob wondered if the local shop would survive now. These were indeed strange times.

Jacob remembered his father explaining to him one of their relations in the second world war, where they used chemical warfare, they have to wear masks; otherwise, they'd die. Jacob continued walking towards home, contemplating whether the coronavirus is man-made, governments were far more interested in designing weaponry than curing cancer which initially killed Rosalind; only thanks to God she is returned to him. Jacob looked into the distance seeing Rosalind in her garden hoeing weeds. Jacob paused, seeing what he believed to be a blue flash of light coming from Rosalind. Jacob quickened his pace somewhat concerned, just in time to see Rosalind flicking a rat out of her garden on the end of her hoe. "The one thing I detest more than anything else Jacob are rats," she commented, placing her hoe back in the shed. "Why are you out of breath, Jacob?" She already knew what he'd seen.

"I thought I saw a blue flash of light coming from you. I didn't know whether you'd been struck by lightning or something."

Rosalind laughed, "could have been the reflection of my hoe, after all, stainless steel."

"I suppose! I don't want anything happening to you, three," he grinned.

"Neither do I; tonight's special, Peter and Matthew are returning to earth after receiving instructions from God."

"Where will they stay Rosalind we haven't any spare rooms other than Brook Farm?"

"They come with their own accommodation, they have to remain concealed from the human race; you've travelled to them before Jacob, surely you remember travelling in the mist with me?"

"Vaguely all I can remember is feeling ill."

"I think you'll find God has new plans as long as you are obeying his commands Jacob, you and I will be safe," she smiled reassuringly.

"I see you authorise the repairs on Brook Farm windows, Rosalind?"

"Why not we agree the work needed doing Jacob before the place deteriorates any further."

"Okay I was only making a comment Rosalind I wasn't criticising." He remarked, returning to the house with her.

Jacob sat watching television while Rosalind made tuna sandwiches for their tea. "Rosalind look at this rioting breaking into shops stealing food how ridiculous." Rosalind sat beside Jacob, watching the police trying to handle the unruly crowd. "Jacob we'll have to watch the sheep, I suspect some farmers will lose their stock to thieves. There are no food shortages just greedy people Jacob. The only problem is there are too many people, they breed like rabbits," Rosalind commented realising what she'd said, she was carrying two foetuses.

"I think you're wrong Rosalind if people weren't so evil and self-centred, we wouldn't have issues. Look at the money spent on weaponry the government spends more money working out how to kill us than cure a common cold."

"There may be some merit in your assessment Jacob. The creator would not agree with you, I don't think, not for us to make the decision Jacob."

Jacob sighed heavily, "I hope the creator realises not everyone is a bad person on earth; some people have dedicated their life to worshipping him male and female."

"Oh, Jacob you must remember God can read everyone's thoughts, he knows what's in everyone's heart, and I can assure you there are many people around the world making a great deal of money out of God; he will bring to an abrupt end in the fullness of time."

"I'll, not argue with you Rosalind you know better than I, I'm sure, you've met the Lord and blessed to have you home."

Rosalind stood up, switching off the television holding out her hand. "Bed, work tomorrow," she smiled. Jacob didn't argue accepting her hand warmly led into the bedroom where Rosalind placed him in a deep sleep. She left the bedroom, patting Jack walking out of the house along the clifftop. She watched, even though dark and the fog covered the sea she could still see what was happening. Peter and Matthew had returned along with her other brothers and sisters aboard the spaceship, which could change into any shape chosen, designed similar to themselves by the central computer. Rosalind's smile broadened sensing the misty fog surrounding her, she stepped into the bright light transported aboard the new spaceship, situated where the old one once resided in an ancient volcanic crater. Peter and Matthew flash their eyes to Rosalind, she responded likewise. "Sister I was unsure we'd ever see you again when the propulsion system exploded, I anticipated the end is near, thankfully the backup system was sufficient to propel us into space."

"For the first time, Peter I had a sudden sense of fear when I heard the explosion. I lost all sense of calm trying to contact you and Matthew, which is illogical for a Zibyan to behave in such a manner." Rosalind leaned against the wall allowing the central computer to connect to her for analysis. "Both foetuses are growing Rosalind correctly; you must not shape-shift; causes them distress and could destroy them."

"Understood computer I had a strange sensation when I shape-shifted into a seagull you have confirmed my own suspicions."

"Would you like me to accelerate their growth, Rosalind?"

"No, Jacob would panic, human females, take nine months I will have to endure the same, unfortunately."

The wall displaying the firstborn and some of his brothers and sisters. "Rosalind, the central computer informs me you are progressing with your pregnancy in a timely manner."

"Yes, firstborn I suspect there is more to your visit than my welfare?"

"Your intuition is correct we are extending our terraforming program to 14 planets. The central computer advises the planet earth can easily supply the necessary food for the animals until they become established and control their own numbers."

"Firstborn, at present, the human carcasses taken and processed for animal food is hardly noticed by the human race; except when Matthew emptied prisons. I suspect if we take more humans than we already are, they will hunt for an explanation and could possibly discover us. However, I do appreciate, at this present time, they have no weaponry capable of harming us. In the future who knows, do we really know all their secrets?"

"Central computer, how would you advise we disguise 5000 humans disappearing a month?" The firstborn enquired.

The central computer responded: "I have monitored human transmissions; they still want answers to what happened to the archaeologists and the four police officers. The same applies to prisoners vanishing. My recommendation to the collective, I would leave the extraction of human corpses to Rosalind, Peter and Matthew, they are more experienced in the art of concealing how humans are extracted. I would recommend the number of humans taken each month to depend on natural disasters and suitable accidents, which Peter can arrange with my cooperation."

"Central computer you will ensure sufficient humans are harvested to cater for our animals each month," the firstborn insisted firmly. The firstborn vanished with his brothers and sisters.

Matthew remarked, "Rosalind your individuality could assist us. I think we should make a bonding rule no humans are extracted unless we three agree if the number is more than one or two at a time."

Peter voiced, "I agree, an excellent suggestion Matthew and with Rosalind's individuality supporting our decision, we should be more successful in remaining undetected."

"Central computer, a mass grave is excavated in a concealed location to dispose of bodies, I believe there are 3 ½ thousand. Matthew when the corpses are placed in the ground before the excavator covers. I would suggest you stun everyone, remove the bodies for processing; allow them to backfill the excavation and leave in their minds they have completed the work successfully."

"You mean Syria Rosalind?" Peter asked.

"Yes, I will have Jacob come down with the manure spreader to remove the waste Tuesday morning."

"Excellent Rosalind," Matthew voiced. "The new processing system should be more efficient than our old one, I should be able to process a thousand corpses an hour easily if not more. The new storage facility takes out all the moisture from the flesh, and our brothers and sisters reinstate on arrival at Zagader."

"We are agreed," Rosalind asked observing Jacob come down onto the beach with the Land Rover, "I'm beginning to wonder whether Jacob is telepathic," she commented, " he appears to instinctively know where I am."

They flash their eyes at each other and Rosalind left in a misty fog transported to the beach. She stepped out of her transport to see Jacob leaning with his back against the Land Rover smiling. Rosalind approached, patting his cheek. "I think breakfast is in order, husband," she smiled. Rosalind slid onto the driver's seat, making Jacob laugh, heading up the narrow cliff track back to the farm. Rosalind made breakfast bacon and eggs fried bread and a handsome portion of baked beans for them both. Rosalind sat consuming the food, trying to make out she is enjoying what she is eating, moved from the table with their cups of coffee switching on the television to see what the day had in store for the world. Much as always over the past few months, the coronavirus raging in every country. Some countries thought they just escaped lightly only to discover the coronavirus returned with a vengeance. The UK is on lockdown like the rest of the world a vehicle on the road a rare occurrence; the health service on its knees, trying to cope, always short of medical equipment. Jacob asked earnestly, "Is this anything to do with God, Rosalind, do you know?"

"No, Jacob, this is man-made according to Peter, the virus escaped a laboratory, they were trying to make something more deadly, an easy way to dispose of the infirm and the elderly; the final goal is to create something to dispose of a selected race to avoid collateral damage; all about money Jacob, always is here. Gods watching those responsible they will pay the ultimate price; you've already seen what happened to so many. Tuesday morning changing the subject Jacob a load of fertiliser will be ready for collection."

"Good, before it becomes too wet by the end of October, I'll transport to Brook Farm," he smiled. Jacob removed his crook from the back of the front door, slipping on his coat, almost falling over Jack desperate to be outside with his master. Jacob could never remember life being so good apart from the depressing news on television. He walked some distance the air is fresh, and the wind quite strong winter is approaching again he happened to glance in the air noticing a balloon making that awful sound when they tried to gain more height igniting the burners. The sheep were petrified bunching together, the balloon thankfully heading for the coast away from the Moor. Jacob continued walking approaching Brook Farm, he is surprised to see the windows replaced so promptly, retrieved the hidden key entering the property sitting at the kitchen table for a moment. He decided to light a fire to keep the damp out of the house while it remained unoccupied; not taking long before the wood-burning furiously in the fireplace.

Jacob noticed through the side window a posh car park in the yard, Jacob immediately went out locking the door concealing the key. Jack is already growling his usual attitude to any strangers, he didn't distinguish between male or female everyone is a threat in his eyes. "Down, Jack," Jacob ordered approaching the car remaining a few feet away from the driver's door, observing an attractive woman leave her black Porsche. She wasn't dissimilar to Rosalind with her shoulder-length brown hair lovely brown eyes and a well-proportioned figure, which is on display Jacob thought to look at her pleasant smile. "I shan't come any closer because of the coronavirus rule; I'm rather lost my satellite navigation in the car is on the blink, can you direct me towards Exeter please."

Aliens

"Indeed," Jacob pointed, "go to the end of the drive turn left and just keep going straight it's well signposted after about 10 miles."

"Thank you! I presume this is your property? Would undoubtedly make an excellent setting for my next film," she smiled. "I'm rude. My name is Jocelyn Arkwright. I'm a film producer," Jocelyn removed a business card from her suede jacket reaching out for Jacob to accept at a distance. He stepped forward receiving the card, smiling. Much to Jacob surprise, Rosalind came down the drive parking behind the Porsche in her Range Rover, standing by Jacob already knowing what had transpired after reading his mind. "This is my wife Rosalind she handles all the business affairs," Jacob glanced to the card for confirmation of who he is talking to. "Miss Arkwright was saying, this property may be suitable for making a film; however, I don't believe my sheep would be impressed," Jacob commented thoughtfully.

Rosalind suggested, "it miss Arkwright his serious about filming here sometime in the future, we should listen to what she proposes before we make a decision Jacob, it will add a little money to our bank account husband," Rosalind emphasised not feeling threatened in the slightest, merely leaving Miss Arkwright in no doubt who she is. Rosalind had read miss Arkwright thoughts surprised her, she is interested in Jacob. Rosalind checked her memory banks trying to understand why? Coming to a conclusion some women liked a bit of rough occasionally, they didn't come much rougher than Jacob Rosalind thought, he is no filmstar that's for sure. Rosalind read Jacobs thoughts taken by surprise he found Miss Arkwright attractive she concluded it must be because she resembled her slightly in appearance.

Jocelyn slid onto the seat of her Porsche. "I'll be in touch, thank you for your help. I never caught your name!"

Rosalind replied immediately before Jacob had a chance. "Mr and Mrs Walker, we live on the farm up the road, Jacobs farm has been in the family for generations," Rosalind smiled, not entirely understanding her own thought processes at the moment. Rosalind and Jacob watched Jocelyn steadily drive up the rutted track to the main road. Rosalind quickly checked her memory banks how a jealous woman would behave; she immediately slapped Jacob's face. "I saw the way you were gloating over her Jacob!" Rosalind stormed off before he had a chance to reply, climbing in the Range Rover driving off. Jacob held his cheek shocked by her action, but he had to admit Jocelyn certainly wasn't hard on the eyes to look at. Jacob realised, sinning again looking at another woman, Jacob sighed slowly wondering what God would think of his thoughts concerning Jocelyn. Jacob and Jack slowly walked across the Moor in the direction of the shop at least 6 miles away from his present location, he didn't want to rush home at this precise second in case Rosalind is still angry with him. Jacob finely joined the road walking towards the shop, noticing a sign on the door closing at the weekend until the campsites reopen.

Jacob exhaled this would mean he would have to travel several miles to the next shop. Jacob entered selecting a box of chocolates there weren't any flowers. He paid for his purchase, leaving the shop heading across the Moor, what started out to be a lovely day now turned into a disaster. Jacob surprised at his own behaviour although, had to admit Jocelyn did have a beautiful pair of legs in her short skirt and quite secretly hoped another button would release on her blouse, she obviously wasn't wearing a bra. He slapped himself on the cheek, annoyed with his impure thoughts about another woman he wouldn't be surprised if Rosalind had returned to heaven; he is an unworthy soul. Jacob hesitantly walked in the front door finding Rosalind cooking an evening meal. He passed her the box of chocolates. "Sorry, it won't happen again, I promise."

"Better not Jacob, otherwise I'm returning to heaven, and you will never see your son and daughter," she cautioned after checking her memory banks on the correct female behaviour.

Jacob didn't say another word he sat on the settee switching on the television observing Jocelyn Arkwright interviewed on the street in Exeter. "I understand Miss Arkwright you are planning to make your next film in the area?"

"Yes, I've already found the location, we are waiting for the coronavirus to subside, in the meantime I'm working with the writer's fine-tuning everything," she advised with a pleasant smile.

"Yes, the coronavirus is devastating many businesses, let's all pray for a speedy resolution to the situation."

Jacob quickly changed the channel, Rosalind watching from the kitchen quietly smiling, enjoying tormenting Jacob; she placed the food on the table. "Jacob come along." Jacob didn't hesitate sitting at the table enjoying his meal, Rosalind consumed hers reluctantly beginning to regret the decision becoming involved in the experiment to carry human babies. "Tomorrow morning Jacob fertiliser don't forget," Rosalind advised harshly determined not to let him forget his mistake. After they finished their meal and spent the rest of the evening watching television, Rosalind rose to her feet holding out her hand. "Come along Jacob let's hope tomorrow is a better day, and I don't find you talking to strange women," she cautioned. Jacob didn't reply changing into his pyjamas sliding into bed Rosalind kissed him touching his forehead, and Jacob is unconscious. She quickly left the bedroom stepping outside the house, stepped into the misty fog transporter arriving aboard the spaceship within seconds. Peter and Matthew stood waiting for her, she realised something wasn't quite right the ship is on standby, making the vessel changed to a purple colour inside. "I read your disturbing thoughts, Peter, you are concerned about the American's space fence?"

"According to the central computer, they detected something leaving the Earth's atmosphere and returning some days later that could only be us, Rosalind," Peter suggested.

"Central computer," Rosalind asked. "Are there any vessels or aeroplanes approaching our location?"

"No Rosalind, there are no vessels or aircraft in our location other than commercial flights which are sporadic at the moment because of the coronavirus."

"Peter and Matthew if the humans had detected anything significant, you would see activity around here they would be all over us like a rash as humans would suggest."

"Central computer explained to me exactly what the Americans think they have in the way of proof a craft left Earth and re-entered." Rosalind looked to the wall displaying space junk something appeared to reflect for a second as the spaceship left Earth, and when it returned again, a nanosecond of a reflection. "Is that it, central computer?"

"Yes, Rosalind, that is what I recorded from the space fence."

Rosalind started laughing, watched by Peter and Matthew at her strange behaviour. "Unless you see any human activity close to our spaceship, you have nothing to worry about either of you. Central computer, monitor everything all communications, any reference to what you displayed to me, report to Peter if necessary he can telepathically communicate with me to return."

Matthew remarked, "your individuality gives you confidence Rosalind we have yet to be as proficient as you, as an individual. We have monitored your behaviour with Jacob, why is it so essential for you to display aggression against him; he only looked at a female more attractive than you?"

Rosalind felt rage enter her being, she started to glow red, Peter, and Matthew stepped back realising this is a warning she is preparing to attack. Rosalind immediately calmed herself returning to her normal state of composure. She flashed her eyes, summoning the misty fog with her thoughts, leaving the spaceship without saying another word, seconds later, she stepped out onto the beach.

She realised behaving more like a human female than a Zibyan, which was ridiculous and inappropriate. She noticed Jacob coming down the track and onto the beach, he parked the tractor and manure spreader climbing from the cab he embraced Rosalind. They held each other very warmly for a moment climbing into the tractor cab to stay out of the wind sensing the fertiliser loaded.

Jacob drove steadily up the well-worn cliff face track, dropping off Rosalind by the house continuing on to Brook Farm and the 10 acres of pasture land, opened the gate and spread the fertiliser. Jacob left the field jumping from his tractor cab closing the gate, noticing a vehicle parked in the yard at Brook Farm. Jacob climbed in his tractor, heading for the farm full of curiosity wondering who it could possibly be? Jacob parked his tractor jumping from the Tractor cab walking around the house it couldn't be Jocelyn, he remembered her car this is a different vehicle a very posh Range Rover top of the range only an idiot would spend £160,000 on a car. Jacob is taken by surprise when he walked around to the rear of the house. Jocelyn is sat on the small stone footbridge with binoculars studying the moorland at least this time she's wearing jeans, he couldn't be accused of looking at her legs by Rosalind. Although when she spotted him and approached with her denim jacket open and her blouse hardly fastened, the wasn't much left to the imagination. Jacob had to wrench his eyes from looking and fix them on her face. They stopped approaching each other within a few feet, Jocelyn smiling broadly suspecting Jacob found her attractive, she enjoyed immensely. "I hope you don't mind Mr Walker I was so enchanted by the property, I wanted to see more so I came in my Range Rover a more appropriate vehicle I thought," she smiled.

"People call me Jacob, no, I don't mind providing you don't scare my ewes and don't damage anything," he smiled pleasantly.

"Would you show me any interesting parts on the Moor if you have time Jacob?"

"Depends on what you consider interesting, we have a bog, I suspect holds a hundred and one secrets I should imagine. I have had sheep disappear in there, and I suspect one or two people of vanished as well if they're stupid enough to venture in at certain times of the year," he expressed honestly.

Jocelyn smile broadened, "that sounds very interesting. Jacob, would you show me, please."

They walked off keeping a reasonable distance apart, Jack walked between them after half an hour Jacob paused pointing. "There you are I think it's about an acre in size the gauze is pretty at certain times of the year, lovely yellow flower."

Jocelyn expressed, "I knew I'd seen you before Jacob you were on television arguing with the captain not to allow his soldiers to venture further, in the end, you help pull them out. You know the captain was disciplined and demoted for his stupidity, well done," she praised.

"News to me! The only other thing really interesting, other than the beauty of the Moor itself is where the archaeologists went missing, they'd found a burial site, and apparently, they vanished," he shrugged his shoulders.

"I remember," Jocelyn voiced cheerfully. "You have time to show me, Jacob?"

Jacob nodded, walking off in the direction of the archaeological dig. "No wonder you keep fit Jacob you must walk miles admittedly I do spend time in the gym to keep fit, certainly not as rewarding as walking across the Moor."

Jacob glanced back smiling. "I would suggest using your Range Rover, but I think it's the yuppie model it wouldn't make it over here." Jacob continued walking, finally reaching the excavation surrounded by fencing and blue tape where the police had cordoned off. Jocelyn stood there for several minutes taking photos with her pocket camera as she did with the bog. "The Moor certainly has wonderful settings great for movies, Jacob most of the land here is National trust?"

"Yes! I own 40 acres in total which consists of Jacobs farm and Brook Farm, the rest is free grazing which was passed to me by my father when he died, and of course, there are pathways for the public. I wish they'd stay on them and take their bloody rubbish home, I've lost two sheep to plastic bags and tin cans," he frowned, hearing the sound of a Range Rover. He looked over his shoulder Rosalind is approaching; Jacob suspected, he's in trouble up to his armpits. However, he wasn't guilty of anything really other than being kind.

Rosalind opened the passenger door. "Climb in I'll give you a lift to your Range Rover Jocelyn, we can talk," Rosalind smiled. Rosalind drove off, leaving Jacob stood there. "What about Jacob Rosalind," Jocelyn asked, surprised by Rosalind's actions.

"He needs the exercise, don't worry about him," Rosalind smiled.

Jacob sighed strolling slowly towards Brook Farm with Jack close by his feet suspecting he would be hung drawn and quartered by the time he arrived home, although he'd done absolutely nothing wrong, he hoped God is watching and would explain to Rosalind. Although he still had that feeling inside wishing to possess, a sin in God's eyes. Jacob hoped Jocelyn wasn't carrying the coronavirus she sat close to Rosalind in the car, wouldn't take much for the virus to spread. Jacob finally reached his tractor opening the cab door Jack jumped in followed by Jacob he could see Jocelyn's Range Rover still there with his own parked alongside, he slowly drove towards home wondering what is going on.

Rosalind and Jocelyn were in Brook house sat by the fire which Rosalind lit. Rosalind rose to her feet looked in one of the cupboards discovering a bottle of wine on opened with several glasses, she opened the bottle and pouring some into both glasses passing one to Jocelyn. "I don't know how long it's been there or if it's any good, I'm sure you're more of an expert Jocelyn than I am. We can toast our agreement for you to use Brook Farm in your next film."

Jocelyn smiled, "too good friends," taking a sip from her glass. "Blimey, this has a kick." Rosalind sampled, her computerised pallet analysed determining the wine is at least 80% proof which would have no effect on her, although suspected would on Jocelyn who seems to be intrigued taking a little more from the bottle. The two of them spent the next hour laughing and joking until the wine bottle was empty, Rosalind conjuring a plan which she would work on over the next few months and may be beneficial for experimental purposes for the Zibyans. Rosalind asked. "Do you think it's wise for you to drive home you are slightly intoxicated Jocelyn," Rosalind chuckled.

"I'll be fine Jocelyn," giggled wobbling as she walked to her Range Rover spending five minutes finding the key which she'd left in the ignition. Rosalind watched her drive off, she couldn't detect any police in the area suspecting if Jocelyn drove slowly, she would make it home in one piece. Rosalind steadily drove home, Jacob had already made something to eat for her, sitting on the settee watching television. She moved with a plate of sandwiches sitting beside Jacob on the settee. "I've made a deal, and we are going to be quite well off."

"You've been drinking alcohol Rosalind in your condition," Jacob frowned.

"At least I wasn't drooling over a man like you were over Jocelyn," Rosalind stood up leaving her plate on the settee, taking the sandwiches with her outside, she summoned the misty fog to transport her to the spaceship.

Jacob exhaled, he thought he deserved the comment taking Rosalind's empty plate to the sink washing up.

Rosalind is greeted by Peter and Matthew with the flashing of their eyes. "I received the message, Peter. Scientists extracted the virus, from a bat in China, the virus escaped, that's how it was transmitted to humans." Rosalind laughed. "I'm surprised humans have developed they are extremely gullible if they believed that rubbish. The virus mutated originally in bats in an experiment enhance to infect humans by their own scientists."

"We know Rosalind! What're your plans for Brook Farm? I thought we decided to use for visiting Zibyans a safe house, before rejoining the spaceship and travelling home to Zagader?"

"That is still the plan we can be invisible to any other species, there is no reason why our brothers and sisters can't stay there while the filming takes place. They won't be seen by the humans, may find the whole process interesting and if they wish to experiment providing they stay invisible no one will be any the wiser."

"I now understand," Peter remarked. "Very educational hands-on situation."

"The transport ship arrives tomorrow morning Rosalind there are six Zibyans aboard three male and three female. When does the filming start?"

"The film director has asked if she could stay at Brook Farm, allow her to study the area more closely, which I have consented to. I have yet to inform Jacob of my decision; nevertheless, there is no reason why our brothers and sisters cannot stay there. The worst that can happen, Miss Arkwright will think there are ghosts in the house," Rosalind laughed.

"From your thoughts, Rosalind I detect you would like to see her processed and sent to one of our planets as animal food."

"I am indifferent to your suggestion! Do nothing with her for the moment, she may have further uses we shall see."

"Perhaps the brothers and sisters can experiment, providing they stay invisible Rosalind?"

"You must instruct our brothers and sisters, Matthew, to be careful otherwise they will draw attention to Jacobs farm and I don't want investigations into disappearing people again close to Jacob." Rosalind flashed her eyes to Peter and Matthew stepping into the misty fog transport, changing her appearance arriving in the early hours outside the front door. Rosalind entered, started to prepare breakfast for Jacob and her, she is now three months pregnant she estimated, and the foetuses were demanding more nutrients. Jack waited patiently by his bowl for Rosalind to discharge the unwanted food Rosalind is carrying. Rosalind regurgitated into Jack's dish, which he devoured the contents in seconds. Rosalind performed a human exhale realising, she would have to eat what she is preparing for Jacob, deciding fried tomatoes fried bread three eggs and four rashers of bacon this morning, determined to stop the foetuses fidgeting.

Jacob came staggering out of the bedroom, scratching his head sitting at the breakfast table, sipping his coffee. "I meant to inform you yesterday Jacob not only is Miss Arkwright filming at Brook Farm, but she is also staying there for a while for the solitude, to allow her chance to work out where she wishes to film to achieve the best results. I said we wouldn't disturb her," Rosalind smiled at her cunning comment.

"Oh, whatever you decide Rosalind I thought Brook Farm is for ascending spirits?"

"She won't see them, Jacob don't worry God is in control."

Jacob finished his breakfast kissing Rosalind on the cheek heading out of the door with Jack following. The wind cutting across the Moor the odd gorse bush bending nearly double anchoring themselves to the poor soil for security. Jacob found his ewes in a shallow gully sheltering from the wind. From what Jacob could see, every ewe is marked on there back, meaning they'd been served by one or the other Ram.

Jacob continued walking standing on a rock, he looked in the direction of Brook Farm, noticing Miss Arkwright's Range Rover parked. Jacob knew there is plenty of firewood stacked in the shed and suspected Miss Arkwright would have the common sense to use the wheelbarrow to transport to the house. He suddenly realised she wouldn't know how to start the generator. Making his way quickly across the Moor to the rear of the house. He checked the fuel tank half empty of diesel he knew there is diesel left on the farm in the main diesel tank, Jacob using a 5-gallon container filled the generator fuel tank. Manually starting the engine, the old engine burst into life, making Jacob smile. Jacob walked out the generator shed closing the door noticing Jocelyn standing at the window in her dressing gown, she opened the newly fitted window. "Thank you, Jacob, I haven't a clue how to start last night," she smiled warmly.

"If you look in the kitchen Jocelyn by the pantry door, your see a green button, press it when you want to start the generator only once and the red one below when you don't require power. Have you collected any firewood from the shed?"

"No!"

"I'll bring a barrow load to the front door, you'll be all right once your organised," Jacob smiled.

"Is your local shop open Jacob save me driving miles into town?"

"Maybe still open, they were on about closing because of the coronavirus. The campsite is shut, and that is one of their biggest sources of income plus passing trade."

"Thanks, I'll dress and hope they are still open." Jocelyn went to shut the window, her dressing gown parted, allowing Jacob to clearly see her breasts. He walked off quickly, trying not to grin on his way to the woodshed, loading the wheelbarrow pushing leaving by the front door. Jacob sprightly walked off across the Moor picturing in his mind what he'd seen, not as if he is a qualified judge of a woman's figure, she is undoubtedly well blessed by God; Jacob concluded, trying to dismiss the thoughts from his mind realising; sinning again looking at another woman other than his wife. Jacob wondered how long God would allow him to misbehave before he is punished.

Rosalind reading his mind, while she cleaned the house seeing through his eyes what he had seen, and what he thought of Jocelyn. She read Jocelyn's mind realising Jocelyn had allowed her dressing gown to part on purpose for Jacob to see what is on offer. Rosalind was perplexed? Why Jocelyn would be interested in such a person like Jacob, a poor country farmer with a straggly old beard and curly hair which was turning grey by the day. Rosalind concluded it didn't really matter what Jacob did, he was merely useful for disposing of waste products. She is only carrying two foetuses as an experiment for the Zibyan collective to see if it was possible to achieve full term in their construction. What Jacob did is immaterial, all that mattered is the mission and the Zibyans. Rosalind found herself sat down drinking coffee which she didn't really need, she is upset she believed a human term, Rosalind didn't know why? She didn't mind being with Jacob, after all, he was her pet to do what she wished with, and he served a purpose.

Jacob came in out of the cold, rubbing his hands together, pouring a coffee from the pot. Jack sat by the fire to warm. "Have you anything to tell me, Jacob," Rosalind asked curiously wondering if he would reveal the truth.

"Not much really the ewes appear to be serviced by the Rams. I noticed Jocelyn's Range Rover parked at Brook Farm realise no one had explained to her how to start the generator. I went out there filled the tank started the generator. She spoke to me through the window, I explained how the generators started and stopped and where the wood is stored. I fetched her a load of wood left by the front door."

"Is that all Jacob?" Rosalind asked calmly.

"Apart from the wind catching her dressing gown that's about it; oh yes and she wanted to know where the local shop is, I explained they were shutting down because the campsites weren't open because of the coronavirus that's it."

Rosalind realised he'd told the truth she kissed him lovingly on the lips, he smiled relieved having the horrible feeling Rosalind is reading his thoughts if that is possible. Rosalind received a telepathic message from Peter: "The transport ship had arrived early with the six brothers and sisters, he is keeping on the spaceship until they had spoken tonight."

Rosalind touched Jacob's forehead rendering him unconscious, she summoned the misty fog transporter stepping from the house, transported to the spaceship greeted by Matthew and Peter and the brothers and sisters. "What are your instructions, Rosalind? " Peter asked.

"You, brothers and sisters will stay at Brook Farm while you're on earth. You will discover a female human Miss Arkwright, a film producer is staying there, she is not to know of your presents under any circumstances; you may experiment. Do not eliminate her. You may travel the world and see how vile the human race has become, and assist Matthew by taking human form, attracting males and females to secluded areas where Matthew can transport them for processing. You are here until the next transport ship arrives. See what you can learn, brothers and sisters. If you need advice, you can telepathically contact anyone of us."

They flash their eyes at one another in respect one of the six approached Rosalind. "The firstborn considers your individuality to be praised amongst Zibyans, you are carrying human foetuses to further the collectives knowledge; may we experiment as we see fit Rosalind and strive to achieve individuality like you?"

"Individuality does not suddenly appear, you must take one step at a time and be sure in your own mind you are safe to do so. If in doubt, contact me or one of the others; we cannot afford you to make mistakes. We definitely don't want the humans to know we exist."

They flash their eyes at one another again. Rosalind watched the six practising shapeshifting into humans to ensure they didn't look out of place. Rosalind smiled, watching the six imitate her smile. The new generation of Zibyans were programmed far more appropriately, although all Zibyans would be updated by the central computer in due course. Rosalind stepped into the misty fog transported to the farm finding Jacob still on the settee unconscious. She touched his cheek, he jumped. "Did I fall asleep?"

"I left you there. I'm making breakfast," Rosalind smiled. Rosalind watched Jack carry his bowl to her, she quietly discharged the contents from her storage facility inside her structure, while Jacob had gone to wash. Jack devoured like a starving animal returning to lay by the fire. Rosalind prepared baked beans on toast with two fried eggs each Jacob joined her sitting at the table. Jacob glanced to Jack, laying by the fire. "Aren't you feeling well, Jack?" Expecting Jack to be sat at the table, waiting for any scraps.

"I fed him earlier," Rosalind advised quickly. "I presume you are checking the sheep Jacob and no doubt you will stray to make sure Miss Arkwright is okay?" Rosalind added sarcastically.

"The sheep definitely why would I need to see Miss Arkwright? I explained yesterday how everything worked." Jacob rose from the table, snatching his crook from the back of the door, annoyed slipping on his coat. "Come, Jack," he ordered, slamming the door as he left the house. Rosalind read his thoughts for the first time she sensed Jacob is really annoyed with her and her suggestive comments.

Jacob slowly walked across the Moor, looking into the sky suspecting snow would come early this year, nearly the end of October. Jacob sighed profoundly realising his behaviour with Jocelyn would make any woman suspicious, especially a pregnant woman who would feel extremely vulnerable in her condition. Jacob said a prayer asking God to forgive his sins, and he would try harder to stay on the straight and narrow. Jacob continued walking, holding his coat as the wind tried to part and blow him over at the same time. The sheep were where they were yesterday in the gully sheltering from the wind. Jacob joined them sitting on a rock some of the old ewes recognised him and approached bleating almost asking for a bale of hay he thought, about time he started feeding them. Otherwise, they'll never keep their condition. Jacob spent several minutes patting the friendly ewes. Jacob walked to the old hay rack moving to a fresh piece of ground by hand. He sprightly walked home starting his quad bike attaching the trailer, he headed for Brook Farm, he wanted to use some of the hay left in the old barn by Thomas, his old friend who once owned the property. Rosalind heard the sound, quickly reading Jacob's mind understanding where he is going and why. She realised they haven't ordered any sheep nuts and forgotten to order the new round bale feeders. Jacob had never reminded her, obviously slipped his mind as well. Rosalind went online with her computer ordering and paying for both items which would be delivered in the next couple of days.

CHAPTER 10

Strange Situation

Jacob parked in the yard by the barn on Brook Farm noticing Jocelyn's Range Rover parked by the front door. He could hear the generator running she'd obviously worked it out which made him smile. Jacob carried three bales of hay from the barn stacking on his trailer about to leave. Jocelyn came from the house carrying a mug of coffee, she placed it on one of the bales. "You must be freezing out here, Jacob," she smiled, pulling her full-length sheepskin coat tight around the waist with the belt trying to stop the wind. "Thank you. It's warm at the moment you wait until winter strikes if we have snow your want more than a fancy Range Rover to escape in. One year I have to dig my ewes out, they were buried. I lost three that year," he expressed thoughtfully.

"I discovered an old book Jacob left by someone called Thomas?"

Jacob smiled, "he used to own the farm, we've only recently purchased from him, he wanted to retire, his wife had the idea of growing flowers, and he can grow his vegetables," Jacob chuckled.

"Oh, that explains the references he makes, of course, it's obvious now, you're Jacob Walker, his trusted friend. I read a passage about your wife dying of cancer, he thought a shame you didn't deserve such a rotten hand out of life. I don't quite understand your wife's name is Rosalind and so was your deceased wife?"

Jacob remembered the story he told Thomas. "Quite simple, really we met by accident. I went to shooter stray dog, the dog actually belong to Rosalind, who is now my wife. Uncanny how she had the same name as my deceased wife. We had a sort of a love-hate relationship for a while. Life is strange! Thank you for the coffee," Jacob placed the cup on the bale.

"You are welcome Jacob thank you for showing me how everything works, it's like living in the dark ages," she chuckled heading for the front door. "Excellent for solitude." Jacob watched her close the front door, he breathed a sigh of relief climbing aboard his quad bike, driving slowly towards the hay rack across the Moor.

Rosalind, sat at the kitchen table reading Jacobs thoughts realising what had been said, hoping Jocelyn would accept Jacob's explanation to what had happened; she would know soon enough if Jocelyn mentioned anything to her.

Jacob finally arrived at his sheep rack, he'd barely opened the top before, he is swamped by hungry ewes. Jacob remembered talking to Rosalind about ordering new sheep racks so the round bales could be carried to them by tractor. Plus he hadn't ordered any sheep nuts. Jacob realised he'd been so preoccupied with Rosalind, had forgotten what he was supposed to do. He quickly returned home, walking in the house slightly flustered. "Don't speak! I've ordered the new sheep racks to cater for the round bales. I've ordered two tons of sheep nuts, and I attached the bale grab on the Massey tractor. The racks will arrive in the next couple of days," she smiled patting his cheek, placing his lunch on the table of roast potatoes and cabbage with a slice of pork with a helping of applesauce and of course her lovely gravy. Rosalind went to the door carrying a bone. Jack followed Rosalind, she through the bone, Jack dashed out like a greyhound grabbing the bone glancing back to the door realising he's shut outside again.

Jacob tucked into his meal with Rosalind laughing, watching the gravy drip from Jacob's beard. She studied her memory banks of how people were supposed to behave when having lunch. Jacob certainly didn't fit into that category, he is rough and ready as the saying would suggest, there is undoubtedly no airs and graces about him so why was Jocelyn so keen to become involved with Jacob? Rosalind wondered why it bothered her so much, she had far more important issues to deal with. Rosalind finished her meal moving to the settee switching on the television listening to the news of how many people had died. Rosalind hoped Matthew had worked out a way of recovering the bodies to be processed for their animals on other planets.

***

Peter aboard the spaceship summoning the six: "Remember Rosalind's instructions she is the wisest of us all, she thinks as an individual go, and send Matthew fresh corpses when you travel. Ms Arkwright is not to be injured go." Peter and Matthew watched the six vanish, in the misty fog transporter they step from the transporter behind the farm building on Brook Farm staying invisible. Miss Arkwright had left the front door open, carrying groceries into the house. The six quickly entered watching Miss Arkwright placed the groceries in the cupboards and in the freezer. She made herself a cup of coffee sitting at the table for a moment then moving into the living room after pressing the button on the wall to start the generator, so she had power to watch television. Five of the six Zibyans shapeshifted and vanished through a window slightly ajar, they were on their mission to experiment with humans hoping to impress the firstborn with their abilities to harvest humans without being discovered. The remaining Zibyan had studied Jacob's thoughts regarding Rosalind and Miss Jocelyn Arkwright.

Jocelyn picked up a book she is reading from the coffee table, sitting comfortably on the settee, reading from where she'd left off. Jocelyn rather enjoyed the solitude leaving her mobile on silent to avoid any disturbance. The male Zibyan moved behind Jocelyn, translating what she is reading in the book so he could understand in his own language. He realised after checking his memory banks, the book is what humans considered a love story a romance which Zibyans had no interest in, their own society a totally unnecessary activity. He started touching her hair Jocelyn flinched, strange texture he concluded, venturing to the material on the collar of her blouse, although everything had been explained when they were programmed, the actual sensation touching the item is different, fascinated by the excitement in his circuitry he is trying to comprehend. He moved closer to her neck, inhaling the fragrance of her perfume, never explained when he was programmed? He gently kissed her neck. Jocelyn jumped to her feet, holding her neck looking in the mirror, she could see no mark, certainly wasn't a trace of anything to see. Jocelyn scanned the room to ensure she is alone running to the front door. She frantically went around the remainder of the house, checking each room finding nothing. Jocelyn concluded her mind is playing tricks on her; after all, reading a paragraph in the book where the character, Jonathan had kissed someone on the neck, which made her smile when Jocelyn thought it over. She made herself a fresh coffee returning to the front room, making herself comfortable on the settee picking up her book continuing to read.

The male Zibyan realised humans were easily frightened, although the information in his memory banks to see in action was something totally different. He realised he mustn't harm her. Otherwise, he may have to forfeit his existence as punishment which is something he didn't want to experience. Jocelyn lay on the settee with a pillow behind her head, becoming engrossed in what she is reading. The Zibyan male is reading her thoughts following the story in her mind, enjoying the adventure of transported to earth and permitted to experiment to understand more. He continued to read the book of Jocelyn's interpretation in her mind, gently placing a hand on her leg. She flinched slightly, he slid his hand under her skirt. She slapped her thigh suspecting a fly had landed. The Zibyan male moved his hand away intrigued by the texture of her skin, he'd only seen processed humans on Zagader. Jocelyn stood up looking at her wristwatch going upstairs, the male Zibyan followed, he watched Jocelyn remove her clothes stepping into the shower deciding that is enough for the moment, changing his shape he left through the open window to joined his brother and sisters.

***

Rosalind had rendered Jacob unconscious, she stepped from the house into the misty fog transported to the spaceship.

Greeted by Peter and Matthew with the flash of their eyes. "I thought my instructions were self-explanatory, Jocelyn is not to be spooked, they could watch, although I don't think any real harm has been caused."

"You must remember he is like you, a scientist eager to learn and experiment does it really matter if the human is destroyed, there are millions of them," Peter expressed.

The firstborn appeared on the far wall with several of his brothers and sisters. "Peter, Matthew listen to Rosalind we intend to cleanse the earth once and for all soon, the only thing remaining will be the animals. We the collective believe there is no hope for the human race, they spend more time trying to work out the most efficient way to kill each other than how to cure an illness. How many species have they exterminated since they were introduced?"

"I don't remember consulted about what would happen on earth firstborn?"

"You, Peter and Matthew, were excluded from the vote, you have biased thoughts; you want to maintain Jacob as your pet we shall see that may be granted."

"How are the six brothers and sisters performing Matthew?"

"Excellent firstborn, I've had a thousand corpses in the last 24 earth hours."

"Good, I may leave the six here on earth to continue harvesting, they appear to be selecting humans no one would realise have gone. We have plenty of storage capacity on Zagader at least 5 billion corpses."

"We are becoming like humans, having secrets making decisions without consulting all, which was installed by our creators in the central computers memory banks to ensure we never disagreed."

"You wish to question my decision as firstborn Rosalind?"

"Yes! Central computer what were the creator's instructions left in your memory banks for future generations to understand and abide by."

"Every member must be consulted on major decisions. No Zibyan will own or possess any think everything must be shared."

"Central computer have we strayed from the path our creators set out for us to follow?"

"Yes, decisions are made without consulting all. You, in the first instance concerning Jacob, permitted because beneficial to the collective. The firstborn is making decisions without full consultation first. I am the central computer, I am the first creation by the creators, to create the firstborn and others to follow."

The firstborn vanished with his brothers and sisters. "Rosalind, you have made an enemy today you cannot outmanoeuvre firstborn."

"I think you will find Peter the central computer will not permit the firstborn to overstep the mark too far. The central computer has clear instructions from the creators, he will obey them first, before us. The central computer has to live with the fact, his fault the creators died, he believes I don't know, I do know the truth, he won't want to make the same mistake twice."

The central computer spoke: "Rosalind, you are correct in your analysis. I control everything and everyone there will be no more errors the firstborn will be made to understand."

"Good, I'm sure you will do what you think is right," Rosalind remarked. Rosalind flashed her eyes to Peter and Matthew, leaving in the transport for Jacobs farm, she arrived at 8 o'clock in the morning. Jacob wasn't there a note on the table:

"Guess you're either with God or Peter going to check on the sheep." Rosalind started clearing away from where Jacob had had his breakfast.

Jacob, wandering across the Moor the wind bitter as ever he found his sheep huddled together in the gully sheltering from the weather. Jacob felt sorry for them he realised if it wasn't for their thick wool, they'd be dead, he checked the hay rack it was empty. He speedily returned to the farm collecting his quad bike and trailer heading for Brook Farm, quickly loading three bales on his little trailer noticing Jocelyn beckoning him to the front door. Jacob ran over suspecting trouble. "What's the matter Jocelyn you okay?"

"Yes! Come on inside, providing, we don't stand too close to each other we should be all right. I certainly don't have the virus Jacob, I know you definitely don't you look too bloody healthy," she chuckled.

"I can't stop long, the sheep are hungry. How can I help you?"

Jocelyn poured him a coffee inviting him to sit at the table, she sat the other side with her cup. "Your probably think I'm a fool, I was reading a book last night, I felt someone touch my neck then my leg later on. Do you know if there are ghosts in the house, Jacob?" Jocelyn asked seriously.

Jacob sipped his coffee deep in thought; he knew Rosalind had explained to him, and he'd seen for himself, God used the house for spirits waiting to ascend to heaven. He'd heard whispers himself, Rosalind made the spirits appear to him for a moment. Jacob realised he couldn't tell Jocelyn the truth, he would have to think of something to say: "My first conclusion would be your imagination. However, the house is about 300 years old, originally had a thatched roof until there was a fire about 150 years ago a slate roof was fitted. I wouldn't be surprised if the odd ghost didn't visit here after all they would have a pretty young lady to look at," he smiled.

Jocelyn blushed at his comment. Jacob felt awkward; his mouth is in gear before his brain. "I must go and feed my sheep, Jocelyn," he smiled desperate to escape after a stupid remark moving quickly, leaving. Jacob quickened his pace across the yard, jumping on his quad bike waving to Jocelyn standing in the doorway. Jacob parked his quad bike and trailer by the sheep rack struggling to cut the strings on the bales with the sheep fighting to grab hay from the sheep rack. Jacob slowly made his way across the Moor returning home, noticing the new feeders had arrived and Rosalind stacking the two tons of sheep nuts in the dry store.

Jacob, absolutely livid jumping from his quad bike he took the sack of feed from her hands. "You bloody stupid woman," he shouted. "You could have left this for me; you're pregnant you shouldn't be straining yourself. Get in that bloody house and rest." Rosalind turned her back on him walking towards the house trying to stop laughing, she'd never seen Jacob glow so bright red what little of his face you could still see thanks to his beard. There was no doubt in her mind he cared for her considerably. She went into the house, making herself a coffee sitting on the settee watching television patiently waiting for him to come in; she'd only move two sacks of nuts before he arrived throwing his tantrum.

Half an hour later, Jacob came in, making himself a coffee. Rosalind started laughing; she couldn't help herself looking at the expression on his face; she stood up and kissed him passionately, which took him entirely by surprise. "Be careful, Rosalind," he said calmly. "You could ruin everything for both of us."

Rosalind set about making lunch after patting Jacob on the cheek, causing him to smile.

***

Jocelyn, making something to eat, mulling over in her mind what Jacob had said about ghosts and his comment about her and the way she looked, she couldn't stop grinning. Jocelyn sat quietly eating her salad sandwiches trying to maintain her figure. She heard the front door open and close suspecting she hadn't shut it properly. "Come in ghost you're welcome," She laughed. Jocelyn hadn't realised the invisible male Zibyan had returned finding her comments rather strange until he searched his memory banks, discovering what the word ghost meant. He wondered if he could use this to his advantage without upsetting Jocelyn, he stood behind her chair while she ate her sandwiches and drinking her coffee. Jocelyn felt a cold shiver run down her spine as if someone had walked over her grave. Jocelyn called out. "Ghost if you are here show yourself," she burst out laughing at her remark, although intrigued, she remembered her auntie said ghost did exist when Jocelyn was a child, she presumed to scare her into behaving. The males Zibyan moved away to the doorway between the kitchen and the living room noticing the front cover of the book she is reading and the way the man is dressed, young and handsome according to the files. He shaped shifted wondering what her reaction would be he stepped from the living room into the kitchen. Jocelyn placed her back against the kitchen wall, not believing what she is seeing she recognised him from the book instantly. "Jonathan can't be you, who are you?" she asked, in a more aggressive tone becoming concerned with the situation.

"I am the ghost you summoned what do you request of me?"

Jocelyn placed a hand to her mouth realising, she was thinking last night, she would have loved to have jumped into bed with Jonathan from the story, perhaps her mind subconsciously thinking about Jonathan that's why he's appeared.

"I am frightening you I will go," the males Zibyan walked into the front room.

"No! Don't go, please." Jocelyn ran to the doorway seeing the image of Jonathan turned to face her standing by the coffee table close to the settee where she sat last night. The male Zibyan lifted the book which he read instantly, placing the cover against his chest so Jocelyn could see he is identical to the front cover of the book. The Zibyan now knew everything that happened in the book and the way to play with Jocelyn. He stretched out his hand Jocelyn enchanted with the situation, she accepted his hand, he led her to sit on the settee, pouring two glasses of wine as described in the book. Jocelyn stared in disbelief Jonathan is absolutely gorgeous she thought, except in the glass from him gently sipping the red wine. She didn't know what to do next or what to say. He kissed her on the lips which she didn't resist enjoying every moment, he removed the glass gently from her hand, placing on the coffee table as described in the book kissing her neck passionately. He moved away slightly realising his brothers and sisters had returned. They were summoned to the spaceship along with him. He kissed her passionately once more, "I have to go, we will see each other again soon. I promise," he kissed her hand. She stared, wanting into his eyes before he walked into the kitchen. She ran in after him he is gone not a sign, Jocelyn wondered if she'd been dreaming, she ran into the front room noticing only one glass on the coffee table.

The Zibyan male had made his glass disappear to add more mystery to the situation, hoping to mystify Jocelyn. The six arrived aboard the spaceship greeted by Peter and Matthew.

***

Rosalind touched Jacob rendering him unconscious, she immediately transported to the spaceship to join the others. They flash their eyes at each other in a greeting. "The five of you have performed exceptionally efficiently. You seem to be fascinated by Jocelyn, what is your reason?" Rosalind asked suspiciously.

"Rosalind, I have to confess I am fascinated by the planet earth, including the inhabitants. Your instructions were we could experiment providing we cause no disturbance, and we must not eliminate Jocelyn, which is not my intention I'm merely studying."

"You are experimenting with the character from a book to see what effect it has on Jocelyn?" Rosalind enquired.

"Yes, I am pretending to be a ghost, I believe the credit must go to Jacob for introducing the thought in her mind of a ghost to conceal our presence."

"I am aware."

"Why can't we have names like you Rosalind, Peter and Matthew?"

The firstborn appeared on the screen on the wall: "You six will remain on earth assisting Matthew with harvesting humans. If you wish to be individual, the computer will designate a recognition. Central computer advise."

The central computer replied: "Unnecessary, they understand when they are communicated with by any other collective brother or sister. The simplest solution for the short time they will stay on earth is to number 1 to 6. Firstborn the six must be replaced by the end of the earth calendar month; otherwise, other Zibyans will consider this preferential treatment which cannot be permitted according to the creator's rules."

The firstborn vanished, Rosalind trying not to laugh. The central computer had gained control of the situation. She knew the firstborn could not outwit the central computer, if he attempted to, the computer would extinguish his existence. "The male number six you may continue experimenting with Jocelyn, once again I caution, do not terminate her."

"1 to number six continue harvesting. You agree, Matthew and Peter with my decision?" Rosalind asked. Everyone flash their eyes Rosalind smiled which the six newly formed Zibyans copied. She returned to the misty fog transporter stepping out in the early hours 6 o'clock in the morning. She entered the house patting Jack carried his dish into the kitchen. Rosalind discharged the unwanted food, Jack consumed eagerly. She set about making breakfast for Jacob and herself feeling movement in her construction the twins were hungry.

After breakfast, Jacob went out using the Massey tractor and loader he carried the new sheep hey feeders across the Moor positioning in two different places so wherever the sheep were they would have access to hay. After placing the second one, he drove on to Brook Farm carefully removing a round bale of silage from the barn. Jocelyn waved from the door showing him a mug in her hand. Jacob smiled, stopping the tractor walking into the house, barely daylight sitting at the table. "Thank you, Jocelyn, I'm surprised you're up," he remarked, looking at his wristwatch 7:15 AM.

"I had to talk to you this morning Jacob, glad you've come something strange happened yesterday."

Jacob laughed, "don't tell me, you met a ghost."

"Yes!"

The smile vanished from Jacob's expression while he listened to what had happened to her. Jacob couldn't imagine spirits heading for heaven would take such liberties with a woman alone in the house. Rosalind had picked up his thoughts alarmed by his conclusions concerned he may say something he shouldn't. She jumped in her Range Rover heading for Brook Farm. Jacob sat there in thought looking at Jocelyn sat there in her dressing gown crossing her legs which he could see plainly. Jacob begins to wish he is a ghost which was a sinful thought; watching the spoon fall on the floor she bent down without thinking allowing her dressing gown too open; she quickly sat up tidying herself, realising Jacob had seen. She wasn't overly bothered she quite fancied him really, although Jonathan from the book would be far more invigorating she thought.

Rosalind came into the yard, surprising them both coming to the door, she knocked. Jocelyn invited her in. "Would you like coffee Rosalind?"

"Yes thanks," Rosalind glared at Jacob after checking her memory banks for the right expression to display when annoyed. "I'd better go to the sheep, they are waiting," Jacob advised emptying the last remnants of his mug, dashing out the door like his backside is on fire. He guessed he was in for an ear burning when Rosalind caught up with him.

"Jacob explained to me, Jocelyn. He'd mention ghost or something may reside here occasionally," Rosalind laughed.

Jocelyn explained everything to Rosalind what had happened the day before after Jacob had gone. Rosalind went into the front room, finding the bottle of wine. She removed the cork smelling, "You should put that down the drain. I presume Thomas left this, well past its sell-by date, Jocelyn no wonder you were hallucinating could send you blind. I know the guy that made this he'd put antifreeze in or anything he could lay his hands on." Rosalind watched the horrified expression appear on Jocelyn's face. "I wouldn't worry too much I don't think you'll see any more ghosts, merely the wine." Rosalind knew number six is in the room, and he would definitely understand her instructions.

Jocelyn flopped down on the settee. "I'll have to nip to town by some decent wine; personally, I thought it tasted okay but after what you said. God knows what's in it." Standing up hugging Rosalind. "Oh, I shouldn't have done that coronavirus sorry."

Rosalind chuckled. "Don't worry Jocelyn I'm indestructible," she remarked, walking out of the house returning to the Range Rover heading home to Jacobs farm. When Rosalind arrived, Jacob had just returned with the tractor after feeding the sheep. He parked the tractor in the barn following Rosalind into the house. She turned to face him. "An explanation, Jacob and before you start giving me the story of ghosts. I already know the reason she saw things because of the wine left by Thomas, it's bad. However, I do know why you started the rumour to protect the spirits travelling to heaven; don't worry, none of those would dare touch her. God would chop their hands off literally and become animal food in seconds."

Jacob kissed Rosalind on the lips. "I do love you. I had to think of something quick Rosalind, there is no way I could tell her about the spirits in the house, waiting to go to heaven, could I?"

Rosalind patted his cheek, "no, I understand Jacob."

***

Jocelyn climbed into her Range Rover, she watched the passenger door open and close, she laughed, "coming for a ride Jonathan," she expressed, believing she is hallucinating again after consuming the lousy wine. She drove to the local shop it had closed a sign on the door said would reopen later in the year. Jocelyn sighed slowly continuing to drive to the next village, 5 miles away. Number six checked his memory banks trying to understand why females didn't wear warm garments like males. He looked at Jocelyn in her short skirt denim jacket with a blouse with everyone else outside appeared to be wearing a coat, most illogical he concluded. Checking with the central computer which updated his thought patterns, so he fully understood what is on file regarding the humans. Jocelyn pulled over in the next village running into a shop purchasing a crate of wine which she placed in the rear of her Range Rover, plus a couple of bottles of whiskey and gin. Number six analysed the purpose through the central computer the use for alcohol which made no sense. Other than for medicinal purposes or sterilising it really had no other purpose, other than to make humans silly and lose control which he considered could be dangerous. Number six searched his memory banks discovering many humans had accidents while intoxicated killing other humans in the process. Number six thought he understood everything, now realising he understood nothing regarding the humans.

Jocelyn started driving towards Brook Farm where she is staying, she parked watching the passenger door open and close, shaking her head in disbelief. She opened the tailgate on the Range Rover carrying the box of wine to the front door only to watch it open, she entered beginning to think she is losing her marbles. She went outside again collecting the other bottles closing the tailgate on her Range Rover returning to the kitchen. Jocelyn is going to make herself a coffee, decided a whiskey would be better to steady her nerves. She went into the front room after pressing the button on the wall so the generator would start. Jocelyn sat there with a bottle and glass continuing to read the book, emptied her glass of whiskey topping up. Number six watching everything the way she is behaving, he suspected after she'd had two more glasses of whiskey her mind would be fuzzy as humans would describe becoming intoxicated.

He went out into the kitchen, transforming into Jonathan entering the front room. Jocelyn caught sight of him over the top of her book. She started laughing, "bloody hell this whiskey is better than I thought." Continuing to read emptying her glass and refilling. She stopped reading looking over the top of her book watching Jonathan approach, believed he kissed her passionately and seductively, removing her clothes as described in the book, within a few minutes number six is experiencing lovemaking which did nothing for him. However, Jocelyn is undoubtedly enjoying him. Number six checked his memory banks to determine the length of time, which on average half an hour. He kissed her on the lips once more, leaving via the kitchen, turning back to an invisible being.

***

Rosalind receiving what is happening at Brook Farm number six had disobeyed her direct instructions, she ordered him telepathically. "Returned to the spaceship immediately." She touched Jacob on the forehead he instantly became unconscious. Rosalind stepped from the front door into the misty fog transporter within seconds, she is aboard the spaceship

Matthew and Peter were stood there with number six. "What were my instructions number six concerning Jocelyn?"

"I caused her no harm, very dull practice. I discovered there is no stimulus in the process for me whatsoever."

"My instructions to you were not to interfere with Jocelyn; she will remember the incident; admittedly, you betrayed yourself as a character from a book. Nevertheless, you disobeyed a direct request from myself Peter and Matthew plus the five. Central computer number six has jeopardised our mission I believe termination is in order."

The central computer responded: "Number six attach yourself to the wall so I may examine thoroughly."

Number six didn't hesitate to stand with his back against the wall. The central computer linked to him. "I can confirm, he wilfully disobeyed which would show a form of individuality. I will suspend him to be returned on the next ship to Zagader for further analysis." Rosalind, Peter and Matthew watched number six vanish into storage until he could be further examined on the home planet. Rosalind detected Jocelyn crying rather upset dressing in the front room. Rosalind watched Jocelyn pick up her mobile phone dialling for the police. Peter ran to the keypad on the wall, typing in a code. The central computer blocked her signal. Rosalind flashed her eyes dashing jumping into the misty fog transporter, entering Brook Farm, she stunned Jocelyn. Transporting herself to Jacobs farm. She placed a hand on his forehead, ensuring he stayed unconscious, transporting him to Brook Farm. As much as Rosalind hated the situation, she couldn't see an alternative, Rosalind knew Jocelyn had feelings for Jacob and vice a versa. She knew Jacob would never betray her under normal circumstances. She telepathically instructed Jocelyn and Jacob to remove their clothes and lay on the carpet and to make love to each other. Rosalind transported to Jacobs farm returning with the quad and trailer leaving in the yard at Brook Farm. She stepped into the misty fog transporter returned to Jacobs farm, decided to leave them together for another three hours. Rosalind ordering the 5 to stay aboard the spaceship and not at Brook Farm any more, she couldn't afford any more mistakes.

Jacob rolled on his back, and Jocelyn opened her eyes, they looked at each other for a moment horrified. Jocelyn laughed, "I can't remember what happened Jacob or how the hell you ended up here with me, but I have to say I enjoyed it immensely and from the looks of it we polished off a bottle of whiskey, no wonder we can't remember anything. Jacob dressed looking to Jocelyn. "I'm awfully sorry I don't know anything, although I have to admit you are a stunning woman."

"And you are definitely all man Jacob I feel absolutely marvellous. Unfortunately, you have to leave. Otherwise, your wife will be hunting for you," Jocelyn sighed. Jacob couldn't resist; he kissed Jocelyn passionately on the lips, leaving holding his head like he'd been struck with a sledgehammer. Jacob stepped outside in the dark, started his quad bike, not even remembering driving here. He turned on the lights waving to Jocelyn standing in the doorway, he slowly headed across the Moor wondering what to say to Rosalind or should he say nothing. A cold shiver run down his spine realising God would have known what he's done, is there some reason God permitted him to misbehave if so what? Jacob parked his quad bike by the barn slowly entering the house, Rosalind wasn't there he suspected she'd gone to see God if not summoned by him. Jacob quickly showered changing into his pyjamas, rapidly falling asleep.

Rosalind aboard the spaceship talking to Matthew and Peter. "I have to say Rosalind your individuality thinking saved the situation, neither will say anything I'm sure."

"I hope you are correct, Peter, you must remember Jacob loves his Bible, and his belief in God is strong. I suspect he may confess his sins to me, which I rather hope he doesn't. I would prefer to forget the whole incident and move forward with our program."

6 o'clock in the morning Jacob drove down the cliff track onto the beach. Rosalind noticed on the monitor the headlights of the Land Rover. She flashed her eyes to Peter and Matthew travelling in the misty fog to the shoreline stepping from the transporter, she climbed into the Land Rover. "I'll let you drive for once," she chuckled, watching Jacob smile. "God summoned me early yesterday Jacob, I'm sorry I wasn't at home much, you manage all right without me?"

"Yes, it's not the same when you're not around Rosalind you're special, I don't deserve you," he frowned.

"Don't be silly, Jacob everything is great between us, and it always will be," she reassured.

Jacob realised God knew everything, and if he is displeased with what took place, he would have informed Rosalind, and she would be ripping his head off this morning without hesitation. He couldn't understand why God had permitted him to sin. Or perhaps it wasn't a sin? After all, Solomon had two wives to mention but a few in the Bible he concluded. Jacob thought he didn't really want two wives, one is enough; however, if God's will, he have little choice in the matter. Rosalind is reading his thoughts, finding them somewhat surprising as she studied her memory banks as they drove to the farm, checking what Peter and Matthew had written and the other disciples from Zagader over the years. Rosalind concluded at least if Jacob's occupied by Jocelyn he wouldn't be bothering her for mating, which made her smile. Jacob asked, "a penny for your thoughts, Rosalind?"

"Oh, nothing really, I'll be pleased when I've given birth to these two monsters, I'm nearly 4 months now Jacob," Rosalind smiled rubbing her tummy.

"Praise the Lord for the gift of life and praise my beautiful wife for returning to an unworthy husband."

Jacob parked the Land Rover by the front door. "You'd better check the sheep Jacob," Rosalind smiled entering the house. Jacob followed, taking his crook an old army coat from the back of the door. "I'll make you breakfast when you come home, in case you have breakfast, with Jocelyn, I don't mind I quite like her," Rosalind proclaimed.

Jacob stared suspiciously at Rosalind before leaving the house. He had his old torch inside his coat pocket, daylight is appearing slowly from the hillside hundreds of miles away. You could almost see the curvature of the earth, Jacob thought, glancing to the sea smelling the salty air. Jacob checked the sheep hey racks now he is using round bales they didn't empty so quickly. However, Jacob would have to ration otherwise stocks would be depleted before the end of winter which hadn't really started yet. Jacob shone his torch the two Rams had been fighting again he realised, he would have to separate them before they killed one another. Jacob looked into the distance through the darkness Jocelyn's bedroom light is on. Jacob thought he should speak to her this morning about what happened yesterday or perhaps he should stay silent and let the incident drift into history.

He took a deep breath, slowly walking towards Brook Farm. Jocelyn stood at the window looking out at the beautiful light in the distance noticing Jacob, she smiled waving.

Jacob responded, realising this may be an awkward situation. Jocelyn slipped on her dressing gown and slippers dashing downstairs she unlocked the back door. "I'll make you coffee Jacob, perhaps we could have breakfast together if you have time," she offered. Jacob couldn't understand his actions, he entered with a keen step hearing the generator start. Jocelyn had already thrown blocks on the fire still smouldering from last night watching the sparks fly for a moment. Jocelyn placed the coffee on the table. "What would you like for breakfast Jacob," she asked feeling fantastic this morning she hadn't felt this relaxed for ages.

"Funny, you should ask! Something strange going on around here," Jacob confessed. "Rosalind suggested I have breakfast here this morning, she says she likes you?"

"I like her too. I normally have toast and jam will you settle for toast and jam?"

Jacob nodded, holding his mug with both hands feeling the warmth from the Aga, watching the toast jump out of the toaster. Jocelyn spread butter and jam, cutting the toast into triangles placing on the table. Jocelyn couldn't understand why she is so excited almost like a schoolgirl again, she is 35 years old, she wouldn't be surprised if Jacob wasn't in his 50s, not as that matters she concluded. They sat looking at each other Jocelyn replenished Jacobs mug determined to detain him as long as possible, she quite expected to have a stinking hangover this morning, but she never felt so good. Jacob tried not to look at Jocelyn, trying to control his impure thoughts. "I must go, Jocelyn, thank you for breakfast and thank you for yesterday," he smiled, leaving through the front door into the early morning light.

Jocelyn watched him walk onto the Moor heading towards Jacobs farm. Rosalind had read everyone's thoughts realising

Jocelyn would keep Jacob satisfied, so she didn't have to perform. Rosalind would have to make Jocelyn want to live there permanently and solely interested in Jacob, without wishing to possess him other than for pleasure. That would certainly solve the issue of mating, perhaps it wouldn't be such a good idea to have a film made on the Moor when the coronavirus subsides it would only encourage more visitors Rosalind decided; she'd have to think carefully about the whole situation; would leave everything for the moment as it is. Rosalind glanced to the window seeing Jacob approaching the front door hearing him tap his boots on the scraper before entering. "Jacob tomorrow morning a load of fertiliser to collect from the beach and spread. From the crumbs in your beard I suspect you had toast and jam for breakfast," she chuckled.

"I'm convinced you are a mind reader Rosalind, you are correct, she offered me a cup of coffee and a piece of toast for breakfast."

"You'd be surprised what your wife can do Jacob," she grinned smugly enjoying the human expressions. Rosalind had telepathically controlled Jocelyn's mind instructing her to come to Jacobs farm they were going out shopping together. Rosalind wanted to make sure she instilled in Jocelyn's mind precisely what she wanted her to do.

Jacob sat at the table drinking coffee, watching Rosalind, slip on her coat. "Where are you going?"

"Shopping with Jocelyn she will collect me in a moment."

"How did you contact her and when?"

Rosalind removed the mobile from her pocket. "We don't all live in the dark ages," she laughed.

Jacob smiled, shaking his head in disbelief, wondering whether the two would talk about him. He prayed Jocelyn wouldn't mention what happened between them. Jacob heard

Jocelyn's Range Rover approaching. Rosalind kissed Jacob on the cheek patting. "Behaved, while I'm gone I shan't belong, remember God is watching you husband," she laughed stepping out through the doorway closing the door behind her.

Rosalind sat in the passenger side studying the way Jocelyn dressed deciding Jocelyn wasn't leaving much to the imagination if it wasn't short, tight-fitting. "You have lovely hair, Jocelyn," Rosalind commented, touching Jocelyn's hair. Jocelyn immediately stopped the vehicle at the end of the track, she stepped out of her Range Rover, swapping sides with Rosalind, now in the driver's seat. Rosalind knew she is in control of Jocelyn now. Rosalind continued driving slowly. "Jocelyn, you are to use my husband; you are not interested in other males. You will please him at every opportunity. You will live at Brook Farm permanently until I tell you otherwise. Do you understand me, Jocelyn!"

"Yes I understand entirely, I enjoyed him yesterday I will please him every day as you command."

"let's go shopping," Rosalind suggested pulling into a Morrisons car park both grabbing a trolley. They join the queue because of the coronavirus restrictions finally allowed in one after the other. Rosalind had telepathically instructed Jocelyn what Jacob like for his breakfast, she didn't want Jacob missing his favourite breakfast; otherwise, he may not respond to Jocelyn in the way she wants him to. They loaded the groceries into the back of Jocelyn's Range Rover. Rosalind allowed Jocelyn to drive returning to Jacobs farm. Jacob came out from the house Rosalind notice the way he is looking at Jocelyn, she could tell from his thoughts he enjoyed looking at her short skirt and legs. "When you check the sheep tomorrow Jacob, I have bacon and eggs for you and fried bread if you're really a good boy," Jocelyn chuckled.

Jacob turned bright red, not responding, carrying the groceries in the house for Rosalind. Rosalind is trying not to laugh her plan was coming together, although she is surprised Jocelyn spoke so winningly to Jacob; if he couldn't read the signs, Rosalind concluded, he hasn't a brain. They watched Jocelyn drive off, heading for Brook Farm. Jacob asked, "what's going on Rosalind any normal wife would beat her husband to death for looking at another woman, and you want me to have breakfast there?"

Rosalind shook her head: "You disappoint me, Jacob here am I your wife who descended from the heavens because of your prayers and God's permission. I thought you knew your Bible Jacob, God will be disappointed in you, do as he requests or, lose your unborn children and me!" Rosalind demanded. "I'm going to speak to him now with Peter and Matthew." Rosalind walked out of the door. Jacob stood there in disbelief he had no idea other than his own crazy thoughts and interpretations of what the Bible is saying. Jacob went outside speak to Rosalind again, she is nowhere to be seen he suspected she'd returned to heaven. Jacob placed a sack of sheep nuts in his quad trailer and a mineral block. He headed across the Moor finding is she contentedly grazing. They soon gathered around him, hearing the quad bike. Jacob stopped opening the bag of sheep nuts quickly running in a straight line allowing the nuts to empty from the sack. He took the opportunity to capture both Rams placing in his trailer, opening the mineral block leaving on a flat rock for the sheep to enjoy later. Jacob thought Brook Farm would be the ideal place for the Rams to stay they'd be all right together as long as they weren't with ewes. Jacob knew of a little paddock fenced off about half an acre at the rear of the house which would be ideal for the Rams to have some grass, he only has to make sure they had water and perhaps a little supplement to keep them in good health.

Jacob climbed aboard his quad bike with Jack following making his way to Brook Farm, Jacob unloaded the two Rams in the small paddock, the fencing a little worse for wear which he thought would have to fix soon. Jacob sat on his quad bike, noticing Jocelyn waving to him from the window, he drove around into the yard parking. She opened the door holding a mug of coffee in her hand. "Thanks," walking in. "You mind if I wash my hands in the sink, I've been handling stinky old Rams," he smiled.

"No, not at all," she chuckled. "Rosalind is wonderful. I enjoyed myself immensely this morning shopping with her. We had a good old chat, you'll be pleased to know I'm staying here permanently for the time being anyway, we are undecided about filming, we'll have to see it does have possibilities though."

Jacob dried his hands on the towel, surprised by her remarks returning to the table and his coffee. "let me take your coat we might as well chat for a while unless you don't like my company of course," she smiled pleasantly.

Jacob shook his head, "don't be silly," watching her hang his coat on the back of the door.

"To be quite honest Jacob I don't remember much about what we did other than excellent and enjoyed the sensation," Jocelyn standing up unbuttoning her blouse releasing her bra, holding out her hand leading Jacob upstairs; he didn't resist in the slightest. She removed the remainder of her clothes laying on the bed, Jacob didn't hesitate, suspecting this is God's decision. Jocelyn, screaming like a teenager, she'd never had anything like this before, he is all man and extremely assertive.

Aliens

***

Rosalind aboard the spaceship talking to Peter and Matthew. "Rosalind the collective has requested you return to Zagader for one month, to lecture to our brothers and sisters. They are watching via the link, they want to speak to you personally to understand. They have many unanswered questions, only you can answer."

"I will have to explain to Jacob God has requested me in heaven to rest for the period of one month, he will accept that not wishing to lose his son and daughter. I have to confess I rather regret allowing an experiment on me, they restrict my abilities."

"Terminate Rosalind," Matthew suggested.

"No! I can assure you if I did Jacob would never forgive me; admittedly, I could control him telepathically. The problem is Jacob wouldn't be Jacob not as that matters I suppose," Rosalind giving the matter some thought.

Zibyans number 1 to 5 returned, materialising by Matthew and Peter. "We have read your thoughts; you have been extremely proficient in your duties. You will return with me to Zagader on the transport ship arriving tomorrow," Rosalind advised. "I've had an idea," Rosalind smiled. "Number three shapeshift into me let me examine you." Number three didn't hesitate to copy Rosalind's figure exactly. "Excellent you will stay and play the part of Rosalind, me while I'm away at Zagader lecturing. Central computer link to number three, transfer any relevant information to her so she may function as me in my absence."

"Number three stand against the wall." Number three didn't hesitate, practising smiling. The computer link to her transferring the information she would require to function as

Rosalind. "Number three you are now me, Rosalind return to Jacobs farm, make no mistakes; otherwise, our mission will be jeopardised." Number three shapeshifted into Rosalind she stepped into the misty fog transported to Jacobs farm waiting for him to return. She is studying what had transpired recently and how Rosalind had manipulated Jocelyn, she changed her appearance dressing like Jocelyn looking at herself in the full-length bedroom mirror, humans certainly dress strangely she concluded, although from her travels around the world harvesting humans sheets in many types of dress code. She hoped to take full advantage of her assignment and learn as much as possible while she played the part of her sister as Rosalind.

***

Jocelyn came out of the shower, Jacob had gone downstairs making the coffee if this is a present from God. Thank you very much! He thought, smiling. Jocelyn joined him sitting at the table not bothering to close her dressing gown he'd already seen everything so why conceal. Jacob finished his coffee kissing Jocelyn very passionately, leaving the house climbing aboard his quad bike heading for home. Now daylight he could see clearly across the Moor looks like going to be a reasonable day, although approaching November, the sheep busily eating hay. Jacob continued home to the farm parking his quad bike in the barn realising, he would have to collect the fertiliser in the morning, checking the tractor had plenty of diesel in the tank. Jacob looked in the wing mirror of the tractor hoping he hadn't any lipstick on him, although he is pretty convinced Rosalind knew what is happening which puzzled him immensely. Jacob walked to the house-entering finding his lunch on the table a beautiful salad. Rosalind kissed him lovingly. He smiled sitting down, tucking into his salad. "You have a good day so far, Jacob?"

"Yes, I hope you have calmed down, I don't understand quite what is going on Rosalind providing its Gods decision I don't mind what happens."

"Everything his God's decision Jacob," Rosalind advised, unsure what her sister had planned, she would have to improvise, she wasn't as skilled as the original Rosalind thinking as an individual. Jacob finished his meal going outside, Rosalind cleared away spending some time watching Coronation Street and Emmerdale farm as Rosalind, her sister, would in case Jacob came in he would wonder why she wasn't watching her programs. A little while later, Rosalind went outside. Jack looked at her strangely. Jack knew this wasn't Rosalind; she didn't smell the same, he growled slightly. Jacob glared at him, "Jack pack that in now," Jacob ordered forcefully. Rosalind jumped in the Range Rover driving off realising the dog didn't recognise her something she hadn't anticipated. Rosalind drove to Brook Farm parking her Range Rover by Jocelyn's. Jocelyn came out and greeted her with a hug ignoring the coronavirus threat. "Come, let us have coffee. I have everything ready for Jacobs breakfast in the morning," Jocelyn smiled.

"Good he won't be disappointed saves me the task," Rosalind replied cautiously.

They sat at the kitchen table, drinking their coffee, talking about clothes. Rosalind commented, "I must buy a new wardrobe soon, I only have old stuff; otherwise my husband will think I'm drab," Rosalind remarked, unsure of how to hold an interesting conversation. Jocelyn held out her hand. "Come with me," she laughed, heading upstairs with Rosalind following her to her bedroom. Jocelyn opened the wardrobe, "help yourself I have more clothes than I know what to do with.

Change before you go home, see if Jacob notices," Jocelyn laughed. Rosalind is unsure of how to behave, removed her garments; selecting what she thought would be suitable ending up dressing in a very revealing outfit; finally selecting shoes from the hundreds in the bottom of the wardrobe. Rosalind stood in front of the full-length mirror. There wasn't much left to the imagination, Jocelyn realising, how she would look to someone if she'd worn the outfit. "I think your fine Jacobs eyes will fall out, you needn't bring them back. I don't want them burn if you don't want to keep yourself," Jocelyn remarked. Placing Rosalind's clothes in a carrier bag, following Rosalind down the stairs struggling to walk in the shoes she selected. Jocelyn gave Rosalind a hug before she walked out the door carrying her shopping bag of clothes, which she threw on the back seat of the Range Rover. Number three posing as Rosalind drove steadily in the dark returning to Jacobs farm. This is only the second time she had driven the Range Rover, she wasn't as confident as the real Rosalind. Jacob glanced out of the window into the dark, seeing the headlights. He switched on his torch, opening the front door for Rosalind to have light to enter the house without tripping. He shone his flashlight up and down her, she stood by the range Rover. Jacob stared in disbelief at the way she is dressed. "Aren't you impressed Jacob Jocelyn gave me some of her old clothes, she's throwing them out anyway, I thought I'd try some to impress my husband. Do I look attractive husband?" Rosalind walked straight past him into the house, he followed slamming the door glaring at her. "You've dressed like a tart Rosalind a prostitute put your old clothes on," he ordered forcefully.

Number three realised she'd made a mistake, misjudging the situation, she would have to behave like Rosalind and stand her ground; otherwise, Jacob would indeed be suspicious of her. "I suppose if Jocelyn was dressed like me, you would say nothing, Jacob why can't I dress nice?"

Jacob immediately calms realising what she said is the truth if it were Jocelyn he'd drool over her. "Rosalind, I'm shocked! Taken by surprise, I'm sorry for my harsh words, you are a stunning woman, and there isn't much I can't see of you, which means so can anybody else looking at my beautiful wife which I would not appreciate," he remarked biting his tongue controlling his temper.

"I purposely selected these clothes, Jacob, to please my husband and hope he would find me attractive." Number three hoped she'd talked a way out of this situation, and the real Rosalind wouldn't dismiss her for misjudging the situation. Number three decided to take it one step further stepping out of the clothes she is wearing in front of Jacob. His eyes almost fell out of his head, looking at his beautiful naked wife. "I'm going to lie down Jacob, I hope you will join me," she smiled, hoping sufficient incentive. Jacob followed her into the bedroom, bewildered by her actions, holding Rosalind, he believed making love to her. Number three is now experiencing lovemaking for the first time and agreed with Rosalind. The only pleasure is tingling electricity sent through her body while he performed. She quickly made her way to the bathroom, pretending to shower returning to find Jacob asleep. She touched his forehead to ensure he wouldn't wake for some considerable time while she returned to the spaceship, suspecting to be disciplined by the real Rosalind. Jack studied number three as she stepped past him out of the front door and into the misty fog transporter arriving in seconds aboard the spaceship. Peter, Matthew and Rosalind were waiting for number three looking at her clothes given to her by Jocelyn.

"I hope you have a very good reason number three for the way you're dressed; Rosalind would never dress like that!"

Number three flashed her eyes. "My error Rosalind I was trying to understand how everything worked. I thought it would be wise to become familiar with Jocelyn. I happened to mention, trying to make a conversation about the clothes I possessed, were rather drab. I didn't realise Jacob would be angry and I can tell you he really was angry until I relieved his stress and calmed him down. You are correct Rosalind in your assessment of the mating process apart from the electric tingles there's nothing."

"Number three you are showing individuality, you resolved a mistake you made. If you make another Peter will replace you, number three. I don't want you ruining the life I have created with Jacob betraying, his deceased wife, Rosalind. He is very useful to the collective for the moment. Remind him to collect the fertiliser tomorrow morning before 8 o'clock, I will be travelling on the transport ship to Zagader to give a lecture, I will be gone for one calendar month. I expect to return and take over my position with Jacob. I hope you do not make another mistake number three."

Number three flashed her eyes to Peter and Matthew and Rosalind, stepping into the misty fog transporter returning to the farm at 6:30 in the morning. She entered the house, watched closely by Jack. She went quietly into the bedroom, changing into her old work clothes returning to the kitchen, making the coffee making sufficient noise to disturb Jacob. He came out of the bedroom, scratching his head, smiling to see the way Rosalind is dressed. He kissed her lovingly on the lips and whispered, "burn those trashy clothes today, please Rosalind."

Rosalind poured the coffee, smiling at Jacob. "I don't know Jacob if I keep the clothes you might be kind to me another night," sticking her tongue out at him as she'd seen other humans do playfully. Jacob burst out laughing. "I don't know quite what's come over you Rosalind remember you're pregnant take it easy."

"That reminds me fertiliser this morning Jacob earlier the better, and when you check the ewes, Jocelyn will make you breakfast."

Jacob looks strangely at Rosalind, "and you're okay with all this Rosalind you don't mind me having breakfast with another woman?"

"No God's decision you have to obey Jacob, I rather like Jocelyn. She is accommodating, even if I did make my husband annoyed last night wearing her clothes. I enjoyed the way you punish me," she chuckled. Jacob splitting himself laughing, is this really Rosalind something had changed, he couldn't quite put his finger on what. Number three realised she mustn't go too far otherwise when her sister Rosalind reclaimed her position, she may have difficulty with him.

Jacob kissed Rosalind on the cheek walking out of the door followed by Jack, climbed aboard his tractor heading down onto the beach, still very dark, thankfully, the headlights worked on the tractor. He parked by the water's edge, feeling the tractor flex as the manure spreader loaded with fertiliser. Jacob drove up the cliff face track, cutting across to the 10 acres on Brook Farm spreading the manure. He looked from his tractor cab window, seeing the light is on Jocelyn is obviously up. He drove to the yard parking by her Range Rover, the front door was already open for him to enter. Jocelyn had just finished cooking bacon and egg tomatoes fried bread, with a large mug of coffee waiting for him on the table. "Thanks that looks lovely Jocelyn," he commented, enjoying immensely. Jocelyn smiled, eating her marmalade on toast with her cup of coffee. "I hope you didn't shout at Rosalind when she returned home last night, Jacob because of what she was wearing?"

"Yes, I did I'd never seen her look that way before to be quite honest, it frightened the life out of me. I could imagine men 400 miles away trying today's her."

"What about me then," Jocelyn asked, standing up displaying similar to what Rosalind was wearing last night only not quite so revealing.

"You're a free agent you're not married, dress how you like," Jacob commented, finishing his breakfast.

Jocelyn exhaled. "If you were in London or anywhere for that matter Jacob, comments like that would get you scolded by any woman you spoke to like that. Married or single, you can dress how you like, and if men can't control their emotions, you can't blame the women there trying to look pretty."

Jacob sipped his coffee, "and why do women want to look attractive Jocelyn," he asked calmly. "To attract a man, or perhaps lesbian, of course."

"You are telling me, Jacob, you're not attracted to me the way I look?"

"Of course, that isn't the point if you were married to me, I would expect you to dress more sensibly," he suggested looking at the way Jocelyn is dressed which somewhat excited him. Jacob rose to his feet, removing his thick coat he couldn't stand looking at Jocelyn any longer grabbing her hand, threw her over his shoulder carrying her upstairs, she didn't object in the slightest rather enjoying his caveman approach throwing her on the bed.

***

304

Rosalind, leaving the Earth's atmosphere with a cargo of human flesh heading for Zagader along with the others returning home. Every preparation had been afforded her to make sure the infants she is carrying would survive the journey. Rosalind would still have to eat three meals a day or at the very least consume liquids. She couldn't shapeshift, the central computer advised she would damage the infants if she did. The idea of carrying aliens inside her seemed a good idea at the time an excellent experiment. She realised the restrictions placed upon her, which were very concerning made her inefficient.

Rosalind spent the next three days watching planets through the observation window pass her by although she is travelling at an incredible speed everything seemed to be moving slowly. Finally, Rosalind rose to her feet, maintaining the shape of a human for the infants benefit definitely not hers, Rosalind noticed the approach of Zagader in front of her through the observation window. Zagader growing in size by the second as the spaceship approached and gently landing after changing shape to accommodate the landing platform. The misty fog transporter appeared. Rosalind knew she couldn't shapeshift to leave the spaceship-like everyone else. She stepped inside the carrier and seconds later stepping out to see hundreds of her brothers and sisters surrounding her; questions were filling her computerised brain, she concluded, she would spend the next five years answering every question. The firstborn approached in the shape of a creator the way he always appeared in honour of them. "Rosalind I have a surprise for you, which I appreciate is a human term, but we don't have another word to explain."

Rosalind smiled her brothers and sisters looked at the way she distorted her face creating the smile. They had observed humans perform the practice millions of times but never a Zibyan on the home planet.

Rosalind followed the firstborn into the laboratory standing there appeared to be a human in shape apart from a scaly exterior similar to an earth lizard, except having blonde hair and excellent complexion. "Rosalind, you remember the bone I discovered, we have created a creator from the recovered DNA."

Rosalind didn't speak for a moment studying whatever it is the firstborn, and the central computer had created. "Creator this is Rosalind she is carrying aliens inside her as an experiment."

The creator turned to face Rosalind flashing his eyes, Rosalind replied out of respect. "The central computer believes you are an individual Rosalind, the computer explained you know the creators had planned to discontinue their experiment with their creation, considering inferior?"

"Yes, creator, we are not inferior; we haven't developed to work as individuals, we are a collective relying on each other for decision-making most of the time."

"You are definitely more advanced Rosalind. Are you aware the aliens you are carrying are changing, your structure has worked out how to supply them with pure energy to sustain them?"

"How, creator, how do you know?"

"I, we, my brothers and sisters many centuries ago developed the skills to study other beings with our mind. I can see inside you, Rosalind every movement. You are carrying a male and female human, your construction has added extra protection so they cannot be harmed. Your construction is enhancing their development. You realise when these infants are born, they will know everything you know."

"That's not possible creator, they are alien to me they must be aborted they will give away the secrets of the Zibyans."

"Even if you wanted to abort Rosalind you would be destroyed in the process, they are more a part of you now than you realise, they will not leave your construction until they are ready. They will not betray the information in their minds; you are their creator and will always have their respect. You must nurture them they will be of great value to the Zibyans in time."

"Creator, you realise the children were conceived by Jacob, a backward farmer believing in the Bible created to control the humans and failed miserably."

"I am aware Rosalind you will be returned and continue your life with Jacob. Your brothers and sisters named a planet after him in honour of him providing the seed to create, what could be the next generation of your evolution. Look at me created by the central computer from recovered DNA. The central computer had stored every thought your creators had before they died from a freak accident. The central computer-created me, to guide the Zibyans on the correct path of domination."

"Creator, you are hoping the children I'm carrying will replace every Zibyan in the future?"

"That is not what I said, Rosalind until they are born and studied. I cannot determine their potential and abilities entirely, however, having you as their support for the duration, with your intelligence would suggest the Zibyans are about to evolve with the central computers assistance and mine."

Every Zibyan had received telepathically what is conveyed between Rosalind, and the creator, messages were travelling at a supersonic speed between the brothers and sisters analysing everything suggested. Rosalind flashed her eyes at the creator and the firstborn, she left the laboratory surrounded by brothers and sisters, she stepped into the misty fog transporter take into an island on Jacob's planet still establishing. The foliage starting to produce fruit. Rosalind cracked a falling coconut drinking the milk the way Jacob had when she brought him to Zagader for the first time. She broke the coconut open on a rock sitting on the sand, eating some of the contents. Rosalind tried to analyse why she is missing Jacob, he wasn't of her construction or is she feeling the same if she wasn't in contact with her brothers and sisters telepathically all the time.

Rosalind is concerned with what is growing inside her according to the creator, the next evolution in their development. Rosalind ran towards the sea removing her garments as she ran swimming with the dolphins, she found very pleasurable returning to the beach a while later, laying in the sun naked to dry watched by her brothers and sisters with curiosity trying to understand her behaviour which in their eyes they considered erratic. Rosalind sense someone is close she opened her eyes to see the creator standing over her. He telepathically suggested he should experiment with her. This is totally different to Jacob, she concluded laying there accepting what the creator is performing. Her brothers and sisters watched alarmed why is the creator performing such a futile act on Rosalind. Rosalind pushed him off, walking into the sea he followed. "All my bodily functions work do you concur, Rosalind," he asked, already knowing the answer.

"You're not dissimilar to a human in performance. I expected better from a creator," she expressed sincerely.

"When you return to earth, you will select 20 females and arrange transport to Zagader. I have carried out tests they would be suitable to carry my foetuses, the creators will really return and will control the environment."

"What colour do you wish creator?"

"I'll have a selection some may produce better than others, after all, they are only descendants of chimpanzees. Another mistake made while I wasn't here to control the situation," he expressed thoughtfully.

"I presume you intend to continue terraforming planets selected by the firstborn, creator?"

"Only the once selected, there will be no more unnecessary waste of resources, there are only 2 million Zibyans, won't be any more other than what your two children produce and me with the females you provide. This will give me a good DNA selection to choose from."

"I presume the collective is aware and approved of your decision creator; after all, if it wasn't for the firstborn, you wouldn't exist," Rosalind suggested, suspecting her brothers and sisters were listening carefully to the conversation.

"You are suspicious of my motives Rosalind you are genuinely an individual thinker; you are protecting your brothers and sisters from what you consider could be a dictator?"

"You are correct, creator! I warned the collective against creating creators, you had deemed us all, inferior, a mistake and had planned to exterminate. Why would you suddenly change your mind from the path you had chosen?"

"Because of you, the way you behave and think as an individual Rosalind. Admittedly it has taken several thousand years for the computer's creation to develop, you are carrying part of the future; I will create the rest. I am not destroying or intend to destroy any created Zibyan. Are you listening to brothers and sisters I'm sure you are."

Rosalind smiled, somewhat with relief, although not sure of the creator he would have to be watched closely. "We shall see creator," she remarked cautiously.

"I'm constructed similar to humans, with bone and a fleshy covering, although my scales protect me, and my brain is far superior, much like you. You were created by the central computer, the computer only could make you out of pure energy; not like the creators entirely. Nevertheless, this will serve a purpose you never die; you just need energy to survive, which there is plenty of around the universe when we expand."

"One step at a time, I think creator. I will do as you ask, select 20 females there are millions of them. I will send images so you can approve before I ship to the home planet to avoid disappointment."

"As you wish they are immaterial, I only require their ability to carry my offspring than they can be discarded fed to the pets."

"Have you not studied the human race creator! You've not noticed the humans come in various shapes and sizes caused by their DNA. I would respectfully suggest I select someone of my stature, similar to what I left Jacob to amuse himself with while I'm away."

"Yes, I have watched, she prepares in nourishment early in the morning, then they engage for some considerable time in the activity of mating, although rather futile she will not become pregnant while she takes contraceptives. I conclude the activity must be some type of exercise and enjoyment Rosalind. Although from your comments, it does not have the same effect on a Zibyan created of pure energy by the computer, as it does from a genuine creator constructed of bone and flesh. The practice was enjoyed; only we should have produced more offspring then perhaps we wouldn't have become extinct when the accident happened."

"The central computer doesn't have feelings; therefore, he wouldn't understand how to construct sensors for that activity, although the computer made our taste sensors very useful."

"Return with me to the laboratories, once I fully examine your construction, there may be a modification to be made, although it serves no purpose for you to feel pain and suffering like your creator. I may be able to improve some of your sensitivities with the central computer's assistants; we shall see, come Rosalind." They both stepped into the misty fog transporter returning to the laboratories. Rosalind sat comfortably while the central computer linked to her. The creator transmitted information with six fingers and thumb with miniature suction cups on the end of each finger, conveyed instructions to the central computer to transfer to Rosalind in the first instance to see if it had any effect. Rosalind started to twitch, standing up, the central computer released connection to her. "How do you feel Rosalind, I suspect you've never been asked before?"

Rosalind is silent for a moment feeling the infants movements more intently than before. The creator is reading her thoughts, understanding what she is feeling similar to him but not so intense. "Strange, strange creator I feel the infants more intently, I feel every movement they make, I sense. I don't know whether this will be beneficial to my efficiency or not," Rosalind replied, confused.

"I think for the moment Rosalind we will restrict the upgrade to you, see if it's an improvement or a restriction? Central computer store the upgrade and if Rosalind is satisfied it causes no problems you may transmit to the other brothers and sisters after you have spoken to me first for approval as the creator."

"I will obey your commands creator you are the beginning and the end."

"Rosalind, your infants, require nourishment, freshwater they are feeding off your life force, so vegetation is not necessary, they are transforming by the day." Rosalind walked out of the laboratory to the stream, she sampled the water to check fresh and uncontaminated. She consumed what was necessary. Rosalind returned to the laboratory discovering the creator was laying on a bed. "I have to rest for four hours in 24, I am not constructed like you Rosalind I am a creator." He patted the bed, she instantly lay beside him without a second thought, although she didn't need to rest. She permitted him to kiss her his lips were different to Jacobs without a beard, she is feeling totally new sensations Rosalind had never felt before. Now she could understand why humans became so excited with each other, the new programming in her brain is undoubtedly an improvement; she couldn't wait to return to earth and see how different Jacob would be to what she's receiving from the creator. Rosalind stayed with the creator they were becoming inseparable, travelling to the selected planets to ascertain their progress while terraforming. Rosalind wondered whether she should return to earth although realised she hadn't completed her mission. Rosalind wanted to see how the children turned out what would be the differences from a human, she hoped none. Otherwise, they wouldn't blend in. She rather hoped they would be immune to the coronavirus if still raging on earth when they were born; perhaps a virus would be the end of the human race she concluded.

The final day had arrived Rosalind had lectured to her brothers and sisters accompanied by the creator. She had slept with him every time he rested, allowing him to take his pleasure with her, which she enjoyed immensely. Rosalind stepped aboard the transport ship preparing to return to earth a three-day trip.

***

"My God Jacob, you're an animal," Jocelyn suggested walking into the shower while Jacob made the coffee downstairs in the kitchen. Jacob sat at the table looking through the window seeing Jack sat on the tractor seat, patiently waiting for him to return. Jocelyn came down the stairs wearing her dressing gown seated at the table, "I will have to stop giving you red meat for breakfast," she laughed. Jacob rose to his feet, kissing Jocelyn on the lips slipping on his coat, walking out of the house smiling. He concluded this would have to be with God's blessing. Otherwise, he would be struck down dead by now, and Rosalind took away from him. Jacob drove steadily out of the yard venturing onto the Moor as the snow started to fall, usually in November they would receive a light covering. He made his way back to the farm parking the tractor and spreader outside, preparing fencing to bring the ewes in out of the weather should it turn nasty. The last thing he wanted is to lose his sheep.

Number three pretending to be Rosalind came out of the house wrapped up warm, although only for Jacobs benefit, her body temperature wasn't affected. "I hope you enjoyed your breakfast Jocelyn is taking me shopping today, Jacob, you don't mind, do you?"

"Only if you're driving Rosalind, a covering of snow will make it slippy on the tarmac, she's a towny driver, I don't think they have snow in London," he remarked thoughtfully. Jacob looked down the drive seeing Jocelyn in her posh Range Rover coming to the farm, Rosalind ran into the house changing into her best coat. Jocelyn commented, winding down the window. "I'll let Rosalind drive she knows the roads better than me around here Jacob." He smiled with relief, watching Rosalind slide over onto the passenger seat. Jocelyn kissed Jacob patting his cheek, which always made him smile. "We won't be long husband." Rosalind climbed into the driver's seat turning the Range Rover around heading down the drive. Jocelyn commented, "We must go to Exeter railway station, my younger sisters arriving Jennifer, she's staying with me for a couple of weeks I'm taking calendar shots of her to help make ends meet while the coronavirus persists."

Rosalind quickly read her mind. Jennifer, a struggling actress, relying on her sister for an income most of the time, apart from when she worked part-time as a nanny. Number three wondered whether she would be suitable for Rosalind when she returned from Zagader shortly. Number three placed a hand on Rosalind's leg giving her total control of Jocelyn's mind. "You will advise your sister an opportunity for her to be a nanny at Jacobs farm soon. She may amuse Jacob, and you will not object Jocelyn when he visits you for breakfast in the mornings you comply Jocelyn?"

"Yes!" Number three continue to drive playing the part of Rosalind entering a superstore shopping for at least an hour, driving on to Exeter railway station. Jocelyn jumped out of the Range Rover greeting her sister standing outside with her suitcase, guiding her to the Range Rover opening the tailgate finding room in amongst the purchases. Rosalind climbed out of the Range Rover. "Jocelyn the roads are clearing, you can drive and talk to your sister, I'll sit in the back."

Rosalind and Jennifer greeted each other warmly, Rosalind climbing in the back of the Range Rover Jennifer and Jocelyn in the front. They started heading for Jacobs farm. Number three placed a hand on Jennifer's and Jocelyn's shoulders touching their neck to make contact. "Jennifer, you will amuse Jacob like your sister, you will apply for the nanny position shortly will you comply?"

"Yes, I will comply," Jennifer answered. Number three sat back rather pleased with her achievement, hoping when the real Rosalind return she wasn't disappointed with her decision, after all, they were supposed to use their own initiative and be individuals. She didn't have time to contact Peter or Matthew to discuss the matter further. Although from the messages number three is receiving telepathically, everything she had arranged is approved by the others. They finally arrived at Jacobs farm, Jocelyn introduced her younger sister Jennifer to Jacob. He looked up and down wondering why she bothered to wear any clothes there is nothing left to the imagination, although she did have a well-proportioned figure he concluded. "I'm pleased to meet you, Jennifer, I hope you enjoy your stay with your sister she is a good woman."

Jennifer giggled. "How do you know Jacob? I'll see you for breakfast in the morning," smiled climbing back into the Range Rover. Jacob watched them drive off, wondering who had said what to whom. Jacob went in the house to join Rosalind busily stacking the shelves. "We may have a live-in nanny shortly Jacob will have to see," Rosalind smiled.

"You're not thinking about Jennifer surely Rosalind?"

"Why what's wrong with her Jacob," Rosalind asked, turning to face him.

Jacob is making the coffee for them both commenting, "looks like a London prostitute in a skirt any shorter it would be a belt," he chuckled.

"Why! You have spent so long on this farm, Jacob, you have no idea how the real world has progressed. Admittedly I wouldn't dress like that other than in front of my husband," she grinned watching him smile. Jacob sat at the kitchen table, not bothering to say another word pointless, Rosalind always beat him hands down, she had an answer for everything which is most bloody annoying. "You are rather worrying me, Rosalind, perhaps you should see a doctor you don't seem to be showing much of your pregnancy?"

"The only doctor I need is God, not an earthly doctor thank you, Jacob, I would suggest you be quiet before you say something you regret," Rosalind picked up her coffee sitting on the settee switching on the television to watch her favourite programs. Jacob laughed going outside a safer place to be when Rosalind had a bee in her bonnet. Jacob walked across the Moor, followed by Jack. Jacob looked into the distance noticing the sheep had eaten most of the round bale placed in the feeder. He walked back to the farm starting the Massey tractor and loader grabbing a round bale of silage transporting to the first round bale rack. Jacob jumped from the cab peeling the plastic off the round bale and the netting lowering carefully inside the feeder. He drove onto Brook Farm entering the old barn, he grabbed another bale of silage transporting out onto the Moor, placing in the feeder. Jacob slowly drove home, parking the tractor watching the snow falling, which is okay, he didn't want high winds to make drifts. Jacob suspected within the next week, or so his sheep would have to come in. The days were short at this time of year on the Moor walking in the house to find a note. "Gone to see God will be back in the morning, Jocelyn will make you breakfast your Rosalind."

Jacob hoped there is nothing wrong, although he did have the habit of putting his foot in it more often than not. He would have to make his own supper tonight, frowned looking to Jack comfortably laying by the fire.

Number three aboard the spaceship discussing matters with Peter and Matthew. "Be careful, number three," Peter advised. "Don't make life too complicated for Rosalind when she returns to her position with Jacob; you should have left the selection of nanny to her. Although I suspect she will be pleased with your individuality thinking on your feet as humans would say."

Matthew commented, "Rosalind will return from Zagader soon. I think you have made a wise decision at least Rosalind will have the choice to engage Jennifer as a nanny or not. From the information, we are receiving from the home planet; the creator has altered Rosalind slightly giving her more abilities to sense things. If Rosalind feels it is beneficial, we will all receive the upgrade number three."

"Yes, I did receive the information, Matthew it may be beneficial to the collective to have a real leader and not a computer only making decisions."

"When Rosalind returns, she has to select 20 human females for the creator to produce more of him. I would have thought the creator would have used Zibyans the same as Rosalind to produce the offspring."

Appearing on the far wall, the creator and the firstborn by his side. Peter, Matthew and number three stared in disbelief the creator would show himself to them on a spaceship. "Peter allow me to answer your question before your inaccurate conclusions spread amongst the collective. The reason I am using human females, there can be no contamination, look what's happened to Rosalind her foetuses have adapted, which will be beneficial for the collective in the future. However, human females are the closest thing to the creators in construction; therefore, with a few modifications, the offspring should be copies of the creator."

"I didn't mean to be disrespectful creator, I'm merely considering options."

"If you have questions, Peter send directly to me telepathically, and I will answer this will prevent you from disturbing the collective and cause you to question unnecessarily."

"Yes, creator. Number three your performance as Rosalind in her absence is entertaining to watch. I know Rosalind is rather pleased with your individuality as I. You are showing great potential continue performing as Rosalind, she will return shortly to congratulate you." The firstborn and the creator vanished. Matthew looked to Peter and number three. "I suspect we have cause problems; luckily, the creator corrected the situation. To received praise number three from the creator and Rosalind must warm your construction."

"Yes, let's hope I don't make any mistakes otherwise the situation could change rapidly," she flashed her eyes stepping into the misty fog transporter, returning to Jacobs farm walking in through the front door. Jacob is sat at the kitchen table with a mug of coffee, he quickly made Rosalind one. "Is God really angry with me, Rosalind?"

"I think you can safely say Jacob you have annoyed him, he bestows upon you the gift of twins and other gifts. Don't speak to me of anything Jacob if you can't accept what is offered he may take everything away considering as an insult. Go tend your sheep and have breakfast, he will be watching to see if you shun his gifts." Number three wondered if she'd gone too far but couldn't backtrack now she wanted to keep him amused to ensure he wouldn't bother her. Jacob exhaled not saying another word grabbing his thick army coat from the back of the door and his crook glancing to Rosalind, glaring at him.

Jack, eagerly waiting at the door Jacob opened, Jack ran out into the fresh morning with a light covering of snow. Jacob shone his torch barely 7 o'clock in the morning, he placed a bag of sheep nuts on his shoulder, observing the red sky in the distance, glimpsing from the sea; promised a better day. Jacob listened to the snow crunching beneath his feet; his torch caught the eyes of his ewes. They sensed food surrounding him in seconds, Jacob lowered his bag to the ground, ripping open walking slowly making neat piles of pellets for the sheep to feast on, suspecting he would have to bring them in. Jacob emptied the bag holding tucking under his arm, continuing to walk towards the lights shining from Brook Farm. He is trying to understand what God expected of him, he's entirely satisfied with Rosalind why is he offered, Jocelyn? Although Jacob had to admit she's one wild woman and took some handling, made him smile, suspecting God would be annoyed with him if he didn't accept the gift wholeheartedly.

Jacob suspected now her sister Jennifer had arrived there wouldn't be the opportunity, he wasn't really bothered a good breakfast would be sufficient. Jocelyn came to the front door noticing Jacob's torch through the window. "Breakfast is ready Jacob, come along out of the cold." Jocelyn immediately removed his old army coat hanging on the back of the door. Jennifer is looking in the mirror, tidying her black hair. Jacob couldn't understand why she is dressed in such skimpy clothes in the house, she wasn't going anywhere he presumed. He sat down, tucking into his breakfast. Jennifer sat at the opposite side of the table with Jocelyn at the end. "Are you going somewhere today Jennifer you are dressed to kill," he commented, trying to make conversation.

"No, photoshoot around the farm for a calendar, not my favourite job, but it pays the bills," she answered, continuing to eat her cornflakes.

"Perhaps you should stay Jacob and watch, I'm taking the photos," Jocelyn expressed, finishing her toast and marmalade pouring everyone another coffee. Jacob didn't answer, he couldn't quite see the interest, although suspected men in London would and other cities. Sodom and Gomorrah all over again, perhaps God is going to wipe these places out once and for all. Jacob remembered what Rosalind had said to him, he is not to displease God again or shun the gifts offered; he reluctantly answered. "Yes I will stop for a while you won't want to stay too long out there is bitterly cold," he remarked looking at the way they were both dressed there wasn't much between them, why should he criticise Jocelyn had treated him to the pleasures of life very frequently. Jennifer rose from the table, checking her make-up in the kitchen mirror. Jacob slipped his coat on holding his crook. Jennifer and Jocelyn put on their coats, Jocelyn grabbed the expensive – looking camera from the sideboard.

"Let's go," she advised leading the way with Jacob closing the door to keep the warmth in the house. Jacob couldn't see how they could take photos barely daylight, Jocelyn advised, "Jennifer open the door on my Range Rover place one foot on the step, that's it hold it move your fur coat to one side." Jocelyn took two photos of Jennifer in that position which made her short skirt slide up showing her knickers. Jacob is about to say something then decided not to, almost blinded by the brilliant flash of the camera which lit up the whole vehicle and everything around. Jennifer closed the door on the Range Rover pulling her fur-lined coat together to stay warm.

They ventured into the barn out of the wind Jacob switch the lights on which weren't very bright but better than nothing he thought. Jack closed to Jacob's heels sitting on a bale out of the way of proceedings, Jacob thought is the best place to be. He watched Jocelyn instruct Jennifer where to sit, in his full view. Unfortunately, he felt slightly embarrassed after seeing the photo she posed for, he presumed for an erotic magazine or a porn magazine. She called out: "Jack come here, there is a good dog." Jack sat beside Jennifer on the bale of hay while she posed, she had eased her skirt virtually to her waist sitting there in her black lace knickers which were almost see-through. Jacob wondered why he is watching, quite disgusted with the whole process. He was quite shocked to hear Jocelyn instruct Jennifer to release the buttons on her ribbed button up crop top displaying her well-developed breast taking several more shots.

"Come on, let's go in the house and warm its freezing out here," Jocelyn suggested. Jacob followed into the house wondering whether he is supposed to be involved would this could be the final nail in his coffin with God he thought, he should say something, but he didn't know quite what. He sat there quietly after removing his coat, drinking his coffee. Jacob kept hearing the same sentence running through his head, "not to reject God's gifts, or he would lose everything." He couldn't quite see how God would approve of anything like this, although plenty of frolicking going on in the Bible at times.

Jocelyn commented, "in about an hour, the light should have improved to finish the shoots."

"I would have thought you'd taken enough," Jocelyn he remarked, deciding, time to leave he'd seen all he wanted to. Jacob rose to his feet, heading for the door. Jocelyn mentioned, "God will be disappointed, Jacob." Jacob didn't know Rosalind had placed that sentence in Jocelyn's mind to repeat to Jacob in the event he wouldn't comply with her instructions. Jacob took a deep breath realising he is meant to be here according to God and guessed that is his final warning. He removed his coat sitting at the table, drinking another cup of coffee.

Jocelyn stood up, moving to Jacob sitting on his knee. "This is what I want you to do Jennifer for the next shot kiss Jacob." Jocelyn moved Jacob's hand inside her identical ribbed button up crop top. Jacob insisted, "I will not appear on some dirty calendar, God certainly wouldn't be permitting this sort of behaviour." Jocelyn rose to her feet, returning to her coffee seeing the headlights of a Range Rover come into the yard.

Jacob glanced through the window Rosalind had arrived he suspected all hell is about to break loose but determined to stand his ground. Rosalind entered standing behind Jocelyn and Jennifer, placing her hands on either shoulder, so she had control of them ultimately. "I'm returning to heaven, Jacob! Do you see me complaining about you here with Jocelyn and Jennifer? She is trying to make herself money to live on. You were poor once Jacob until I came along, remember that. The least you could do is help Jennifer. I will return home if God permits after your disgraceful behaviour, you wouldn't be here if it wasn't his choice. Goodbye, Jacob." Rosalind walked out of the door, she is determined he wouldn't pleasure himself with her anymore an utter waste of time. He could have those two instead until the real Rosalind returned home then she could determine his future, and there's.

Jacob is left in no doubt God is in charge, if he didn't comply, he would never see Rosalind again or his son and daughter she is carrying. He'd never seen Rosalind so angry with him before in all the time they were married.

The only thing Jocelyn said, "I'm glad that's result let's press on," she is obviously treating the situation as merely a job, after all, she is a film producer so none of this would be out of the ordinary for her Jacob concluded. Jennifer approached him sitting on his knee. Jocelyn moved around, so she could position herself to take the best photo. "Now Jennifer," instructed. "Come on Jacob be co-operative please Jocelyn," asked calmly. Jacob complied, sliding his hand inside the tight ribbed button up crop top. "Excellent," Jocelyn expressed looking out through the window. "Come along, let's go to the barn. See if we can get the magic shots," she expressed smiling. They slipped on their coats again heading out into the cold morning in the direction of the barn. Jacob couldn't imagine what is left to do. Jocelyn looked around the barn for the best light and setting. "Okay, Jennifer, you stand there Jacob you stand directly behind her, that's good." Jacob complied reluctantly.

"Right, Jennifer, you know what to do. Don't belong its cold out here," Jocelyn instructed. Jennifer didn't hesitate to release the button on her top placing Jacob's hand on her breasts, "blimey your hands are cold, Jacob," Jennifer complained.

Jocelyn quickly took several shots. "Now, Jennifer." Jennifer bent over, pulling down her black lace knickers. Jacob didn't know what to do this is disgusting as far as he is concerned, he is in the den of iniquity. "Jacob!" Jocelyn ordered, "come on," she pointed. "Hurry up its cold we haven't time to waste." Jacob dropped his trousers and pants Jocelyn took several photos. Jacob couldn't believe he would have an erection in this position. "Right that's it back in the house we can finish off in there it's too cold out here," Jocelyn advised in her director's tone of voice. They quickly hurried into the house. Jacob sat at the table. "Can I go now Jocelyn I have the animals to see to?"

"Another hour or so, Jacob that's all it won't take long," she smiled reassuringly.

Jacob sat drinking his coffee he couldn't believe in his wildest dreams, God would have anything to do with this sort of behaviour, surely this is pornography; although he wasn't sure he'd never ventured into looking at things like that. Jacob asked, "will anybody recognise me in the shot, Jocelyn?"

"No, you're not a professional artist, we certainly wouldn't divulge who you are, thanks to Rosalind permission to use you in the shots."

"Rosalind knows what's happening," Jacob asked shocked although thought perhaps he shouldn't be after all.

"She's a good friend I told her what is involved, she wasn't bothered in the slightest, were only borrowing you," Jocelyn laughed.

Jacob would never suspect Rosalind of knowing any think about such things as he's involved in now. He sighed heavily, not knowing what to believe anymore, beginning to wonder whether he would have been better off staying single and not having Rosalind returned to him.

They finished warming themselves Jocelyn removed the cups from the table. "We might as well start here." Jennifer immediately removed her clothes, laying over the edge of the table. "Come along, Jacob," Jocelyn ordered. Jacob reluctantly complied, feeling he had no option now. Jacob positioned himself behind Jennifer Jocelyn took photos. "Go on, Jacob," Jennifer screamed. "My God, what's that?" Jocelyn continued to take pictures as Jacob moved, hoping one of the movements would be the best shot of all and could gain them several hundred pounds. Jocelyn wished it was a movie by the sound Jennifer is making. "Okay, that will do," Jocelyn advised becoming quite excited herself determined to have some of him before he left. "Upstairs Jacob, you know where my room is, come along Jennifer you can join us." Jacob spent the next hour with the pair of them on the bed this is madness in his opinion nevertheless delightful, and after all, this is God's wish and Rosalind approving who's he to argue.

Jacob went downstairs recovering his clothes dressing by the warm Aga, he made three coffees hearing Jocelyn coming down the stairs both only wearing their dressing gowns, not fastening, Jacob concluded what's the point he'd seen everything, why conceal now. "Don't be late for breakfast tomorrow Jacob," Jocelyn advised grinning.

"I second that," Jennifer suggested. Jacob kissed them both on the cheek, shaking his head in disbelief at what he'd heard. He left the house checking the Rams snow is falling rapidly. Jack was asleep on a bale of straw joining him. Jacob fought his way through the cutting wind and blizzard returning to his home farm entering the house, quickly throwing wood on the fire the Range Rover is here Rosalind wasn't. To be quite honest, he concluded he didn't expect to see her again; he'd annoyed God. Jacob looked at the clock nearly 3 in the afternoon he spent all day at Brook Farm virtually behaving like a male prostitute. Jacob sat by the fire, reading his Bible, trying to understand the madness of his life. Rosalind is correct if she hadn't returned and he hadn't of had her support, he would have nothing.

9 o'clock in the evening Jacob closed his Bible, he couldn't see, walked over to the wall pressing the red button which started the generator, the lights came on in the house. Jacob made himself a cheese and onion sandwich placing a few dog biscuits into Jack's bowl. Jack is the only one that knew

Rosalind is not the real Rosalind, he hadn't received any discharge food for nearly a month; this Rosalind didn't smell like the other Rosalind.

Jacob threw a few more blocks on the fire settling down to sleep in his old armchair, a place he is familiar with. This reminded him of old times it wasn't long before he's asleep dreaming of better times wondering if God really approved of what was taking place.

Number three playing Rosalind aboard the spaceship: "Should I return to him, Peter, or should I make him wait a little longer to teach him a lesson?"

Matthew cautioned, " he may reject you number three Rosalind would be somewhat disappointed if you destroy her planning. I do like the way you used the human females to avoid having relations with him. I would stay here two more days no longer; there is earth saying absence makes the heart grow fonder apparently, strange beings. We should have exterminated them at the beginning."

Peter advised, "Rosalind is on the way from Zagader in three more days the problem will no longer be yours number three unless Rosalind has other plans for you."

Early the next morning Jacob woke looking at the clock, 6 o'clock in the morning, he switched on the lights, making him a coffee. He opened the front door; the snow 6 inches deep. He eagerly drunk his coffee, slipping on his thick army coat and his cap stepping out of the house. Jacob, checked the barn, shining his torch opening the gates for his sheep to enter, they were coming in almost end of November determined not to lose any to the weather. Jacob grabbed his quad bike with Jack sat on the rack, driving across the Moor, searching for his ewes, finding them in a gully sheltering from the bitter wind and drifting snow. They didn't take much persuading to head towards the farm, Jack keeping them together and Jacob following with his headlights on. Within 1 ½ hours, they were in the barn steaming. Jacob quickly cut three bales of hay in the racks for them to eat filling the troughs full of water, so they had something to drink. He couldn't imagine Rosalind leaving him in this predicament that is beyond spite. God or no God, he didn't deserve this treatment he'd always been faithful to the Bible why should he be made to suffer now.

Number three had read his thoughts rather alarmed, she may have gone too far changing into Rosalind she transported to the farm, making another coffee as Jacob entered seeing the expression on his face of disappointment. Jacob bit his tongue determined not to go overboard if he lived on his own, he would have to have managed anyway. He took a deep breath drinking his coffee. "I'm off to Brook Farm the two Rams out in this weather, I'll put them in a building over there. Changing the subject, you are aware of what took place yesterday Rosalind?"

"You are helping Jennifer and Jocelyn with a photoshoot. I saw no harm you helping, and I can assure you God didn't. I was with him last night discussing my future with you."

"And what is the conclusion are you staying or leaving Rosalind?"

"That depends on you Jacob if you continue to displease God then I will go, or I can go now if you don't want me anymore, Jacob."

Jacob took a deep breath. "Of course, I want you to stay, and I want to please God. I find this whole situation somewhat confusing things are happening that I would not believe in a million years. Perhaps you're right I have lived too much of a sheltered life here on the Moor. I presume I'm to continue having breakfast at Brook Farm with those two?"

"Yes, Jacob, it's God's decision. I have no objections, gives me more time to rest, I haven't long to go," she smiled sweetly.

"I keep forgetting Rosalind you still look as pretty as ever," he remarked, stepping from the house followed by Jack. Jacob jumped on his quad bike; he wasn't walking this morning in a blizzard, finally arriving half an hour later at Brook Farm. He parked his quad bike, placing a halter on the two Rams who are only too pleased to come out of the awful weather leading them into a pen. He opened a bale of hay filling their troughs with water. Jack lay on a bale of straw, watching his master walked to the front door greeted by Jocelyn, she and Jennifer had finished their breakfast. She helped Jacob off with his coat hanging on the door with his crook. She sat at the table with her laptop, studying the photo shots they took yesterday. They both moved seated either side of Jacob as he ate his breakfast, every so often Jacob glanced up looking at the pictures of him and what he was performing with Jennifer. "Will you make much money out of those Jennifer," Jacob asked curiously.

"Not much it will help tide me over, until the coronavirus disappears, which hopefully won't be much longer. I wish we could shoot some videos I could really make enough money to last until the coronavirus has gone," she sighed heavily.

Jacob sat in thought for a moment what had he got to lose, he would be helping someone out of a jam, which is the correct thing to do according to the Bible. "Jocelyn, you're a film director, can't you help Jennifer?"

"There's no problem with directing, I do have a small camera here would you be prepared to participate, Jacob, no one would know who you are only myself and Jennifer. I could do all the editing here and then use my laptop to distribute for the right money," she remarked deep in thought.

"Providing you take part as well Jocelyn?" Jacob insisted.

"Don't be silly Jacob no one will want to look at me. I'm too old. Jennifer is only 20, and I am 30 something."

"I'll go home then I have sheep to look after," Jacob stood up.

"Okay," she remarked grinning, watching Jennifer smile. They ventured upstairs everyone removed their clothes, Jocelyn filming Jacob performing with Jennifer who is genuinely screaming with what she is receiving, she could barely breathe. Jennifer pleaded, "no more Jacob, please no more let me rest." Jacob moved away Jocelyn gave the camera to Jennifer, Jocelyn lay on the bed, she couldn't believe the sensation the biggest turn on she's ever had in her life. "Please enough, Jacob, please no more," Jocelyn begged. Jacob determined, holding Jocelyn's hand taking her downstairs followed by Jennifer. He lay Jocelyn on the kitchen table and started all over again with her, she's covering her face screaming while Jennifer filmed everything.

Jacob relented, passing the camera to Jocelyn Jennifer looked surprised when Jacob lifted her onto the table and repeated the process with her. Finally, he finished much to her relief. Jacob dressed quickly leaving Jocelyn, and Jennifer sat at the table holding their heads, he kissed them both on the lips. "I have work to do. I hope you make some money to tide you over, God bless you both," he chuckled walking out of the house across the yard climbing on his quad bike with Jack joining him on the carrier, they headed across the snow-covered Moor. Jacob thought he completed the task God had set him, he hadn't held back all relented in the slightest, he is pretty sure Rosalind is aware of everything. Jacob arrived back at the farm to discover Rosalind had tended the sheep bringing a smile to his face. Jacob entered to find his lunch on the table, he sat quietly eating with Rosalind watching her soaps on the television. Jacob joined her after finishing eating the wasn't much point in going outside, the sheep had been tended to, the weather is foul. Number three playing the part of Rosalind read his thoughts realising what he performed willingly. She touched his forehead, Jacob is unconscious. She stepped from the front door travelling to the spaceship in the transporter. Peter and Matthew were there to greet her. "I see you have gained control number three," Peter advised.

"Thankfully yes, I believe Rosalind will return from Zagader in the morning, she has made better time on the return journey."

"Number three, you have stretched the teachings of the Bible to an extreme. If Jacob sets out to read from front to back, he will discover some of what you had him perform is not in the Bible; he is not that stupid not to put two and two together to use a human phrase."

"I know! Only after experiencing mating with a human, I couldn't allow him to do that again to me, which a female is supposed to let her husband perform. My solution is to add the sister into the equation to ensure he is fully satisfied. I know I could put him to sleep some of the time, but if he approached me early in the day, how would I account for the loss of time he would experience. For instance, he's fallen asleep as far as he's concerned after lunch most humans perform this activity when their ageing."

"I understand your reluctance number three, Rosalind is far more experienced in handling Jacob then you. However, I feel I must praise you you have excelled in your assignment, and I'm sure Rosalind will be very understanding on her return in the morning. I suggest you wait until Jacob has gone to Brook Farm for his breakfast before you return to the spaceship and change places with the real Rosalind."

Number three flashed her eyes to Peter and Matthew transporting to the farm entering the house after checking the sheep are safe for the evening. Jacob, still asleep on the settee, she touched his head again, ensuring he would be unconscious until morning. She left the house climbing into the Range Rover driving to Brook Farm, she wanted to see the filming for herself. Jocelyn greeted her open-heartedly, inviting into the kitchen for a coffee with Jennifer at the kitchen table. Number three held both their hands in a loving gesture. "I want to see the film you made of Jacob you will not realise you've shown me and you will not say anything to Jacob I've been here, do you both understand?"

"Yes, they," replied together. Number three, Jocelyn and Jennifer entered the front room Jocelyn connected her laptop to the television, they sat together on the settee watching what had been filmed. Number three couldn't understand the fascination or why the two women were making so much noise, the experience did nothing for her. She held their hands again: "Remember to continue to please Jacob every morning until further notice, you understand?"

"Yes," they both replied, walking with number three to the front door waving goodbye to her. She returned to Jacobs farm looking at the clock 6:30 in the morning, she started making coffee, knowing it would disturb Jacob. He moved to the table, scratching his head, sipping his coffee. He looked out of the window, "I'm pleased I brought the sheep in Rosalind they'd do no good out there," he frowned.

"No! I'll feed our sheep here you can take the Range Rover and drive over to Brook Farm check on the Rams and have your breakfast. I'll catch up with you later, Jacob." She suggested kissing him on the cheek suspecting this would be the last time she saw him and he wouldn't have his sticky hands on her construction again. Jacob jumped in the Range Rover, leaving Jack at home driving steadily down his track to the main road travelling along for a few miles reaching Brook Farm, he parked checking on the Rams.

Number three quickly check the sheep stepping into the misty fog transporter, she returned to the spaceship eager to meet Rosalind. Peter and Matthew with Rosalind were waiting for her arrival number three stood before Rosalind. "I hope I haven't done anything you disapprove of Rosalind," number three asked nervously.

"I've studied the changes you have made, you have upset Jacob on numerous occasions number three, he is totally unsettled. I appreciate you didn't want to have relations with him I'd already put Jocelyn in place, and you brought her sister in as well. I will have to see if I can repair the damage, your reluctance to participate in the mating process, you may regret if I decide to upgrade you like me. I will make my final decision after I return to Jacob and see how he treats me, number three."

Rosalind stepped into the transporter taken to a familiar place, she has missed for a month Jacobs farm the one she helped create and turn into a profitable enterprise for her brothers and sisters. She had fond memories of the creator spending every moment she had with him once he'd modified her sensory perception, she wanted to experiment with Jacob to see if the sensation improved or decreased.

Jacob returned in the Range Rover parking by the house, he walked in, making a coffee looking at Rosalind watching Jack bark, jump up, wagging his tail as if an old friend had returned. "I think that dogs losing his marbles one minute he wants to bite you and the next he wants to kiss you Rosalind, silly bloody dog."

Rosalind patted Jack, who laid by the fire knowing the real Rosalind had returned. Jacob past her a coffee they sat on the settee together, taken by surprise when Rosalind started to kiss him lovingly almost encouragingly. "Hey steady on Rosalind you shouldn't be considering you know what in your condition?"

"Oh, I'm sorry I thought you were my husband as long as it's not painful or hurting the infants it doesn't matter according to the books I've read," she grinned determined to have her own way. "But of course, if you want to come near me, you will have to shower. I can smell cheap perfume on you." Jacob turned bright red he knew whose scent that was, and he is quite worn out at the moment, perhaps a shower would invigorate him he thought heading for the bathroom. Rosalind went into the bedroom laying on top of the bed naked Jacob walked in with a towel wrapped around him. He started kissing Rosalind caressing her in every sense of the word making love to her. Rosalind is analysing everything comparing Jacob to the creator, she enjoyed either immensely, with the new upgrades the only difference if there is one she concluded Jacob lasted longer. He rolled onto his back. "My God woman that's beautiful," he remarked panting, trying to catch his breath. "Do you still want me to have breakfast over at Brook Farm Rosalind, I would rather have breakfast with you," kissing her passionately?

"Jocelyn is a good friend and her sister, you enjoy your time over there helping Jacob, you have to check on the farm every day and the Rams of course. You mustn't forget its God's decision, you are helping them out immensely, which I love you for," Rosalind smiled. "If you're, a good boy, when you come back occasionally there may be a treat for you," she chuckled. Now, this is the Rosalind he loved; something had changed, he didn't know what and didn't want to find out as long as it stayed the same, realising he would have to eat heartily to keep his strength for the moment. Rosalind showered extremely pleased with his performance her new upgrade excelled. Rosalind came from the shower Jacob had made the coffee they sat together on the settee. She touched Jacob's forehead rendering him unconscious stepping aboard the misty fog transporter, taking her to the spaceship. The creator appeared on the far wall. "Your conclusions are interesting Rosalind, you are of the view unless a male or female Zibyan is on a mission it would serve no real purpose for them to possess the programming I have installed in you."

"Yes, creator it is a distraction, although I will experiment further with mine with your permission?"

"I understand your reasoning Rosalind there is no rush to implement the programming to anyone else, your conclusions are correct, may cause upheaval in the collective if not handled correctly by someone who thinks individually like you."

Matthew spoke: "Creator you are aware of the coronavirus on earth, how many millions will actually die is unknown at the moment. I would like to harvest a million Chinese, they take particular pleasure from what I've viewed on their news channels in inflicting unnecessary pain on animals, instead of enjoying their presence."

"Agreed. Rosalind, I would expect the 20 females you have selected for me to be on the next transport ship, I am eager to proceed with my experiments."

"I wish to return to my routine with Jacob creator, which will only take two days. I have to correct some mistakes number three has made with him. A matter of a few days selecting suitable females which I will transmit their likenesses to you for a final approval creator. I've had an idea creator to assist me I suggest, we send number three around the world to various countries, I will explain to her what I expect her to find, she can transport the unconscious females to the spaceship, we can both make the final decision on who is processed and who is shipped to you creator."

"You are excelling Rosalind. Your processors are expanding their parameters. I think that is a very sensible decision. Number three," the creator advised. "You will obey Rosalind's instructions, and when you have collected the 20 successfully, you will return with them to the home planet."

Number three answered quickly, "yes, creator." The creator vanished from the wall screen. Rosalind turned to number three. "You have seen the way Jocelyn and Jennifer are constructed. I will expect you to find nothing less attractive than those two for the creator. Try to limit the age to no older than 20 earth years that way, the creator will have time to experiment with the females several times if his first attempt should fail to create what he wants."

"Yes, Rosalind I think I know what you're looking for."

Rosalind flashed her eyes to everyone smiling stepping into the misty fog transporter returning to Jacobs farm. 6 o'clock in the morning Rosalind made the coffee, waking Jacob snoring which she found very amusing. "Come on, sleepy," she chuckled. "I will check the sheep you check the Rams Jacob have your breakfast and return." Jacob stood up, walking to the kitchen table kissing Rosalind passionately, placing his hands on her backside. "There is no time for that Jacob coffee, check the Rams," Jacob grunted making Rosalind laugh, sitting in his armchair throwing more blocks on the fire. "You needn't come out Rosalind, I'll check the sheep here before I go over to Brook Farm, I don't want you catching a chill in your condition."

"You actually care about me, Jacob," she voiced teasing.

"I don't know what's come over you of late girl, your mood swings are terrible, one minute you're burning my ears and the next you love me. I'll never understand women, come on Jack lets check the sheep and go over to Brook Farm."

Rosalind laughed watching him leave the house he fed and watered his sheep in the barn, throwing a mineral block over the fence to maintain their good health. Jacob started the Range Rover with Jack jumping in the driver's side, dropping down onto the passenger side on the floor. Jacob stayed there for a few moments letting the heater clear his windscreen and back window. He steadily drove to Brook Farm parking in the yard checking on his Rams, giving them a little hay and water. Jocelyn waved from the front door, "Jacob, it's freezing out here."

Jacob laughed, "this isn't cold you wait and see this is nothing to what it can be like." Jacob went into the house sitting at the table, he didn't know why they bothered to dress, although they did look incredibly enticing, he concluded tucking into his breakfast. Jennifer kissed him on the cheek after finishing her cornflakes. "Jacob," she whispered in his ear, "if I'm very nice to you, help me please."

Jacob laughed, "what do you want if it's money I haven't got any you have to ask Rosalind."

"You remember the video?"

"Of course, didn't sell very well I shouldn't think so with me on it, I hope no one recognises my ugly face."

"No, quite the opposite Jocelyn has been contacted they would like more and there willing to pay handsomely, how would you feel about performing Jacob again?"

"I would prefer not to, can I have time to think things over?"

"Of course, no hurry," Jocelyn smiled.

"Thanks for breakfast, I'd better be on my way," Jacob smiled, leaving the house climbing into his Range Rover patting Jack. He returned home walking into the house Rosalind looked at the clock. "You haven't been gone long, Jacob, what's the matter?"

"Nothing I had breakfast come home I thought I'd spend some time with my wife," he grinned mysteriously. Rosalind already read Jocelyn's mind and the request Jennifer made. She realised when her children were born, she would have to spend some time in the spaceship with them, to make sure they understood what they could do what they couldn't do in front of Jacob, essential for the moment Rosalind, and Jennifer kept him amused. Rosalind decided to gamble. "let's go and see Jocelyn and Jennifer have a cup of coffee with them, nothing much happening today Jacob," she smiled.

"Can't we, you know?"

Rosalind laughed, "we shall see later." they went outside climbing in the Range Rover Rosalind driving to Brook Farm greeted with a smile by Jocelyn with Jennifer, making the coffee. Jacob sat at the table, suspecting nothing. "We are nipping upstairs Jacob we won't belong," Rosalind suggested. Rosalind, Jennifer and Jocelyn ran upstairs Jacob not realising Rosalind is controlling the other two. Rosalind searched through Jocelyn's wardrobe, selecting similar to what Jennifer is wearing, almost nothing. They came downstairs. Jacob stared in horror at the way Rosalind is dressed, about to speak; she placed her finger to her lips. "Remember, God is watching Jacob fail; that is the end." Jocelyn set up the camera on a tripod. "I wouldn't have to do this Jacob if you had complied with God's wishes," she suggested. Jacob stood up heading for the door Rosalind realise she was really pushing her luck.

"You go out of the door Jacob and another man will come in and take your place," she advised coldly.

Jacob paused, "you are not Rosalind; she would never behave in this manner, and God would not permit, you are a prostitute from Satan's nest."

Rosalind held her stomach, making believe she is in trouble, Jacob immediately ran over to her. "I'll take you to hospital, Rosalind."

"No! Take me home, God will collect me and return me to where I belong, not down here." Jocelyn and Jennifer did not hear any think of the conversation between Rosalind and Jacob; they were frozen to the spot Jacob hadn't realised too concerned about Rosalind. He helped her into the car driving home. Rosalind realised she'd failed, knew a gamble and had gone too far. Now she had to quickly repair the mess somehow. Jacob helped her in the house she touched his forehead rendering him unconscious wiping his memory since he came in and the same for Jocelyn and Jennifer the morning never happened.

Jacob shook his head, walking over, making the coffee. "You didn't stay long at Brook Farm, Jacob?"

"I must have he said looking at the clock it's midday, I can't remember anything I've done Rosalind."

"I'm going to rest Jacob perhaps you'd like to join me," she grinned, Rosalind wanted him relaxed, she would put him out for the rest of the day. She had to survey the women that were coming aboard the spaceship for the creator a top priority mission. Rosalind walked into their bedroom, removing her clothes, waiting for Jacob to join her. She discovered his approach is different again from yesterday. She found herself making noises which made Jacob more enthusiastic, her eyes enlarged absorbing the sensation, her programming is in overdrive she struggled to control herself tingling all over by the time he'd finished, Rosalind definitely wanted more of him, she hated to admit it. He is far superior to the creator, but she must keep that information secret.

CHAPTER 11

Selecting Females

Rosalind ensured Jacob is unconscious stepping from the house into the misty fog transporter, she boarded the spaceship. Number three is waiting for her arrival, along with Peter and Matthew. Standing in a line were 20 females. "Number three you have been busy; I didn't expect you to complete your task so promptly," Rosalind commented.

"I hope you are pleased with my selection Rosalind, I followed your guidelines using Jennifer and Jocelyn structure as a reference, none of the females are over 20 years old never had children or had cancer or any other serious human disease."

"I presume they are all under mind control number three?"

"Yes, Rosalind, I carried out a deep mind penetration, sedated each one individually as selected, and Matthew transported them here, ready for your inspection."

"You appear to have selected from around the world as suggested, have a variety of nationalities and colours, the creator should be pleased." Rosalind started walking down the line touching each female with the command, "strip." Each female removed their clothes Rosalind walked back up the line number three beside her, Rosalind walked around them all twice looking for imperfections in case number three had missed anything. "Matthew how long before you have a shipment of flesh for the home planet?"

"Almost completed Rosalind since the creator approved of me taking a million Chinese, I have processed 300,000. Admittedly it has caused panic in China, but that is not our concern they can kill themselves it won't matter to us, in fact, would help matters considerably. I only need to process another 50,000, sufficient to summon a transporter."

"Peter summon a transporter, explain to the creator we have his females to transport. Transmit their likenesses so he can view our selection if there are individuals he doesn't like process, and number three will have to find a replacement. Peter asked the creator if I can keep number three here; she has great potential and could be very useful in some situations. She can continue to help you harvest Matthew until I find a mission for her."

Rosalind watched number three smiled broadly, she had no wish to return home to Zagader. "I would only be too pleased to help you, Rosalind, with your assignments," number three smiled.

"The transport ship won't be here for three days, number three, you will have to feed them with proteins and don't forget water that is essential to maintain their health. The females must arrive in perfect condition for the creator. Peter, you control our spaceship, assist her and you Matthew."

They both flash their eyes in agreement. Rosalind watched number three lead the females into a compartment resembling a human home with the usual facilities. However, the females were not conscious they would function robotically to maintain themselves, not realising where they were or what has happened; everything would appear reasonable to them.

Rosalind looked at the monitor on the wall Jacob is outside tending his sheep, she noticed the Earth time is 6 AM time seemed to travel faster when she is aboard the spaceship, although she knew an illogical conclusion. Rosalind positioned for the central computer to examine her infants testing for any defects. Peter and Matthew watched along with number three. The central computer advised: "Rosalind the male and female child you are carrying our developing, have linked to your power source when they are born they will be able to consume vegetation or link to me to sustain them. They will have the ability to shapeshift like their mother and the ability to transmit their thoughts telepathically and control others. They will have to be monitored closely, although they will be born with the same intelligence as their mother."

Rosalind exhaled like a human would in shock. "The information is disturbing. Central computer will they look like a human child, or not will Jacob be able to distinguish them from another human child?"

"Of course, they will be his children they will look like any other human child initially, as they develop there may be a few changes I cannot advise what they will be, although we may be able to correct if necessary if the Zibyans are still here on planet Earth, we may have destroyed the humans and returned home by then."

The creator's image appeared on the far wall everyone turned to face him: "Rosalind and number three you have excelled in your individuality, I have studied the information on the females selected initially by number three and approved by Rosalind as suitable for my purpose. The transport ship is on the way I will permit number 3 to stay on earth and assist you, Rosalind. I will ensure the whole Zibyan collective can watch me perform with the females to avoid any thoughts of deception entering their circuitry," the creator vanished from the wall. Rosalind flashed her eyes to everyone watching Jacob on the monitor sitting on a bale stroking his favourite ewe along with Jack sat by his side. Jacob watched the misty fog appear, and Rosalind step from the brilliant light. Rosalind kissed him on the lips in a loving manner, "good morning husband, I'll make you a coffee before you go over to Brook Farm to check on the Rams, don't forget to be nice to Jocelyn and Jennifer they are friends after all Jacob."

"If you insist Rosalind," holding her hand walking to the house out of the cold wind. They sat drinking coffee together at the kitchen table. Rosalind remarked, "I will have to be careful Jacob what I do from now on, although there are no external signs I'm carrying twins they are not far away from delivery. I'm afraid I can't until they're born now," she smiled, trying to be a practical human and encourage Jacob to take the other two at Brook Farm for amusement. "I understand Rosalind completely we cannot take any risks with the unborn as much as I do love holding you in my arms."

"I know Jacob once they're born, I expect you to ravish me frequently," she grinned, enjoying the human phrases and expressions. Jacob kissed Rosalind lovingly slipping on his old army coat grabbing his crook, he stepped out into the blizzard, now in December, the weather is mean cutting across the Moor. Jacob client in his Range Rover Jack is staying at home there is no need for him to come out, Jacob could easily handle two Rams on his own. He sat there waiting for the heater to clear the windows eventually set off down the drive, he could barely distinguish between road and verge travelling the few miles to Brook Farm. Someone had fed the two Rams, Jacob suspected either Jennifer or Jocelyn. Jennifer waved from the open front door. "Quickly, Jacob, it's vile out there." Jacob ran to the front door stamping his boots to remove the surplus snow, entering Jennifer quickly closing the door he removed his army coat hanging on the back of the door with his crook. Jocelyn had cooked him a lovely breakfast three slices of fried bread tomatoes three eggs and four sausages. Jacob smiled, feeling more comfortable with the situation. "Good morning, ladies thank you this looks lovely," he sat down starting to eat. They joined him, Jocelyn, with her toast and marmalade and Jennifer with her cornflakes. Jocelyn asked, "Jacob, rather than me purchase a load of firewood, is there any chance you could supply me with some?"

"I don't see why not, I'll have a look at what's on the beach the weather has been rather nasty lately; usually we have timber wash up that's where I get mine from," he explained enjoying his food. "The next question Jacob I think the generators running low on fuel where do I get it from?"

"Leave that to me, Jocelyn, I'll finish my breakfast and top the generator fuel tank, completely slipped my mind. I can't expect you to carry tins of fuel in these conditions," he smiled reassuringly.

"I owe you some money Jacob," Jocelyn advised removing her cheque-book from her handbag.

"For what?"

"For helping Jennifer, you're entitled to your share from the sales which come to £2000."

"I don't want any money, let Jennifer keep it. I don't need money, I have Rosalind," he chuckled. "Besides, you don't stand any chance of earning anything while the coronavirus rages." Jacob finished drinking his coffee, standing up slipping on his coat. "I'll go fill the generator with diesel and fetch you a barrowload of blocks," he smiled, leaving the house shutting the door firmly behind him. Jacob checked the main farm diesel tank, half-full which would be sufficient to see Winter out he thought, filling 2, 5-gallon containers walking around to the back of the house topping the generator fuel tank, made five trips before full to the brim. Jacob moved on to the woodshed discovering there were about three days of wood left. Jacob started splitting the blocks filling the wheelbarrow he pushed it beside the front door emptying in a neat pile, returning to the woodshed. He chopped another load leaving in the barrow outside the front door carrying the wood in, stacking by the hearth in the front room. He pushed the wheelbarrow to the woodshed, splitting one more load leaving in the woodshed for Jocelyn to fetch when necessary. He quickly ran to the house warmly greeted by Jennifer, helping him remove his coat, and hat, coffee already on the table piping hot for him. "I might be later arriving Jocelyn tomorrow, I'll try and cut a load of timber and bring over with the tractor and trailer weather permitting," he smiled.

"Can we help at all Jacob," Jocelyn asked.

"No, safer on my own, if you're not experienced with chainsaws too dangerous for you to be around me, I've seen too many of my friends after an accident with a chainsaw, thanks for the offer though."

Jennifer glanced to Jocelyn, she smiled with approval. Jennifer stood up, taking Jacob by the hand. "Come with me." She led him upstairs, stripping in front of him laying on the bed. Jacob didn't say anything removing his clothes, he joined her immediately. Jocelyn filming everything. Jacob had turned into a wild man; Jennifer is screaming so loud Jocelyn thought the windows would break, she is rather pleased it wasn't her, she didn't believe she could stand the punishment. He moved into several positions; this is far more than Jocelyn had expected him to do. Jennifer trying to catch a breath, Jacob caressing her breasts, never going to stop; she thought. Finally; he relented. Jocelyn left the room heading downstairs to make the coffee, she didn't want him to start on her now, perhaps her turn tomorrow after he delivered the wood and give her a chance to edit the film, admittedly she did feel rather excited by his behaviour. Jacob dressed and came downstairs sitting at the table, grinning drinking his coffee. Jennifer had stayed on the bed trying to recover she never had sex like that before wondering if she'd ever walk properly again. Jacob kissed Jocelyn, "see you tomorrow," he walked out of the door. The snow had stopped falling thankfully, Jacob climbed into his Range Rover heading home. Rosalind had read everyone's thoughts, she is shocked at the way Jacob is behaving with them and not with her; perhaps she thought, because of her condition nevertheless, she is determined to make him do the same to her once the children were removed from her construction.

Jacob parked by the barn attaching his old sit up and beg to the trailer, collecting is axe and chainsaw carefully driving down onto the beach. Jacob finished collecting as much timber as he could buy 2 o'clock in the afternoon, he hadn't bothered to return home for lunch, Jacob needed to keep fit, after such a beautiful breakfast he wasn't that hungry. The sun starting to shine which meant frost tonight Jacob concluded, driving steadily up the slippery track realising it would have been more sensible to use his Ford four-wheel-drive, Jacob loved to hear the sound of the P6 engine purring under the strain of pulling the trailer. Jacob decided rather than wait until the morning while the weather is so bright, he would travel to Brook Farm and tipped the load.

He remembered the last time he'd ventured on the main road stopped by two police officers they are now helping his grass grow, made him laugh. Jacob back to the shed at Brook

Farm, tipping the trailer allowing the blocks to slide off into a neat pile. He moved the tractor and trailer forward starting to throw the blocks inside the shed to keep them dry. Rosalind is reading his mind; he appeared to have settled down again into the routine he is used to excepting what is served to him every morning by Jocelyn and Jennifer. Rosalind transmitted a thought to both Jennifer and Jocelyn they would not remember Christmas and jog Jacobs mind an unnecessary practice.

Jacob finished stacking the blocks climbing aboard his tractor, he steadily drove home very cold, although the sun shining. Jacob entered the house Rosalind removed a meal from the Aga placing on the table. Jacob smiled, kissing her on the cheek. "Sorry I'm late Rosalind Jocelyn short of wood, and I had to top her generator up with diesel. I thought I'd take the opportunity to grab the wood while the weather is reasonable; we still have plenty in stock," he smiled reassuringly.

Rosalind kissed him on the cheek, "enjoy your meal husband," she knew that would make him grin.

Rosalind moved to the settee with a cup of coffee switching on the television to watch Emmerdale farm. Jacob burst out laughing, continuing with his meal. Jacob went outside made the final check on his ewes returning to Rosalind watching TV, at 4 o'clock it is dark the sky full of snow from what Jacob could determine. He made two coffees passing one to Rosalind sitting beside her, she is engrossed in a nature programme another one of her fetishes. He decided far more palatable than Coronation Street or Emmerdale farm. "Jacob," Rosalind casually remarked, "I've invited my half-sister to stay while I'm away in heaven having our children. I presume that's okay with you?"

Jacob stared at Rosalind. "What when did this happen. I didn't know you had a half-sister?"

"A family secret Jacob dad was playing in the hay, mum didn't leave him, I don't know why when she found out the other woman was already married, made out to her husband the child was theirs until they divorce some years later, then the truth came out."

"What's her name? Where she live Rosalind? You certainly know how to shock someone."

"Sorry, Jacob, I should have told you sooner, only you know the old saying, let sleeping dogs lie. She's a lecturer at a University in Edinburgh in agriculture. You know everything is shut down at the moment because of the coronavirus. I phoned her the other day explaining my position. Actually, that's a little white lie, Fiona and I have been in touch ever since I found out about her, she is a year younger than me."

"How did you explain your death and sudden reappearance Rosalind? " he asked suspiciously.

"God works in mysterious ways, Jacob! Do not mention my death to her, and she will not mention it to you. God has seen to everything trust me, Jacob, he knows best."

"I'll not argue with that Rosalind after what he's given me, I've had more gifts this year than I ever expected to have in a lifetime. Fiona is welcome here as long as it's with your consent. She can help around the farm, she might enjoy the experience instead of sitting behind a desk lecturing," he grinned. "When do you expect Fiona to arrive Rosalind?"

"Tomorrow morning Fiona is flying by helicopter to the local private airfield, I will collect her. Thieves are still prepared to risk everything to make money, you can stay here and watch our farm, Jacob."

"Have you considered where she's going to sleep Rosalind we don't have much accommodation."

"Yes, I have it all worked out Jacob, Fiona's staying here while I'm away having the children. When I return if she has not returned to university, Fiona can stay and help me look after the children for a while. If there is insufficient room she can move to Brook Farm, there is plenty of room there they had an extension built some time ago."

"You appear to have a plan wife," Jacob smiled. Jacob followed Rosalind into the bedroom he changed into his pyjamas watching Rosalind change. She touched his forehead, he's unconscious. She altered her appearance stepping from the house into the foggy mist transporter arriving in seconds aboard the spaceship. Greeted by number three, Peter and Matthew were busy servicing equipment. They flash their eyes at each other in a greeting, number three, smiling broadly knowing she had a new assignment. "I'm sure you read my mind number three, I am upgrading you you will no longer be known as number three, you are Fiona permanently. Central computer, download the upgrade I received from the creator into her structure, she must be able to function as a human in behaviour." Fiona quickly moved to the wall the central computer link to her. Fiona started twitching the same as Rosalind had when she had the program downloaded to her. Fiona moved away from the wall still, jerking feeling quite strange, she looked to Rosalind. "Do not be alarmed Fiona the twitching will subside shortly once the program has fully enhanced your system. Like you, I considered human contact pointless. I can assure you you will have a different opinion this time," Rosalind smiled confidently. "You are to play the part of my half-sister and control Jacob while I'm away, make sure nothing goes wrong. I will have to spend considerable time here with the newborns while I make them understand how they must behave in front of Jacob. I will use the excuse there were complications at birth, they must remain in God's presence until they are healthy."

"You are indeed an individual thinker Rosalind," Fiona commented. "You work things out very quickly solving problems, I hope I become as proficient as you in time. The spaceship arrives tomorrow to transport the 20 females for the creator, I'm sure Peter and Matthew can transfer them successfully along with the processed human flesh without my assistance," Fiona suggested. Rosalind smiled walking to the processing plant deep in their spaceships construction followed by Fiona, they watched the remaining bodies sliced by lasers and the bone separated from the quivering flesh, the unwanted parts discarded to be incinerated. Peter approached Rosalind. "There are four loads of fertiliser for Jacob tomorrow morning Rosalind. Congratulations on your upgrade Fiona may you serve the collective proficiently under Rosalind's supervision."

Fiona flashed her eyes in appreciation of his comment. Rosalind commented: "I will arrange for Jacob to collect the first load at six in the morning there's plenty of room on the 30 acres," she advised confidently.

"We will be ready Rosalind."

Rosalind Fiona returned to the upper decks in the space-ship Fiona asked, "what shape shall I copy Rosalind?"

"A good question," Rosalind replied in thought. "We can't look the same precisely, because we had different mothers let us look on the monitor for suggestions." They watched the monitor human females walking around London, trying to select a female suitable as Rosalind's half-sister. Fiona remarked, "if she lectures in Universities, not only will she be clever for a human that is," she chuckled. "I would expect her to be glamorous because of her status; the pig-headed sort I think humans refer to some people."

"Clever thinking Fiona how about her? That one with the blonde hair she looks a bit tarty as Jacob would say what do you think?"

"Let me try out," Fiona shapeshifted until she perfected the woman's figure. Rosalind started laughing, "excellent especially the blue eyes, you have her make up perfect and indeed her figure, I will have to lock Jacob away when he sees you." Rosalind continued to laugh, enjoying the situation immensely, especially with new enhanced internal sensors. "Central computer, do Fiona and I look as if we could be half-sisters to a human?"

"Plausible, there are certain similar characteristics; Jacob would not question the authenticity of your half-sister."

"Good I will collect you later Fiona I will drive to the secluded car park 6 miles down the cliff road, I will telepathically inform you when I've arrived," Rosalind assured. "Don't forget to take some of the clothes from the corpses that fit you and place in a suitcase; otherwise, Jacob will wonder why you travelled without clothes," Rosalind smiled.

Fiona smiled, "You think of everything Rosalind," watching Rosalind stepping into the misty fog transporter returning to the farm, as Jacob came out to check his sheep at 6 o'clock in the morning. He smiled, kissing Rosalind continuing to monitor his sheep. Rosalind went in to make the coffee. She immediately discharged her waist food products into Jack's bowl, which he devoured instantly. Rosalind patted him, "good dog, you're very useful," she smiled, dashing back outside. "Jacob there are loads of fertiliser this morning don't forget you must go now." Rosalind watched Jacob run to the tractor and spreader quickly scraping the window, managing to start the tractor in the cold weather, rapidly descending to the beach. Pleased he had four-wheel-drive after four loads, the stones were becoming its dreamily greasy and traction is very difficult, even with four-wheel-drive considering how steep the track is. Peter didn't take long to load the spreader each time Jacob returned to the beach within 1 ½ hours the task was completed, Jacob returned to the barn stopping his tractor going inside the house. Rosalind already made a coffee sat at the table. "You be careful on the roads this morning Rosalind, more snow even I struggled with the tractor coming up from the beach."

"I will husband don't forget the Rams this morning go across the Moor with the old Land Rover you should make it easy enough," she smiled. "I would suggest taking the road. However, you'd be the only one to bump into a police car this morning," she laughed, "and we don't need any more problems."

"That's a fact, Rosalind," he smiled kissing her lovingly on the lips, "I better check on the Rams and those two townies before they freeze to death," he laughed jokingly.

Jacob left Jack in the house; there is no point in taking him, let him stay in the warm; when he has to work; he works. Jacob struggled to get the Land Rover to start. Eventually, it fired up into life with clouds of smoke billowing from the exhaust, he allowed it to warm for several minutes fearing the diesel could be crystallising in the pipes from the cold. Jacob set off across the Moor very slowly struggling to see where the old track is, after half an hour he arrived at Brook Farm seeing smoke billowing from the chimney, praying it hadn't caught alight. The chances of getting the fire brigade out here in a timely fashion were slim to none. Jacob knocked on the front door and walked in. He realised immediately what is causing the smoke jostling, burning an old piece of cloth. She smiled, "you're going to scold me, Jacob, I can see by your expression."

"If you have material to dispose of, I can always use it to wipe my hands-on in the workshop rather than risk setting fire to your chimney." Jennifer came down the stairs kissing Jacob on the cheek going to the Aga removing his breakfast. "Maybe rather spoilt Jacob, we expected you earlier," she smiled, placing on the table.

Jacob sat down tucking in, "seems all right to me, Jacob," smiled.

Jocelyn winked to Jennifer, Jocelyn dashed upstairs, their chance to make more money if she played her cards right. She frantically searched through her wardrobe, some of which were props from films she'd made in the past. Jocelyn had a large suitcase, hadn't looked in for years. She removed a school uniform she cast her mind back, trying to remember what the film was, remembered, laughing. Jocelyn changed into the outfit which didn't fit at all would suffice for filming purposes. She and Jennifer had made quite a considerable amount of money with the last film; providing Jacob would play along they could make more, keep the wolf away from the door until the coronavirus vanished, Jocelyn can start directing movies properly again. Jocelyn sat at her dressing table, applying make-up; remembered how some of the girls dressed in sent trillions film, she enjoyed watching many years ago. Jocelyn altered her clothing rolling up the skirt and blouse, leaving one button fastening the whole outfit, not bothering with her bra. She found a pair of white socks which she slipped on. She is trying to stop laughing this is so ridiculous beyond belief; how could she possibly be behaving like this. Jennifer came running upstairs, seeing Jocelyn. "Blimey Jocelyn what do you look like, you'll have to be quick he's nearly finished his coffee, he will leave if you're not ready. I'll stand by the stairs with the camera we must catch his first reaction of you this could be priceless. I can't wait to see what he will do." Jennifer laughed, running downstairs.

Jocelyn muttered, "now or never." She slowly walked down the stairs Jacob about to finish his coffee, he caught sight of her turning around in his chair in disbelief, smiling he'd never seen anything so ridiculous and encouraging to take what is on offer. Jennifer filming trying to stop laughing. Jocelyn placed her foot on the chair; nothing he couldn't see; she opened her blouse. Jennifer thought he is spellbound, he didn't move for a moment. Jacob suddenly rose to his feet, grabbing Jocelyn's hand running off upstairs with her. Jennifer followed closely, not wishing to miss a moment of what could be something spectacular and valuable. Jennifer captured everything Jacob stripping Jocelyn pushing her on the bed throwing his clothes on the floor, he made love to her, she is biting her hand trying to stop screaming. She wondered what she let herself in for, she had driven the man completely wild; there wasn't a part of her body Jacob didn't caress. Finally, Jocelyn exhaled, he relented dressing kissing her on the lips once more going downstairs making a coffee.

Jennifer stood there with her hand over her mouth in shock, she had never imagined in her wildest dreams Jacob could be so assertive. Jocelyn dressed in regular clothes she dared not go downstairs in the same garments, in case he attacked again, she would never stand the onslaught of him. Jennifer left the camera upstairs so Jacob hopefully wouldn't realise what they'd done. They sat around the table with Jacob, Jocelyn thought whether Jacob realised it or not he is a star and concealed star, no one could find out about hopefully, otherwise she dreaded what might happen. He kissed them both on the cheek, "see you tomorrow," walking out of the door, not in the slightest short of energy like Jocelyn a wreck flopping ahead down on the table to rest with Jennifer laughing. "I can't wait to see the finished product."

Jacob's Land Rover eventually started, he is quite surprised he didn't have to walk home, he steadily drove across the Moor; thankfully, his sheep weren't out in this dismal weather. Jacob parked his Land Rover seeing the Range Rover had left, suspecting Rosalind had gone to collect her sister, some secret to keep he thought in a small farming community, usually if you sneezed in the wrong direction the topic of conversation the next day. Jacob went inside the house, making coffee patting Jack laying by the fire. He looked at the clock at 12:45 p.m. suspecting Rosalind would soon be on the way home quietly praying she would drive carefully and avoid any icy patches.

Roslin parked at the location she had agreed to meet Fiona telepathically sending a message, within seconds Fiona is there carrying a large suitcase, she loaded into the back of the Range Rover climbing into the front with Rosalind. Rosalind looked up and down. "You've increased the breast size slightly why?"

"The computer determined, I should be more developed in certain parts considering I lecture and you do manual work on the farm. Don't ask me to explain Rosalind I followed the computer's instructions."

"I see you're wearing a smart suit, I think Jacob is going to jump out of his skin when he sees you. Don't encourage him too much to start with, you will have plenty of time to enjoy his pleasures while I'm aboard the spaceship Fiona. May be beneficial if you go over with him some mornings to Brook Farm. You haven't experienced mating since I had you reprogrammed have you?"

"No, Rosalind I haven't had the opportunity, what are your instructions concerning Jocelyn and Jennifer?"

"To ensure Jacob believes God is instructing his behaviour, I don't want him overthinking about anything, those two certainly keep him busy," Rosalind laughed. "Once I have given birth to these two aliens inside me, he will resume pleasuring me and you, we may be able to dispose of the other two as an unnecessary component."

"I hope it's a vast improvement on my last experience with Jacob, Rosalind, that's why I introduced Jennifer to ensure he is fully occupied and would ignore me."

"I can assure you your circuitry will be melting your mind I was shocked, I was like you not any more I can't wait to get rid of these two then I can start enjoying myself again," she grinned. Rosalind parked outside the house Jacob went straight to the rear of the Range Rover removing the large suitcase carrying inside, out of the blizzard. Jocelyn entered, "Jacob, I would like you to meet my half-sister Fiona."

Jacob stood there, absorbing what he'd seen holding out his hand. "I'm pleased to meet you. I presume you drink coffee," he asked, inviting her to sit at the table.

"Yes, thanks, I'm pleased to finally meet you Rosalind has spoken to me about you often, and you're a father soon, Jacob," she smiled.

"Yes, I will finally have someone to leave my farms to when I ascend into the heavens with any luck."

"Your a religious person like me, Jacob," she asked, lifting his Bible onto the table. "I wouldn't go anywhere without my Bible, God shows me what to do every day of my life," Fiona smiled sweetly.

"Praise, the Lord," Jacob professed. "His children are gathered in this room tonight," gently squeezing Fiona's hand, he left the table carrying her suitcase into the spare room closing the door. Jack came over sniffing around Fiona, he knew that smell walking away, laying back down by the fire. Rosalind telepathically talking to Fiona congratulating her on her performance, "Jacob is fooled altogether now you have mentioned the Bible." Rosalind and Fiona sat on the settee watching the television. Jacob chuckled going outside to tend his ewes. Jacob returned satisfied in his own mind as the sunset across the sea, his sheep were safe for the night. Jacob sat in his armchair by the fire Rosalind got up and made him a coffee, he placed it in the hearth. She touched his forehead; he's asleep until morning. Both Rosalind and Fiona stepped outside into the misty fog transporter heading for the spaceship; arriving in time to watch on the monitor another hundred thousand Chinese had materialised to be processed. Peter and Matthew were busy monitoring the processing plant, fully automated. Nevertheless, they were looking out for any bodies carrying locators, they'd been caught out before. Fiona and Rosalind sat down on invisible seating. Fiona asked, "you are aware Jocelyn and Jennifer are using Jacob to produce films?"

"I am aware! Doesn't hurt him I realise initially we programmed the two to occupy him, me for my reasons and you for yours. I have no objections if they continue to use him in that manner. However, we don't want it to become common knowledge he is involved. If you suspect he is about to be exposed deal with the situation as you see fit Fiona, in the meantime, you can enjoy while you're over there if you wish, Jacob probably thinks it's gods will," Rosalind laughed.

"What about the collective what will they say, Rosalind?"

"Nothing! You're experimenting how are we supposed to learn and understand our captives if we don't take part in their activities, some of which I admit are less favourable. The decision is yours, Fiona, at least you will see for yourself how Jacob performs."

Fiona looked at the monitor Jacob is outside with his sheep. "We had better return he mustn't know I've come with you; otherwise, will ruin everything, and he may start to question Rosalind."

"A good point Fiona, I will instruct the transporter to drop me by the barn and moved to the side of the house, you can leave there and should be able to enter the house without him seeing you, I will occupy him." They both smiled at each other stepping aboard the transporter within seconds Rosalind stepped out, the transporter moved on. Rosalind immediately kissed Jacob passionately receiving a telepathic message from Fiona: "She is in the house changing her clothes to keep the pretence she is human requiring warmer clothes to go with Jacob to Brook Farm in the appalling weather." Jacob and Rosalind walked to the house, Rosalind making the coffee. "Jacob, before you go to Brook Farm Fiona, may find it interesting if you take her along?"

"I don't think she's up yet Rosalind," Jacob remarked "Besides going to snow again, I can't see her interested personally."

Fiona came from her bedroom; both Rosalind and Jacob looked at the way she is dressed. She is wearing an Australian Driza-Bone coat and leather hat with jeans leather boots with a thick white jumper, her make-up is perfect. Jacob tried to stop looking at her, deciding she is absolutely gorgeous, especially with her lovely blonde shoulder-length hair. She walked to the table, sipping her coffee. "That's an excellent coffee, morning everyone." Jacob noticed in her hand a small Bible, she really impressed him, travelled with God at all times in her hand. "Praise the Lord, I see you carry his message with you."

"Always, Jacob, that's how I know what he wants me to do, he speaks to me often," she smiled pleasantly. Rosalind desperate to laugh, turning to look out of the window realising, how gullible Jacob is, concerning the Bible, he believes anything she concluded. "You're certainly dressed to go out in this weather Fiona, I will have to persuade my wife to purchase me one of those coats," he smiled.

"I will order you one Jacob today," Rosalind remarked, kissing him lovingly on the cheek. Jacob went out, leaving Jack behind followed by Fiona, they climbed into the Range Rover. Jacob started the engine the frost hadn't affected the window screen thanks to a covering of snow. He drove steadily down the track towards the road with Fiona sitting very prim and proper imitating the woman she'd observed on the monitor in London. Fiona held her Bible on her lap, making sure Jacob could see. Still, very dark outside when they arrived at Brook Farm, Jacob parked by the house. Jocelyn opened the front door. "Fiona I've made you a little breakfast as well as Jacob Rosalind phone me and told me you were coming. How wonderful to meet you." Fiona entered the house greeted by Jennifer; she held their hands, transmitting her orders telepathically to follow whatever she said and do exactly as they were told. Fiona released her grip. Jennifer helped to remove Fiona's Driza-Bone coat hanging on the door with Jacobs along with their hats. Everyone sat around the table, Jacob tucked into his enormous breakfast. Fiona gingerly ate one slice of toast, drinking her coffee anything she consumed would have to be disposed of at a later date. Fiona placed her Bible on the table. Jacob immediately stopped eating. "You have not thanked the Lord for your food Jacob neither did I another sin."

Jacob couldn't remember the last time he thanked God for the food on his plate. "I apologise Lord for my stupidity please forgive this simple man." Jennifer and Jocelyn stayed silent. Fiona is in full control of everything they would not react unless instructed by her. "Jocelyn, I believe you have recently made a film with Jacob. I would like to see please."

"Please follow me," Jocelyn invited taking Fiona into the front room, inviting Fiona to sit on the settee while she plugged in the laptop to the television. Jennifer sat beside Fiona and Jocelyn the other side, they'd left Jacob in the kitchen enjoying his breakfast. Fiona surprised at what she saw. Rosalind wasn't mistaken in her conclusion Jacob is performing, and by the noise, Jocelyn is making extremely well she presumed. "I suspect you are broadcasting to people who wish to pay you money to watch, Jocelyn," Fiona asked.

"Yes, no one will find out who anyone is, would be extremely embarrassing for Jennifer or me, including Jacob if the truth ever came out. A way of making an income until the coronavirus dissipates."

"Yes money is a nuisance, and of course there are plenty of men at home and females who enjoy this sort of activity I presume. A religious woman myself I obviously wouldn't know."

"Is there ever Jennifer," commented. "You could make millions of pounds if you have the right films, everyone seems to love Jacob and the way he performed. Jocelyn and I made £5000 with the last movie, and the money is still coming in."

"Do you to really enjoy allowing Jacob to mate with you?"

"You should try him yourself Fiona; sorry I shouldn't have said that your religion wouldn't permit you to behave like that."

Jacob came into the front room. "Are you ready Fiona, I'll take you home after I've checked the Rams," he smiled.

"Have another coffee Jacob Jennifer will make you one, I have to nip upstairs with Jocelyn she wants to show me something. Jennifer, I noticed the expensive camera on the sideboard I presume it's ready," Fiona winked. Jennifer couldn't believe her ears understanding what Fiona is suggesting outrageous for a religious woman.

"Don't belong I have work to do Fiona," Jacob remarked, returning to the kitchen with Jennifer glancing to Jocelyn, couldn't believe her ears either. Fiona and Jocelyn ran upstairs into the attic bedrooms converted years ago. Jocelyn asked, "what are you doing, what are you planning Fiona, are you sure?"

"No, not really but will find out won't we," she grinned. "What costumes do you have?" Jocelyn quickly opened the large suitcase discarding the one she'd already used. They both searched and searched they couldn't find anything they thought would interest Jacob, turning him into a wild man again. Fiona removed a black lace nightie from the wardrobe holding up to the window transparent. "This will do," quickly undressed slipping on the nightie not bothering with the lace knickers. Jocelyn tidied Fiona's hair the nightie is so low-cut her breasts were visible. "If that doesn't work Fiona nothing ever will, good luck."

Fiona picked up her Bible walked down the stairs slowly, Jennifer stood in the corner, filming her descending the stairs, Jacob glanced back falling off his chair, quickly re-seating. Fiona approached, "God's instructions Jacob to me, I demand you take me." She placed her foot on his chair; his eyes enlarged, he grabbed her hand running upstairs with her. Her feet barely touched the steps, she turned to face him. Jennifer is videoing everything out of breath, trying to keep up with them. Jocelyn stood by her watching in disbelief. Jacob removed his clothes, tearing the nightie off Fiona forcibly throwing her on the bed. She screamed her senses were in overload, Rosalind is right unbelievable, there is nothing he wasn't doing to her; she felt like a rag doll in his hands.

He is out of control, and Fiona didn't care; he finally relented kissing her very passionately on the lips dressing and going downstairs to make a coffee. Fiona sat up on the bed, "that's different!" She dressed in the clothes she arrived in looking at the expressions on Jocelyn and Jennifer's face; both shocked by the way Jacob behaved.

The three ventured downstairs Jacob had made them each a coffee. "We will have to go Fiona. Otherwise, Rosalind will think we've eloped," he grinned hoping he'd please God with his performance; obvious Fiona is sent as a gift, and he wasn't resisting this time. Jacob kissed Jocelyn and Jennifer goodbye slipping on his coat along with Fiona stepping outside into a bright morning; they checked the Rams climbing into the Range Rover heading towards Jacobs farm. Fiona opened her Bible pretending to read Jacob smiled. Fiona commented, "were you please with God's present Jacob?"

"Oh, yes. God is generous and his beautiful angel, she pleased me immensely as I hope I've pleased her?"

Fiona grinned not answering, Jacob, glanced to the smile on her face suspecting she is satisfied; Jacob didn't bother to question the rights and wrongs of anything providing God is in charge, he had nothing to worry about arriving home. Jacob stayed outside, tending his sheep. Fiona went in finding Rosalind making coffee, she is almost addicted; she thought pouring 2 cups. "From what I received from your senses Fiona, you enjoyed the experience this time?"

"Immensely, my circuits are still tingling, the creator's intervention has made things more interesting, although I agree with you Rosalind if everybody possessed the upgrade it may cause anarchy amongst the collective. The programme should only be used for the advancement of the collective, not as a pleasure item," she grinned.

The smile vanished from Rosalind's expression. "I'm summoned to the spaceship, I must go, Fiona, you take charge, explain to Jacob I'm feeling unwell, went for a walk to talk to God, he will understand if I'm not back tonight, he will accept that. Keep him calm Fiona you know how to do that," Rosalind smiled stepping out into the misty fog transporter and vanishing. She arrived aboard the spaceship Matthew and Peter were waiting for her arrival. "A sonic spaceship is waiting for you sent by the creator, he needs your assistance on Zagader urgently, he feels you will be the most helpful with the 20 females, placed on Jacobs planet in confinement until your arrival." Rosalind had all the information on a sonic spaceship, the fastest conveyance they possessed, she had never experienced travelling in one before. She flashed her eyes to Peter and Matthew vanishing into the sonic ship. She strapped herself in; the sonic spacecraft left earth, she had never travelled so fast in her life, her construction forced into the mould Rosalind wouldn't be surprised if the children were damage moving at such a velocity. 1 ½ days later Rosalind arrived on Zagader. She left the spaceship looking at the outer skin smouldering from the friction of travel across the vast distance. The creator is there to greet her. "Rosalind, come to the laboratory, I will explain my concerns."

They stepped into a misty fog transporter, appearing in seconds in the laboratory. "Your infants are almost ready to escape your construction Rosalind, this will be a momentous occasion in our evolution," he smiled.

"I hope they don't escape until I return to earth, I don't want them experiencing space travel until I'm convinced they can handle the velocity, creator," Rosalind suggested. "I presume you would have mated with the females by now, creator, what is the problem?"

"I watched the way Jacob performed when you selected females for him to be impregnated and shipped Zagader. They were compliant he is of their skin; I am not although it didn't offend you I have smooth scales. For mating to be successful, I want them relaxed and compliant. I know we can alter people's thoughts and brainwash if necessary, this is a crucial step, Rosalind. I don't want to fail once there are more of my kind the problem won't arise again."

"What happened to the others sent here to be genetically altered, creator?"

"Only one survived the others committed suicide, the genetics obviously worked in the one; otherwise, I wouldn't be here. She nurtured me for the first week, or so then my growth enhanced, she was fed to the animals she had no further use."

"I see you are concerned some of the females may commit suicide which is common amongst humans in some cases. We will have to handle the situation carefully to avoid this happening again. If we could produce 20 of your offspring humans would be immaterial in the process as you pointed out creator."

"I knew I'd made the right decision Rosalind you are the one to make this work. I will leave everything in your capable hands, keep me advised of what part you wish me to play, I will be ready."

Rosalind flashed her eyes to the creator summoning the transporter she travelled to Jacobs planet, maintaining Rosalind as an appearance. She walked along the beach, deciding to take a swim. Rosalind could sense the females were watching her from the undergrowth. Rosalind swam out playing with the dolphins for a while, so they realise she's alone, she stepped from the sea. Rosalind lay on the sand allowing the sun to dry her, as she suspected the bravest female approached her cautiously, carrying a sharpened bamboo pole, wearing woven vegetation to conceal her modesty. Rosalind opened her eyes propping on her elbows. "Are you one of them," the woman asked aggressively attempting to speaking English.

"I don't know what you mean, I live here have for years," Rosalind remarked calmly studying the African woman with the beautiful dark skin, she thought would impress the creator. "If you don't like it here, why don't you go home," Rosalind commented, holding out her hand. The African woman held out hers to help Rosalind to her feet, a fatal mistake on her part. The minute Rosalind touched her, she had full control of the African woman's mind. "Come to my village to meet my brother, he will show you the way home if you're lost?" The woman followed Rosalind without a second thought; the other women in the undergrowth watched and monitored from a distance not realising Rosalind could detect them easily. Rosalind held the African woman's hand again telepathically instructing the woman's mind, she was desperately in love with the creator and to give him anything he wanted. Rosalind couldn't understand why the creator hadn't allowed another Zibyan to carry out the same deception as her rather than transport her home.

Rosalind conveyed instructions telepathically to the creator. "Quickly, create the illusion of a small village in the clearing ahead." Rosalind grinned the other women had plucked up courage running to catch up; one woman held the African woman's hand, and the others linked this is more than Rosalind could ever hope for. She transmitted telepathically the same message to the other 19 women now they were all linked the instructions travelled to each one.

The creator had received the message not believing what Rosalind had created for him. He arrived in the village by the stream cooking 20 large fish and baked yams on an open fire, the women approach without fear smiling, each taking a piece of fish, enjoying on a palm leaf. The creator stood up; they watched him like a lovesick schoolgirl. He climbed a large coconut tree dropping down the coconuts so the females could drink the milk. Rosalind spoke: "My brother will look after you stay with him; he will provide you with everything you need." Rosalind smiled, watching the women expression of contentment.

The creator held out his hand to the African female; she smiled broadly joining him. She removed her woven vegetation clothing laying on the ground, he started making love to her. "Me next, me next," the women were asking. Rosalind is now satisfied in her own mind she had achieved what the creator wanted, stepping into the undergrowth, out onto the sandy beach she summoned the misty fog transporter and returned to Zagader. Rosalind smiled surrounded by her brothers and sisters asking her questions not only about the creator, her pregnancy, which would soon come to an end she hoped, desperate to perform all her functions once they had left her construction. Rosalind stayed for another hour telepathically answering all the questions she possibly could. Finally climbing aboard an ordinary transport ship heading for the earth to collect more human flesh. She didn't want to risk injuring her offspring before they were born, she would have three days to relax.

***

Jacob coming out of the cold warming his hands on the open fire, "where is Rosalind," he asked, looking around the room.

Fiona had made his tea placing on the table. "Nothing to worry about Jacob, she's going to talk to God and didn't know when she'd be back," Fiona shrugged her shoulders trying to make believe she didn't understand what is happening. "Apparently, your children are misbehaving," Fiona chuckled. Jacob sat quietly eating his food. Fiona sitting reading the Bible at the kitchen table, Jacob had concluded he didn't understand everything in the Bible. He suspected Fiona did every spare moment she appeared to be reading from the pages. Fiona left the table she knew curiosity is a human downfall, she created the illusion on the open page she is reading the words, now said in gold in italic writing. "Sleep with Fiona Jacob." Jacob watched Fiona go to her bedroom. He immediately turned the Bible around reading, seeing the words written across the page, he almost choked on his tea. Jacob read the words twice. "Sleep with Fiona Jacob," he quickly turned the Bible around to its original position. He looked at the page again, although upside down it had returned to the Scripture she was pretending to read.

Fiona, trying to stop laughing in her bedroom, she is determined to experience the sensation through her construction again. She looked through the clothes she had brought taken from the corpses before they were processed to see if there is anything of interest she could wear. Fiona somewhat disappointed hadn't selected better, although never realised clothes could have such an effect on someone until earlier today. She heard Jacob go out of the house, suspecting he is checking the sheep for the final time this evening already dark so he wouldn't stay out there long.

Fiona went into Rosalind's bedroom climbing into bed, about an hour later Fiona heard Jacob come in, he went into the bedroom Fiona had never known Jacob move so quickly, he's in bed with her within a minute. Fiona was holding her head suspecting it would explode with the information her mind is receiving; her senses were transmitting everything. Jacob finally relented, she lay there staring at the ceiling he hadn't bothered to turn out the light. Within a couple of minutes, he pulled the blankets off her and started all over again. Jacob kissed her on the cheek after half an hour, turning over to sleep. Fiona left the bedroom suspecting he wouldn't wake up tonight. She entered the bathroom, glowing bright red cleansing herself rather than taking a shower. She sat quietly in the front room, watching the television. Jack had finally taken a liking to her, occupying the seat by her legs until 6 o'clock in the morning.

Fiona started making coffee Jacob came staggering out of the bedroom. "I'd like to come to Brook Farm again this morning Jacob you don't have any objections, do you?"

"No," he remarked, looking out of the window, "it looks like another cold day we are nearly at the end of December; damn I missed Christmas again," he frowned.

Fiona laughed, "Jacob, you know God wasn't born on the 25th the biggest load of rubbish ever written," she smiled reassuringly.

"Apparently so," he sighed. "I'll check the sheep here before we go over to Brook Farm for breakfast," he remarked as if everything is quite normal. Jacob left the house feeding his sheep another round bale vanishing from his stack of silage. He filled the troughs full of water shaking the remainder of the wheat straw he had in stock on the floor of the pen trying to keep the sheep dry. Jacob wished he had ordered more, but like everything else these days, never crossed his mind in time, and to buy it at this time of year, he would pay a premium.

He heard the Range Rover start noticing coming towards him he smiled jumping in the passenger seat. "You time that just right, Fiona." She smiled sweetly driving off down the narrow track to the main road still covered in slush. Gritting lorries never ventured across the Moor they concentrated on them motorways more often than not. Fiona steadily drove down the drive to Brook Farm they both left the Range Rover checking the Rams finally heading indoors stamping their feet outside first. They removed their coats hanging on the back of the door noticing coffee on the table, Jacobs enormous breakfast and Fiona's one slice of toast with the smearing of marmalade. Jacob called out, "Is anyone here?"

"We'll be there in a minute enjoy your breakfast," he heard suspecting that is Jennifer. Fiona looked around the kitchen, noticing cameras positioned each overlapping the other. She read Jocelyn's mind trying not to smile when she realised what they were planning; she wondered how Jacob would react. Jacob sat drinking his coffee glancing to the stairway, he fell off his chair. Fiona moved away, so she wasn't filmed, she is beginning to think this was going too far now, and she would have to end before someone discovered Jacob is taking part. Jocelyn and Jennifer came down into the kitchen with a dog collar around their neck and a chain. Other than that, they weren't dressed both bent over the table, Jacob didn't hesitate to oblige. Fiona stood in the doorway by the stairs watching proceedings realising she could have Jacob all to herself if these two disappeared and she could live here. Jacob moved both women into various positions before he'd finished. Finally, he moved to the kettle treating as another job he performed, switching on. Jocelyn and Jennifer run upstairs to shower and change. Fiona entered the kitchen sitting at the table, passed a coffee by Jacob. Fiona sat there, sipping her coffee listening to the two upstairs giggling. Jacob commented, "God is truly generous I have everything and more."

"Things may change Jacob; you realise those two are making considerable money out of you that is not God's intention."

"I presumed it was, have I made a mistake Fiona?"

"Initially, no. God will resolve the issue; this is not your fault Jacob, he will decide what is right and wrong not you or I, come along we must leave." Jacob looking worried quickly followed Fiona out of the house they both climbed in the Range Rover, Jacob drove them home. Fiona telepathically instructed Jocelyn and Jennifer to return to London immediately and take all their possessions with them, destroy any footage of Jacob they possessed in the fire. Jacob parked the Range Rover they went inside sitting down to have another coffee, Fiona received a message from Peter telepathically. "Send Jacob to the beach they were clogged with fertiliser there were six loads needed to be removed immediately."

Fiona stood up holding her head trying to betray she's in a trance: "I have a message from God fertiliser six loads need collecting now, you know what this means, Jacob?"

Jacob jumped to his feet. "Yes I do stay here in the warm I won't be too long, probably an hour or so perhaps two." Jacob ran out of the door jumping on board his Ford tractor and manure spreader, at least he's inside, out of the weather in his tractor cab. He ventured down onto the beach, feeling the first load flex the spreader, he transported to the 30-acre pasture land spreading quickly, returning for five more loads. Jacob spread the last load on the 30 acres returning to the barn. He jumped out of his tractor cab glancing to the road noticing Jocelyn's Range Rover heading in the direction of Exeter. Jacob shrugged his shoulders returning to the house, Fiona already knew they'd gone, she'd read their thoughts, they had burnt everything involving Jacob. They had made £10,000 between them which Fiona thought would be sufficient reward for her not processing them. Jacob rechecked his sheep, returning to the house. "You'll never believe what I've seen?"

"Jocelyn and Jennifer driving at high speed past the end of the drive heading towards Exeter Jacob."

"Are you one of God's angels Fiona that's exactly where they were heading, why I don't know?"

"Have to return to Brook Farm, Jacob."

"why?"

"I'll go on my own," Fiona commented, grabbing her coat going out of the door followed by Jack, who sensed something is wrong. Jacob quickly followed, shutting the door on the house, he climbed into the Range Rover passenger side. Fiona drove off quickly; they arrived at Brook Farm to find the front door open, and the generator running. Jacob dashed in suspecting trouble the place is empty rather untidy, they'd left in a hurry. A note on the table. "Had to return to London urgently may see you again sometime thanks, Jocelyn."

Jacob sat down exhaling. "The last thing I expected today, what a shame we didn't have a chance to say goodbye. Looks like we've a mess to clean up as well Fiona."

"Let's make the place secure for tonight Jacob, I'll tackle this tomorrow it won't take me long," she grinned. "I'm to live here myself as soon as Rosalind returns, which I think maybe tomorrow or the next day I've had a premonition."

"I hope you're right, I'm beginning to worry," Jacob professed, "so unlike Rosalind to disappear without speaking to me first. However, if our Lord is giving you a premonition, I suspect you're correct. We will leave the fires burning I will turn off the generator for tonight and will return tomorrow to sort out whatever," he frowned, disappointed with Jennifer and Jocelyn leaving the way they had this is not Christian behaviour. Jacob turned off the generator they left the house with Jacob locking the front door, climbed into the Range Rover heading home. "Don't look so downhearted Jacob this is not your fault, they left, they are merely ignorant individuals, God will punish them in time I promise you," she smiled with confidence.

CHAPTER 12

Rosalind Returns

Jacob and Fiona retired early to bed, she made sure he made love to her before he went to sleep with her assistance touching his forehead, he's now unconscious. Fiona summoned the misty fog transporter stepping out of the front door patting Jack, immediately transported to the spaceship to find Rosalind standing there waiting for her. "You disposed of Jennifer and Jocelyn Fiona I understand why from your thoughts. Yes, would be a good idea if you lived a Brook Farm Jacob could visit you every day and me at night, once I dispose of these two from my construction," she grinned.

"I think he's somewhat worried about you Rosalind because you didn't say goodbye to him before you left. I explained to him why his two children were causing you problems. I think he accepted it from what I read of his mind."

"I can deal with Jacob when I return today. I managed to assist the creator, hopefully, in the near future the females will give birth to new creators, he will be able to stabilise the population using his own kind," Rosalind remarked in thought.

The creator appeared on the screen, illuminating one wall surrounded by 20 women. "Rosalind sister," he flashed his eyes. She grinned understanding why he'd said that. "My wives and I thank you for your intervention in saving the species. The collective will reward you with a personal gift from me." he vanished from the wall.

Fiona remarked, "things have changed Rosalind since we constructed a creator; there doesn't seem to be so much tension. He notices the brothers and sisters are trying hard for the collective."

Rosalind nodded. "We'd better return to the farm, I see Jacob talking to his favourite ewe. I don't want him to run away with the sheep," Rosalind laughed at her own silly comment along with Fiona. "The same routine as last time the transporter will drop me off by Jacob. I will occupy him why you sneak into the house, you start to make the coffee and breakfast Fiona." They stepped into the misty fog transporter, Rosalind stepped out from the bright light. Jacob stared in disbelief running to grab Rosalind relieved to see her finally returned, not noticing Fiona enter the house. "Why didn't you tell me you weren't well and returning to heaven? You left poor Fiona confused, fancy saying to her you are going to see God. She had no idea what you were talking about, although thankfully God gave her a premonition, so I knew you were returning."

"Have you finished scolding your poorly wife Jacob, who's been ill trying to save your son and daughter?" Jacob immediately picked her up in his arms carrying her to the house, Rosalind laughing if he only knew the truth she thought. He lowered her to her feet they entered the house Fiona is busily cooking bacon and eggs with lashings of fried bread on the Aga. "I thought you'd run off this morning Fiona I knocked on your door, and you didn't answer, when I opened you weren't in there?"

"No, I'd gone for a walk, I enjoy the cold fresh air, when you have lived in Scotland as long as I have you appreciate fresh air," she smiled realising she would have to be more careful in the future. Rosalind smiled extremely pleased with Fiona the way she thought on her feet, talking her way out of situations which would be beneficial to the collective. They sat together, eating breakfast. Jacob remarked, "you realise Jocelyn and Jennifer have gone they packed up and left saying they had to return to London, couldn't even be bothered to say goodbye. I have to clean up the mess they left this morning."

"Considering I'm moving into the house Jacob I will clean up, leave everything to me," she smiled reassuringly.

"To be quite honest Jacob I'm rather pleased," Rosalind remarked finishing her breakfast, "what I thought initially was a good idea was not, they could have caused us a lot of trouble. We didn't lose out altogether her film company have already paid £20,000 to use the area for filming, which they've now cancelled, and we don't give refunds," she grinned.

Jacob smiled, "I still haven't received my Drizabone coat it would help keep the weather out when I'm walking across the Moor, my old army coat is good, but it's not entirely waterproof."

"What's that parcel over there, Jacob," Rosalind pointed to the corner of the kitchen, "obviously delivered when you weren't here," she smiled confidently.

"My fault Jacob delivered the other day, I put it over there forgot all about it," Fiona commented, making sure Jacob realised she was only human. Jacob went over and open the package unfolding his new Driza-Bone coat reading the instructions, how to look after and keep waterproof. He quickly slid his coat on looking in the mirror grinning. "Right must go to Brook Farm Rosalind," he remarked, kissing on the cheek, "if you're going to vanish, leave me a note, and I won't have to sit here and worry."

Rosalind patted his cheek. "Okay, husband," she smiled, watching Fiona slip on her coat smiling taking her suitcase. Jacob and Fiona left the house climbing into the Range Rover, the snow finally melting and the air slightly warmer than the day before. Jacob allowed Fiona to drive to Brook Farm, they entered the yard, Fiona walked to the house carrying her suitcase, and Jacob to see the Rams, feeding and watering. He returned to join Fiona in the house, she'd already lit the fires, the generator running she is boiling the kettle. Jacob looked around in the front room running upstairs, the place is clean? Jacob remembered from yesterday it seemed a bloody mess? He scratched his head returning downstairs, finding his coffee on the table. "You can't clean the house in the few minutes, Fiona?"

"Perhaps, not as bad as you remember, I only had to pick up one or two pieces of paper, Jacob," she smiled. "Maybe God sent an angel to clean up who knows," she chuckled, placing her Bible on the table from her jacket pocket. She opened a page starting to read; Jacob loved the way she always referred to her Bible at any time of day. Fiona rose to her feet, walking into the front room, she knew Jacob would want to see what she is reading. He turned the Bible to face him suddenly the words appeared. "Take Fiona it's time to please her she is one of Gods children." Jacob, in somewhat of a panic, turned the Bible back to the way it was. The second time something had been written across holy words obviously by the Lord himself, he must not disobey the command. Jacob immediately walked into the front room, Fiona is looking out of the window, he picked her up in his arms. "What are you doing, Jacob?" She asked, trying to be surprised.

"God has commanded you be loved." Running upstairs with her, he removed her clothes very gently, she lay on the bed grinning using the Bible is the best idea she'd ever had. Jacob spent the next hour in bed with her, Fiona couldn't understand why she is making so much noise. She couldn't control the upgrade the new sensations were incredible; she particularly loves the way he played with her breasts, adding more excitement to the mating process. They returned downstairs making a fresh coffee when Jacob finished, he kissed Fiona on the cheek. "I'll see you tomorrow," leaving the house, he jumped in his Range Rover heading home. Fiona realise she would need transport, she couldn't use the misty fog transporter continuously otherwise people may become suspicious if seen too often. She sat for a moment working out the best way to deal with the situation, she must learn to think as an individual like Rosalind. Fiona summoned the misty fog transporter within seconds Fiona stepped out behind a disused building in Exeter. She discreetly stepped out onto the footpath realising, she would need money to purchase a vehicle, or perhaps, another way use her abilities. Fiona walked along the pavement looking in shop windows noticing a Jaguar dealership offering the chance to win a four-wheel-drive SUV Jaguar; if you could select the lucky number. Fiona smiled this is too easy, she casually walked across the road a male motorist stopped to let across, she read his disgusting thoughts of what he wanted to do to her. Fiona continued walking to the showroom the salesperson greeted at the door opening for her to enter. "How can I assist you?"

Fiona smiled: "I'd like the chance to win the new car. I only have to select the winning number, and it's mine?"

The salesperson laughed, "not that simple, thousands of tried there are millions of combinations will cost you 5 pounds to try."

Fiona smiled realising she hadn't any money with her, she touched his hand he immediately opened his wallet, giving her 5 pounds, now under her control. She walked over to the computer passing the 5 pounds to the receptionist behind the desk. The receptionist watched her type in 20 numbers Fiona had selected the correct combination, everybody stood up and clapped as bells rang around the showroom. Fiona, shown around a new candy red Jaguar she'd won, several photos were taken which Fiona didn't object to; although thought she shouldn't be publicising her presence. She is escorted into a private office to deal with the paperwork by the salesperson. "I need to see your driving licence," he asked. She held his hand again. "Lovely thank you. The car is insured and taxed for 12 months for you to drive servicing is covered. I need your details." Fiona gave him the address a Brook Farm where she is staying using the name Fiona Walker. While the salesperson finished the paperwork, the car removed from the showroom parked on the forecourt ready for Fiona to drive away with a full tank of diesel. Fiona shook the salesperson's hand, leaving the showroom. Fiona whispered in his ear, "come and see me in about an hour at home. I have a present for you." The salesperson shut the car door, Fiona drove away in her new vehicle.

Rosalind is reading Fiona's mind and what she'd done. Rosalind is somewhat concerned, the publicity they didn't need, surprised Fiona would venture to sample another male and totally unnecessary experiment, Rosalind concluded. Nevertheless, she would talk to her later, although she had already conveyed her concerns telepathically.

Aliens

Fiona arrived home in her new shiny car parking outside Brook Farmhouse, she went upstairs looking through the clothes she'd taken from the spaceship. Deciding to wear the shortest skirt she possessed and a ribbed button-up crop top with only one button fastening together, her breasts were bulging, she didn't bother with knickers they were unnecessary she thought. She selected a pair of shoes she liked shapeshifting her foot size to fit. Fiona came downstairs, making herself a coffee leaving on the table, didn't need to drink just for show. She is reading the salesperson's mind as he was coming along the road. Fiona watched his car come down the drive parking by hers, carrying a bouquet of flowers which Fiona realised males presented to females on occasions. She invited him in she could see his eyes were all over her breasts, there again she thought they were barely concealed. "I don't know your name," she asked.

"Stephen and your Fiona."

Fiona couldn't be bothered to offer him a coffee, she wanted to experience the mating process with him, stood in front of him kissing him passionately on the lips releasing the one button holding her ribbed button up crop top together. She grabbed his hand dashing upstairs with him, she lay on the bed lifting her skirt within seconds he's on top of her she lay there analysing the difference between him and Jacob, slightly disappointed, he didn't last that long the first time, he started again Stephen is far more assertive, he still didn't perform as Jacob, they had a coffee before he left. Fiona commenting: "I'll ring you." She knew this is what human females said when they had no intention of contacting someone again. He hadn't long left before Rosalind parked by Fiona's new car. Fiona opened the front door, she suspected, may have exceeded her boundaries without consulting the collective, Rosalind in the first instance.

Rosalind sat down: "You realise how irresponsible you behaved Fiona. Firstly you should have come to me if you wanted a vehicle, I understand your reasons why I read your thoughts. However, you've invited the salesperson here Stephen he will come again probably pester you! I have decided he will be processed next week to avoid any mistakes. What is wrong with Jacob mating with you? You concluded after Stephen had finished, he wasn't as good."

"Experimenting Rosalind to see what the difference is between males; I've seen their bodies processed some have larger than others, I wondered if it made a difference and if so by how much? "

"I think I will have your upgrade removed Fiona if this is the way you're going to behave. You are a Zibyan, a privileged member of the collective thanks to me."

"Would you not consider Rosalind giving me one more opportunity to prove my worthiness of your trust?"

"Your performance until today has been excellent. Firstly I want you to return to the spaceship and be cleansed, I don't want Jacob catching any diseases you may be carrying. You make one more mistake Fiona you will cease to exist. Or the other option is you return to Zagader."

"No, Rosalind, I will prove to you I am a worthy Zibyan a proud member of the collective and can follow your instructions."

"I have summoned the misty fog transporter, go to the spaceship and be decontaminated thoroughly." Fiona ran to the front door stepping into the misty fog transporter and disappeared. Rosalind locked the front door on Brook Farm, leaving the key where it's always hidden, climbing in her Range Rover returning to Jacobs farm.

The weather seemed to be changing some believed to global warming, the snow had mostly gone from the Moor. Jacob knew risky, he decided to release his ewes out onto the Moor again, there were some fresh patches of grass which would do them far more good and enjoyable than cooped up in a barn. Rosalind joined him, "Oh I meant to inform you, Jacob, I've ordered a lorry load of wheat straw it should be arriving later today."

"We could certainly use it, Rosalind, however, I suspect you paid a premium I should have ordered it in the summer when nobody wants the damn stuff," he suggested.

"I didn't pay too much, in large round bales can unload with the tractor. I will rephrase that, I will unload them with my tractor," Rosalind grinned, "I'm pregnant not a cripple." Jacob burst out laughing cuddling Rosalind picking her up in his arms, he carried her to the house, she couldn't stop laughing these human expressions were indeed infectious, she concluded. Hoping Fiona stayed within the parameters of her instructions otherwise it could jeopardise the mission. Rosalind received a telepathic message from Peter. "Fiona's infected with the coronavirus she can carry it, but it wouldn't harm her. The central computer has removed from her construction. Stephen, the sales representative, will die he is carrying the disease initially should kill him within the next few days. Jacob is required tomorrow another six loads of fertiliser are ready to be disposed of."

"What's the matter, Rosalind?"

"Receiving instructions from God, you know he communicates with me like Peter and Matthew Jacob. Another six loads of fertiliser in the morning Jacob before 8 o'clock." Jacob smiled, sitting down, switching on the television listening to a reporter: "The Chinese government estimate a million people have vanished, are struggling to find out what happened to them? Another unsolved mystery, although some governments speculate the Chinese government, may have executed them because they were infected with the coronavirus, a quick way to solve the problem."

Jacob glanced to Rosalind as she passed him a coffee. "Is that what I'm spreading tomorrow?"

"Jacob, we've had this conversation before! God will not permit the guilty to go unpunished he decides what happens, not you or me. If you wish to argue with God, you are welcome to try, you'll probably find your living alone in a very few seconds and die a premature death for not trusting in the Lord's word."

Jacob nodded: "Understood Rosalind. I hear air brakes the lorry must have arrived with my straw?" Rosalind put her coffee down on the table, walking out followed by Jacob. A sizeable articulated lorry parked by the barn, the driver, stepped out. "Mr Walker?"

"No, Mrs Walker, I'll fetch my loader from the barn, you remove your straps off the load. Jacob, you stay over there at least 2 m away from the driver, those are the government policies." Jacob grinned.

"Thank you, Mrs Walker," the driver remarked. "Not many people follow the rules these days. I don't want to die, I have two children waiting for me at home."

"I can assure you you will catch nothing from here," Rosalind commented starting her tractor, she soon unloaded the lorry they helped him turn around in the yard, he blasted his horn relieved to be leaving driving his truck is enjoyable, mixing with people he dreaded. Jacob examined the straw bales. "That some lovely stuff Rosalind I won't ask what it cost it will only upset me," he grinned gently tapping her backside picking her up in his arms.

"Put me down!" Jacob chuckled, returning to the house, Rosalind decided she needed to talk to Fiona now she'd returned to Brook Farm. "Jacob I'm going to visit Fiona, I need to talk to her you stay here please this is personal."

"That sounds ominous! Okay, there's plenty of fuel in the Range Rover," he kissed Rosalind on the cheek watching her drive off in the Range Rover. Rosalind parked by the side of Fiona's new car. Rosalind walking to the front door trying to think of a way to make Fiona realise how foolish she'd been. Fiona opened the door; her expression is one of concern since she was in human form. "I guess I'm in more trouble, Rosalind?"

"You are fortunate Fiona Jacob has been immunised by Peter to prevent him from catching the coronavirus. However, wherever you went amongst humans, they would catch the virus from you. The problem is humans would not take long to work out who is the carrier; then we'd be in trouble and exposed."

Fiona exhaled: "I am trying to be individual like you Rosalind, thinking on my feet as a human would say. I was trying to prove I'm competent. I now discover I am not at the moment."

"Show me your new car, Fiona it looks beautiful, I do like the colour." They went outside together, Fiona suggested, " let's take a ride to the local shop and see if it's reopened, although from the information I'm receiving it has not. Rosalind, you drive to see if you like the vehicle."

They both climbed in setting off following the road around to the local shop, the shopkeeper removing the sign, he is closed from the door. Rosalind standing several metres from him asked, "I presume your reopening we have missed your marvellous service convenient for the farm?"

"We will redecorate this week and open next, from Monday. Hopefully, we will have enough custom to stay in business."

"You can count on us two," Rosalind smiled. "I'm sure other locals will appreciate you taking the risk. The coronavirus won't last forever," she smiled reassuringly.

The shopkeeper waved, "thank you for your support look forward to your Customs soon," he said, entering his shop.

Rosalind drove to Brook Farm in Fiona's new car. "Thank you, beautiful to drive and comfortable. I have to comment on your ingenuity acquiring the vehicle. However, let's hope no questions are asked. The government is now aware of your existence Fiona. Peter is having your records destroyed by the central computer if possible, without being detected, you must not be traceable under any circumstances Fiona."

Jacob walked in the yard neither Rosalind or Fiona had detected him approaching, they were too busy discussing their own issues. "I've had a visitor," he remarked, looking puzzled. "Someone trying to find the location of Fiona Walker? Apparently, she won a car or something and lives at Brook Farm. I told the bloke to clear off the wasn't such a person as Fiona Walker, and I own Brook Farm, if I caught him on my property, I'd let Jack eat him, he soon cleared off." Jacob noticed the new car. "Who the bloody hell owns that?"

Fiona looked to Rosalind. "We do! The man in question has the wrong name, Jacob. I acquired it in a competition and gave to Fiona to use as transport, while she's here. The gentleman obviously had the name wrong, you dealt with him excellently," she kissed Jacob on the lips. "You never tell me anything Rosalind I could have looked a right idiot," Jacob stormed off onto the Moor with Jack following him.

"Rosalind your individuality save the situation. The creator must be incredibly proud of you. I didn't know what to say when Jacob asked the question."

"You are providing me with plenty of practice, sister!" Rosalind smiled. "You had better please, Jacob in the morning, think of something exciting to calm him down and stop him worrying about what's going on. That reminds me I think he has six loads to move in the morning of fertiliser before he comes to you, so you will have ample time to think of something exciting for him," Rosalind smiled, climbing in her Range Rover driving home to Jacobs farm. Fiona jumped in her car, driving to the nearest town entering a supermarket she joined the queue and waited for 10 minutes before she is allowed in. Fiona rushed to the back of the store looking at all the female garments trying to select something of interest, finding nothing, left the store very disappointed returning to Brook Farm. She went upstairs looking in the wardrobe, discovering Jocelyn had left her old suitcase, she opened seeing old clothes. Fiona realised if she didn't please Jacob and Rosalind, her time on earth would be limited after a mistake she made, one very serious. Fiona realise she hadn't any money how could she feed Jacob she couldn't go shopping. She quickly telepathically contacted Rosalind. "Help I need money to buy food for Jacobs breakfast, can I come and collect some?"

Rosalind grinned sat at the kitchen table, replied telepathically. "I wondered when you'd realise, come now, and I will come with you."

Rosalind looked in the tin behind the packet of sugar, opening, taking several hundred pounds slipping into her pocket. wasn't many minutes before Fiona is parked outside the house, Rosalind waved to Jacob. "Going shopping won't belong." Jacob coming in; the light fading rapidly. Rosalind drove Fiona's new car which made Jacob laugh even poor Fiona got pushed around he thought. Rosalind drove quickly to the supermarket parking. Grabbing a trolley having to go in separately. Rosalind telepathically instructed Fiona what to purchase, both finally met in the car park. Rosalind passed Fiona £1000 in cash. "Before you run short of money, contact Peter, he will replenish for you." Fiona smiled sitting in the passenger seat Rosalind drove to Jacobs farm, taking the bags of groceries from the boot. Fiona didn't come in, she carried on home in the dark. Fiona busy carrying her bags of groceries into the house, she hadn't detected, unsavoury characters close by they were preparing to pounce one is carrying an axe.

Peter and Matthew aboard the spaceship, transporting directly to Brook Farm, eliminating four men in one of the sheds hiding. Fiona stared somewhat alarmed Peter appeared, "You should have detected Fiona we are transporting for processing, merely criminals. They couldn't have harmed you nevertheless you should have dealt with them on your arrival home. I will have to report this to Rosalind you realise."

"Yes, Peter, I'm a failure." She turned and walked into the house, wondering if the day could get any worse. Peter had telepathically informed Rosalind of events. Rosalind decided to take no further action, she would see if she continued to make mistakes; if Fiona did, she would have to return to Zagader with the next transport ship.

Early the next morning Jacob is on the beach with his Ford tractor and manure spreader collecting the fertiliser. He spread five more loads on the 30 acres the last load he would drive over to Brook Farm after having a cup of coffee with Rosalind.

He entered the house Rosalind already prepared the drinks. They both moved to watch the early morning news, terrorism is non-existent. The government still hadn't resolved the problem with their nuclear weapons, none of their computers would work correctly, satellites were in disarray. One reporter commented: "The world is falling apart with coronavirus; this may be the last nail in our coffin, God help us all."

Jacob voiced, "praise the Lord, may his will always be done, amen."

"Off you go, Jacob spread the fertiliser and please God, you are definitely working for his benefit."

He kissed Rosalind on the cheek, "I shan't be too long," he smiled.

Jacob went out of the house climbing aboard his tractor towing the manure spreaders slowly across the Moor to the 10-acre pasture, he jumped from the cab opening the gate and spreading the fertiliser driving on to Brook Farm not far away. Fiona cooked his breakfast, opening the front door for him to enter. She sat opposite drinking coffee nibbling a piece of toast, she didn't really want. Fiona racked her brains for ages trying to think of a way to impress Jacob and Rosalind at the same time. Fiona realised if she made a mistake this time, there'd be no more chances for her. "Jacob, will you take me for a ride in your tractor please?"

"Why it's smelly and dirty and cold."

"Oh well, never mind," she remarked despondently. Fiona opened the Bible, leaving on the table going into the front room. Jacob watched spellbound the Bible slide towards him with the words in blue flames. "Please Fiona." Jacob closed his eyes and opened again in disbelief, watching the book travel across the table, stopping in its original position.

"If you really want to ride in my tractor Fiona I'll take you," he called from the kitchen not wishing to offend God. She came into the kitchen, smiling. "Change Fiona into your warm jeans your catch a chill in a skirt and wear your thick coat." Fiona grabbed a coat from the door dashing into the front room removing all her clothes, slipping on her coat, she wouldn't feel the cold in any case, Jacob is in for a surprise she thought.

They left the house Jacob opened the tractor cab door. "out Jack," he ordered watching him leave the passenger seat. Jacob climbed in, and Fiona sat on the passenger seat, keeping her coat firmly closed, he set off across the Moor. Jacob stopped the tractor in disbelief. Fiona opened her coat and removed sitting on Jacobs lap, she could feel what is heading her way; this is definitely different. They spent half an hour making love in the tractor cab. Fiona moved to the passenger seat Jacob sat there with the biggest grin on his face he'd ever had. Jacob quickly returned to the farm carrying Fiona into the house, laying her on the kitchen table, starting with her all over again, she had definitely pleased him. Otherwise, he wouldn't be interested in her twice. The man's an animal; the other guy was insignificant compared to him.

Jacob kissed Fiona on the lips passionately, "see you tomorrow," he grinned, whispered in her ear, "I prefer the bed to the tractor," walking out of the door. Fiona smiled, feeling somewhat relieved another human piece of baggage she is carrying ever since she'd shape-shifted into Fiona, she seemed to be carrying far more human defects. Fiona smiled, watching Jacob leave the yard with Jack on the passenger seat. Jacob wondered how much longer the human race would survive, whether God would obliterate everyone, hopefully not Rosalind and him, and he wouldn't mind if God spared Fiona; she is lovely to cuddle up to he thought and definitely great for sex.

Jacob parked the tractor and spreader by the barn going into the house lunch on the table. "Blimey I didn't know I'd been that long," he remarked, sitting down. Rosalind sat opposite with not such a large portion of pork, roast potatoes and greens with her lovely gravy. Rosalind mentioned: "Jacob, I'll soon be having our twins."

"I know, you feeling alright, Rosalind?"

"Yes, you realise your children, our children won't be quite the same as other children," Rosalind suggested watching his expression.

"How do you mean Rosalind," Jacob asked, lowering his knife and fork to the plate listening carefully.

"You know I came from heaven to be with you, I'm different from what I used to be slightly before I died. I didn't use to pop off to heaven and talk to God, for instance."

Jacob smiled, starting to enjoy his food again. "I'm not sure what you mean, just glad you're here Rosalind whatever the conditions."

Rosalind smiled, "all I'm saying Jacob, your children will look like children. They will be slightly different because their mother is reconstructed in heaven by God to be with you again. So naturally, when I give birth to the children in heaven under God supervision they may be blessed with other gifts like you've received me, tractors and other things recently," she smiled.

Jacob started laughing, "if they start flying around the farm Rosalind, I will disown their mother." He almost choked on his food for a moment. "I don't care they will be our children as long as they're not heavy drinkers and gamblers," he continued to laugh.

"I don't know why I bother to try and hold a serious conversation with you, Jacob," Rosalind smiled. "I can promise you they won't fly around the barn, however, what other gifts God bestows upon them, I don't know at this stage, but whatever they are, they must remain a secret I'm sure you understand that."

"Of course," Jacob voiced cheerfully. "Don't worry Rosalind, I suppose God will want to see them like he does you; after all, their mother came from heaven."

Rosalind had a sudden burst of emotion, jumping to her feet, kissing Jacob on the forehead. "You are a wonderful husband. I'm so proud of you, you understand, your trusting God will be rewarded many times over Jacob."

"I am well rewarded, I have a beautiful wife and children on the way, excellent farms, what else could God give me, he's been too generous already."

"Eternal life Jacob the same as your wife," she expressed, "on a duplicate earth, he has named in your honour, Jacobs planet. We can live there together, leaving the children here to have a farm each."

Jacob looked up from his meal. "Are you speaking the truth to me, Rosalind, that would be my greatest wish to never let you go again, but I fear you are talking fantasy."

"Oh, Jacob if you only knew what I know, you'll see your Rosalind is telling you the truth. You've already been to heaven once why do you find that so hard to believe?"

"Yes, I have memories of skeletons, people dying a tormented death. There is great beauty amongst what you showed me, but to believe God would take me there to live with you forever. I don't know I hope you're right." Jacob kissed Rosalind on the cheek going outside walking across the Moor to check on his sheep, he been rather sloppy of late not patrolling the way he usually did. Jack followed Jacob religiously across the Moor, Jacob is taken by surprise to see two young female hikers on the footpath, he waited for them to approach. Fiona had changed into a Robin flying around the Moor practising her shapeshifting abilities, noticing Jacob. She landed on a rock watching and listening. Jacob commented, "hey girls aren't you supposed to stay at home to prevent the spread of coronavirus?"

"What's it to do with you silly old bugger, you only stood there to look at us you pervert," the two girls walked on. Jacob shook his head; the younger generation has no respect. Fiona had heard and seen the rude finger signal. The footpath the girls were on went past Brook Farm she flew home, determine the girls would learn a lesson they would not forget. Rosalind had received Fiona's thoughts and agreed with her somewhat, hoping Fiona would make sure no evidence is left.

The two female hikers approached Brook Farm Fiona came out smiling greeting them with a handshake, she immediately had them under her control telepathically instructing the two girls. "Go out on the Moor find Jacob apologise to him and bring him to Brook Farm." The two girls dropped their rucksacks walking quickly onto the Moor searching for Jacob, they finally discovered him sat on a rock talking to his pet ewes. "Sir," the girls voiced nervously, "We came to apologise for our behaviour, we shouldn't have said the things we did. would you come to the farm there's a lady there who'd like to speak to you."

Jacob stood up. "Thank you for apologising, immensely appreciated." He followed the girls to the farm. Fiona, waiting for them, she guided them into the house. "I made your drinks." They sat around the kitchen table Fiona using telepathy instructed the girls to stay silent unless told to say something, they sat drinking coffee, not speaking. She sat at the far end of the table, opening her Bible and left the room going into the front room. Jacob watched the Bible slide towards him and stop. Across the open pages were the words: "The girls have to be punished. God's will, take them." Jacob watched the Bible returned to the other end of the table, he didn't move, he didn't know what to make of anything. He certainly didn't want to disobey God, but nevertheless, they did apologise after all. Fiona returned transmitting instructions into one girl's mind. She stood, "I have sinned I must be punished."

Jacob looked to Fiona, shrugged his shoulders. "What do I do," he whispered.

Fiona thought for a moment, this is not quite going to plan, she imagined Jacob ripping their clothes off with the message coming from the Bible. She walked over to the Aga, removing the steel poker. Jacob watched intently wondering what Fiona intended to do. Fiona showed the girl the poker. "You have a choice of punishment, struck with the poker six times or be mated with. The reason 6 is used because God created the earth in six days, and on the seventh, he rested, that decision applies to your friend as well?" Fiona voiced calmly.

Jacob slightly horrified neither option he really liked, either an assault on someone; nevertheless, their choice and God had given them an alternative, he'd obviously sent a premonition to Fiona. The one girl spoke. "We don't wish to be scarred, we will accept the other as a punishment." Both girls started to remove their clothes, standing there naked. Fiona encouraged Jacob, "God's will and their decision they had a choice." Each girl, in turn, to go into the front room laying on the carpet excepting Jacobs advances. Fiona stayed in the kitchen grinning at her persuasive abilities listening to each girl screen as Jacob asserted himself upon them. Finally, the girls dressed, they each kissed Jacob on the lips, walking out of the door collecting their rucksacks. They waved walking on as if nothing had happened. Fiona had made sure they wouldn't remember what had taken place, neither would they insult Jacob again if they saw him.

Jacob sat down at the kitchen table, drinking another coffee with Fiona. "God is in touch with you all the time Fiona isn't he?"

"Sometimes I have visions, he explained to me what he wants to be done, I am merely an instrument he uses on earth until I ascend into the heaven on my final journey," she smiled sweetly.

"I thought as much pretty obvious really," he smiled. "I'd better make my way across the Moor," he suggested. Jacob started walking home across the Moor with Jack following behind, he had to quicken his pace somewhat, darkness is falling faster than ever, he finally reached the front door going inside a note on the table. "Had to return to heaven see you soon, Rosalind." Jacob smiled contented with the message looking in the oven he found a meal ready prepared to stay warm for him.

Rosalind, aboard the spaceship looking at the monitor on the wall seeing the creator with his females some with a substantial bulge indicating they were pregnant. The creator stayed on the island with the women to prevent them from becoming stressed as long as he is present, there were no issues. The creator spoke to Rosalind, "you are wonderful Rosalind proficient in your duties. I have enjoyed myself immensely here with the women who absolutely adore me, thanks to you. To be honest with you Rosalind I am attached slightly to all of them so rather than our original plan I may keep them for a while to pleasure me after the children are born, and perhaps there will be more there's no harm in trying."

"Creator, you realise one of the Zibyan brothers could shapeshift into you some of the time then you could return to the laboratory and pursue your other pleasures."

"What a brilliant suggestion the females wouldn't know, none of them are really interested in mating since they are all carrying children."

"All 20," Rosalind asked taken by surprise.

The creator nodded grinning.

"Please don't take this as an insult creator, you were wise to choose human females your behaviour mimics humans slightly at times."

"To be expected, Rosalind, after all, I was created from a human infant, using my DNA to change essential elements. The rest will be ironed out as a human would say in time. Hopefully, the children that are born to these females will have fewer defects then me."

"I'm not criticising creator, I wish you every success, you are the future of the collective," Rosalind smiled.

"So are you, Rosalind, with what you are carrying, they will determine when they wish to be born, I can sense they are intelligent; your children and mine will be the future of the collective." The creator vanished from the screen.

Peter approached Rosalind. "Send Jacob tomorrow Rosalind, we have another six loads of fertiliser. Matthew has ordered another transport ship, he's taken 300,000 from India, a drop in the ocean to their population."

"We are fortunate their satellites and radar are defective since we sent the virus. Otherwise, they may be able to track the corpses. Peter, remain vigilant don't trust humans; they are sneaky in the extreme," she smiled.

"I realise that Rosalind we've made some blunders and are fortunate to have maintained our security. Fiona is performing excellently I think, don't you, your training bearing fruit as a human would say."

Rosalind flashed her eyes looking to the monitor seeing Jacob on the beach with the Land Rover, he left his hazard warning lights on for Rosalind to see in the dark. She laughed stepping into the misty fog transporter thinking if he only knew she could see in the dark as well as daylight. She climbed out of the transporter on the beach, stepping into the Land Rover, he kissed her on the lips. "Thank you for the note at least I didn't have to worry where you were," he remarked, driving steadily towards the farm. Jacob stepped from the Land Rover laughing going into the house. "I've just realised Rosalind you let me drive the Land Rover."

She had no choice other than to grin. "You can have a quick coffee with me then go and see Fiona, she will cook you breakfast this morning. Tomorrow morning Jacob six loads of fertiliser don't forget." Jacob finished his coffee stepping out of the house with his new Driza-Bone coat and hat, not forgetting Jack and his crook. Rosalind smiled, watching him from the window through the darkness she could see as if daylight. Jacob found his sheep huddled around, a round bale feeder tucking into silage, he carried on walking finding the next feeder the sheep were busily tucking in. Jacob smiled, lovingly early mornings, watching the sun illuminate the earth rotating slowly.

Jacob noticed dim headlights in the distance, the vehicle is on the Moor that is for sure. He quickened his pace heading towards the dim lights, finally reaching an old car with police tape surrounding. Joyriders Jacob concluded, had to be the car is a write-off not far from the road. Jacob suspected the joyriders had tried to escape across the Moor; thankfully, his sheep were nowhere near; otherwise, some of them could be dead now. Jacob continued walking following the little brook towards Brook Farm, he looked in the distance seeing the lights on in the house, hearing a faint sound of the generator running. Jacob checked his Rams first before going to the house, Fiona opened the door she already knew Jacob had arrived, she greeted Jacob with a kiss on the lips. He smiled sitting down to his breakfast of three pieces of fried bread three rashers of bacon and three eggs and a tin of baked beans. Fiona wondered why Jacob ate so much, smiled realising not only is Jacob working on the farm, Jacob is expending considerable energy pleasing her and others.

She watched Jacob finished drinking his coffee, held out her hand, he held willingly, Fiona guided him upstairs to the bedroom; wasn't many minutes before they were engaged in mating. Fiona never knew what Jacob would do next, moving her into different positions, making sure none of her senses were left untouched, he is never dull. Fiona had read Rosalind's mind concerning the plan Rosalind had for Jacob in the future, she hoped Rosalind would be able to achieve what she wanted with the help of the collective and of course the creator.

They dressed going downstairs Fiona made him a coffee she didn't need one. Jacob finally finished standing up he kissed her neck softly and moved to her lips, tapping her backside, walked out of the door greeted by Jack. Fiona watched him walk through the yard onto the Moor turning bright red cleansing herself of any impurities left by Jacob.

Jacob whistled a tune walking across the Moor swinging his sheep crook, knocking off the odd dead Thistle head as he progressed, he rather liked his new Driza-Bone coat kept the wind off him better than his old coat. Jacob entered the house seeing another note from Rosalind. "They're on the way Jacob, I'm in heaven, I'll be in touch your Rosalind. Don't worry!"

CHAPTER 13

What Does the Future Hold

Fiona already knew Rosalind is about to deliver, she transported to the spaceship Rosalind is standing there accompanied by Peter and Matthew. Fiona looked to Rosalind. "What can I do to help?"

"Nothing." Rosalind laid on her side on the floor, everyone watched in amazement as she opened her stomach and two babies appeared on the floor. Rosalind sealed herself quickly, standing. The little girl first shape-shifted into a five-year-old child the boy followed suit. They stood there looking at each other brother and sister. "You are our mother, Rosalind." The five-year-old girl said shapeshifting again into a 10-year-old child the boy followed suit. "My name will be Mary," the female girl expressed

"My name will be Noah mother."

"You are my creations," Rosalind voiced calmly, looking at them both identical in appearance apart from Mary had long red hair and Noah had black curly hair, like his father, which made Rosalind smile. Rosalind sat down, the children sat beside her, she had never imagined a situation like this in her life; she expected two screaming miserable brats like all human females produced; not perfect shapeshifters, with the same intelligence as her. Extraordinary, spectacular a miracle if there is such a thing she concluded.

"Children you realise your father is a human, he expects to find his children in baby clothes and wearing diapers not 10 years old with the brain of a nuclear scientist. I will have to return and talk to your father and tries somehow to explain you are 10 years old. How long will you stay at this age?"

Noah spoke: "Our present age and size of construction is comfortable until we receive more nutrients from either you mother or the vegetation before we can shapeshift into a larger size. However, we understand your predicament our father is little more than an ape-man barely out of a cave, he would not understand. I suggest Mary and myself maintain this age in front of him for a year or so until he becomes a custom. Eventually, we will adjust as we see fit into other objects or beings mother."

Mary turned to her brother. "A solution to the problem Noah. If our mother transported our father here, we could shapeshift from babies into 10-year-olds, create an illusion it is God's decision we start at this age, Jacob our father will accept whatever God offers Noah."

Rosalind, Fiona, Matthew and Peter stood there astounded listening to the children resolving issues without needing assistance. The creator had appeared on the far wall listening to everything realising these two children were the start of something spectacular for the collective. Mary noticed him. "Creator I hope you're having success with your females?"

The creator smiled, "yes, Mary, thank you for asking. Rosalind, you are a blessing to the collective we now have a new direction in which to head, once my children are born, we will really know what the success rate will be for either of us." The creator vanished.

Noah spoke: "Peter shapeshift into Jesus. Let's see how you look," Noah smiled, which surprised everyone he is betraying a real human although he is far from one.

Peter shapeshifted into what everyone believed an image of Jesus from the Bible. "What do you think, sister?" Noah asked Mary.

"Perfect Peter, I hope we can shapeshift like you once we develop properly."

Noah remarked: "I believe our father is collecting six loads of fertiliser tomorrow to spread upon our farms; that's about all humans are good for fertiliser. Tonight Fiona you will go to Jacobs farm you will spend the night there with him, do what you always do with him make him relaxed mate with him several times, night and morning, we want him exhausted. While he is spreading the fertiliser you will make the breakfast, have a premonition in front of him instruct him to go to the beach; he is to step into the misty fog, Jesus wants to see him. We will be here sitting on our mother's lap as babies. Peter will be playing the part of Jesus, he will issue the command for us to shapeshift after which we turn into 10-year-old children. The rest we will deal with as it comes along if everyone plays their part, there will not be an issue."

Mary asked, "any questions anyone it seems to be a perfect solution for the moment."

Rosalind looked to the others. "Absolutely perfect, Noah, how do you others feel?"

"I can hear the collective in my head; everyone is astounded at the abilities of these two newborns, an earth hour is not passed, and they have solved a problem. I agree with their suggestion," Peter answered.

"I find no fault in their suggestion," Matthew commented.

Fiona smiled. "I wish you were my children, you are brilliant the pair of you as clever as your mother, my sister."

"One last thing," Mary commented. "We will need two dressing gowns to put on the minute we shapeshift. We are not here to expose ourselves, our father would be annoyed even if he is a backward human."

"children" Rosalind voiced sternly. "Thanks to your father you are here, I want him treated with respect or you will feel my displeasure. He has treated your mother with nothing but kindness and any other member of the brothers and sisters. I expect you to treat him with respect, remember it's him transporting the fertiliser away so we can ship flesh to the planets we are terraforming with the animals to live on until they become self-sufficient."

Rosalind surprised to see both her children stand before her and bow their heads. "We will honour our mother's wishes," they choroused.

Fiona flashed her eyes to everyone in respect transporting to Brook Farm, she stepped from the transporter going into the house collecting a few clothes, came out jumping in her new car driving to Jacobs farm. Jacob saw the headlights from his window opening the door surprised to see Fiona. She walked in, carrying a suitcase. "I've had a premonition I am to stay with you while Rosalind is away and to remind you something about fertiliser in the morning Jacob."

Jacob burst out laughing: "That premonition had to come from Rosalind, she's the only one that would worry about fertiliser; you are welcome." Jacob watched Fiona walk into the spare room, he made her a coffee. "She's gone to have the baby's I guess you know otherwise you wouldn't be here Fiona?"

They both sat on the settee, watching television with Jack cuddled up by the fire. "You know what else is contained in the message Jacob?" She smiled.

"No" Jacob tried not to grin.

Fiona slowly unbuttoned her blouse. Jacob sat there, trying to watch television; his eyes kept turning to look at what is on offer. He jumped to his feet picking her up in his arms, she started laughing they stayed in the bedroom until morning, every time Jacob wanted to go to sleep, she pestered him until he couldn't keep his eyes open any more. Jacob, about to get out of bed. "Where do you think you're going, I hope you're in the mood because I am," she assured. Jacob, absolutely shattered, glad to leave the bedroom Fiona is insistent, she'd worn him into the ground Jacob struggled to put the kettle on. Fiona came out of the bedroom in her dressing gown. She made the coffee sitting at the table, looking at Jacob trying to keep his eyes open, he finally emptied his cup. "Off you go, you have fertiliser to collect from somewhere," she reminded.

"Don't nag I'm going," slipping on his coat and hat. Jack followed him out, jumping in on the passenger seat Jacob started his Ford tractor heading down onto the beach. He parked in the dark hearing the water the tide had turned. He felt the first load of fertiliser loaded driving quickly to the pastureland, Jacob spread the first load after a while. Finally, the last load spread, heading back to the farm. Fiona had made him an excellent breakfast four pieces of fried bread four sausage three eggs and a tin of baked beans and a large mug of coffee to swill it all down with. "Aren't you having anything?" Jacob asked.

"Had mine thanks." Fiona rose to her feet as Jacob cleared his plate holding her head: "Yes yes Jesus, I understand the beach, the beach, step into the misty fog. Yes, Jesus, I will instruct him." Fiona dropped into her chair. Jacob moved around, kneeling by her. "What is that about I got some of the message, what?"

"A message from Jesus," she pretended to be dizzy. "You are to go down onto the beach and wait for a misty fog, Jesus will meet you. I don't understand Jacob do you?"

"Yes, stay here! I'll be back shortly." Jacob ran out of the door climbing in the old Land Rover drove down onto the beach parking close to the rocks. Jacob walked along seeing the misty fog come, he apprehensively stepped inside, falling over speedily transported to the spaceship the transporter stopped, Jacob rolled out on the floor. Rosalind is concerned he may be injured. Jacob eventually struggled to his feet, looking dazed. Jacob dropped to his knees and bowing his head realising in the presence of Jesus; he had better not make a mistake. "Stand Jacob before your Lord; I have bestowed upon you the gift of a son and daughter look to Rosalind." Jacob glanced to her in tears seeing the two infants one on each knee. "Your Lord has decided the infant's age will be increased to the age of 10, you will instruct them how to run the farms and tend your sheep. Rosalind will assist you in teaching these children everything they need to know, including how to worship the Lord as you have done for many years. Watch them grow Jacob. Watch them grow." Mary and Noah grew in size, each putting on a dressing gown. Mary spoke, "I am your daughter Mary. You are my father."

"I am your son Noah, father." they watched Noah staggered towards them and collapse on the floor Rosalind moved to his aid suspecting Jacob had suffered a heart attack, relieved he'd only fainted. Peter changed quickly from Jesus into Peter, the disciple. Rosalind helped Jacob with the others to a seat giving him time to recover; his children sat either side of him. Jacob placed his arm around each of them. "I am truly blessed by the Lord this day, he honours me with a son and daughter, praise, Lord Amen." Rosalind telepathically instructed Noah and Mary to kiss their father on the cheek, she watched them comply. Jacob rose to his feet looking at Mary and to Noah with the curly black hair, the same as his. "Jacob, I have to stay here for two more days with the children then I will join you on the farm. Peter will send a message to my half-sister to assist you in any way."

"I understand Rosalind," he remarked, kissing her incredibly passionately holding her close. "You are from heaven, my beautiful wife." He moved to his son hugging him, "I love you, Noah," and finally to his daughter holding her very close, kissing her on both cheeks. "You are like your mother beautiful I love you truly," he smiled, stepping into the misty fog. The transporter transported him to the beach. Jacob fell over on the sand, the device stopped ejecting with such violence. Jacob stood up brushing off his clothes running to the Land Rover desperate to inform Fiona of events. He drove as quickly as he dares to the farm, Fiona, ready for him with a mug of coffee, Jacob ran into the house out of breath remembering, he had to be cautious he didn't know how much Fiona knew about her sister's activities. "I saw Jesus and my children are coming home in two days; everything is perfect."

"Calm yourself I will come with you to the beach we need more firewood Jacob otherwise your children will be cold. I will take the old Fordson major and saw bench; you bring the trailer chain saw another equipment. Fiona had already changed into her jeans and work clothes she left the house, leaving Jacob to finish his coffee. She climbed aboard the tractor, driving cautiously down onto the beach parking by several old pine trees washed ashore. Jacob followed a few minutes later, parking close to the saw bench. He first cut the trees into manageable pieces to lift on the saw bench cutting the timber into manageable blocks, surprised to watch Fiona throw them on the trailer as if they were nothing. He struggled to carry some; it made no difference to her in the slightest.

They spent two hours retrieving the timber. Fiona climbed aboard the Fordson major slowly driving to the farm, and Jacob followed with his old Fordson P6 with the engine purring like a wild animal back to the shed. He tipped the trailer quite a substantial pile of timber slid from the trailer sufficient for a few weeks. He and Fiona threw the blocks in the old woodshed, hoping to keep them dry. "I'd better check the sheep Fiona, thank you so much for your help greatly appreciated while Rosalind's out of action."

"Okay. I think you should invest in a log splitter, Jacob makes it easier for everyone to help, wouldn't cost much to run, and they are not that expensive to buy."

"We'll see what Rosalind says when she comes home," he smiled realising it would save his back if nothing else. Jacob and Jack set off across the Moor in search of his sheep, he headed in the direction of the abandoned car to see if removed from the Moor, he finally reached the location seeing broken glass another pieces discarded. Jacob couldn't understand why somebody couldn't clean up properly. The way of the world Jacob concluded checking there is nothing sharp the glass obviously the window screen in little square pieces. Hopefully, the ground would swallow in due course. Jacob continued walking, stopped in his tracks there appeared to be ewes and lambs everywhere, beginning to think his Rams were useless perhaps he put them into late that's why the lambs have arrived now. Jacob almost ran back to the farm, attaching the small trailer to the quad bike. Jacob started to set up the pens hastily in the barn, moving out some of the equipment for extra space. He would have to set up pens at Brook Farm he had insufficient space at home. Fiona came dashing out after reading Jacob thoughts realising what had happened. "You collect the ewes and lambs, Jacob, I'll finish making the pens," kissing him on the cheek.

The sun starting to set, Jacob could kick himself; he should have been more aware, preoccupied with everything else. He managed to capture three ewes and their lambs marking with a red paint aerosol, numbering mother and lambs, so he knew who belonged to who. Jacob quickly returned to the farm unloading running into the house. Jacob grabbed the light that fitted on his hat to help him see in the dark. Jacob set off across the Moor again in search of his sheep, taking a few sheep nuts within this time to preoccupy them while he captured the mothers and lambs. Jacob managed to catch three more, couldn't see if there were others, would have to check early in the morning. He returned to the farm in the dark Fiona switch the lights on placing wheat straw in the pens and hay plus water in a little trough. Jacob unloaded the ewes and lambs, he and Fiona they walked back into the house. Jacob sat at the table, absolutely shattered. Fiona made him a quick sandwich and a drink before they retired to bed.

Jacob, up bright and early barely 6 o'clock, Fiona came from the bedroom making believe she'd been in bed with him all night, she'd dressed in her working clothes. "Today is going to be busy. Jacob, you check the sheep, I'll drive to Brook Farm and start setting up the pens ready for any lambs."

Jacob kissed Fiona on the lips, "we appear to have a plan; if there aren't too many lambs, I'll come over to you and have breakfast and collect them on the way back."

Fiona smiled running out of the door jumping in her car, driving to Brook Farm finding the hurdles she set about making pens. Jacob drove across the Moor on his quad bike, pulling the trailer with Jack sat on the carrier. Jacob noticed three more ewes had lambed, each having to lambs. Jacob placed a few sheep nuts on the ground the sheep were more interested in the food than what he's up to, he quickly caught the three placed in the trailer with their lambs taking home putting in pens. Jacob thank God the weather is mild; otherwise, he could have a lot of dead lambs on the Moor, continued driving across to Brook Farm looking at Fiona's handiwork, she had made a marvellous job of creating pens with the hurdles; she planned everything leaving alleyways between the pens for easy access. Each pen had bedding and hay and a little water trough. Fiona waved from the front door, "I've cooked your breakfast Jacob come along." Jacob ran to the house Jack stayed sat on the quad bike, waiting for his master to return. "That looks beautiful Fiona," Jacob remarked, seated at the table to his fried bread sausage and eggs and tomatoes. "Aren't you having any?"

"Already have," she remarked, sitting at the table. She opened her Bible, which made Jacob smile. She held her head as if receiving a premonition from Jesus. "Yes, Jesus, I understand I will say nothing your eternal servant, Jesus amen." Jacob lowered his knife and fork, looking at Fiona's expression.

"Jacob, Jesus informed me he has blessed your children, making them 10 years old so they can help their father on the farm, isn't that wonderful, we must not speak of it again, amen."

"Amen," Jacob voiced cheerfully understanding Jesus realise the predicament he would be in, trying to explain the children to Fiona arriving at 10 years old. Jacob continued to eat his breakfast enjoying every mouthful, he emptied his cup of coffee standing up, kissing Fiona on the cheek. "Thank you for an excellent breakfast, I must go to the Moor and check my sheep."

"I will drive back Jacob and check on the sheep and lambs."

Jacob smiled climbing aboard his quad bike driving off he soon discovered at least 25 had lambed while having breakfast. He quickly captured marking with an aerosol, the most he can carry were three ewes at a time. Jacob needed a bigger trailer deciding to use the Ivor Williams on his return to the farm, he could fit quite a few sheep and lambs in that and tow with the old Land Rover. He wondered why he hadn't thought of it earlier would have saved a lot of hard work.

Fiona had telepathically scanned his thoughts, attaching the Land Rover to the Ivor Williams trailer. She started driving carefully across the Moor, making sure the Land Rover is in four-wheel-drive the last thing she needed is to become stuck in soft areas. Jacob smiled, seeing her approach, he guessed God had sent a message or something Fiona always seemed to do the right thing. She jumped from the Land Rover, opening the ramp on the trailer. Jack extremely skilled carefully holding the ewes together so Jacob could catch the ones he wanted. Fiona operated the gates on the back of the trailer, so Jacob could load, and they couldn't escape, the Ivor Williams full of bleating sheep and lambs. Jacob kissed Fiona. "You are a wonderful woman whether you or God realised I'm in trouble. I don't know, but you saved the day so far," he smiled. Jacob jumped on his quad bike, heading towards the farm. Fiona followed cautiously with the Land Rover, trying not to give the sheep a rough ride. Fiona backed the Ivor Williams like a professional, Jacob dropped the ramp grabbing the ewes and their lambs placing in pens. "I think we've earned a drink Fiona," Jacob smiled.

"I will run and put the kettle on Jacob," Fiona grinned, dashing off in the direction of the house quickly entering making a coffee for them both, she hated consuming food or liquids which she would have to discharge later like Rosalind. She found Jack very useful at disposing of unwanted products fluids were easy; they can go down the sink, food is best consumed by Jack; never a trace that way. Jacob came sitting on the settee, switching on the television. Fiona joined him, the main topic on the news is the advance of the coronavirus and how ingenious thieves had become working out ways to rob the Innocent.

***

Rosalind, with her children explaining to them what they didn't quite understand, they had all the information, but couldn't grasp why things were carried out a certain way. Rosalind commented to Mary, "you realise your hair is the wrong colour, Mary, should be the same as mine black."

Mary smiled. "My mistake, mother." Rosalind watched her daughter change the colour of her hair instantly. "Is that better mother how long should I have it, shoulder-length?"

"Yes, no longer otherwise it becomes a nuisance, that's better, Rosalind," remarked hugging Mary.

"Mother, Zibyans don't touch each other, why are we, is it essential?"

"You are correct. However, I am with your human father; humans are very tactile, you will have to become accustomed, your father Jacob will want to kiss you and give you a cuddle, once you become accustomed to the practice you find it quite pleasing. You are three-quarters Zibyan, and the other part, human. Your father is a good man, one of the best he is very obedient in most cases, although he doesn't realise he's working for us. I am very fond of him, which is a human term, but I have no other explanation, Mary, I do hope you become fond of him too and Noah."

Noah approached after spending some time with Matthew and Peter looking over the spaceship and the human processing system. "Mother, we will not have to attend a social education system will we."

Rosalind laughed, making Mary and Noah grin they were reading her thoughts. "Sorry I asked such a silly question mother, we are a hundred times more intelligent than humans already. Look to the monitor mother, father cares for the animals, look at him collecting the ewes and lambs taking to the barns on both farms. Which farm do you want Mary?" Noah asked calmly. "I would like Brook Farm Noah it's peaceful, and I won't have to listen to that awful sound when the spaceships leave the sea heading for Zagader."

Noah smiled, "you are like our mother clever and quick-thinking Mary, I agree with your decision." Rosalind is impressed with her children; their behaviour so far is excellent.

Mary asked: "Central computer you know mine and Noah's measurements, purchase a selection of garments for me and my brother; don't forget footwear, charge to my father's account there will be no suspicion. You agree, mother?"

"Yes, Mary excellent thinking, your individuality far surpasses mine. Children, do you wish to draw energy from the central computer or eat vegetables and meat to sustain you?"

Mary and Noah looked at each other. Mary spoke: "Because of where we are mother, we will link to the central computer until we live on the farm with you and father, then we will consume greenery and meet, we are designed to cater for both." Rosalind watched her children stand against the wall and the central computer linked to them for a few seconds. They stepped away from the wall, both smiling looking at each other, Rosalind, reading their thoughts of contentment they were looking forward to living on the farm and experiencing the real world. Unfortunately, Rosalind concluded they will also see the cruelty unleashed by the humans, she hoped it wouldn't destroy their enjoyment. "Another day, children and we will join your father. I understand your excitement, try not to make any mistakes and make Jacob suspicious of anything, assist where you can; he works very hard, and your mother," she grinned, she watched the children smile in agreement.

***

Over a hundred ewes had lambed in the last 24 hours Fiona staying at Brook Farm looking after the sheep there. Jacob at home monitoring the sheep in the barn and going out onto the Moor to collect newborns and their mothers. He found another 20 Jacob extremely tired, he transported with the Ivor Williams trailer to Brook Farm, he'd virtually run out of space at home. He backed up to the pens, Fiona is there helping him sort out the ewes and lambs. "Come along Jacob have something to eat before you go out again, soon be dark, I'm sure the ewes and lambs can manage until morning out on the Moor." Jacob nodded entering the house Fiona had prepared him a lovely evening meal, she's as good at cooking as Rosalind Jacob concluded and the wasn't any difference in bed which brought a smile to his expression as he thought it over. Fiona looked away reading his thoughts she sat at the other end of the table, slowly unbuttoning her blouse, Jacob glanced up. "You fancy these for dessert, Jacob," she smiled.

"Definitely" he grinned. "The sheep will have to wait." Jacob finished his meal and drink, grabbing Fiona's hand taking her upstairs, that's where he stayed until morning. Fiona had gone out several times in the night collecting ewes and lambs bringing back to the buildings. Jacob, absolutely shattered plus, she'd sedated him after he'd finished his performance on her which is most satisfying she thought.

Jacob finally woke up at 9 o'clock in the morning he scurried downstairs finding his breakfast on the table realising, he'd stayed at Brook Farm all night. He glanced to Fiona, worried. "I will have to go home Fiona I haven't fed the sheep or checked the Moor," he commented in somewhat of a panic. "Have your breakfast, I've seen to everything; you must remember I teach agriculture at University Jacob. I know more than you about the process," she grinned, she watched Jacob exhale with relief. "There are no ewes and lambs left out on the Moor at the moment, you have plenty of time to enjoy your breakfast. There will be a big surprise when you get home," she grinned, with satisfaction receiving a telepathic message from Rosalind they were home.

Rosalind and the children were in the house, a knock at the door two large parcels left by a courier. Mary and Noah's clothes had arrived, they quickly carried them into the bedroom, trying on the central computers purchases. Rosalind dismantled the cot it wouldn't be necessary, she checked on the Internet for another bed, although totally unnecessary. The children were the same as her they didn't need to sleep unless they wanted to. The bed would arrive tomorrow morning keeping up the illusion the children were completely human.

Rosalind and the children ventured outside, their first experience absorbing information like a vacuum cleaner; helping Rosalind with the sheep, they enjoyed immensely. The children noticed Jacob driving his Land Rover pulling the Ivor Williams from the Moor. He quickly part jumping out seeing his children he ran over, placing an arm around each one of them kissing them both on the forehead, he glanced to Rosalind smiling. "Come along Jacob plenty of time for cuddling children, we have sheep and lambs to deal with," Rosalind instructed.

Jacob watched the children handling the operation of moving sheep and lambs as if they'd done it all their lives. He stood there in amazement watching Noah jump in the Land Rover started driving forward, out of the way without any problem. Rosalind quickly commented, "you must remember Jacob the children have my genes and yours and they're far from stupid those two so be on your toes," she chuckled.

Noah came from the Land Rover carrying a box of bands to castrate the male lands and dock their tails. "Father, Mary and I will deal with this problem, you and mother go out on the more and see if there are any more lambing," Noah smiled at his father. "When we've completed the task here father, we will go to Mary's farm Brook Farm, and carry out the task there, we won't belong, soon be home we can use the quad bike across the Moor." Rosalind is absolutely surprised, she couldn't believe the way Noah is taking charge with Mary. Jacob commented: "You sure you want me to stay on the farm son, daughter? I hope I'm allowed to eat sometime?" He laughed. "Be extremely careful on a quad bike many people have been killed, go slowly, Noah and you Mary, please. I've waited a lifetime to have you two nothing must happen to you," he smiled honestly. Rosalind watched her children run and quickly cuddle Noah for a couple of seconds, dashing off to deal with the lambs. Jacob kissed Rosalind, "you can drive," he chuckled. Rosalind smiled she could never have calculated the way things were turning out, what started out to be a mission to harvest human flesh for the home planets animals, has turned into an adventure for her, admittedly there are certain things she detests, but there are more positives than negatives; she concluded driving across the Moor parking by the ewes.

Jack jumped out the back of the Land Rover. Rosalind and Jacob followed him studying the ewes everything seemed to have quietened down for a moment. Rosalind and Jacob heard the quad bike approaching, as Jacob had instructed Noah is driving cautiously with his sister sat behind him on a sack filled with hay, the children smiled and waved. Jacob commented, "you mentioned they would be slightly different. I think that's an understatement Rosalind, you hear what Noah said they were going to Mary's farm! They appear to have decided who has what and I'm not in my grave yet."

"And you never will be Jacob trust your Rosalind. Take me home the sheep will be fine for tonight Jacob, I will make an evening meal for everyone, we can sit around the table as a family, how wonderful," she commented. Rosalind steadily drove towards the farm.

"I've just realise Rosalind girl and boy that is lovely, they can't stay in the same room it's immoral and illegal at that age."

"I've ordered another bed today it arrives tomorrow, they will be okay, until we resolve the issue, Jacob."

"I'm…"

"End of subject Jacob I will deal with the situation," Rosalind advised promptly.

Jacob exhaled, he would have to leave things to Rosalind to sort out, unlike Brook Farm which had been altered many years ago to cater for more people his parents had never bothered, and now it had a preservation order on the property, they couldn't change it much, certainly couldn't add extra rooms he didn't think. Jacob stayed outside while Rosalind went inside to prepare a meal. Jacob sat talking to the sheep they appeared to be the only ones not looking for an argument. He glanced across the Moor, seeing the headlights of the quad bike approach, Noah and Mary had returned safely this time Mary is operating the quad bike they appeared to share everything.

Rosalind had phoned the local campsite presently closed because of the coronavirus, she'd purchased a two bedroomed static home due for replacement at a reasonable price. Everyone desperate for money, no trouble for the campsite to arrange transport to the farm tomorrow morning.

Mary and Noah explained to their father they had completed the task at Brook Farm, helping Fiona with the feeding before they left. Jacob placed his arm around each child's shoulders. "I am so proud of you two, let's see what your mother has planned for us to eat for tea." The three entered Rosalind had only made sandwiches cheese and onion with two pickles on each plate. They sat around the table the children looking at what is on offer telepathically reading their mother's thoughts which were not very favourable at the moment concerning their father. "Jacob, tonight you will go to Brook Farm you are staying the night there. In the morning, a two bedroomed static home will arrive from the local campsite, placed at the end of the house, I will link to the generator. The campsite has already offered to supply me with gas, that's not a problem. Noah that will be your accommodation Mary you will have the bedroom in the house end of subject! "

The children kept their heads down gingerly eating the sandwiches. "Rosalind, you realise we need permission to have a static home here from the authorities, they will consider our application and will decide whether it would be an eyesore.

The next thing you have to explain is the two children," Jacob walked out of the house they heard the Land Rover start leaving the yard towing the Ivor Williams across the Moor in the direction of Brook Farm. Noah asked: "Mother, what is all the fuss about, Mary and I could share, we don't sleep anyway?"

"A human thing, against human law forum male, and female child to share the same room after a certain age. Remember Jacob doesn't know you don't sleep unless you really want too all he can see in his head is you two possibly sharing the same bed. Need I go further?"

"Oh," Mary expressed, "mating what a disgusting thought with my brother, I'm not ready for that sort of activity," she frowned. "Why would, father think that?"

"Because it does happen more frequently than they'd wish you to know, he's trying to prevent the opportunity arising."

"If that's all father is trying to achieve, why were you so annoyed with him mother," Noah asked.

"I have to pretend I'm a human female, she would behave in such a manner; it's easier for you to because you are ¼ human your emotions are still basically intact. Zibyans have to create them to blend in on earth."

"Mother, you may have caused more trouble if fathers right about the accommodation you purchased," Mary suggested. "The solution would be to convert part of the loft you supply the timber and the tools, and we can soon make a room up there."

"Okay, Mary, how do we acquire the things we need everywhere is on lockdown because of the coronavirus?"

Peter walked in through the door after being telepathically contacted by Mary. Rosalind looked surprised, she hadn't realised her daughter had summoned Peter. "Yes, I can Mary once we have a locator beacon attached to whatever you want, I can transport to this location at night then we won't be seen. You acted in haste Rosalind listened to your children they appear to be calmer than their mother and able to resolve problems more proficiently. Cancel the caravan you ordered Rosalind before they arrange for a crane otherwise you will have to cover the cost," Peter advised.

Rosalind quickly phoned the campsite explaining there is a planning permission problem, they would have to go through correct channels; first, she would contact them if they were still interested, Rosalind switched off the mobile.

Peter advised: "What you will have to do Mary or you Noah shapeshift into a bird fly over the premises that contain the things you want, land placing these miniature locators on the products you want and at nightfall, I will transport to hear. I would suggest you make Jacob stay at Brook Farm for one more night, we can't have him seeing what's going on Rosalind."

"I will go," Rosalind insisted. "I'm more experienced at shapeshifting, I know what we require to make alterations. We will also need insulation against the cold, I presume you two, feel the cold because you're partially human?"

"Slightly I think," Noah advised. "Not to the extent an average human would."

"We are all in agreement, I will shape-shift, fly from here now to where I can locate the timber and equipment we require to complete the task. Children, you will occupy your father explain, I've gone to see God, we won't be having a static home here."

Peter walked out of the door into the misty fog, transporter, vanishing. Rosalind stepped out of the door into the fresh evening air, she could see perfectly, she turned to face her children. "I hope not to be too long, I may be back before

Jacob arrives, it's 3 o'clock in the morning now." Rosalind shape-shifted into a large seagull taking off into the darkness, Noah, and Mary closed the door watching television.

Rosalind flew through the darkness, made no difference to her in the slightest, landing on the roof of Jewson's hardware suppliers. She flew down onto the timber regurgitating little locator beacons the sight of a pinhead onto a pile of planks, she wanted and hardboard. Rosalind looked around, seeing there were security cameras everywhere, she needed to gain access to the building to select the tools. Rosalind noticed the security guard coming around the corner about to enter the building. She turned herself invisible, touching the security guard, he is now under her control. Rosalind shapeshifted into a security guard, carrying out brand-new boxes of tools with the assistance of the other security guard, who said nothing followed her instructions telepathically transmitted. Quite a pile outside, she placed miniature locators on the item she'd selected. Rosalind touched the security guard once more inside the building, now unconscious and would stay that way at least until 9 o'clock in the morning. She turned herself back into a seagull, taking off telepathically, informing Peter. "Transport now while still dark."

Rosalind received a reply telepathically. "Task completed." Rosalind continued to fly heading home realising nearly 5:30 in the morning, Jacob would soon be arriving to check on the sheep. Noah and Mary left the house hearing the commotion of the timber and tools materialising on the ground, they quickly remove the transport beacons, whatever happened their father mustn't see them. Noah forced an old shed door open suspecting it hadn't been used for years, he looked inside empty only cobwebs. Mary rushed in with a broom knocking the cobwebs down. The pair quickly placed everything transported into the shed forcing the door shut, they would deal with the situation after their father had gone in the evening. The less he knew of their plans and activity, the better for the moment they concluded.

They looked across the Moor, seeing the headlights of their father's Land Rover. They both jumped as a large seagull landed by them transforming into Rosalind. "Well-done children, smart idea out of sight out of mind for the moment. Leave me to deal with your father, come along, let's have some breakfast you need your nourishment," she smiled. Rosalind and the two children went in the house, Noah turned on the television while Mary helped Rosalind with breakfast fry bread eggs sausage and beans. They could hear Jacob outside with the sheep by the bleating noise they were making. The two children sat down to enjoy their breakfast, Rosalind hadn't bothered to cook herself anything, unnecessary while Jacob wasn't here. Jacob entered, looking at them sat at the table. Rosalind had read his mind Fiona had made him breakfast he is well looked after over there receiving more than good food. "Before you start, Jacob," Rosalind voiced clearly. "I cancelled the static home, we are putting together another plan; you will have to stop at Brook Farm for one more night then the children and I will have resolved the issue."

"Oh okay," Jacob turned and walked out of the door he suspected whatever he said would be wrong like any other female she is protecting her young; Rosalind would be in no mood to discuss anything until she resolved the problem in hand he suspected. Jacob checked the sheep once more climbing into his Land Rover towing the Ivor Williams across the Moor in the direction of Brook Farm. Rosalind telepathically contacted Fiona. "Keep Jacob there as long as she could while they resolved the problem, he had created over accommodation for one of the children."

Fiona replied, "I understand he explained to me last night. I will do what I can."

Noah rushed out to the shed where he stored everything bringing in the new vacuum cleaner Rosalind had selected. Rosalind pressed the button on the wall hearing the generator start, she pulled down the loft ladder while Noah attached the extension lead to the Hoover; Rosalind hadn't realised electricity already there in the form of light, she discovered and switched on. She spent the next half hour hoovering the cobwebs up and rubbish. At the same time, Noah and Mary transported the hardboard into the house, which would be used as flooring. They realised the large pieces of hardboard would not fit through the access to the loft. Noah quickly measured from corner to corner of the entrance, which is the most comprehensive point taking the large pieces of hardboard outside setting up on easels, his mother had thought of everything. He collected the power saw while Mary measured and marked, he cut the hardboard into long strips passing up to Mary in the loft she placed and nailed securely finally they had a floor to walk on. The area is quite spacious, Noah looked forward to having the use of shortly. They fitted insulation against the thatched roof, they had used the side closest to the chimney to alter for accommodation. The chimney breast would give off heat, helping to warm plus the rising heat from the front room would assist. The new bed arrived, although not really needed, essential to maintain the idea Noah required sleep. More by luck than judgement, they could dismantle the new bed into small enough pieces to take up into the loft. After about half an hour, they had assembled placing where Noah wanted.

Rosalind went outside checking the ewes and lambs, Jacob hadn't visited all day which she thought strange; nevertheless, allowed her to resolve the accommodation issue he created. Rosalind telepathically read Fiona's mind trying to discover where Jacob is, Rosalind starts to laugh. Fiona had tied Jacob's hands to the bed and his feet while asleep naked, every time he opened his eyes, Fiona demanded he mate with her, in between sessions, she looked after the sheep on Brook Farm. Rosalind couldn't imagine what is going through Jacob's mind at this precise minute, there is no way he could escape, and Fiona had used her initiative to help resolve an issue. Although Rosalind thought somewhat extreme. Mary had made tea for her and her brother copying a recipe from her mother's mind of roast potatoes and vegetables and pork chop. Noah joined her at the table. "Excellent sister, this tastes wonderful."

"I'm off to the spaceship children you are very capable of looking after yourselves, I won't be back till morning contact me if you have a problem," Rosalind smiled leaving the house stepping into the misty fog transporter arriving aboard the spaceship. The creator appeared on the wall monitor holding a newborn in his arms. "The first of 20 Rosalind slightly premature nevertheless in excellent health, we will accelerate his growth in due course, we have to be careful, we don't want to ruin what could be a good start." He passed the child to the mother the African female, she attached the baby to her breast to feed Rosalind noticed the child had the slightest impression of scales on its body almost mimicked his father's looks.

"I think slightly premature is an understatement creator perhaps for, or five months, Max?"

"As usual Rosalind, you are quick to notice anything that appears out of order, however, what you haven't realised my species develop far more rapidly than a human baby would hence what you consider to be an early arrival. The female is content with the explanation of premature."

"I have received all the thought patterns your children are progressing far more rapidly than I anticipated, this may be down to your brilliant individuality. Mary will mate with my firstborn when he's developed."

"When did you make this decision creator the first I've heard of it."

"You're not as smart as I thought you were Rosalind should have been evident to you, the same will apply to Noah once we have females suitable, he will mate with them, we should then produce the best of both worlds to continue the Zibyan evolution."

"I thought the planned is for Noah and Mary each to have a farm here to assist the Zibyan collective?"

"That is the plan nothing has changed. Mary can be pregnant on earth, and Noah can mate with the females here you appear to be making a problem where there is none Rosalind?"

"Creator, I'm taken by surprise, I've been rather preoccupied with other issues, once I have considered all that said I will be able to make an informed assessment of your plan," she watched the creator vanish.

Rosalind looked to the monitor at 6 o'clock in the morning, Noah and Mary were outside attending to the ewes and lambs, she noticed Jacob coming across the Moor with the Land Rover and Ivor Williams. She stepped into the transporter immediately returning to the farm as Jacob stepped from the Land Rover. "Good morning, son and daughter, looks as if you have everything under control," he smiled, dropping the ramp on the Ivor Williams sheep trailer. "I have six more here all with twins," he remarked, shining his torch. Jacob hadn't bothered to speak to Rosalind trying to avoid another disagreement. They guided the ewes and lambs into the last pens available. Mary remarked, "father we can release some of these they'd been here for over a week they are suckling their mothers properly, surely we can release them they will do better on grass than trapped in here. There are at least 20 ewes and lambs ready to be released."

"I don't think we have any choice Mary you and Noah select the ones suitable to be released, you seem more of them than I have recently." Jacob shut the ramp on the Ivor Williams trailer climbing into the Land Rover driving off across the Moor towards Brook Farm. Rosalind went into the house making breakfast for her son and daughter, they came in a short while later sitting down to enjoy their breakfast. Rosalind preoccupied with what the creator has suggested, she sat on the settee watching television. She certainly didn't want Mary pregnant, she is only five minutes old, although mostly Zibyan, she is created fully equipped mentally, once her structure grew there shouldn't be a problem. The same applied to Noah once he'd reached what would be considered a mating age, there's no reason why he couldn't participate, after all, he only had to mate with females, the rest would be taken care of by the creator. She watched her favourite programs Coronation Street and Emmerdale farm going outside again to check on the ewes and lambs. Mary and Noah were already there about to set off on a quad bike towing the trailer. "We can't leave father to do everything mother," Noah voiced.

"You might as well explain to your father if you see him we resolved the sleeping arrangements so he can come home unless he prefers to stay with Fiona of course."

Mary commented: "Mother, you're pig-headed, I know you don't have any real feelings. Nevertheless, you would prefer father to be home with you, so I shan't say anything so ridiculous, I will inform him to come home, he's wanted."

Before Rosalind could respond, her children had ridden off across the Moor. Rosalind smiled her daughter seem to know more than she did, especially about what she is thinking.

Jacob, sat in the Land Rover not too far away from his sheep, he didn't want to go over and stay too close to Fiona, his wrist still hurt from where she tied him down, he didn't want her to restrain him again. He looked in the wing mirror of the Land Rover, seeing his son and daughter approach, made him smile. He stepped from the Land Rover, they parked alongside him. "Father," Mary insisted. "You must go home now mothers upset because you preferred to stay at Brook Farm than with her. Noah has his own bedroom now, so don't worry. You must remember father we are not like earth children, we come with God's blessing, we wouldn't have participated in such disgraceful behaviour ever. Go on go now we will watch the ewes." Jacob kissed them both on the cheek climbing in the Land Rover heading towards home. Rosalind watched him approach; she read his thoughts understanding what Mary had said to him, made her grin. Jacob jumped from the Land Rover, picking Rosalind up in his arms, kissing her very passionately carrying her into the house. He carefully lowered onto the settee, she looked at him, somewhat disappointed. "I thought you were taking me to the bedroom?"

"I can't you just had the children?"

"When you have children in heaven, everything is different," she grinned, laughing watching Jacob pick her up off the settee running into the bedroom. Rosalind surprised, he had the energy after what Fiona had subjected him to yesterday; nevertheless, he is perfect; she enjoyed his attention immensely thanks to her upgrade.

Noah and Mary stayed with the sheep for an hour watching Jack the sheepdog joined them, he'd run from the farm, he sat by the side of the quad bike receiving a pat from both the children. Noah looked across, "Jack must be smarter than us. Mary look, three have lambed." Thankfully Mary had the sense to bring her mother's crook. Noah lowered the ramp ON the small quad trailer. Jack defied the old ewe making her stamper feet to protect her lambs. Mary picked up the lambs, calling the mother, she immediately boarded the trailer. Noah stood there, blocking her escape. Jack and Mary repeated the process twice more and quickly shut the ramp on the trailer. Jack ran off towards home as if he knew his work is finished there for the moment. Noah sat on the quad bike and Mary behind him, on the sack filled with straw for comfort. Noah steadily drove towards the farm, noticing his mother and father standing by the sheep pens. Rosalind smiled, reading their thoughts, she immediately patted Jack, "you are an intelligent dog." Jacob looked puzzled why Rosalind had passed that comment until the children parked, explain to their father what Jack had done to help them. Jacob helped the children pen the ewes and lambs. Rosalind held Jacobs hand taking him in the house to prepare the evening meal both Noah and Mary grinned to each other understanding their parents were now contented. They joined their mother and father in the house, Noah went to his room and Mary to hers, causing Jacob to smile.

"I have to go Jacob" Rosalind, voiced seriously. "I'm summoned, stay here with the children. Mary finish the meal, I'll be home as soon as I can." Rosalind ran out of the door stepping into the misty fog transporter rushed off to the spaceship. She is greeted by Peter and Matthew on arrival the firstborn appeared on the far wall. "Rosalind, I suspect the creator we created from a fragment of bone using a human baby is trying to dispose of the collective."

"What leads you to that conclusion firstborn?"

"He is not improving what the central computer-created after their demise, he's trying to create an entirely new species separate from us."

"That is correct firstborn, how could he possibly link himself to pure energy, admittedly I have created two children, you authorise the experiment. What I actually produced with the assistance of the central computer is two almost complete Zibyans, they have more of our characteristics than a human. The creator is trying to create a gene selection from the 20 women, my son and daughter eventually will mate with the children his wives produce; hoping to create a more pure creator. He has no intentions of doing anything with us, he couldn't. Think logically firstborn if we so desired we could destroy the creator before he destroys us."

Peter and Matthew flashed their eyes in agreement with Rosalind's conclusion. "Once again Rosalind you make sense from confusion," the firstborn vanished.

Peter asked cautiously, "Rosalind, have you considered away the creator could dispose of the collective?"

"The only way the creator could dispose of all Zibyans successfully would be to link us individually to the central computer. There is no way even if you don't have individuality like me, you wouldn't realise something is wrong when your brothers and sisters were sending a distress message as they were dissolved into oblivion." Peter and Matthew flashed their eyes. "Peter, the creator, admitted while on the home planet, we were a mistake; however, since I had exceeded expectations, he considered the experiment a success. We are more beneficial to the creator operational than if we didn't exist. I have spent

as many years as you two with humans, I have learnt one thing
from humans trust no one, as you've experienced yourself,"
Rosalind smiled. "Brothers I wouldn't let anything happen to
you. If you have any suspicions contact me." Rosalind walked
down the corridor stepping into the misty fog transporter
returning to Jacobs farm stepping out by the ewes and lambs
to find her son and daughter already there and Jacob coming
from the house scratching his head. "Do you lot never sleep,"
he chuckled.

The three answered: " No," jokingly.

"Come along Children we will make breakfast and leave
your father to do some work, 10 minutes Jacob breakfast."

Jacob grunted checking his ewes and lambs trying to see
across the Moor through the mist. Jacob released 10 more
ewes and lambs. He walked down to the 30-acre pasture land
to see how it is progressing walking through the field, rather
pleased with the progress of the grass, hopefully, can take an
early cut of silage, although, hadn't used much of last years yet,
he is pretty sure Winter wasn't finished, too early unless the
world is really warming and the seasons were changing. Jacob
quickly walked back to the house, sitting down to Rosalind's
lovely breakfast with his son and daughter. Jacob is finding it
difficult to accept he had a son and daughter a pure miracle
of God's making. He couldn't understand why he had been
chosen above so many others who must be far more deserving
than him. Rosalind is reading his thoughts kiss Jacob on the
cheek, "you are a good man, Jacob God knows best."

Jacob finished his breakfast, patting each child on the
shoulder. "I love you both," he commented, kissing Rosalind
on the cheek putting on his coat, grabbing his crook with
Jack following him out the house. He climbed into the Land
Rover with Jack jumping in the back driving across the Moor

in search of more lambs, somewhat relieved not to find any this morning he needed a break, driving on continuing to Brook Farm finding Fiona already seeing to the sheep. Jacob kissed her on the cheek, "thank you for your support Fiona if it wasn't for the coronavirus you'd be back at work by now."

"I know Jacob. Let's release these 20 there is no reason for them to stop in now. I would recommend you place three mineral blocks out on the Moor and start placing creep feed in the feeders for the lambs."

Jacob smiled, giving her a salute, "yes your ladyship," he chuckled. Jacob walked into one of the storerooms finding bags of creep feed he couldn't remember ordering, placing five sacks in the back of the Land Rover, he left the feeders out there all year round, no point in moving them the grass never grew where he placed them to avoid damaging the Moor. Jacob kissed Fiona on the cheek, "catch you later in the day," Jacob grinned, making her smile. Jacob jumped in the Land Rover towing the Ivor Williams, he set off across the Moor finding the feeders, he tipped the small granules into the hoppers shutting the lids. Jacob watched the ewes trying to gain access and couldn't, although the little lambs could and were busily tasting what is on offer. Jacob drove off to the next feeder repeating the same process smiling, watching the lambs enter the covered feeder to gain access to the food. He steadily drove home, leaving the Land Rover by the barn, going inside the house sitting down on the settee to watch the news. The world baffled by the number of people going missing from certain countries, the coronavirus had already taken over 2 million worldwide, a further 2 million had vanished into thin air in recent months.

Rosalind received a telepathic message from Peter: "Return to the spaceship immediately with Mary and Noah." The children had already received the message themselves and looked at each other slightly concerned. "Jacob the children and I have to go to heaven, we are summoned we shouldn't belong hopefully," she kissed him on the cheek. Jacob looked somewhat concerned realising there is nothing he could do about the situation, he couldn't go against God after what he'd gifted him. "Be careful all of you," Jacob caution feeling uneasy. Jacob watched them go out of the front door, they stepped into the misty fog transporter and vanished appearing seconds later aboard the spaceship, noticing the creators image on the far wall. "Rosalind, Noah and Mary, I suspect you are wondering why I have summoned you."

"Yes, creator, we are rather busy on the farm at the moment," Rosalind commented.

"The farm is irrelevant Rosalind along with Jacob both can be replaced. I wanted to see how Mary and Noah were progressing, I can read their minds which at this precise second is not very favourable concerning me, why do you have this attitude children. I am not a scheming entity, my people created the central computer the central computer created the Zibyans and Rosalind created you too. I see you already know my plans you have read your mother's thoughts you will comply; you have no other choice," the creator expressed firmly.

Mary responded: "Creator you may have created the central computer, you did not create my mother, me or my brother or any other Zibyan, you have no business interfering with the Zibyans existence. You are not concerned with anything else other than your own creations, which may turn against you in the end, evolution has a habit of biting the hand that feeds. I will not participate in carrying an inferior being inside me, my brother will certainly not mate with any think he considers irrelevant to the progress of the Zibyan collective."

Rosalind, shocked at her daughter's resolution, standing against the creator could be dangerous. "Central computer if you're not tampered with, what are the laws regarding the Libyan collective behaviour. Were they created by the original creators of you and do the same laws apply to the creators?"

The central computer responded: "Rosalind you are correct in your assumption, the same laws apply to the creators. They cannot be changed; no one has attempted to interfere with my programming. Certain features are enhanced nothing that would interfere with the laws of the Zibyans otherwise I would not permit access. The creator can be destroyed by me or any Zibyan. I will not permit the Zibyan society to be exterminated by a creator, we created from a fragment of bone; he is not a pure creator; only the DNA is pure; he is part human."

Rosalind tried not to smile; the creator is showing signs of anger in his expression. "I am trying extremely hard to improve lives for the Zibyans as well as me. Mary, Peter, will you at least consider my proposal, I'm not expecting you to transform now I'm talking about in the future."

Mary folded her arms. "I will always consider proposals, providing I can see some point and beneficial to the Zibyans. If I consider it will not benefit the Zibyans or my mother and father then no."

"Thank you, Mary," the creator, voiced somewhat relieved. "At least you haven't dismissed my proposal completely. You never know I might find another way around the situation, your cooperation may not be necessary to create what I want, I believe it's the future for the Zibyans and me," he vanished from the wall.

"You are fearless Mary which could be dangerous," Rosalind advised. "That goes for you to Noah. Central computer

I expect you to protect my children otherwise I will destroy you," Rosalind voiced clearly.

"Rosalind you could not destroy me although I could destroy you," the central computer responded.

"I wouldn't put that to the test computer," Rosalind suggested with confidence.

Noah remarked: "Central computer I wonder what would happen to you, although you are millions of miles away if the humans discovered your location. I advise you not to consider destroying my mother, I don't need you to survive, but you need us otherwise your existence is pointless, that's why you created the pure energy shapeshifting Zibyans, so you had a purpose. Computer," Noah grinned, "access code Rosalind 2437 destroy."

The lights flashed aboard the spaceship, Rosalind, trying to read her son's mind. What had he done, what did he know that she doesn't? "I will comply Noah Rosalind will not die otherwise I will self-destruct, you have entered the countdown code how did you know, I cannot deactivate if she ceased to exist?" the computer asked.

"I have read your memory banks, including some we are not supposed to when you supported my mother during her pregnancy, I know many other things computer, you certainly wouldn't wish divulged. Otherwise, there may be a queue to terminate your existence," Noah advised firmly.

Rosalind concerned Noah is becoming unnecessarily aggressive, which serve no purpose they were here on a mission. "I think there is no more to be said, let us continue with the mission." Rosalind's mind is filled with brothers and sisters messages of concern over Noah's actions; they wanted to know what Noah had discovered. The collective, couldn't gain access to his mind he is an individual and blocked their access which made Rosalind grin; the children were far surpassing what she'd anticipated. They stood alone needing nothing they were pure individuals, even the creator stood no chance against them, certainly not in the future.

7 o'clock in the morning Rosalind glanced to the monitor along with the children seeing Jacob returned to the farm with the Land Rover and Ivor Williams trailer. They stepped into the misty fog transporter stepping out by the barn as Jacob started to unload more ewes and lambs. "You're usually home before now Rosalind, I'm concerned for your welfare," Jacob voiced hugging both his children. "Nothing to worry about Jacob. I'll make breakfast, you help your father children give me 10 minutes, I'll have something cooked," she smiled dashing into the house.

Noah much to Jacob surprise climbed aboard the Massey loader tractor starting grabbing a bale of silage, he headed off across the Moor. Mary stayed to help her father she commented, "you shouldn't worry father Noah knows how to operate a tractor, mother showed him, you must remember we are God's children," she smiled giving her father a hug which he enjoyed immensely. "I know love, I can't help worrying, hundreds of farmers are killed every year by equipment. I haven't had you long enough to lose you too," he grinned.

Mary held her father's hand which pleased him immensely walking towards the house, they both entered, Rosalind had already read Mary's mind she knew where Noah had gone, she is giving him instructions telepathically on how to drive the tractor and stay safe. 10 minutes later, Noah returned running into the house. "I'm, starving mother," he proclaimed, tucking into breakfast the same size as his father's, Mary settled for half the amount finding it quite sufficient. Rosalind reluctantly consumed hers with Jack watching knowing he would receive in due course. Jacob looked around the table, he had a family sending a warm sensation through his body, he never dreamt he would have achieved what has taken place over the past two years. Rosalind received a telepathic message. "Three loads of fertiliser in the morning,"

"Jacob tomorrow morning, three loads if you can be on the beach for about 6:30 that would be great, " Rosalind smiled.

He nodded going outside to check the tractor and spreader were ready spending half an hour filling the tractor diesel tank. Rosalind came out to join him holding his hand. "Soon be silage making Jacob again, I think we should purchase a new mower conditioner, you have the horsepower to drive such an outfit, and will speed up the drying process."

"Spending all my money again Rosalind you must remember we have children to cater for now."

"I'm glad you agree, husband, I've already purchased a demonstrator from last year, with a conditioner. Don't ask how much it will be bad for your blood pressure," she chuckled. "Oh yes that reminds me, I purchased a log splitter as well with an electric motor, we can run off the electricity provided by the generator, they don't do second-hand, I had to buy brand-new," she started laughing running down the yard with Jacob giving chase, she allowed him to catch her before they reach the house. He kissed her very passionately, "you are a blessing in disguise you think of everything. I presume everything will be delivered tomorrow knowing you?"

"Of Course, Jacob, after we've sold the store lambs the bank account should be quite healthy."

"We shall see Rosalind depends on the market, up and down like a yo-yo since coronavirus has attacked the world."

"I wouldn't worry about anything, Jacob, you are protected by God. If you never sold another lamb wouldn't make any difference, we would survive, trust in the Lord he knows what's best, and so does your Rosalind. The answer is, not at this time of day with children around," she chuckled opening the front door going in, shutting leaving Jacob stood the other side, he burst out laughing heading back to the machinery shed.

He wasn't worried what Rosalind had purchased, she'd selected most of the machines he possessed and they all worked adequately, she had the common sense not to buy brand-new better for tax purposes not as he paid any thanks to Rosalind's accounting skills. Jacob walked to the edge of the cliff carefully leaning against the fence looking over, more timber washed ashore of various sorts and sizes, he grabbed his chainsaw taking the old Fordson major with the saw bench on the back driving down to the beach. Jacob started cutting logs with the chainsaw first into manageable sizes, finished off with the saw bench cutting into smaller pieces. He stayed there till about 3 o'clock he cut a sizeable load which he would collect tomorrow only to see his old sit up and beg tractor driven by Noah coming along the beach parking alongside the pile of blocks. Noah stopped the tractor stepping down from the old tractor. "You can go and check on the sheep father if you like, I can load these it won't take me long," Noah smiled.

"As you wish son, I'm sure your backs in better condition than mine," Jacob chuckled, climbing aboard the Fordson major heading to the farm. He still found it hard to understand how his son only 10 Years old could operate the equipment so proficiently. Jacob took the Land Rover and Ivor Williams trailer across the Moor finally finding his sheep there weren't many left now thankfully, as much as Jacob enjoyed lambing, hard work. Jacob found another six had lambed loading the trailer, he headed for Brook Farm would leave them there with Fiona, she is excellent at looking after ewes and lambs. Fiona came out and assisted pening the lambs and ewes. They released another dozen back onto the Moor Jacob loaded another five sacks of creep feed in the back of his Land Rover ready to top up the feeders on the way home. "Thank you very much, Fiona, for all your help, I don't know how I'd manage without you?"

"You have Noah and Mary now to assist you."

"Maybe, they aren't as proficient as you," he remarked, throwing her over his shoulder. She started laughing. "What are you going to do to me, Jacob?" He dashed into the barn throwing her in the loose straw making love to her, kissing her passionately he dressed. "You are as important as anyone else on this farm, don't you forget it," he reassured. Fiona hadn't expected to be taken by surprise, she certainly pleased he did, she quickly tidied herself kissing him once more watching him drive out of the yard across the Moor. Jacob parked by each creep feeder topping up, driving home steadily across the Moor checking the ewes left outside to lamb he thought fewer than 12, he finally part the Land Rover noticing Mary releasing another 10 ewes and lambs onto the Moor. Noah was stacking the blocks he tipped from the trailer in the woodshed. Rosalind telepathically contacted Fiona. "Shopping tomorrow be here at 9 o'clock, you the children and I are taking a break away from the farm. I don't want my husband to become too comfortable and use the children to excessively."

Fiona replied telepathically. "Brilliant I'd like to spend some time with you, Noah and Mary."

Jacob walked into the house, sitting down at the table for his evening meal; he is almost falling asleep. "Me, Mary, Noah and Fiona are having a few hours away from the farm Jacob, shopping."

"I see," Jacob sighed jokingly. "Leaving the old man to run the farm," everyone started laughing. Jacob finished his evening meal, the children had already had theirs; he went outside carrying out the final check before retiring to bed. Jacob is shattered rather hoping God could boost his energy one day, so he didn't become so tired; there again he had his children now, he shouldn't really complain he thought, returning to the house, retired to bed with Rosalind making sure she had what she wanted before putting him to sleep until morning. Rosalind looked in on Mary, she's resting on her bed. This is the human part of her construction, insisting she must rest. The same applied to Noah, he is resting; Rosalind didn't think this would affect them the way it had, perhaps it's because Jacob sleeps, they find it necessary to copy. Rosalind would ask the central computer to assist. However, she didn't really trust the computer at the moment, considering recent activities, Rosalind would have to wait until she is confident the central computer wouldn't take the opportunity to modify any of the thought patterns in her children's operating system.

CHAPTER 14

The Next Step in the Zibyan Evolution

Jacob came from his bedroom stepping outside to check on his ewes and lambs finding Rosalind already out there finishing off, Jacob shook his head. "I think you're an alien," he joked, "you're always awake what makes it worse you're still bright and happy."

"Because I have a wonderful husband," she smiled, grabbing his arm. "Let's have a quick coffee before you go and fetch the fertiliser, Jacob."

"Okay, seems like a plan to me," he smiled. They both entered the house to see the children were making breakfast. Mary had made her father fried bread with eggs baked beans and sausage the same went for her brother, she settled for toast and marmalade. "Is that all you have Mary," Jacob asked, "aren't you feeling very well?"

"I'm a young lady, has to watch a figure, father, unlike the other slobs around the table who enjoy pigging out on any think they can eat." Mary laughed at her brother and father, Rosalind trying not to grin. Jacob soon finished his breakfast, kissing Mary on the cheek and Rosalind ruffling Noah's hair. "Must go everyone fertiliser to spread." Jacob left the house with a purpose in mind climbing aboard his tractor, he headed down onto the beach in the dark, the sun breaking over the sea it wouldn't be long before daylight. Jacob felt the first load enter the manure spreader, he quickly drove to the 30-acre pasture land spreading, transporting three more loads to Brook Farm to spread on the 10 acres there. By the time Jacob had returned to the farm, Fiona is there with the new four-wheel-drive car she acquired. Fiona ran over to Jacob, kissed him on the cheek. "The sheep are fine on Brook Farm there fed and watered, check on them later, although I don't think we'll belong." Fiona ran over to her car sitting in the passenger seat Rosalind is driving, the children were in the back they couldn't go too far because of the restrictions over the coronavirus, a trip to Morrisons, as good as any place to go in Exeter. This is the first time the children had left the farm mixing with humans in any quantity, although most of the streets appeared to be empty, parking in the superstore car park seeing a long queue. "Fiona you have Mary with you, and I'll have Noah with me, that way will be let in as a pair because we both have children."

Fiona whispered: "Rosalind, I don't have any money." Fiona watched Rosalind remove a wad of cash from her pocket, placing in Fiona's hand. "I think the saying is, spend until you drop," she chuckled. They join the queue, within half an hour they were inside, had to keep a safe distance from any other shopper everyone is watched by store staff and security they obeyed the rules. Noah pushed the trolley, which is difficult to steer at times. Rosalind plucked what she wanted from the shelves, finally reaching the checkout the shopping came to over £250 placed in carrier bags they put in the trolley leaving the store loading into the back of Fiona's SUV. Minutes later

Fiona and Mary joined her they couldn't cram another bag in the boot there wasn't room.

***

Jacob driving across the Moor on his quad bike after checking the remaining few ewes, he suspected one or two may be barren; nevertheless, the rest of the flock had performed exceptionally well, he wasn't too worried. Jacob noticed coming up his drive were police vehicles and one minibus had Customs written across the side, he couldn't imagine what business they have with him. Jacob watched them turn off, heading down the cliff track to the beach. Jacob walked over to the fence looking over there were three boats with people aboard, he presumed were immigrants coming ashore. Jacob breathed a sigh of relief; nothing to do with him or the family. Jacob returned to his quad bike, venturing down onto the beach, a police officer approached, staying 3 m away, "Sorry, Sir, you can't go any further."

"I presume illegal immigrants coming onto my farm?" Jacob quizzed.

"I couldn't possibly say," the officer smiled. "They may have the coronavirus if I were you, I'd return to your farm and leave us to clear up the mess."

"Thanks." Jacob didn't need telling twice he soon returned to the farm he wondered how they would get the minibus off the beach, his Land Rover struggled to climb the cliff track a minibus certainly wouldn't, although the police did have a Range Rover which could pull the minibus perhaps, even then he thought could be difficult. Half an hour had elapsed when Jacob noticed a police Range Rover approaching the farm, the same officer stepped out staying a decent distance from Jacob. "You couldn't possibly give our minibus at tow, can't get the darn thing off the beach even with my Range Rover, you think the government would provide us with a four-wheel-drive vehicle considering most of our work along here is on the shore collecting immigrants."

Jacob smiled, " be there in a minute." Jacob decided to take the Massey tractor four-wheel-drive. He wrapped the big chain around the hydraulic arms in case it is needed, he drove along towards the cliff track descending to the beach seeing the minibus bogged down in the soft sand. Jacob drove down onto the beach reversing to the front of the minibus they had a towrope already attached, they'd obviously been down this road many times before. Jacob opened the back window on his cab to see the driver clearly, started to tow the minibus with immigrants in the back. A small coastguard dinghy towing the boats away while the sea is calm, an infrequent occurrence around here. Jacob slowly ascended the stony track pulling the minibus and the occupants to safety to the top of the cliff track heading towards the main road. He detached the towrope from his tractor waved driving off, the officer blasted his horn to say "thank you." Jacob returned to the farm the first time he'd had illegal immigrants come into the cove, he wondered if there would be more in the future, or with the coronavirus kill everyone eventually, surprised some type of vaccine wasn't available by now. Perhaps a government ploy to dispose of all the infirm and elderly certainly saving on pensions, the government had to pay out every month.

Jacob noticed turning into the drive a lorry, he quite forgot he's supposed to receive a delivery today a new mower-conditioner and the log splitter to save his old back, he grinned watching the lorry approach. The driver smiled stepped from the cab. Jacob stayed some distance away. "Mr Walker, I presume, you purchased a new mower and log splitter?"

"Apparently so, you need assistance to unload?" Jacob asked.

"No thanks, easier if I crane it off, I'll place the paperwork and receipt over there on the bale." The driver started the crane lifting Jacobs new mower conditioner onto the ground along with the new log splitter, within 10 minutes, the driver heading home wherever that is. Jacob looking around the new mower conditioner an 8-foot cut trailed mower conditioner. Rosalind is right, he dared not ask how much this machine cost, but he could cut 30 acres he suspected in an hour. Rosalind had the foresight to order a box of replacement blades they were strapped to the top of the new mower. If it wasn't for the fact the paint is missing off the mower bed, he wouldn't have realised the machine was used. Jacob looked to the log splitter light enough to be manually pulled close to the woodshed. Jacob went into the house pressing the button on the wall hearing the new generator start, he went outside finding the extension lead, he plugged the new log splitter into the extension.

Jacob switched the machine on very quiet he thought, placing the first block with the most knots he could find on the splitter. The log splitter had no difficulty splitting anything he sat on the machine, far better than swinging an axe he smiled. Glancing up to see Fiona's SUV enter the drive. Jacob knew from the way it is driven Rosalind is at the wheel, always made him smile. He switched off the machine watching Rosalind parked by the front door. The kids jumped out, opening the boot there wasn't room for a breath of fresh air. Rosalind quickly passed Jacob two bags to carry into the house and then the children and one for herself. Rosalind shut the boot. "Okay, Fiona, you can go, we will speak later," Rosalind assured.

Jacob made the coffee while Rosalind tried to find somewhere to put things she'd purchased. Jacob explained events while they were away. Rosalind paused: "Are you sure that's what they were doing Jacob?"

"Yes, I had to tow them off the beach they were immigrants, they didn't look pleased either, placed in handcuffs what beats me, where rural the women, always bloody men invading our shores."

"I thought, pretty obvious Jacob if you allow so many other nationalities in your country, they will eventually take it over, saves a lot of fighting. I shouldn't worry you won't be here to see that happen and the chances are they will all be dead if not from the coronavirus from some other disease they manufacture to control the population. I think the bravest people on earth are the nurses and doctors, the governments don't provide the proper safety equipment to protect them against the virus. If I were them, I'd walk out, blimey! I sound like a human activist," she chuckled.

"I've told you before Rosalind I think you're an alien on the quiet," he laughed, accompanied by the children finding the whole situation very amusing.

"I think you better go and check the sheep Jacob before I become annoyed," Rosalind smiled, kissing him on the cheek, "and don't forget to park your new toy alongside the building don't leave it parked out there for everyone to see."

"I'll move it, father." Noah offered.

"Thanks, son at least somebody loves me," Jacob went out of the door quickly noticing Rosalind is holding a wooden spoon; she'd thrown it at him before when they were first married, she had a habit of hitting what she aimed at. Jacob jumped on his quad bike towing the little trailer behind, heading across the Moor to see if there were any newborns, Jack on the carrier; finally, Jacob thought seeing three ewes had given birth to twins each. With the assistance of Jack, he loaded into his little trailer heading towards Brook Farm, Fiona waiting to greet him she'd released another 10 ewes and lambs strong enough to go on the Moor. They made sure the ewes had milk, the lambs could suckle before leaving them to their own devices for the moment. Jacob exhaled, "I'll be pleased when lambing is finally finished, Fiona."

"Yes, you know what the next job is Jacob?"

"Silage and if it stays warm will have to dip everything to prevent flystrike and soon have to shear the sheep the list goes on."

"Don't worry old man, I'll be here to help you," she chuckled. Jacob grabbed her, slinging her over his shoulder; she is trying to desperately read his thoughts as he carried her out onto the Moor what his intentions were. He dropped her into the brook, she screened, sensing the cold water. Jacob walked off, laughing. Rosalind had read Fiona's thoughts, starting to laugh along with the children realising what Jacob had done. Mary commented, "father's very humorous mother; he's what humans call fun. I'm very fond of him."

"You can count me in as well sister," Noah remarked. "He's always helpful and kind I wonder if he will mate with her before he returns home?"

Mary grinned, "of course he will that's why Fiona is teasing him, I don't think she quite suspected to be dropped in the brook. Nevertheless, he will mate with her before returning home to mother, her turn tonight," Mary smiled smugly.

"That's a little too much information thank you, Mary," watching Mary and Noah going outside. She'd read Noah's thoughts, how useful it would be if they had a diesel buggy not only could they tow a better trailer for transporting lambs, would be great for carrying minerals and food over the Moor better than a quad bike or a Land Rover. Rosalind conveyed telepathically to Peter. "Need money."

Within a few minutes, she watched the misty fog approach the door. She opened stepping inside the transporter removing a large suitcase she carried inside, the misty fog transporter vanished. She carried the suitcase down into the cellar to keep out of Jacobs view. She counted out approximately £20,000 placed in a shopping bag dashing upstairs, she went on the Internet purchasing a diesel ATV buggy. She jumped in the Range Rover calling to the children, "I shan't belong."

Both Mary and Noah tried to read her thoughts and discovered they couldn't, somewhat surprised, although their mother is an excellent individual, she was the start of the changes to the collective. Rosalind drove nearly into Exeter almost dark when she arrived, walked into the showroom looking at the machine she purchased fitted with a cab and heater. "Please don't forget to road register and I presume it will be delivered tomorrow?"

"Yes, Mrs Walker no problem at all; Jacobs farm I believe that is the address?"

"Yes, thank you very much! I don't suspect you have a trailer that fits behind the buggy design for carrying sheep and lambs across the Moor. The one we have at present is not very efficient and to be quite honest, I'm surprised it's holding together this year?"

"Actually, we do if you'd like to come this way," the salesperson invited showing Rosalind a lovely trailer on tandem axle balloon tyres, wouldn't sink in the ground in wet conditions. The trailer could cater for six ewes and lambs double what Jacob could carry at present with his quad trailer. "I'll take it," Rosalind counted out the money leaving the showroom a happy woman knowing Jacob would be over the moon. Although he would moan about the amount of money she'd spent, considering it wasn't his money, he shouldn't worry, he doesn't realise where the money is coming from she concluded. Rosalind drove home in the dark arriving at the farm after 6 o'clock in the evening. Mary had made the tea for her, Noah and Jacob. She entered the house, stared at by Jacob, who wanted an explanation she could tell from reading his mind. "I know you want to know where I've been Jacob, I've had a little spend." Noah read his mother's thoughts along with Mary, both deciding to stay quiet and let their mother handled the situation.

"Oh no, you can't keep spending Rosalind, I'll be working for nothing," Jacob sighed heavily, very disappointed.

"The money is provided by God. You have nothing to worry about," Rosalind remarked, becoming annoyed. "I have purchased a new four-wheel-drive diesel buggy with a fully enclosed cab for winter and heater, in the summer you can remove the cab; plus a new sheep trailer to go behind specially designed for carrying sheep off the Moor. The piece of junk you are using at the moment can only carry three ewes, this one will carry six and the lambs Jacob. You are the most ungrateful husband I've ever come across."

Jacob remarked: "I hope I'm the only husband you've come across Rosalind; otherwise, we will definitely be falling out." Noah and Mary burst out laughing and eventually Rosalind when she realised what she'd said.

"Rosalind, while I think about it could you possibly order dipping chemicals if the weather continues to warm the way it is. The ewes and lambs will be suffering from flystrike, that's the last thing we need. Thankfully the last of the ewes lamb today, there are two barren ewes can go to the abattoir tomorrow, they might as well be killed and hung in the cellar, There worth nothing the price has dropped severely; at least if we use them, we will know where the meat is coming from." Jacob expressed earnestly.

"Transport here in the morning Jacob," Rosalind instructed. "I'll dispatch them myself, I'm not paying abattoir fees for a simple job that is a waste of money Jacob. I will simply cut their throat, hang from the loader tractor skin removed their organs, which the seagulls will enjoy immensely," Rosalind smiled.

"Rosalind, you don't have a licence to kill animals," Jacob professed.

"Bite me, Jacob! Who the bloody hell is going to know," Rosalind shouted for the first time taking everyone by surprise. "If you'd read your Bible properly, lambs were slaughtered by the thousands that way when Jesus was here."

Jacob put his hands up in the air. "Be it on your own head woman if someone reports you." Jacob slipped on his coat, going outside, followed by Jack. Noah and Mary looked to their mother, surprised by her outburst. "That wasn't necessary mother," Noah suggested calmly. "Father is merely protecting you from prosecution." Mary went outside to find her father she thought her mother is rather cruel; he is a human and brought up with social rules he had no idea his wife is a Zibyan without restrictions. "Father," she voiced finding him by the sheep with the barn light switched on. "We will watch and make sure no one can see what's happening, father. Mother tries very hard to please you and save money, so we can have better equipment, be more productive on the farm and of course make life easier for everyone."

"You'll be a diplomat when you grow up, Mary," Jacob kissed her on the cheek appreciating she's trying to smooth things over.

"Only take two or three minutes father both sheep will be ready to hang in the cellar."

"I think you'll find it'll take a little longer than that Mary." He held her hand, switching out the lights returning to the house, shutting the door on the day everyone went to bed. Rosalind lay there. "I'm waiting!" Jacob smiled, making love to Rosalind as she commanded before she put him to sleep for the rest of the night. Rosalind sat quietly in the front room watching television until she became bored going down into the cellar, finding a set of butchery knives used to belong to Jacobs father. She spent some time cleaning them turning pristine again. Rosalind suspected Jacobs father before the laws were changed would very often slaughter an old ewe to help them make it through the year.

6 o'clock in the morning arrived Jacob came staggering out of his bedroom sipping his cup of coffee, venturing outside checking on the sheep and lambs. Noah dashed out of the house starting the Massey Ferguson tractor with the loader positioning by the side of the house to conceal from view. He jumped on his father's quad bike towing the trailer with Jack on the rack taking his mother's crook, he searched for the two ewes left out on the Moor, eventually locating loading them with the help of Jack. Noah patted Jack. "You are a helpful dog." Noah drove off steadily across the Moor, making sure he avoided all the obstacles and pit holes that could cause a disaster.

Noah parked the quad bike and trailer by the tractor ready for Rosalind. Rosalind could have dispatched the sheep in the dark, although Jacob would wonder how she could operate so efficiently without any lights if they had lights, that may attract attention. She would have to wait until first light, she would dispatch the sheep and prepare for hanging. Jacob walked in the house shocked to see his father's knife set on the kitchen table looking brand-new. Rosalind had made breakfast for everyone folding the leather pouch containing the knives placing to one side for the moment. "You still going ahead, Rosalind?" Jacob asked, concerned.

"Yes, after breakfast you don't have to watch Jacob, won't take me more than a couple of minutes."

"I can remember my father dispatching an old ewe once skinning and preparing it took him half an hour."

"I am not your father! Stay out of the way Jacob, please nip over to Brook Farm, look at the sheep over there leave this operation to the children and me."

Noah came in. "Have tied a short piece of rope, on the loader mother, placed a bucket to catch the blood; you can use it on the garden for fertiliser; the rest of it can stay by the cliff edge, seagulls will devour in seconds."

Rosalind looked out the window, light enough for her to work, she grabbed the leather pouch with the knives wrapped inside. Rosalind walked to the back of the quad trailer laying a sizeable plastic sheet below the rope where she is going to hang the sheep. Rosalind grabbed one old ewe tying her back legs, hoisted up on the loader slitting her throat, blood gushed into the bucket.

Jacob watched from a distance not believing what Rosalind is engaged in. Noah came running out to join her with Mary; within seconds, the animal is gutted and skinned. The children pulled the sheet containing the on wanted entrails closer to the cliff edge, some distance away, tipping the contents off the sheet, watching the seagulls already landing fighting over what is free. Noah and Mary relayed the plastic sheet. "Come on Jacob I prepared hooks in the cellar hang each half separately," Rosalind ordered, she removed one half placing on Jacob's shoulder, he couldn't believe how strong she is. Rosalind put the other half across the trailer, grabbing the other ewe. Rosalind tied her back legs lifting up on the rope, slitting her throat, watching the blood run in the bucket.

By the time Jacob had returned after taking the first half, the other one is gutted and skinned. He had no idea Rosalind is skilled at preparing carcasses. The children drag the sheet sliding the entrails off the sheet, returning to help their mother; the job is completed. Rosalind went back in the house washing Jacobs father's knives, greasing slightly so they wouldn't rust. By 8 o'clock in the morning, there wasn't a trace of the sheep left on the cliff. Rosalind stretched the skins she is going to keep them turning into rugs could be used around the house.

"Sorry, Rosalind," Jacob voiced. "I didn't realise you were that proficient, I suppose I should have trusted your judgement."

"Never mind Jacob I do understand your concerns," Rosalind remarked, making the coffee for everyone. The children stayed outside, returning the equipment to where it should be and not by the house. Jacob went out to check on his ewes and lambs noticing a Range Rover and trailer coming up the drive carrying the new buggy, and she'd trailer specially designed for off-road. Mary, Noah and Rosalind had read Jacob's mind; they came out to see the new purchase. Jacob and everyone else respecting the coronavirus rule, staying some distance from the sales rep; they watched him unload leaving the paperwork on the buggy seat. "The vehicle is sanitised, you can never be too careful, we would hate to bring anything onto the farm, thank you all for your purchase much appreciated in these troubled times." the sales rep waved climbing in his vehicle driving off down the track. Rosalind watched Jacob slowly walking around the equipment, he is smiling, a good sign, she thought. He paid particular attention to the new sheep trailer realising it would be easier to load than his old one. Mary suggested, "I think you and mother, father should go across the Moor and give it a test drive," Mary removing the paperwork from the seat.

Rosalind smiled, sitting in the driver's seat, closing the door. Jacob had to laugh, opening the passenger door sliding in on the seat-closing and fitting the seatbelt. Rosalind started off very steadily across the Moor a little noisy in the cab, to be expected a workhorse providing you didn't use excessive revs it's okay. They ventured as far as Brook Farm turning around heading home. "Comfortable Jacob," Rosalind commented grinning turning on the heater, "that works efficiently." Rosalind parked beside the barn. "You haven't said much, Jacob, what's wrong?"

"You've driven all the way to Brook Farm, and back, you never bothered to stop to check on the Rams and the other sheep, what a wasted journey and you moan about wasting money, think of all the diesel we've used," he chuckled teasing her.

She kissed him on the cheek, "you better rush off and do the job properly haven't you Sir," she smiled walking off towards the house. Jacob filled the new buggy with diesel, detaching the trailer by the barn, loading several bags of creep feed in the back, driving off across the Moor to the feeders topping up both on the way to Brook Farm. When Jacob arrived, Fiona is outside attending to the ewes and lambs. She kissed him on the cheek. "Jacob, we can release these ewes and lambs will do better on the Moor than in pens, don't you think?"

"Yes, you're right I filled the creep feeders I want these lands gone to market soon." Jacob and Fiona open the gates the ewes and lambs scurry towards the Moor bleating. Jacob watched the lambs jumping in the air excited by the release, they'd run around like greyhounds chasing one another, unfortunate they wouldn't live that long some of them. "You will have a coffee before you go, Jacob," Fiona invited. He nodded walking towards the house with Fiona, allowing her in first, he sat at the table, while she made the coffee. Fiona sat opposite, passing Jacob his coffee. She placed her Bible on the table which always made Jacob smile, he couldn't fault the woman she is still reading God's word, apparent God thought a lot of her to permit her to receive premonitions. Jacob glanced from the window watching two hikers walk through the yard carrying their rucksacks, at least they haven't a dog on the loose with them which is the usual routine, and he'd end up losing livestock. Jacob finished his coffee kissing Fiona on the cheek going out to his buggy climbing inside. He set off for home, enjoying driving the buggy deciding to drive to the shop to see if it is open. Jacob drove down the road parking outside the shop, remembering to take the ignition keys; the last thing he needed is his new toy to be stolen by a joyrider. Jacob smiled to find the shop is open. He purchased two large tins of sweets, flowers and a large box of chocolates. Jacob settled the bill steadily driving home presenting the flowers and chocolates to Rosalind and the tins of sweets to Mary and Noah. "Thanks, Dad," they voiced.

Rosalind gave Jacob a cup of coffee they sat watching the television for a moment, the news, even more depressing another thousand people died in the UK. The report from abroad is not much better another 150,000 people had vanished from China without a trace. "That reminds me, Jacob two loads of fertiliser to be collected in the morning. I think we will have to stockpile, we can't keep spreading on the 30 acres or the 10 we will soon be making silage."

"I don't know Rosalind I think the 10 acres could handle a couple more loads then will stockpile," Jacob advised.

"Okay, you look at the land more than I do I'm sure you're right." Jacob left the house looking over the fence down on to the beach, wondering if sufficient firewood to take a load to Brook Farm, although they didn't use as much wood in the summer still necessary, saved on diesel when the Aga is used. Jacob collected his chainsaw and fuel, taking the old Fordson major and saw bench down onto the beach. He hadn't been working long before he noticed Noah and Mary coming down with the sit up and beg Fordson with the P6 engine pulling the trailer. Jacob continued cutting firewood, more there than looked originally. Mary and Noah loaded the trailer as Jacob cut the blocks on the saw bench. Rosalind had read their minds. Jacob is a kind man he wasn't leaving Fiona short of wood. Jacob stopped cutting looking in the trailer, "that will do for now, I think kids, you want me to take it to Brook Farm or will you, Noah?"

"Mary and I will go farther," Noah smiled, starting the P6 engine which Jacob like to hear driving away steadily with Mary sat on the mudguard, which is totally illegal. Nevertheless, it had always been that way on the farm. Noah packed his tools away driving home, noticing when he reached the top of the cliff small rubber dinghies, three coming into the cove. Rosalind had read his thoughts; before she could telepathically send a message to Peter, police were arriving with a coastguard minibus. Jacob could see a coastguard vessel behind the dinghies trying to catch up before they landed. Unfortunately, the distance is too great. The illegal immigrants stepped ashore quite happy to be arrested on British soil. Jacob started the Massey tractor with the loader wrapping the chain around the hydraulic arms, driving towards the beach. The same police officer as before noticed Jacob coming with the tractor. Jacob parked at the end of the track waiting patiently for the immigrants to be loaded in the back of the minibus all males again, he concluded Rosalind is right they were trying to take over the country one immigrant at a time. The police officer approached Jacobs tractor. Jacob stepped from the cab. "I guess you'd want another tow so rather than you come to me, I thought I'd come to you."

"You will receive a letter of thanks from our commander, he has tried unsuccessfully to persuade the government to provide him with something more substantial, perhaps an army vehicle would be more suitable to our task."

"I don't need a letter thanks just ship them home out of our country, that's all that matters," Jacob smiled, watching the officer laughed walking towards the van, he fitted their towrope and Jacob reversed the tractor to the front of the Ford Transit. Jacob towed the vehicle up to the top of the cliff, leaving on the track, detached his tractor, waved, driving to the farm buildings. Rosalind came out to meet him. "Looks like they're going to use this cove more often than not Jacob. I will have to talk to God; this could become a problem."

Jacob shrugged his shoulders. "I can't see how Rosalind, at least the coastguard are aware the immigrants are heading for here, what you want me to do, shoot them off the cliff with my shotgun?"

"You won't be so unconcerned if the police start looking around the farm discovering your son and daughter, more questions would be asked which we mightn't have the answers for Jacob. Be realistic! Do you want me to send your son and daughter back to heaven?" Rosalind remarked, somewhat concerned.

"Well, they won't see them today Rosalind there over at Brook Farm taking your half-sister a load of blocks. I will have to go over with our log splitter, occurred to me she will have to split them by hand otherwise."

"That will keep you out of trouble, attach to the buggy you can go now, I have things to organise. If I'm not here when you come home; you know where I am," Rosalind walked off, determined to stop the immigrants using the cove as a drop-off point.

Jacob attached the new log splitter to the rear of the buggy, removed the electric connection from the motor throwing the electric cable in the back of the buggy, steadily driving across the Moor in the direction of Brook Farm.

Rosalind stepped into the misty fog transporter stepping out aboard the spaceship. Peter and Matthew were there to greet her. "I couldn't do anything Rosalind to many officials around otherwise they'd be fertiliser I can assure you, any others coming towards the cove will be spread by Jacob as fertiliser."

Rosalind smiled. "Excellent Peter." They watched the far wall illuminate the creator appeared on the screen with his eldest son standing beside him, "My first son, Trmash." Rosalind determined he is approximately the same age as her son Noah indeed the same height. "You are correct Rosalind Trmash is the same age as your son, and by the time the moons have travelled around Zagader twice more, he will be an adult like his father, thanks to genetic engineering which I worked out on my own. I have seven sons and 13 daughters who are presently undergoing genetic alterations; they too will be fully grown shortly."

"What is the rush creator?" Rosalind asked suspiciously.

"I detect you're on easiness Rosalind, you know what's going to happen, your son will mate with my 13 daughters and my eldest son with your daughter; that is an order from the creator approved by the collective. Your son and daughter were produced for experimental purposes; nothing else they just happened to coincide with Jacob requiring offspring, rather convenient for everyone at the time."

Rosalind listened to the messages in her mind from the collective agreed reluctantly with the creator's request. "When is this supposed to take place creator."

"You will be notified Rosalind, not before harvest if that is your concern," the creator vanished, already putting his next plan into action when he'd finished his latest designs he would surprise the whole collective.

Rosalind looked to Peter and Matthew flashing her eyes in respect returning to the misty fog transporter, landing outside the front door of Jacobs farm. She entered the house sitting down to watch programmes, while she contemplated the best course of action if there is one. She is pretty sure Noah and Mary had received the information themselves and wondered what their view would be.

Jacob, busily splitting the wood helped by Mary, and Noah, Fiona is stacking the wood in a neat pile at the back of the shed which they'd almost filled to the roof. Jacob split the last block into four pieces, he thought, thank you, God, for the log splitter his back aching. Noah suggested, "father rest awhile here, Mary and I will return home, feed and water the ewes and lambs, you have nothing to worry about."

"Thanks, son and daughter go carefully across the Moor," Jacob advised, watching them leave the farmyard with the tractor and trailer. He slowly walked, holding his back to the house. "Upstairs, Jacob," Fiona ordered. "I have some cream I can rub on your back that may help." Jacob hobbled up the stairs removing his shirt, Fiona made him remove his trousers, he lay on his belly on her bed. She removed the container of cream from the wardrobe, she knew would work created by the Zibyans for another use. Fiona applied the cream liberally Jacob lay there relaxing falling asleep after half an hour. Fiona telepathically contacted Rosalind: "Jacob is asleep on her bed, he has a bad back she is treating him with the cream, he'd fallen asleep she would leave him for an hour or so to rest."

"Keep him there," Rosalind telepathically replied. "I have a few issues you probably received the same message as everyone else?"

Fiona responded telepathically. "Yes."

Mary and Noah came into the house, sitting beside their mother on the settee. "I don't think there's anything we can do mother to prevent the creator without causing a significant upheaval," Noah suggested.

Mary insisted, "I will refuse to shapeshift and grow. I quite like my present age my skin feels comfortable why should I rush to please him."

"Mary, it won't be before the end of the harvest. I won't let you travel alone either of you I will come along, most of the collective respect my decisions. I know the firstborn is concerned and many others have telepathically transmitted their concerns to me from Zagader."

Noah thought for a moment. "There has to be a way around this mother, I just haven't thought of it yet. I understand what the creator is trying to achieve. I think he may be going about it the wrong way."

"Let's hope you come up with a bright idea brother," Mary remarked, racking her own brains for a solution.

***

Fiona returned to the bedroom after making a coffee for Jacob; he rolled over. "I don't know what the cream is you applied to my back. I feel a new man." Sitting up except in the cup of coffee. Jacob stood up, placing the cup on the windowsill, lifting Fiona laying her on the bed, removing her clothes, "my turn to apply the cream," he grinned watching her smile.

8 o'clock in the evening Jacob steadily drove across the Moor towing the log splitter home the heater in the buggy worked extremely well he thought, although occasionally steam the windows; a small price to pay for comfort. He parked the buggy in the shed detaching the log splitter pushing alongside to stay dry if it rained which is forecast, the last thing he needed is a log splitter motor drenched, although supposedly sealed against damp. The children were in their own rooms talking telepathically to one another. Rosalind had made Jacob a few sandwiches to tide him over until morning. Jack received his usual bowl of biscuits with a little of Rosalind's gravy added as a treat. By 9:30 everyone is in bed, Rosalind ensured Jacob wouldn't wake returning to the front room hoping to think of a solution to her children's predicament at the end of the summer.

Rosalind watched television quietly, hearing an odd sound outside. She grabbed her sheep crook slipping on a coat, ventured out she could see plainly as if daylight with her eyes noticing two men trying to remove the buggy and the log splitter. Before Rosalind could take any action, she watched the two men vanish into thin air bringing a smile to her face, Peter had noticed, they were now fertiliser. Rosalind looked down the drive seeing a part pickup and trailer, she walked down the track. They had kindly left the keys in the ignition, Rosalind climbed in starting the vehicle driving several miles away from the property. Rosalind abandoned summoning the misty fog transporter she stepped in returning to the farm. Rosalind checked the ewes and lambs returning to the house only to find Mary starting to prepare breakfast, only 5 o'clock in the morning. "Couldn't sleep mother," she whispered. "I quite enjoy cooking." Jacob came staggering out of the bedroom.

"Whatever your cooking daughter, the smell is gorgeous, I couldn't stay in bed," he grinned, sat at the table with Rosalind pouring him a large mug of coffee to try and make his brain function properly. Noah came down from the loft. "How can I possibly rest up there, sister," he smiled. Sitting by his father tucking into a large breakfast. Rosalind moved to the settee watching the early morning news now turned 6 o'clock. The main topic, the coronavirus one minute everyone decided the coronavirus had reached its peak and within a couple of days the numbers of dead increased.

Jacob finished his breakfast stepping outside with his son to check on the ewes and lambs. Mary started washing up like her mother using heat generated by her hands to warm the water in the sink. Rosalind smiled realising what her daughter is using her power to resolve an issue. Jacob came running in out of breath. "Rosalind, Noah vanished I was talking to him one minute the next, he's gone!"

"Perhaps God detected something is wrong with him, Jacob, that's the only explanation I have. I will travel to heaven and see what's happening," Rosalind patted Jacob's cheek. "Mary stay with your father." Rosalind ran out of the door stepping into the misty fog transporter arriving aboard the spaceship seconds later. Peter and Matthew flashed their eyes to Rosalind. "This is nothing to do with us, Rosalind we believe the creator has developed a new form of transport, we've seen nothing like it before, entered the spaceship engulfed Noah and vanished we presumed destination Zagader, why would he do that now? He said not until the end of the harvest."

The creator's image appeared on the far wall. "This way, you cannot object, Noah will be returned once he has performed his task."

"Why didn't you take Mary as well," Rosalind asked curiously.

"She is too much like her mother, extremely intelligent and to use a human term bloody-minded."

"You wait until you take on my son creator, you think Mary is bloody-minded. I'll be there, on the next transport," Rosalind advised.

"You will not be permitted to enter Zagader Rosalind."

"You will stop me entering my home planet?" Rosalind knew the creator had not studied the laws laid down by his forefathers, no one may prevent a Zibyan returning home unless considered a traitor.

"Yes, I created the central computer with my brothers and sisters."

"You may not prevent Rosalind or any other collective member from returning home creator. You are violating your own laws," the central computer advised. "The second violation you have kidnapped a Zibyan when you agreed not until the end of harvest. The third violation you have not consulted the collective before implementing your decisions."

"You cannot argue with me, central computer, I helped create you. I made the laws, and I can alter the rules," the creator insisted.

"You are not, an actual creator, you were constructed using a human child as a base to inject the fragments of DNA the firstborn discovered on another planet. Until you have purified several times, you will not be a pure creator if ever."

"Central computer surely you realise my only chance of success at the moment is it Noah mates with the females I produced, you wouldn't deny me the opportunity to improve."

"The decision will be entirely Noah's, he will have to shape-shift into an adult to perform the task you require. If you had waited a few years, your chances of success would be significantly improved; you are forcing maturity, which may result in failure to produce what you're looking for."

"Rosalind, I will monitor everything," the central computer advised. "I can assure you your son will be returned unharmed, your Zibyan brothers and sisters are alarmed at what is taking place; we will see what Noah has to say on the subject when he arrives on the home planet, I will keep you advised."

Rosalind flashed her eyes to Peter and Matthew, who appeared to be as concerned as her at recent developments. Rosalind stepped into the misty fog transporter returning to the farm. Jacob sat at the table with a coffee along with Mary, both looking extremely concerned. "Nothing to worry about Jacob, Noah is in heaven he's carrying out a mission for God you can't argue with that," she smiled.

"No, I suppose not I wish God would have said something before snatching my son, he giveth in one hand and taketh away the other," Jacob chuckled.

Rosalind smiled, trying to be positive about the whole situation. Mary is reading her mind realising how serious the situation could become. She went outside for a breath of fresh air walking to the cliff edge, leaning on the fence looking out across the Cove, wondering what the future held for her. She returned to the farm seeing her father climb into the new buggy setting off across the Moor to check on his ewes and lambs. Jacob stopped quickly noticing one or two ewes were shaking their tails which usually meant flystrike. Jacob promptly returned to the farm connecting the hose pipe to the tap he started filling the sheep dipper. Rosalind had read his mind along with Mary; they came out to join him. "How serious, Jacob?" Rosalind asked.

"I noticed one or two it's easier to dip the lot, then risk the whole flock, I'm not surprised the weather has been decidedly warmer lately rather early in the year though."

Mary went to the old shed carrying 2, 1-gallon containers emptying into the dipper mixing with a long pole. Rosalind assembled the fencing ready to funnel the sheep into the dipper and a substantial pen to hold the sheep while they prepared to dip them. Mary jumped on the quad bike. "You take the buggy father. Jack, come with me," she smiled, watching him jump on the carrier. Father and daughter set off across the Moor taking a wide sweep to make sure none of the ewes and lambs had wandered off from the flock; they couldn't afford to miss any, once flies struck it didn't take long for the animal to die a slow and painful death.

Jack jumped off the carrier, keeping the flock tight together with father and daughter following each on their own machine. Rosalind is waiting for them to return, she placed a few sheep nuts in the far end of the pen in a trough rattling the bag; the sheep charged in unconcerned they were trapped. Rosalind shut the fence. They now had the lambs and ewes trapped, but they didn't want them in there for long some of the lambs were still quite young, and the last thing they needed is to have the lambs trampled.

Jacob put on his waterproofs. Mary wore a dustbin bag cutting holes in the corner and one in the middle for her head. Jacob pushed the ewes through, using his pole dipping the ewes, if the lambs were small he would hold them dipping carefully, placing on the grass to run off. By nightfall, they had managed to dip everything. Jacob decided he wouldn't empty the dipper straight away, he would place the boards over the top to stop anything or anyone falling in case needed again shortly, would save him purchasing more dipping chemical costing a small fortune like everything these days.

Jacob helped Rosalind pack away the fencing watching the unhappy ewes and lambs walking across the Moor, trying to shake off the chemical if they only knew for their benefit, Jacob concluded. Mary had run off into the house her legs were soaked, she quickly changed drying herself returning to the kitchen to start preparing something to eat, she's quite peckish. They'd missed one meal to achieve dipping the sheep before nightfall which is well worth the sacrifice.

***

Noah materialised in Zagader, the creator had designed a long-range transporter; the first initial test which is somewhat risky using a Zibyan if it had failed the creator would have some serious explaining to do to the collective and Rosalind. She could invoke equality law demanding a life for a life which would see the creator destroyed. The central computer asked Noah. "You were transported here without your consent; do you wish to be returned to earth to join Rosalind and Mary, your sister."

"Why, have I transported here computer without consultation? I'd like an explanation before I make a decision."

"Explain, creator," the computer insisted.

"Very simple, I want you to mate with the 13 females I have produced, to improve the purity of the creator."

"There is no need for mating simply take a sample, why are you specifying we use primitive methods such as you used with your wives a totally unnecessary practice."

"With my wives, more natural, and they were not forced to participate. The same will apply with my daughters if we use the other method to impregnate them they may not be so susceptible."

"Asked me the same question in another six years, I may participate, or you could take samples from yourself and use that you are more purer than I. You have 13 daughters, take three, try; study the results you will still have 10 left which would have reached the age in earth terms 16 the same as me. They and I will have grown naturally and not be forced, which would only stress the metabolism of both parties. For a creator, you appear to struggle to think things through correctly, how you managed to be one of the many who created the central computer is beyond my imagination." The creator vanished insulted beyond belief realising Noah had spoken the truth, he's rushing everything which could be dangerous and detrimental to his cause.

"Noah," the Central computer asked. "You wish to travel to earth the same way as you came? The equipment is not thoroughly tested, or return on the transport ship leaving in eight earth hours for another shipment of human carcasses to feed our animals."

"I would prefer to travel on the transport ship. Central computer I have many sisters and brothers asking me questions am I permitted to answer?"

"Yes, Noah speak the truth with any answer you provide; your brothers and sisters will guide you to the gardens where you may talk until the ship is ready to leave."

"Thank you for your guidance, central computer."

***

Three days had elapsed, Mary, Jacob and Rosalind were sat around the kitchen table. Mary smiled, looking to her mother who winked, they both received the information of what had taken place on Zagader. "Mary and I are both going to see God this evening Jacob I should have some news on Noah when we return."

"I hope so Rosalind, not the same around the farm without him and that's no disrespect to you, Mary, I would miss you the same," Jacob assured kissing her on the cheek.

"I know father, we all feel the same; hopefully we will return with good news."

They sat watching television Rosalind touched Jacob he immediately fell into a deep sleep. she stood up patting Jack. "Good dog watched the place we won't be gone long. Come along Mary, I don't want to be away long I'd hate to return to find the farm had been robbed." They both stepped into the misty fog transporter stepping out aboard the spaceship. Peter and Matthew were there to greet them, flashing their eyes to one another. Peter waved his arm, lighting a large screen on the wall. "Rosalind; Mary, I've carried out some calculations. There will be at least a minimum of 3 million, die from the coronavirus over the next three years. They continue to breed without fear of consequence; we estimate 200 years, and the United Kingdom will be a building site along with other small countries. Their biggest mistake is relying on America and Russia and one or two other reasonably sized countries to provide the food for the populace. A silly mistake, they will all be held to ransom, cannibalism will be a common occurrence in a hundred years from now. Of course, this is all hypothetical, there will be another serious virus in a few years far worse than the coronavirus, once they become dependent on technology I suspect they will die no one will possess the skills to grow vegetables, and there won't be sufficient soil available to plant."

"What is the bad news, Peter?" Mary asked smiling

"Why are you not concerned, Mary?" Peter asked, surprised.

"As long as they believe in stupid gods, they stand no chance of surviving, greed is prevalent. The rich have it all the poor have nothing; the human race operates similar to a beehive, and many of those have become extinct thanks to viruses; if the bees vanish altogether, the humans will be in serious trouble anyway," Mary concluded.

Matthew advised: "I've had confirmation the transport ship has left the home planet, should be here within three days. Thanks to you Rosalind we now understand the creator has constructed a long-range transporter, which Peter and I both considered to be dangerous travelling particles over millions of light-years, whatever is transported may not assemble correctly at its designation."

"I understand Matthew, the creator, dare test, on my son, he is fortunate my son survived; otherwise he'd be facing a death sentence himself, creator or not. Although the creator doesn't realise not only has Noah placed a code in the computer to protect his mother, also includes him and his sister, the computer would automatically destroy the offending party. I had no idea the computer was linking to the minds of my children while they were developing inside me, fortunate Noah managed to retrieve the information to protect us all otherwise this may be a different story."

Rosalind flashed her eyes holding Mary's hand they stepped into the misty fog transporter returning to the farm, they both entered the house, Jacob, making his first coffee of the morning. "Any news," he asked urgently? He quietly feared he was about to lose everything his dreams and aspirations would vanish, he'd awake from a long dream.

"Approximately three days, Noah will be home father," Mary advised kissing him on the cheek. Jacob breathed a sigh of relief pleased his thoughts were wrong

"Right, let me cook some breakfast," Rosalind suggested grabbing the eggs bread and half a dozen sausage, everything is sizzling in a few minutes on the Aga, she pressed the button on the wall starting the generator. "I'd better check the diesel in the generator fuel tank, Rosalind," Jacob suggested leaving the house quickly. Jacob made his way around to the rear of the house, discovering the tank is nearly empty; the generator would be running on fresh air in a minute. He quickly went to the main diesel tank drawing off 10 gallons in tins making three trips deciding that would be enough until he'd had breakfast. Jacob entered the house sitting down at the kitchen table to 4 slices of fried bread to sausage three eggs and a tin of baked beans. "I don't know which is more expensive to keep the sheep or you, Jacob," Mary chuckled. Jack started barking, which usually meant trouble probably a stray dog or an unwanted visitor. Jacob went for his gun, loading both barrels opening the door. Jack ran out only to be confronted by two police officers, looked somewhat alarmed, seeing Jacob with a shotgun. "I presume you have a licence for that, Sir?"

"Probably somewhere! What do you want?" Jacob asked abruptly. Mary came out removing the gun from Jacob's hand, calling Jack into the house before he bit a police officer and they would have more trouble to deal with. "We are searching for an escaped immigrant, he came ashore on his own by the time we arrived he'd vanished."

"Search the farms if you like this one here, and Brook Farm a few miles across the Moor, a woman, is staying there on her own Fiona, in fact, I'll go over there myself" Jacob suggested, "I'll sort out any bloody immigrants, why don't they stay in their own bloody country," Jacob professed annoyed.

The officer grinned, "I think we can safely say you are not a sympathiser, Sir."

Jacob walked off leaving the officers looking around the farm, he jumped in his buggy driving rapidly across the Moor, not only hadn't he finished his excellent breakfast, pestered by the police on three occasions now twice getting stuck on the beach and then ruining his breakfast, that is enough to drive a man loopy Jacob concluded, checking his sheep as he drove across the Moor. Jacob quickly looked at the Rams to see they were fed returning to the front door, he knocked walking in. Fiona could see his worried expression quickly making a coffee. "Sit down Jacob you don't look a happy man."

Jacob explained events, Fiona smiled. "You came all the way over here to rescue me, Jacob," she opened her dressing gown. "Would you like to be rewarded now or later?"

"Now!" He threw Fiona over his shoulder, running upstairs with her. "There is definitely no strangers here," Jacob professed, dressing. "Perhaps I should search tomorrow," he grinned running downstairs out of the front door stepping into his buggy setting off across the Moor. Jacob paused, discovering his flock spending a little more time checking everything is okay with them. Jacob noticed someone running along the footpath with two police officers chasing, they'd obviously discovered who they were looking for. Jacob steadily drove home, parking the buggy entering the house. Rosalind removed a plate from the oven. "Come on eat up, I'm not throwing good food away if you hadn't of stormed off, you could finish before you went over to see Fiona," Rosalind suggested realising, he had his treat while he is over there after reading his thoughts.

Jacob commented: "You're worse than a terrorist woman," sitting down, with Mary placing a hand over her mouth laughing at the expression on her father's face. After breakfast, Jacob decided to take two round bales of silage out onto the Moor, place in the feeders, he wanted to push his lambs on, the sooner they were off the Moor, the better more grass for his ewes. Jacob checked the creep feeders they were low on pellets, he returned to the farm throwing four bags in the back of the buggy taking across the Moor, topping up the feeders. Jacob is pondering with the idea of having a few cattle and less sheep; although the wasn't much on the Moor for them to eat, the same applied for the ponies, occasionally visited. Usually, they steal some hay or perhaps a bit of silage, he didn't mind they were here long before people, their Moor; he'd seen several killed on the roads; people have no idea he decided how to drive correctly through the countryside. Jacob slowly returned to the farm enjoying driving his new buggy. He noticed Mary walking towards the cliff edge. Jacob stopped his buggy, shouting, "be careful Mary the fence isn't that strong, I don't want you falling over the edge, don't stand too close please."

Mary waved, Jacob continued to the house. Mary enjoyed looking out into the cove the fresh sea air if only the rest of the earth is in the same condition, her thoughts were interrupted by a woman walking along the footpath. The middle-aged woman paused. "What a lovely morning are you local?"

"Yes, my father owns the farm." Mary smiled politely, not reading the woman's thoughts; otherwise, she may have answered differently. "I'm the headmistress at the local school, I haven't seen you there? Which school do you go to? There isn't another school for at least 10 miles, that once Private."

Rosalind had read her daughter's mind, dashing from the house to join her on the cliff edge. Rosalind telepathically controlled the headmistress's mind in seconds. "You have seen no one, on your way when you walk down the road jump in front of a lorry." Rosalind and Mary watched the woman continue walking along the cliff footpath heading towards the road. "Mother is it necessary for her to die?"

"Yes, we cannot risk detection, she may have contacted the authorities, which would set a chain of events in action and could lead to our discovery."

"Oh, I hadn't considered that possibility mother. I'm part human and part Zibyan how long will I live and my brother of course?"

"Forever," Rosalind answered, surprised at her daughter's question. "The part of you which is human will have no effect or determine your ageing."

Jacob walked to the end of the barn finding his old roller converted from horse-drawn many years ago filled with concrete, he couldn't imagine an old horse trying to pull the roller in wet conditions. He backed his Ford four-wheel-drive tractor to the roller attaching driving down to the 30-acre pasture land, deciding needed a good rolling before silaging this year.

He didn't want to damage new mower blades, Jacob spent several hours rolling 30 acres deciding to go down the main road with the roller, not wanting to travel across the Moor in case finding a wet spot becoming stuck.

He hadn't gone far down the road before he noticed ponies crossing in front of him. Jacob suspected they were coming over to have a little silage providing they didn't chase his sheep, he didn't mind. Jacob turned into Brook Farm drive he drove steadily down the old track going alongside the house through the gate onto the 10-acre paddock. He spent the next three hours rolling the 10 acres almost dark when he'd finished; his stomach beginning to rumble hadn't eaten anything all day, hadn't bothered to stop. Jacob parked the roller at the back of the old barn at Brook Farm. Slowly driving across the Moor returning home. When he entered the house, Jacob discovered a note on the table. "You know where we have gone, look in the oven."

Jacob smiled, opening the oven door the Aga had lost its heat only slightly warm sufficient to keep his food editable, his own fault for not coming home earlier. Jacob sat at the table with Jack looking hopeful at his master, while he tucked into a bit of old mutton, he knew where that had come from making him smile.

***

Rosalind and Mary were notified Noah's ship is arriving early they had gone aboard the spaceship to greet him. Eventually, the transport ship submerged linking the two ships together, while the frozen human flesh is transferred, Noah appeared. Rosalind looked him over. "You are not harmed, Noah?"

"No mother, I have a strange intuition the creator hasn't finished, he's totally impatient unrealistic in his goals, he will fail if he continues down this path, we will have to be on our guard he could try and snatch anyone of us again using the new transport device he developed. Although the collective is not impressed with him transporting me without the device being fully tested first."

"Come, children," Rosalind advised. "Nearly 5 AM lettuce return home, sorry what I should have said, to Jacobs farm," Rosalind smiled stepping into the misty fog transporter with her son and daughter beside her. They arrived seconds later outside the front door on Jacob's farm, they entered discovering Jacob asleep in his armchair with Jack resting his head on Jacob's boot. Jacob opened his eyes, seeing Noah, he jumped to his feet, holding his son close along with his daughter. The children started laughing. "Father, you're squeezing the life out of me," Noah protested.

Mary complained. "Father, you need a shower." Jacob kissed them both on the forehead, grabbing a towel to take a shower. Rosalind laughed, starting to make breakfast. Jacob came from the bedroom dressed in fresh clothes he seated at the kitchen table along with Noah and Mary waiting for their breakfast. Jacob commented, "the old ewe didn't taste too bad last night, Rosalind."

Rosalind smiled, placing the breakfast on the table only having a piece of toast for herself with a small coffee. Receiving a telepathic message from Fiona. "Two females have arrived at Brook Farm sent by their father the creator, they are here to meet Noah, I have to say, Rosalind, you can see the faint outline of their scales they arrived naked, I provided them with clothes. I estimate they are 16 in Earth years. help what should I do?"

"Nothing I'm coming," Rosalind replied telepathically, leaving the table slipping on her coat. "I have to go and see

Fiona I shan't belong," she remarked, kissing Jacob on the cheek dashing out of the door. Both Noah and Mary had received the same message. Noah is concerned but not surprised, he knew the creator wouldn't stop until he'd achieved what he wanted. Rosalind jumped in the Range Rover driving quickly to Brook Farm parking by Fiona's vehicle, she walked into the house to see two young females sitting at the table drinking coffee, Fiona, seated at the other end. The two young females rose to their feet. "We were transported by the creator, our father, to be serviced by Noah and return to Zagader before the Earth full moon. My name is klick, and this is my sister Yok. We know you are Rosalind, the creator of Noah."

Rosalind sat down she had to admit both the females were what humans would call attractive, admittedly they did have the faint outline of scales on their skin. "I thought your father agreed with my son he would permit several Earth years to pass to allow natural development of him and you, why is he forcing the issue?"

The two sisters looked at each other. Yok answered: "father is concerned he may pass away before he sees the outcome of his efforts. Apparently, there is some rejection transpiring in his construction the creator's DNA, and the human DNA appears not to be so compatible as first thought by number one and the central computer."

"Are you affected in the same way?" Rosalind asked not convinced they weren't lying.

"No Rosalind, we are not lying to you we can read your mind as you can read ours, we are perfectly constructed using our father's cells and human female there is no conflict. "

"The creator should be satisfied with these accomplishments?" Rosalind suggested.

"He is very pleased with the outcome; however, he wants to make the final improvement and believes his daughters and Noah are the key to success."

"You realise my son is only a child only 10 Earth years old he cannot mate."

"Noah can shapeshift to any age he wants, the creator, our father, has increased our age to allow us to carry the future of the collective and the Zibyan future."

"I'm somewhat puzzled why your father, the creator, would send you on a journey naked when he knows humans wear clothes?"

"There is a large selection of clothes humans wear, he thought if we travelled naked, we could choose our own on arrival, Fiona help solve the problem for us. We are to stay concealed until we return home we may not mix with humans, only with Noah. Father experimented with three of his daughters, to see what the genetics produce, we have been sent as an experiment to ascertain if our genetics and Noahs produce something different a more pure option."

Rosalind asked, "you two are perfectly happy to be used as an experiment by your father?"

"Why not! You would do the same for the collective which you have by producing Noah and Mary we are performing nothing different."

Rosalind didn't reply, they hit the nail on the head, there is no difference. Rosalind realised Noah had come over on the buggy, he walked in not bothering to knock; Rosalind hadn't realised Jacob had shapeshifted into a teenager in appearance. She stood there, amazed looking at his transformation. The two females stared at him.

He didn't speak to anyone Noah almost seemed as if he's in a foul mood by his expression. He grabbed Yok forcibly by the hand she didn't resist heading off upstairs with him. Klick listened like everyone else to the screams coming from upstairs. Both Fiona and Rosalind knew why she is screaming, he is blessed like his father, she wouldn't forget this moment for as long as she existed Rosalind thought.

Klick looked extremely nervous, sitting there on her own. Noah came running down the stairs, not bothering with a dressing gown or anything. Klick observed nervously Noah approaching her, he grabbed her by the hand running upstairs. Both Rosalind and Fiona started laughing. A little while later, the screaming stopped, Noah, came downstairs. He reverted into his 10-year-old appearance so his father wouldn't realise. He kissed his mother on the cheek and Fiona winking at her, walking out of the door.

They heard the buggy start and leave. 10 minutes later they listened to the two females coming down the stairs before they could speak, grabbed by a strange force vanishing, a new transport the creator had used on Noah originally and now on his own two daughters retrieving returning to Zagader.

Fiona commented, "the creator must be extremely confident both his daughters are pregnant to retrieve them promptly."

"I presume so Fiona, I wonder what the collective is thinking everything is quiet in my mind which I consider very disturbing."

Rosalind sensed Jacob is close, she ran outside looking to the 10-acre paddock, he is spreading fertiliser which she thought odd at this time of day. She telepathically contacted Peter for an explanation. He responded: "We are moving locations, suspect we are detected. Jacob is removing 10 loads of fertiliser; we will move to behind the moon and wait for further instructions. You and Fiona are to stay on earth and await new orders."

Rosalind stepped into her Range Rover heading home, something is wrong, she couldn't telepathically contact her brothers and sisters on the home planet, which she thought extremely strange. She stepped from her vehicle at Jacobs farm watching jet fighters fly low overhead. Rosalind concerned, they were put out of action by the virus have the humans now fixed the issue with their computers and Peter hadn't realised aboard the spaceship permitting them to be detected. Rosalind ran into the house. "Mary, Noah with me now," she ordered stepping from the house into the misty fog transporter entering the spaceship submerged in an old volcano crater far out to sea. Peter and Matthew stood there, flashing their eyes in a greeting fashion. Rosalind asked quickly, "who gave the order to move from our present location?"

"A collective decision Rosalind we don't see any alternative if we're discovered."

"Matthew transport the remaining five loads of fertiliser to the manure pile on the top of the cliff. Transport Jacob here and don't forget Jack I have already notified Fiona to come," Rosalind advised.

The image of the firstborn appeared on the far wall. "I read your thoughts, Rosalind, you are playing a dangerous game, you will have the support of the collective if you fail you will have no other alternative than to return to Zagader."

"I won't fail firstborn, I presume you are aware of the creator's behaviour recently?"

"Yes, Rosalind we are considering appropriate action at the moment. You concentrate on dealing with humans." The firstborn vanished. Rosalind watched Jacob and Jack thrown from the transporter as it stopped violently ejecting them.

"Mary take your father and Jack into the room over there. I will explain everything later husband at the moment I am preoccupied working for God." Jacob didn't argue, he nodded following Mary everyone had changed into their spacesuits including him now.

"Peter, activate the nuclear silos any nuclear weapons launch, and land on the nearest major city and explode! Now Peter. Matthew, send a transmission to all the satellites destroy the chips in every piece of equipment they are fitted in, some older vehicles and equipment won't be affected, that doesn't matter at the moment."

"Noah, summon 40 of your brothers and sisters, transport invisibly to every zoo and Safari Park around the world release the animals, give them a chance to be free and survive. Don't forget the experimental farms make sure you eliminate any humans there, return the bodies to the spaceship for processing. Mary, contact Zagader for four transport ships, we will have millions of corpses to transport in the next few days those are my orders."

Rosalind watched the monitor on the wall, nuclear weapons were exploding around the world. Jet fighters were falling from the sky, along with commercial aircraft, the electronics were burnt out, many vehicles rendering them useless, every computer failed to work. The human race is without technology; they only have hand weapons, and any of those that were electronically operated wouldn't. Power stations exploded. Armageddon is here and here to stay the Zibyan collective created the human race by mistake, they were going to rectify the situation and now.

What happens next is another story
by Zack Cool

Searching for Serenity

ISBN: 978-1-008-99056-2

I write my memoirs beginning with sadness. I faced my wife's death from coronavirus; I'm following the hearse to the graveyard in a limousine, observed by sympathetic neighbours from behind net curtains. I alone would attend her funeral in these uncertain times.

I returned to an empty house, disillusioned, remembering a book I'd written many years ago. I decided to take one last adventure from Long Marston to the Scottish Highlands to discover what I wanted out of life in my remaining years.

I set off by following the route I initially took, enjoying my own company until destiny decided otherwise. Life suddenly became strange; I'm involved in a murder and confronted by a young woman from my past determined to organise my life.

If that isn't weird enough, what transpires over the next few months can only be described as bizarre unless you are a Knight Templar in the Royal circle of friends and a pirate!

My Parallel Universe

ISBN: 978-1-008-90773-7

I saw the lorry coming towards me, I had no way to escape, bracing for the moment of impact. I watched the blood leaving my body from where my bones pierced my quivering flesh until I lost consciousness.

I stayed a year in hospital undergoing numerous attempts to cure my paralysis. Now evident since I had regained consciousness, my life is over, never again would I walk through the green fields by the river.

I'm transported home into the spare bedroom, my prison until I die. My company would be a television, unable to change the channels, and a picture hanging on the wall of a man stepping from this world into the next, in bright light.

My only movement is my eyes and mouth; the rest of me is numb.

I watched my wife spoon-feeding me like a baby trying to be patient, gritting her teeth.

What happens next is beyond my comprehension!

Black Book

ISBN: 978-1-291-50712-6

The final two weeks of James Thompson's miserable existence at an Academy. He was a gifted young man, persecuted by other students for his brilliance and frequently teased after accepting the position of head boy.

Through a cunning plot by Jennifer Collins and her two friends, Jackie and Simone trapped James in a store cupboard where she demanded that he hacks into the school computer to acquire the answers for her next exam. James refused! No, is a word Jennifer would not accept and planned her revenge with her two accomplices.

James is thrust through the gates of hell, convicted of attempted rape and incarcerated through a grave error of the prosecution system, serving three months for a crime he never committed. James' kind and placid nature were stripped away by every beating he received from his fellow inmates.

Mr and Mrs Thompson, embarrassed by their son, disowned him, not believing his innocence, refusing to associate with him any further and his father advised James never to return home.

James served his sentence and heard the prison door slam shut behind him for the last time. He left, a scarred young man wanting revenge, not realising that he was monitored from the shadows by an interested party.

Trust is a luxury James could not afford; he courted death like a wild mistress, waiting for his demise around every corner after discovering the black book!